HOSTAGE QUEEN

Freda Lightfoot

This first world edition published 2010
in Great Britain and in the USA by
SEVERN HOUSE PUBLISHERS LTD of
9–15 High Street, Sutton, Surrey, England, SM1 1DF.
Trade paperback edition published
in Great Britain and the USA 2010 by
SEVERN HOUSE PUBLISHERS LTD

British Library Cataloguing in Publication Data

Lightfoot, Freda, 1942–
    Hostage Queen.
    1. Marguerite, Queen, consort of Henry IV, King of France,
    1553–1615 – Fiction. 2. Catherine de Medicis, Queen,
    consort of Henry II, King of France, 1519–1589 – Fiction.
    3. Saint Bartholomew's Day, Massacre of, France, 1572 –
    Fiction. 4. France – History – Wars of the Huguenots,
    1562–1598 – Hostages – Fiction. 5. Historical fiction.
    I. Title
    823.9'14-dc22

ISBN-13: 978-0-7278-6888-6   (cased)
ISBN-13: 978-1-84751-231-4   (trade paper)

Severn House Publishers support The Forest Stewardship Council [FSC],
the leading international forest certification organisation. All our titles that
are printed on Greenpeace-approved FSC-certified paper carry the FSC logo.

Mixed Sources
Product group from well-managed
forests and other controlled sources
www.fsc.org Cert no. SA-COC-1565
© 1996 Forest Stewardship Council

Typeset by Palimpsest Book Production Ltd.,
Grangemouth, Stirlingshire, Scotland.
Printed and bound in Great Britain by
MPG Books Ltd., Bodmin, Cornwall.

'Let no man say that marriages are made in heaven; the gods would not commit so great an injustice ... All the harm that ever came to me in life came through marriage, the greatest calamity that ever befell me.'

Marguerite of Navarre

Author's Note

The life of Marguerite de Valois was so full of drama, romance, intrigue and danger that very little in this story needed to be invented. I have nonetheless used my imagination to interpret her reaction to events, her love affairs, and to fill any gaps. Much that was written about her was pure malice or propaganda, rather than factual history, and I have done my best to stay true to what seemed most likely. Although they form the background to her story, this is not a history of the Wars of Religion, rather the effect upon them by one woman. While historians agree that the seed for the Massacre of Saint Bartholemew was sown in the talks at Bayonne, there is some dispute on how much was pre-planned. I have made my own decision on this, which I feel is logical. Where these are known, I have used a person's actual words, modifying them slightly to suit the modern ear.

Margot's Family Tree

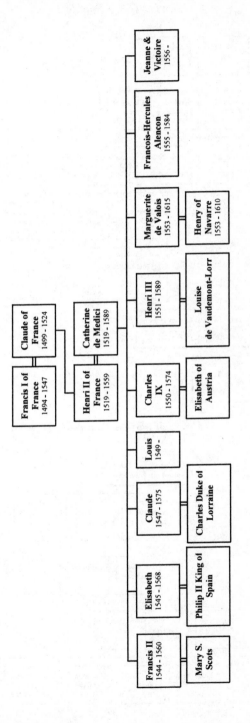

Henri of Guise Family Tree

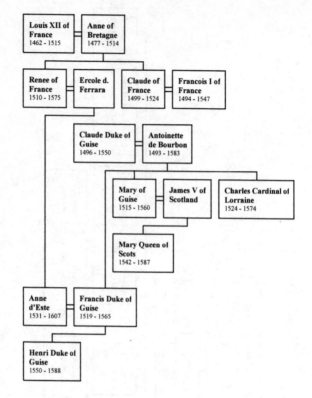

Henry of Navarre's Family Tree

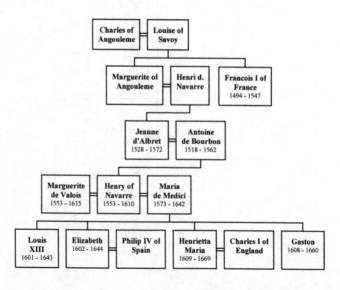

Part One

Pawn in a Royal Game

Bayonne 1565

Summer 1565

The hot summer sun seared through the drawn curtains of the litter as the cumbersome vehicle trundled with bone-aching slowness through the French countryside, every jolt jangling Margot's already shredded nerves. A fly buzzed annoyingly around her flushed cheeks and she flapped it impatiently away. The clink of harness, the clomp and thud of hundreds of tired feet from those walking alongside, pounded ever louder in her ears, making her head ache. She felt hot and sticky and cross, for once uncaring of her appearance, of her rumpled gown and the fact that her dark curls hung in damp tangles instead of shining with their usual luscious richness.

Margot was bored. She longed to be out in the fresh air, galloping across the open countryside, not forced to sit demurely beside her governess breathing in the sweaty stink of horses and baggage mules from the confines of her mother's litter.

However luxurious, however pretty a shade of green were the plush velvet cushions, it felt very like a prison.

Occasionally some incident would occur to enliven the journey: a brawl or a duel, which Margot always found entertaining. So when she heard the screams and sobs and heart-rending wails coming from some distance behind them, she couldn't resist poking her head out between the curtains to see who was making such a din.

'Sit still, child, and stop fidgeting,' Madame de Curton chided.

Ignoring her governess, Margot asked a young groom riding alongside what was amiss.

'Some court lady has been discovered in an indiscreet *affaire*,' the boy confided. 'She has been abandoned at a roadside convent to reflect upon her folly.'

Margot felt a surge of pity for the poor woman, and turning to her governess, chestnut eyes blazing in outrage, cried, 'Is that not the cruellest way to treat a wife?'

'It is not for us to judge, child.'

'But why should a husband be allowed to spread his favours as he wishes, but not his wife?'

Madame de Curton stifled a sigh of exasperation. She was not above indulging in a little gossip and scandal herself, and after more than a year of travelling any diversion to break the tedium was welcome. Stalwart that she was, even she had grown weary of the jolting to her ageing bones. But while she might sympathize, or even agree with her young charge's passionate defence of the poor lady, it would be wrong to say as much.

'Because that is the way of the world, dearest. A lady must at all times conduct herself with propriety and modesty, and of course obey her lord.'

'But that is so unfair!'

Numbering almost a thousand souls, the Royal Progress comprised some of the noblest Catholic lords in the land, Princes of the Blood and great officers of state. Loyal as she was to the crown, Madame was the first to accept that their brilliance was displayed more by the splendour of their robes and the length of their private retinue, rather than the virtue of their morals.

She smiled fondly upon her charge. 'You might do well to learn the art of obedience yourself, my child. Now close those curtains and sit still.'

The entire court was on the move: maids and cooks, guards and grooms, doctors and priests, the usual hangers-on seeking favours, merchants and charlatans who would join this seemingly endless royal progress for a part of the journey, staying in local inns if they could find rooms available, before returning home exhausted and often much the poorer for their efforts. Rogues and pickpockets lurked amongst the crowd, local peasants came to gawp, children and feral dogs ran alongside, excited by this long caravan of people that stretched for miles. It was as if a whole town had suddenly got up one morning and decided to take a walk together.

This great procession had been planned by Margot's mother, Catherine de Medici, who loved nothing more than to devise magnificent tours in order to display the wealth of the realm and impress the people.

The baggage for such a large number of persons was considerable, for they must needs be accompanied by huge wagons and mules loaded with trunks of magnificent clothes, and all the paraphernalia needed for the many masques and pageants held en route. Then there were the oak beds and silken sheets, washbasins, trenchers, linen, trestle tables and gold plate for banquets that were required by the royal family on their travels.

Today, Catherine had ridden south to Bayonne on one of her finest horses to get everything ready for the reunion with her eldest daughter, Elisabeth, Queen of Spain. Margot was filled with excitement at the prospect of seeing her sister again, and said as much to her companion.

'Why could I not ride with the Queen, my mother? You know I ride well, Lottie, and it would be such a relief to escape the litter for a while.'

'Her Majesty does not have time to linger over admiring the scenery or picking pretty flowers. She has important business to attend to.'

'What sort of business? Not the war again?'

The nation had been torn apart by civil war for years, and Margot knew that the Queen believed it essential that France should be seen to triumph. Her aim was to bring the two opposing factions, Catholic and Protestant, to a greater tolerance of each other at a local level. She had driven the cavalcade through province after province, town after town, bestowing smiles and false promises, or stern admonitions, as the fancy took her.

It mattered not that the court often shivered under winter snows, forded turbulent rivers, ploughed through fields thick with mud, or, now that summer was here, fever and disease stalked them daily. Margot was only too aware that any inconvenience must be suffered in silence, as it was of vital importance for the people to see her brother, King Charles IX, now that he had reached his majority at fourteen.

'I trust not, sweeting,' Madame said. 'Her Grace must prepare for the meeting with King Philip of Spain, and there is to be a marvellous water picnic by way of celebration. You will enjoy that, will you not? You know how you do love to dance. Now, what shall you wear?'

Instantly suspicious of this diversion, which was a favourite tactic of her governess when faced with an awkward question, Margot's eyes flashed with rebellion. 'I'm too hot to care.'

'You must care,' Madame de Curton gently scolded. 'The Queen Mother likes you to dress well, as she herself is always supremely elegant and magnificently attired.'

Margot thought her mother looked like a fat old crow in her habitual widow's black, however bejewelled, but then she was in the mood to be as difficult as possible. She might even refuse to attend yet another masque and go hunting instead, except that she loved her darling Curton dearly. Her beloved governess was an intelligent, remarkable woman who had taught her well: not simply the more traditional female skills but literature, philosophy, Latin and Greek, in addition to her religious devotions. At least the Queen had ensured a proper education for her children, even though she'd shown them little affection in the process.

It was to Madame de Curton that Margot had turned for love, which she'd received in abundance. The governess was fiercely protective, keeping her fully informed of all that was going on, essential in this mischievous court of plots and double-dealing. Margot was never quite certain whom she could trust since her own brothers continually squabbled, their childhood bickering and petty jealousies turning bitter and dangerous as each vied to wear a crown.

Now she heaved a dramatic sigh, for her resistance was mostly sham, in keeping with her ill humour. There was nothing she liked better than to dress up and look pretty, but she had no wish to give in too easily. 'The Queen my mother constantly accuses me of being difficult, light-minded and frivolous, which is not true at all.'

Madame de Curton smiled as she stroked Margot's damp curls from her hot brow. 'It is most certainly true that you have an inquisitive mind, sweeting, and display far more spirit and intelligence than is perhaps quite appropriate for an obedient daughter. Now tell me, which gown do you favour?'

Margot pouted. 'I may choose the orange gold, since that is my favourite colour.'

'I believe Her Majesty would prefer you to wear the silver tissue, far more appropriate for a young princess on such an important occasion.'

Margot gave a shrug of careless agreement, bowing to her mentor's superior knowledge in such matters. These extravaganzas were commonplace in court life, yet her keen mind warned her she'd been neatly sidetracked, and she resolutely returned to her unanswered question.

'Then if it is not the war which concerns my mother, what is the purpose of this so-important meeting?'

Madame picked at a thread on her gown, avoiding the girl's probing gaze. 'They are to discuss a marriage proposal.'

'For me?'

'It is time. Your sister Elisabeth was betrothed at thirteen, only a year older than you are now.'

Margot fought to keep her voice steady as she asked the most vital question of all. 'And who is the proposed groom?'

The governess manufactured a bright smile. 'Why, none other than King Philip's own son, Don Carlos.'

Physical discomfort paled into insignificance by comparison with this shocking discovery. For several long moments Margot could not speak. It was as if every breath had been knocked from her body. She felt dizzy, close to fainting in the suffocating heat of the litter. Margot regarded her governess with frightened eyes, her voice barely audible.

'Don Carlos, Philip's mad son? Are you saying that the husband whom the Queen my mother has proposed for me is insane, a hunchback who likes to roast rabbits alive?'

Charlotte de Curton quailed beneath the intelligent, furious gaze. It was indeed typical of the Queen's manipulative nature to leave the difficult task of telling her youngest daughter the decision about her future to a third party. The woman known as Madame Serpent did not soil her own hands with unpleasantness when others could do it for her. Yet none of her own children, certainly not Margot, would dare to stand against her. The governess's eyes softened as she sought to offer some comfort, however small. 'I am sure rumour exaggerates his condition. He suffered a terrible accident as a boy by falling down a stone staircase, which almost killed him. You should feel nought but compassion.'

'I feel more for myself.' A sick fear lay like a lead weight in the pit of Margot's stomach. 'Were not the doctors obliged to drill a hole into his skull to relieve the pressure on his brain, which left him sorely damaged? I have heard the tales, Lottie, that he tortures dogs and cats, even horses, simply for the pleasure of it. I was also told that, fearing he might progress to humans, his father keeps him close at home. Has my mother taken none of this into account?'

Madame de Curton fixed her gaze on a fly crawling up the warm curtain, unwilling to answer this question either. 'You are Marguerite de Valois, the third daughter of Catherine de Medici and King Henri II, a Princess of the Blood and a Daughter of France. Of course you must marry where the Queen your mother deems appropriate.' As if this excused such an abomination.

Margot's response was barely audible. 'I marvel at this fresh proof of her devotion.'

'Do not take it to heart so, child. There is more to consider than your wishes.'

'My mother never considers my wishes. She may claim to love all of her six surviving children equally, yet everyone at court knows she cares nought for me. The Queen hates me because I possess the good health and strong constitution she covets for my brothers, whom she much prefers, in particular Henri, duc d'Anjou. He has ever been her favourite.'

The governess could not deny that Anjou was the apple of his mother's eye. Nothing was too much trouble for this favourite son. He must have the finest clothes, the choicest meats, sleep only in a warmed room, be pampered and cosseted by all of the Queen Mother's women, her *dames galantes*, the bevy of beauties, or flying squadron, as they were mockingly called. But then Anjou always did love to be the centre of attention, even as a small boy when he would pose in his silks and satins before them all. It was no surprise to her that he played on his mother's love while he patiently, or perhaps it would be more correct to say *im*patiently, waited to succeed his brother to the throne, should that poor boy's uncertain health overtake him.

'Anjou is the heir,' she reminded Margot now, wishing to be fair. 'Therefore he is bound to be the favourite. And you are a foolish young girl who thinks of nothing but amusements: of dancing, hunting, and the like.'

Margot straightened her spine. 'I enjoy parties and dancing,

I cannot deny it, but I have little inclination for setting myself off to advantage by dress, or exciting admiration of my person and figure. Certainly not in order to marry with a madman.'

'You will be expected to do your duty.'

Margot responded with passion. 'I *will* do my duty, so far as I am able, but I tell you, Lottie, even if my mother drags me to the altar, I will refuse to marry unless I like the husband she chooses for me.'

Words which were to come back and haunt her.

Margot waited anxiously at the quayside at Saint-Jean-de-Luz for her sister to arrive, her slender body afire with outrage as much as the early summer heat. Elisabeth was due at midday but the hour came and went and so stifling was the day that several soldiers collapsed and died, suffocated in their own armour. Margot glared at her mother, half wishing she would do the same.

She knew that the Queen too disliked the heat, as it made her perspire profusely because of her heavy build. Even the leafy arches she'd ordered to be erected offered little in the way of shade. A stout woman in her forties, Catherine de Medici was dressed from head to foot in funereal black, as had been her custom since the death of Margot's beloved father some six years previous. She stood impatiently fanning herself, using the fan she kept pinned to her girdle for that purpose, the young King by her side, together with her favourite son Anjou, and Henry of Navarre, their cousin. François-Hercule, as always, kept close to Margot, being the youngest and least prepossessing of the Valois brothers, and not liked by their mother.

It was five years since mother and daughter had last seen each other, and they had never been close even before Elisabeth had left France to marry at fourteen. Surely, Margot thought, the Queen Mother must be acutely aware that this once timid girl was now wife to the most powerful prince in all of Christendom, one whom she feared more than any other. Watching her keenly, Margot thought that mayhap she did look somewhat anxious. Her round, olive-skinned face glowed pale and sickly beneath the widow's veil, although she was clever enough to keep her hands quietly clasped at her waist, giving no tell-tale sign of nervousness.

Anxious over the proposed marriage, Margot's own mood continued to sour, and the prickle of sweat beneath her armpits, which must surely be marking her pretty gown, wasn't helping. She'd quarrelled again with her governess this morning, Madame insisting that a union between the Houses of Valois and Hapsburg could only add to the strength of France in the Catholic world.

'The Queen favours this marriage simply in order to restrain the power of the Guises,' Margot had cried, desperation making her tone bitter, and her whole body tremble with fear. If only she dared to discuss the matter with her mother, but however confident she might be with everyone else, Margot always felt clumsy and dumbstruck in the presence of the great Catherine de Medici. She could only vent her spleen upon poor Lottie. 'I see no reason to pick a quarrel with so noble a family. Indeed, Henri has been my particular friend for years, as you well know, Lottie.'

Charlotte de Curton had clicked her tongue by way of reprimand. 'Do not presume to question your betters when you know nothing of politics, child. No more do I. You must put that young man from your mind.'

Now, as she watched the fishing boats come and go in the harbour, Margot knew this to be quite impossible. How could she, when she loved him so? When every part of her ached to be done with childhood and have Henri pay proper court to her. She had loved him since she was but four or five years old, and he a few years older. She'd been sitting on her father's knee watching the Prince de Joinville, as he then was, playfully jousting with the Marquis de Beaupreau. The King had asked which of the two she would choose as her *chevalier*.

'The Marquis,' had been her pert response.

'Why so? He is not the handsomest.'

It was true. The Prince de Joinville was tall and blond, and his friend dark and not nearly so striking. But, young as she was, Margot had known better than to add to Guise's arrogance. 'Because the Marquis is better behaved, while the Prince is always making mischief and thinks himself master over everyone,' she'd retorted, making her father laugh.

Yet were she allowed the opportunity, she would favour him still. And why should she not? He was courtly, eloquent and charismatic. Descended from the great Charlemagne himself, with the royal blood of the Capet line running through his veins. Surely a worthy champion for a Princess, as well as being handsome enough to quicken any young girl's heart.

Margot knew that they were meant for each other, and longed to be free to marry her *chevalier*. Yet how could they ever hope to come together if her mother so feared the power of his family that she would rather sell her youngest daughter to a madman?

She was a Valois, a Daughter of France, as her darling Lottie kept reminding her, with no control whatsoever over her own life.

Margot was but twelve years old and she shivered with foreboding.

Catherine had no intention of selecting a husband for her daughter from any other motive than diplomacy. Until the tragic death of her eldest son, François II, who had inherited the crown from his father Henry II, the Guises had been in a high position at court because the young King's charming and spoiled wife, Mary Stuart, Queen of Scots, was one of their girls. The House of Guise had held the power then, not herself, the King's own mother. Catherine had become regent only when Charles, merely a boy of ten at the time, had ascended the throne.

François and Mary had loved each other dearly, but while the young widow was still in mourning it had come to her knowledge that the Guises were approaching the Spanish King for a new marriage for the girl. Catherine had been outraged, for any such match would have resulted in too strong a union between the House of Guise and Philip of Spain. The Guises coveted the throne of France, wishing to supplant her power with their own. Consequently, Mary had been dispatched back to Scotland, and the Queen Mother was now offering her own daughter in her place, determined to forge whatever links she could with the mighty Spain.

After two hours of waiting the royal barge at last approached, and with joy in her heart, Catherine stepped forward to welcome her daughter. She was surprised and delighted by what she saw. This dark-eyed beauty bore little resemblance to the shy child she remembered from the royal nursery, her girlish figure now that of a woman, beguiling and curvaceous. Catherine was relieved to note that her complexion remained unmarked by the small-pox she'd suffered shortly after reaching Spain, and that she had the tall graceful bearing of all the Valois. In a black velvet gown trimmed with jewels, slashed to reveal embroidered scarlet satin sleeves, she seemed aloof and somewhat remote. The timid young girl had indeed turned into a magnificent Queen.

Elisabeth wept softly as they embraced, before turning to greet her siblings. While soft kisses and salutations were exchanged, the troops released a cannonade in salute.

Catherine felt a surge of pride in her daughter even as her gaze flicked over the assembled lords and Spanish nobles, seeking a face which was clearly absent, as she had feared it might be.

There had been doubts for some weeks that Philip may not keep his promise to attend the meeting. Rumours at court had been rife, and although such gossip ceased whenever Catherine drew near, the reason for His Majesty's absence was plain. Philip II disapproved of her too tolerant attitude towards religion: the fact that she was willing to pacify alleged heretics rather than see France torn apart by yet more civil war.

Addressing her daughter, Catherine coolly enquired, 'He did not come then? Do you not see that your husband's suspicions will lead us straight to war?'

Elisabeth's response was not only impassioned but regal. 'What cause have you to believe that the King mistrusts Your Majesty? Only evil-minded people could give you such ideas.'

'My dear daughter, you have become very Spanish.'

'I am indeed Spanish, as it is my duty to be so. But I am ever your daughter, the same that you sent to Spain.'

Catherine's smile barely touched her round, slightly protruding eyes. 'I trust you will always recognize your duty to your mother.'

Elisabeth looked discomfited, the innate fear of her mother still present despite her new regal status. 'My husband the King sends his apologies, and his emissary, the Duke of Alva, a soldier and statesman of renown, in his stead.'

Right on cue, the gentleman himself, stern-faced with a long nose and a beard, stepped forward to bow over the Queen's hand in courtly fashion.

Catherine barely managed an icy smile, striving not to reveal her fury and disappointment. She had hoped not only for a marriage for Margot, but also a union between her darling Anjou and the Dowager Queen Joanna, Philip's own sister. Despite the difference in their ages, a match would help to unite the two nations. Instead of Philip, she would now be obliged to deal with this odious little man with an even greater reputation for harshness and cruelty than his cold-hearted master.

The day of the water picnic dawned hot and humid, and Margot felt sticky with the summer heat, even in her silver tissue, and excited at the prospect of the celebrations ahead. It was to take place on the Isle of Aiguemeau on the Adour River.

The Queen Mother had spent many tiring weeks preparing for this most important day, ordering alcoves to be built, each one containing a round table to seat a dozen revellers, with the royal dais raised on four banks of grass at one end.

Pretty shepherdesses dressed in cloth of gold and satin, after the fashion of the different provinces of France, tripped and danced across the meadows. Mermaids draped themselves in artistic decadence upon the rocks, while imitation dolphins playfully disported themselves around magnificently decorated barges. Margot was enchanted. It was a fabulous display, no doubt intended to demonstrate that France was a rich and powerful nation.

The Duke of Alva looked on unimpressed.

The royal party, including this unwelcome interloper, had been carried upriver on the royal barge, accompanied by satyrs and nymphs playing their pipes and flutes and singing their songs of welcome.

He was old, Margot decided, older even than her mother, and thin and erect like a soldier. His face was long and hollow-cheeked, the skin like yellow parchment, the brown eyes shrewd and piercing, and his long beard much speckled with grey. Most striking of all, she recognized a sardonic cruelty in the way his lip curled. Margot thought that her mother might need all her diplomatic skills to deal with such a man.

She watched almost with sympathy as Catherine leaned over to show the Duke an artificial whale leaking red wine from a supposed wound, pointing out how grand King Neptune looked as he rode his chariot pulled by sea horses. Alva glanced disdainfully at the scenes being enacted on the river. Nor did he appear to be listening to a word the Queen said, behaviour the great Catherine de Medici was certainly not accustomed to.

Yet Margot felt more sympathy for herself. She was in an agony of emotion, anxiously awaiting her fate. Would she be wed to a madman, or could she continue to hope and dream of Guise? Her heart skipped a beat at the prospect.

An army of servants brought cold meats to the tables: the jambon de Bayonne, duck and pigeon, foie gras, fine cheeses and custard tarts. As she nibbled on a sweet pastry Margot could barely drag her gaze away from the two Queens, her mother and sister, as they sat huddled together in close conversation. One moment they were squabbling with icy coolness, the next smiling, kissing and embracing each other. Like everyone at court, the young princess was skilled in the art of eavesdropping, an accepted part of court life and often the only way to survive.

'Do you think,' she whispered to the ever-present Madame de Curton, 'that these talks yet touch upon me?'

'They are discussing the Huguenots, which is far more important.'

Margot stifled a sigh.

She must try to be optimistic. She was young, after all, with an immense appetite for life. Her natural exuberance would always come to the fore and allow her to hope. Besides, the stern dissatisfaction in her mother's face seemed to indicate that the discussions were not going well.

Catherine's voice rang out momentarily above the hubbub. 'Philip should never doubt the strength of my faith. I am the niece of a pope, after all, and when orphaned as a young child, spent some of my most formative years being educated by nuns.'

'His Grace the King wishes me to remind Your Majesty that he has no desire to be the ruler of heretics.'

So Madame was right, they did still talk of religion. Was that good or bad? Margot was a great admirer of her mother's skills in pacifying the religious fanatics of either persuasion, but the fierce Duke of Alva looked very much a persecutor rather than a peace-maker. He seemed eager to prove that his master, surely the most powerful monarch in the world, was ready to stand against the Queen Mother, if needs be.

A frightening consideration, even to Margot, a mere girl.

The royal children had grown up through the first turbulent wars of religion. When Margot had been but seven or eight even her brother Anjou had flirted with Calvinism for a while, simply out of a desire to follow the fashion, ever a weakness of his. He would constantly tease and plague her, ordering her to replace her rosaries and Book of Hours with the Huguenot prayer book, and on one occasion had even thrown it into the fire.

Despite her tender age she'd stood up to his bullying, remaining firm in her devotions. 'I would suffer whipping, and even death, rather than be damned,' she'd told him, tossing her dark curls, eyes blazing.

Fortunately, neither fate had been called for. Madame de Curton had taken her to the Cardinal of Tournon who recommended she hold fast to her faith and provided her with a new Book of Hours, to replace the one that was burned. Anjou had continued to mock her childish piousness, yet she'd steadfastly ignored him. And once their mother had learned of her favourite son's misguided fancy, he'd been sternly brought back to his true calling.

Surely no one would dare to view the Queen Mother's tolerance as a sign of weakness. She was without doubt a strong woman, a clever and wily diplomat, prepared to bend events to her will. A Medici no less. She was, after all, a woman who did not balk at selling off her own child in marriage to a madman.

The music had started and in a fury of frustration, Margot flounced out of her seat and succumbed at last to join the dancing. Much to her displeasure she found herself partnered with Henry of Navarre. They were dancing the pavan, surely one of the simplest dances in all the world, yet this oaf could not seem to train his great clumsy feet to keep time with the music. She took a step to the right in the fashion of the dance, soft round arms lifted gracefully, their two hands clasped. Henry took two forward, realized his mistake and attempted to rectify it by leaping back into line but misjudged the move and collided with his partner, tripping over her train and almost knocking her over. Margot was furious.

'This is intended to be a dignified dance, meant to herald the entrance of the gods and goddesses in their triumphal chariots,' she remonstrated with him, as she brushed the dust from his shoes off the hem of her gown. 'You are a graceless clod who should never have been allowed out of the farmyard.'

Henry laughed, as if it were all a great joke. 'I do my best to learn the ways of your fine French Court,' he grandly informed her, black Gascon eyes sparkling with mischief. 'But I fancy you may be right. Hunting boar in the forests of Navarre suits me better than these mincing steps.'

Grabbing his hand, Margot gave him a shove back into line. '*Now* we take the double step forward. Do please pay attention. It's perfectly simple if you follow those in front of you.'

'What a pair we make,' he chortled, as they successfully accomplished the next few steps without incident.

Margot inwardly groaned. In just a few months they would be back in Paris where she hoped Henri of Guise would be waiting for her with the same eager impatience she felt to see him. If only he were by her side today, instead of this gawky cousin of hers, yet another Henry, although he liked to spell his name with a *y* in the English manner. But then he was little better than a peasant, for all he called himself the Prince of Béarn.

She glanced at her companion with disdain, thinking that he certainly couldn't match Guise for looks. He had a dark tangle of unruly hair, styled in the fashion of the provincial Nérac, long nose, and large deep-set eyes, which admittedly sparkled with his customary good humour. He was infuriatingly good natured, an affable fellow with a droll wit and not without some intelligence, but his manners and Béarnaise dialect were really quite uncouth. She and her brothers often teased him, calling him the boor, mountain goat, or *canaille* of Béarn. A disreputable rogue forever with his eye on the girls. Even now, while he danced with her, his attention was on the trim waist of that pretty shepherdess, rather than watching his own feet.

Henry had been living at the French Court for some years, ever since his mother had taken up the cause of Protestantism. Since Jeanne was now the accepted leader of the Huguenots following the death of her husband, and her son was in line for the throne of France after Margot's brothers, all of whom were known to be sickly and had not yet married and produced heirs, there was little trust between the two queens. The Queen Mother operated on the principle that while she kept the future King of Navarre under her personal care, there would be less risk of any nasty surprises from his mother.

'You're far too young to be lusting after maids,' Margot scolded as Henry again missed a step when his gaze followed a pretty nymph tripping across the meadow.

'I am but seven months younger than you, and since you are considered old enough to be betrothed, why cannot I at least look?'

'My betrothal is none of your business.'

'Is it not? I confess I am agog to hear the outcome.' He leaned close to whisper in her ear. 'Has it been decided? Are you to be sacrificed?'

Now it was Margot who missed her step, and she could very easily have slapped him as she mumbled that it was far too early in the negotiations to know anything.

'My late father, the King of Navarre, seemed to think it might be a good idea if you and I made a match of it. What say you to that? Better an oaf than a madman.'

Margot glared at her country cousin as they stepped delicately to the left, almost in tune with the other dancers. 'I dare say he did, considering he was ever ambitious for his only son. Sadly you are destined to be disappointed. You can be certain that you will never gain the throne of France through me.'

Henry gave her a measuring look. 'Would I not make a better king than mad Charles, or that scented fop, Anjou? And as for your precious Alençon, the deceitful dwarf with his pockmarked face, no one could accuse him of having regal presence let alone the wit to rule a country. I, at least, am in the best of health, which cannot be said for any of your brothers.'

Margot's cheeks, along with her temper, blazed dangerously. 'How dare you speak of my royal brothers in that uncouth manner! They at least are not so low-born as to scramble over rocks barefoot. Nor do they smell of horses.'

Henry grinned. 'Good honest sweat from a day out hunting is surely a better scent for a man to wear than violet powder. Besides, my grandfather made sure that I was raised to be hardy. My cradle was the carapace of a turtle, and it is said that when I was but a newborn babe he wet my lips with garlic and good Jurançon wine to make sure I was a true Béarnais.'

'Oh, you are certainly that,' Margot snapped, sighing with relief as the music stopped and the dance came to an end. 'For my part, you may return to your precious Navarre and never set foot in the French Court again. Fortunately, our paths are not destined to cross once I have been found a husband, and none will be more pleased about that than I.'

But as she stormed off, chin high, the sound of his laughter following her, some presentiment made her wonder if that were indeed true.

Increasingly anxious, Margot slipped into the seat beside her sister. Elisabeth had seemed very grand and grown-up now that she was Queen of Spain, but Margot felt in her heart that she was still her beloved sister and was grateful for her concern and love, since she saw little of either sentiment in their mother.

'Has my future yet been decided? Could you not speak on my behalf and insist this match is a bad one?'

But Margot saw at once, by the sorrowful expression on her sister's face, before even Elisabeth shook her head in sad regret, that she had no more power than herself. Margot burned with silent outrage. What control did any of them possess over their own lives, their own destiny? None. Both she and her sister were mere pawns in a royal game of chess.

Elisabeth squeezed Margot's hand, softly urging her young sister not to be anxious or cast down. 'Do not fret; I too was originally betrothed to Don Carlos but married Philip instead, and see how well it has turned out for me.'

Unconvinced, Margot ached to dispute this argument, but Catherine suddenly stood up, casting her a quelling glance as she drew the Duke of Alva away from her youngest daughter's flapping ears. As always when confronted with the terrifying ire of her mother, Margot's small rebellion withered and died.

Watching them stroll away, Elisabeth dropped her voice to a whisper. 'My dear little sister, you will grow into a great beauty. It is no wonder that our mother is already seeking a husband for you, but much can go wrong with such delicate negotiations in these early stages. I am certain there will be any number of other likely suitors lining up for the honour of winning your hand, all eager to marvel at your flawless skin, your prettily rounded cheeks and those sparkling chestnut eyes.'

Margot's spirits instantly lifted, and her heart glowed with renewed hope. Her sister's words filled her with a sudden burst of optimism, a reassurance, albeit false, that she might truly have the world at her feet and she would not, after all, be obliged to marry a sadistic maniac. She may even be allowed some small say in her choice of husband.

Besides, she was excited and fascinated by the festival, entranced by the beauty of the ballet, the excitement of the jousting. The sun glinting off the lances reminded her of another joust, and a happier time. Why couldn't she choose her own *chevalier*, one with whom she was so perfectly suited?

Margot fleetingly wondered if Guise would be at court on their return, and if he had missed her while she'd been away.

Tables were now being cleared, and, with the feasting over, a troop of musicians, habited as satyrs, appeared out of an opening in a rock magically illuminated by hundreds of candles, whilst richly attired nymphs descended from above to form a final dance. Both girls were enchanted, but before either could join in the merry-making, the heavens opened, drenching them in seconds and half drowning the poor mermaids. There was utter pandemonium and confusion as everyone made a dash for the boats.

Elisabeth and Margot picked up their skirts and ran with the rest, slipping and sliding in the mud in their satin slippers, squealing with giddy laughter, their sudden uplift of spirits unquenched by the sorry turn in the weather. Margot secretly viewed the rain as a prophecy, one which might dampen the Queen Mother's hopes for her, as surely as it had this magnificent pageant.

The moment Mass was over the following morning, the negotiations began in earnest. First Alva approached the King, but soon realized that he must talk to the horse master and not the donkey, and arranged for Elisabeth to present him once more to her mother.

Catherine welcomed Alva to her apartments in the royal *chateau* close to the harbour at Bayonne, ensuring that all doors were firmly shut before they began their talk. Elisabeth and Charles were also present.

Throughout the water pageant she had attempted to present her case for a union between their two houses. Alva had been deliberately obtuse, refusing to discuss anything but the perceived threat from heretics.

Catherine knew him to be a fanatic. Like his master, Philip of Spain, the duke was obsessively determined to destroy Protestantism. Catherine's aim was simple. She needed peace for France, and the Huguenots were the only rival to her power. The question was: should she follow the example of the extreme Catholics and pursue them with the sword, or offer an olive branch? As ever, she dithered over making a decision. For all her following of the black arts, she was a Catholic. How could she change the habits of a lifetime?

But the Huguenots were a powerful party, their faith spreading throughout France, their armies led by men of great standing. Moreover, they had powerful friends in Protestant England and in the Low Countries, who were not likely to remain idle were she to attempt to crush them. Neither could she risk war with Spain. Catherine was prepared to go to any lengths, make any promises, however insincere, in order to avoid such a calamity.

With her diplomatic skills newly sharpened after a good night's rest, Catherine approached the knotty problem of marriage contracts with fresh vigour. But every attempt was blocked by Alva. At last she sighed and gave up.

'I see that you want us to arrive at religion.'

'I own it,' he agreed. 'It is the whole point of our discussion.'

She kept her hands quite still in her lap, as the nuns had taught her. It was vital that she appear relaxed and serene, that she not reveal by the smallest flicker of irritation that she was reaching the limit of her patience.

'Philip does not seem to appreciate how I have managed to maintain peace by accepting that Protestantism is not a crime. While acting as regent to my son Charles the King, I have agreed to allow Huguenots certain rights of worship, albeit restricted to open fields outside of certain towns, and to private estates of the Huguenot nobles, but—'

Alva brusquely interrupted. 'To permit liberty of conscience by allowing as many varieties of religion as there are fancies in the minds of men can only stir up grievous treacheries and rebellions. Such pacifications have caused grave disquiet to the Catholics.'

Not least the Guises, Catherine thought with some satisfaction.

In truth, being prone more to superstition than religious zeal, she was interested in her own power rather than those of either faith. Her one objective was to keep her sons secure on the throne, and in order to achieve this happy state she would sup with the devil if needs be.

Catherine fervently believed that her first duty was to her children. Hadn't the great prophet Nostradamus himself assured her that each of them would one day wear a crown? The prophecy had become her guiding star in her quest for power ever since.

Claude, her eldest daughter, had proved to be something of a disappointment – far too docile and gentle for her own good, yet claiming to be happy and content as wife of the Duke of Lorraine. But Elisabeth was Queen of Spain, mother of the Infanta Isabella, and hoping for a son next time.

Charles had the dark good looks of all the Valois, and Catherine knew she must get him married soon, perhaps to Elizabeth of England. The boy had once fondly hoped for a match with Mary of Scotland, but his fancy for the girl was fading and she expected little resistance from him to take the older Queen. England was a prize worth having.

While the boy King was physically strong, loved hunting and all field-sports, his health remained uncertain. Catherine suspected he had the same lung disease that had claimed his late brother, François II. He had a nervous disposition and was worryingly weak and unstable. Clever he may be, but if his wishes were thwarted by the smallest degree, his golden-brown eyes would grow fierce, his manner turn brusque and uncivil, which could quickly deteriorate into a temper tantrum. He showed no sign of growing out of these childish fits; rather they seemed to be getting worse, often caused by jealousy of his brother Anjou.

It was becomingly worryingly obvious that he too was tainted by the sins of his forefathers.

Catherine accepted these flaws with resignation as she did not expect the boy to live long. When Charles ultimately succumbed to the disease that had claimed his late brother, Anjou, her favourite,

whom she loved more than life itself – almost as much as she
had loved his father – would be ready and waiting to take his
place on the throne and claim his due rights.

Anjou, in Catherine's opinion, was beautiful. At fifteen he was
tall and slender, looking more Italian than French with his olive
skin, long dark eyes and gracious mouth. His hands were as white
and shapely as a girl's, which, young as he was, he showed off to
best advantage with sparkling rings and bracelets. Effeminate he
might be, and some would say already showing signs of perversion, yet he was the cleverest of all her sons, brave and eloquent.
Catherine believed that with her guidance, this most adored child
would one day make a fine king.

Far better than François-Hercule, the Duke of Alençon, the
fourth and youngest of her sons, who lacked the regal presence,
height, and handsome good looks of his older brothers. As a child
the poor boy had suffered from a bout of smallpox which had
left him sadly pockmarked. He had a tendency to be cowardly
and deceitful, although Margot frequently defended him, saying
it was only as a means of defence against the dreadful teasing he
suffered at the hands of his siblings. Catherine supposed that in
his favour it must be argued he was far less fanatical than his
older brothers; more moderate in every way. He took after herself
in that respect at least.

And, of course, he adored his sister, as did they all.

Each of her sons was jealous of the amount of attention she
gave to the other. The gossip-mongers claimed that the attachment
was unhealthily close, which caused Catherine much amusement.
Even if it were true, it wouldn't trouble her in the slightest. A
woman who had watched her husband make love to his mistress
through a spy hole in the floor of her own bedchamber could
never be accused of being a moralist.

As for Marguerite, given the pet name of Margot by the King
her brother, she was indeed a Queen of Hearts with her dancing
eyes, pale silken skin, dark shining curls and neat little figure. A
wanton little madam. Pretty enough to turn any man's head, even
her own brothers.

Through her children Catherine had found power, and she
intended to make full use of it, including taking advantage of her
daughter's famed beauty to win yet another crown for the House

of Valois, as well as bring peace to the realm. No matter what the cost.

The discussions continued, concluding the following morning in the palace's long gallery. Out by the harbour courtiers lazily dined on crab, *moules* and sardines, enjoying the hot summer sun. Servants hurried to and fro, sweating in the heat as royal barges were prepared and restocked in readiness for departure. But within doors the four delegates slowly paced the length of the cool, pillared corridor.

The young Queen of Spain kept her eyes on the ground, saying little; nor did Charles dare to utter a word as he trailed in the steps of his mother. Catherine was at her most magnificent, her customary black robes appearing strangely ominous amongst the shadows, like some creature from the netherworld. Alva was equally sombre in his Spanish garb.

Catherine broached the subject of the royal marriages, countering every argument the Duke brought against them. Little progress was made as he again held up her attitude towards the new religion as a difficulty, speaking with bitter hostility.

'King Philip wants to know whether or no you are going to remedy this religious business. Shall he count upon your son the King, or shall he act by himself? To ascertain this is the only reason why your daughter has come to Bayonne.'

Cold fury sharpened her tone as Catherine reminded the Duke that neither country could afford war. 'Spain certainly cannot from what I hear of the state of King Philip's treasury. I offer no promises to deal differently with the Huguenots. It would be an impossible task without inflicting great risk to the state.'

'Then I do not see how we can make progress on this matter.'

'I fear His Majesty fails fully to understand my position.'

'He understands it perfectly.'

Catherine's hands instinctively clenched with fury, and she quickly hid them in the folds of her gown. 'Have you brought any Protestant Lords with you today? I thought not,' she said as the Duke snorted at the very idea. 'It is perhaps a pity that neither of us thought to do so. Were I to do anything rash following this meeting, they would be bound to assume that we plotted against them, that our discussions today were concerned with their elimination and not a marriage union between the Houses of Valois and Hapsburg.'

The Duke's ambition and cruelty was all too evident in the sourness of his expression and the harsh nature of his reply. 'My mission is to ensure Your Majesty adopts a far more active anti-Huguenot policy. King Philip will offer every assistance, and I am confident will show all due appreciation, once that is achieved.'

'Ah, so now we come to it. What is it, exactly, that His Majesty requires?'

'No matter whether by fire or sword, the roots of evil must be cut away. His Majesty demands the immediate expulsion of the Huguenot ministers on pain of death, a ban on Huguenots in public office and . . .' A slight pause before he issued his final demand. '. . . the heads of their leaders: Condé, Rochefoucald, Andelot. And Coligny.'

Catherine's round eyes widened. Disposing of lesser men was never a problem to her, but she had no wish to dip her hands in the blood of princes, or the great lords of the kingdom. Such lengths would be considered only as a last resort. 'Coligny? How am I to take such a man?'

'The Admiral has been like a father to me,' protested the young King, unable to keep silent any longer.

Alva barely glanced at the boy. 'He is a Huguenot. No matter what the cost, these heretics must be dealt with. You are surely not a woman lacking in imagination, nor one to balk at their disposal. The destruction of Huguenots in France and Spain is essential. Death of their leaders is the only sure way to achieve that, by whatever means seem expedient. Otherwise . . .' Here his eyes narrowed and hardened as he paused for effect. '. . . my royal master must needs consider more drastic measures to bring France back into the fold.'

Catherine's expression was glacial as she prudently made no reply to this implied threat.

'The head of one salmon is worth the heads of a thousand frogs.'

It seemed that the talks were over, a conclusion reached and a course of action set in motion which would surely have far-reaching consequences. The party of four left the gallery, anxiously turning over their separate thoughts, unaware that hiding in an alcove the entire time had been the young Henry of Navarre, who had heard every word.

'The head of one salmon is worth the heads of a thousand frogs. That is what Alva said, Mother. I heard him with my own ears.'

Following the talks, the huge, unwieldy cavalcade had gone back on the road to proceed north through thick pine forests to Nérac. This was the home of Jeanne d'Albret, Queen of Navarre, and the stronghold of Protestantism. The town stood astride the river Baïse, north of Toulouse in the gently undulating country of Aquitaine.

Whenever they'd stopped to rest in towns along the way, the young King and the entire French Court had been deeply shocked by the sorry state of the desecrated churches and ruined monasteries, evidence of Huguenot zeal. The instant Catherine came face to face with the Queen of Navarre, she'd ordered Jeanne reinstate the old religion and make recompense for the vandalism.

His mother's response had been dry. 'You cannot plant by force what will not take root in the ground.'

Now the colour drained from her angular face as she learned the full extent of Catherine's betrayal, although Henry could see how she attempted to disguise her fear from him, her only son. 'You have learned to spy in the French Court then, my Enric?'

He gave his easy laugh, wanting to reassure her. 'It is a requirement. I managed to hide without them seeing me. Knowing we would be calling at Nérac, I wanted to tell you what it was they discussed so secretly.'

His heart had beat loud in his ears as he'd crouched in the alcove, unable to think what excuse he could offer were he to be discovered. Fortunately the group had been too absorbed in their conversation to notice him. Henry was afraid of the Queen Mother, and dreaded to think what she might have done had she caught him spying on her. Yet she could equally well be amused by his antics. Like any plump, jovial lady, she would laugh out loud at the way he chased the girls, at his oaths and coarse jokes, and the manner in which he swaggered about court, aping his royal cousins. Now he puffed out his chest with youthful pride.

'Am I not a diplomat, Mother?'

She kissed his brow. 'You are a true prince.'

Even though he had spent many years away from his beloved
mother, he remained very protective of her. Jeanne d'Albret was a
formidable woman, stern and righteous, single-minded in her cause
and a born rebel. At twelve years of age she'd had to be carried
to the altar in order to be married to the German Duke of Cleves
in spite of her defiance. The marriage was never consummated and
was eventually annulled. Her second husband, Antoine of Bourbon,
she had loved with all her heart. Unfortunately the sentiment had
not been returned, and he had never been faithful to her.

He'd died an ignominious death, being hit by a musket shot
whilst relieving himself at the Siege of Rouen, done as a gesture
of contempt to his enemies, and had forfeited his life as a result.
It was almost a fitting memorial for a King with a ripe sense of
humour. One Henry felt certain he'd inherited.

Finally freed from the bitterness of a loveless marriage, Jeanne
had thrown herself heart and soul into the new faith, becoming
a fanatical Puritan, surrounding herself with black-gowned ministers who conducted endless prayer-meetings. His mother had
come to despise luxury and revel in austerity and privation;
callously driving out priests and nuns from her land, forbidding
Papist ritual and did not hesitate to have churches pillaged and
destroyed. The Catholics might see her as a ruthless, despotic
heretic; Jeanne saw herself as simply observing the tenets of her
faith.

Since then Catherine had insisted Henry live at the French
Court. He knew that his mother missed him and longed to have
him home with her in Nérac, and to return him to the Huguenot
religion. He wanted that too. He went through the motions of
taking Mass with his royal cousins, but was indifferent to it.

'You know that I remain loyal to the reformed faith,' he assured
her now, as he had done many times in the past.

In truth he had no strong feelings either way. Henry felt no
passion for religion, couldn't quite understand this fanaticism of
hers. For some reason he could always see the other point of view,
and certainly wouldn't risk his life for a doctrine. Since he was
brought up to be a Huguenot, both by his mother and his tutor,
Gaucherie, then that is what he was, but he could just as easily
have been a Catholic. Wasn't there but one God? What did it
matter how He was worshipped? Why was one way right and

another wrong? And why did Catherine de Medici see the Protestant faith as a threat?

Jeanne listened with increasing alarm to the tale he was telling her. Some mischief had been hatched at that chateau amidst the semi-tropical, hot-house atmosphere of the Bay of Biscay. But she gave no indication of these thoughts to the young prince.

'You should join the hunting party, my son. The fresh air will bring the colour back to your cheeks, grown pallid by court life, I fear.'

Henry returned her warm embrace, basking in her approbation, yet he was equally eager to be out in the sunshine, as a certain dairy maid had caught his eye. He knew his mother was afraid he would grow up to be a licentious libertine like his father. Henry thought she might well be right, but why should he care? He loved women, whatever their age or class, whether court ladies or peasant girls. And if the desire to make love was in his blood, wasn't that better than making war? He strode from her privy chamber feeling proud of his achievement. Not such a country clod, perhaps.

Margot was bubbling over with happiness, not only because she would be with Guise back in Paris in a few short months, but Madame de Curton had smilingly informed her that she was, after all, to be spared marriage with a madman. The meeting at Bayonne had not been the success Catherine had hoped for, and the talks with Alva had ended in failure so far as the marriage proposals were concerned. Since these joyful tidings Margot had thrown herself wholeheartedly into the dancing and merry-making, even if it was only at the provincial Court of Nérac.

She thought the town pretty enough with its red-roofed galleried houses, and she loved to walk in the Queen's gardens along the banks of the wide River Baïse with its stone bridge and ancient mill. Today she was out following the hunt, riding lazily along the forest trails of the Landes de Gascogne, the tall oak and pine seeming to go on for ever. Margot kept to the back of the main party on her white palfrey, simply enjoying the freedom and the cool breeze in her hair, when Henry brought his horse to her side and challenged her to a gallop.

There was nothing Margot loved more than a dare and she

normally would have welcomed any adventure to break the tedium, yet she hesitated. She hated to be outshone, and this high-bred horse was trained to amble with a smooth gait over long distances. Beautiful as the animal was, she certainly wasn't made for a fast gallop.

'I think not. Pray ride with the other silly young boys, if you are bored.'

'Don't tell me you're afraid you might lose?' he teased.

'I am afraid of nothing, certainly not an oaf like you.'

'Or are you nervous that you may get lost?'

'Of course not.'

'If so, you need have no fear. This is my country. I know it well. And everyone knows me.'

'Every peasant, I dare say.'

Henry smiled. 'Indeed, and every farmer, every woodsman, every milkmaid. Have you not heard them hail me? They call me *noste Enric.*'

'Our Enric?' Margot scornfully mimicked. 'No doubt because no one else would ever lay claim to you.'

'Not even you?'

'Particularly not me! I'd sooner die than . . .' The words were no sooner out of her mouth than a wild boar suddenly charged out of the undergrowth in front of them, startling both Margot and her horse. Cursing, she fought with the reins to bring the skittish animal back under control while desperately attempting to maintain her seat in the saddle.

Henry put back his head and laughed, but when he reached out to grab the reins and help steady her mount, she turned on him like a spitting cat.

'I can manage perfectly well, if you please. Unlike the countless pretty girls who fawn at your feet, I need assistance from no one, least of all from *you.*'

This seemed to amuse him all the more. 'I'm thankful to hear it, since a Princess of France must surely be both brave and steadfast, although she must of course obey her husband, once she has one. If you were my wife, that would most certainly be the case.'

Cheeks flushed bright pink, and not simply from the effort of bringing her mount back to a steady gait, Margot responded sharply. 'Only if a husband were worthy of respect, which you would not be. I should never do as *you* ordered me. Fortunately, I never shall be your wife, so the point will not be put to the test.'

'We may yet be obliged to consider the possibility, since you are back on the market. Would you not care to be my Queen?'

'No, I would not! Your clothes are outmoded, your manners worse than a peasant's, and your breath smells of garlic.'

Henry laughed. 'Of course it does, I'm a Gascon.'

'That does not mean you must be quite so vulgar.'

But he was no longer listening to her. One of her mother's *Escadron Volant* trotted her horse by them at precisely that moment, a pretty brunette with green eyes. Henry instantly lost interest in their sparring and galloped off in pursuit of the girl. Margot was furious. How fickle that boy was.

The moment she was alone Jeanne reached for quill pen and ink, wasting not a moment in sending a message to warn her fellow leaders of this threat.

Condé she knew to be ambitious, brave and cunning, a military genius, and as a Bourbon Prince more than ready to claim the throne were King Charles to be deposed. Hump-backed he may be, but far from repulsive in either appearance or character. For all his brilliance he had a weakness for women, who responded easily to his charm and his merry blue eyes. Such antics did not endear him to Coligny, the Admiral, who considered his colleague morally unstable, being himself of a more serious nature.

Jeanne would consider any threat to the leaders' safety as tantamount to a declaration of war.

She wrote and dispatched the letter with all speed before returning to the entertainment planned for her guests.

Looking about her, Catherine remarked, 'There are so many nobles here that every evening in the ballroom I could fancy I was still in Bayonne, if only I could see the Queen, my daughter. And everybody dances together: Huguenots, Papists and all, so smoothly that it is impossible to believe that they are as they are. If God willed that they were as wise elsewhere as they are here, we should at last be at rest.'

'We would indeed, Your Majesty,' Jeanne agreed, but both queens knew this to be a dream that neither would see fulfilled.

* * *

Gaspard de Coligny read the letter from Jeanne in his beloved rose garden at the family home, the Château de Châtillon-sur-Loing. He was a sober, kindly, family man who loved his wife, his children, and his garden almost as much as he did his religion and his country. He'd enjoyed a pious and simple upbringing with his three brothers: Pierre, who had died young, Odet who had become a cardinal, and Andelot whose career was very much parallel to his own.

He had no love of war and no appetite for torture, unlike some of the generals, nor did he tolerate insurrection within the ranks: no pillage, robbery, loose women or dice games. He made stout laws for his troops and did not flinch at ensuring they were kept, considering himself tough but fair; a solemn and ruthless advocate of justice, as well as a ferocious foe on the battlefield. Because of this, his men honoured and followed him.

Coligny read the Queen of Navarre's warning with the kind of stoic indifference one would expect from an old soldier. Later in the day he received another message from the Queen Mother, which troubled him more.

'Her Majesty is demanding that you go to court and take part in a reconciliation with the Guises,' Téligny informed him, his tone brittle with anxiety. He was the son of a respected Huguenot family and a young soldier whom Coligny had taken into his home for training in arms and the art of diplomacy.

'Does she indeed?'

The Guises had seen him as their enemy ever since the murder of the head of their house, Francis, duc de Guise, two years ago in 1563. The murder had been committed by one Poltrot de Méry, a Protestant who had sworn he was Coligny's agent, no doubt under torture as he'd later retracted his confession. Despite there being no sound evidence the Guises remained convinced of Coligny's guilt. Paris too was ready enough to believe the charge, being Catholic and passionate in their support of Francis's son, the dashing young Henri of Guise.

Poltrot had been swiftly and publicly despatched, torn into four parts by strong horses whipped to north, south, east and west, but Coligny had so far escaped unharmed, if still an object of loathing to the Guises.

Now he could not help but wonder what game the Queen

Mother was playing by demanding this reconciliation. Clearly she saw the enmity between the two families as a danger to the nation's peace, and perhaps to the King. But one could never be sure with Catherine that she might not be playing a double game: that she wished for the appearance of peace between them, while at the same time with her serpent's guile she made other plans.

'Have I not sufficiently demonstrated my innocence by proving the money I paid to Poltrot was for a horse?'

'The Guises claim to possess an incriminating letter.'

'Yet they have never produced such a document, because it does not exist.'

'They must see that you are not the kind of man to involve yourself in treachery. You are upright and honourable. Why do they not remember how friendly you once were with Francis?'

A wistful sadness crept over the older man's face as he smiled in recollection. 'Indeed, that is so. Did I not keep him well supplied with the pick of the crop of my best melons?'

'It would be unwise for you to go to court, Monsieur.'

'My relationship with the King has ever been a good one,' Coligny demurred, while privately acknowledging Charles was weak with little power. 'And the Queen Mother depends upon me to negotiate a union between His Majesty and Elizabeth I. As Admiral I am also responsible for strengthening the royal navy. She relies entirely upon my service.'

Téligny remained obdurate. 'I still do not recommend you answer her call. The court is a dangerous place at this time for those of our faith, and for you in particular. Does not the Queen of Navarre's letter warn you to take extra care?'

Coligny rested a gentle hand upon the young man's shoulder. 'I welcome your support, Téligny, as always, but you know as well as I that if the Queen Mother summons me to court, I must obey.'

Leaving Henry with his mother for a short visit, the court journeyed on through western France, through Bordeaux and Nantes, accompanied by a large body of men, which proved wise as they were frequently heckled and jeered by Calvinist fanatics in this very Protestant region. By November they reached Angers, and from there they sailed up the Loire, stopping at various chateaux en route, including the Queen Mother's favourite, Chenonceau, till they reached Moulins, where the planned reconciliation was to take place.

Catherine hoped this might be the day to act on the promise she'd made to Alva. She would welcome the opportunity permanently to separate Coligny's clever military brain from those able shoulders of his.

But there were too many of them, and they came well armed, bristling with suspicion. There would be other opportunities but today she must smile and dissemble, and keep the peace amongst these dangerous rivals.

She watched with interest as they warily circled each other. Coligny and the Prince de Condé on the one side, and the entire Guise family, including Anne d'Este, widow of Francis of Guise, on the other. The two families had not been in the same room together for months, convinced as they were that the man really responsible for the murder of the head of their House was Coligny, and not Poltrot.

The greatest amongst the Guises now was the Cardinal of Lorraine, that sly old fox who spent far more time with his many mistresses than reading the scriptures. His nephew, the handsome young Henri de Guise, was largely ignoring his Bourbon rivals as he sat whispering with Margot.

These powerful men thought themselves so grand, so supremely important; the Guises with their eye on the throne arrogantly challenging her power. Coligny determined to oppose the orthodox religion of the realm. She meant to teach them all a little humility.

Catherine curled her lips into a practised smile. 'My dear friends, it is good to see you all gathered here together. Without question we all mourn the death of your leader, the great Francis of Guise, victim of a cruel and cowardly act. But for the sake of France we must strive to banish this resentment that exists between your two houses. My one wish is to see you reconciled.'

Charles said, 'We wish to officially acquit our dear friend Coligny of any part in the great warlord's tragic death. Let us see this matter settled.'

There was a short, tense silence as nobody spoke, nobody moved.

'Come now, Cardinal,' Catherine urged. 'We require you to offer a kiss of reconciliation, of forgiveness for the ill feeling between you, which a man so pious as yourself should have no difficulty with. Think of it as necessary for the good of our nation.'

'I bow to your greater wisdom, Madame,' the Cardinal dryly responded, 'since you always put the good of the nation before your own.' With these insincere, ambiguous words, and beneath the cold, watchful gaze of the Queen Mother, he stepped forward towards his bitter rival.

Coligny stood pale faced, his hand on his sword, carrying out the order with obvious distaste. When it was done, both men stepped quickly away from each other. It was a theatrical display which fooled no one.

Catherine next turned to the Cardinal's nephew, the young Henri, Duke of Guise. Face flushed with youthful defiance, he refused point-blank to play the game.

'You ask too much. I cannot betray the memory of my father, not even to please Your Majesty.'

Catherine considered the heartfelt passion in the boy's face, his rigid stance with his hand on his sword, as was Coligny's still, and knew she had lost. She noted how the rest of his family stood proudly behind him, emphasizing by their very stance that although their great leader was dead, they nonetheless had a fine replacement in the form of his son. The meeting had turned into a farce. For all her efforts, her clever acting and dissembling, nothing had been achieved.

Henri and Margot walked hand in hand in the park. 'How could I betray my father's memory? You know how I loved him, how I have sworn to take revenge for his murder.'

Margot pulled Henri down on a grassy sward to hold him in her arms, breathing in the warm scent of his skin, loving him, swearing her complete support as emotion overcame him over the loss of the father he loved so dearly.

'You are right, my love. How could you risk it? I thought you so brave to stand up to my mother the Queen like that. It was unfair of her to attempt this nonsense of a reconciliation. The order certainly did not come from the King. Charles has far too much sensitivity.'

The young man dashed the tears from his eyes, embarrassed by this show of weakness. 'I hate Coligny. The coward should own up to his crime. Poltrot was but a half-witted youth of twenty, clearly acting under orders. My father didn't stand a chance. He wasn't even wearing his usual coat of mail, and was shot in the back by an arquebus.'

'I remember that my mother offered her finest surgeons, sitting by his bedside at the camp until he breathed his last,' Margot said, combing her fingers through Guise's fair curls as she leaned against the hard strength of his shoulder.

'Poltrot said Coligny had offered him one hundred écus to do the job. What price is that for a life? My father's life, for pity's sake! A hero, a warlord.' Too agitated to sit still, the hot-headed young man broke free from her embrace to stride back and forth in a fury of impatience. 'I know Coligny swore on his life that he did no such thing, that he was innocent, but I do not believe him. He is a liar! The plot came directly from him. He freely admitted that Poltrot was one of his men, but it is no defence to say that he would never have trusted the gibbering fool to carry out such a task. The fellow's very idiocy might have been considered a defence.'

Margot frowned. 'I am sure you have every right to be angry, my love.' Whatever the rights and wrong of the case, Margot wished he would stop ranting and railing, and hold her in his arms.

Guise swung about, fists clenched, eyes burning with hatred. 'And do you know what else he said? That although he was inno-cent, he nevertheless regarded the duke's death as the greatest benefit which could have befallen the kingdom, God's Church, and in particular his whole House. What kind of remark is that to make about *my father*?'

'Despicable!'

'It fills me with rage to think of it. I'd rather run the black-guard through with my sword than kiss his cheek.'

'You can kiss mine.'

He looked at her lovely face, at the glittering promise in her chestnut eyes, then put back his head and laughed. Gathering Margot tightly in his arms, he kissed her cheek, her lips, her hair, the smooth silk of her throat. 'At least I have you. Know that I love you, Margot.'

Warmth spread through her as sweet as honey. 'I know it. I carry your love in my heart every day.'

'They may allow us to marry in time; we can still hope.'

'There is always hope, and I shall ever love you.'

'And one day – one blessed day – I shall have my revenge on Coligny.'

Part Two

LOVE AND WAR

1567–1572

September 1567

The royal family were enjoying a sunny autumn holiday at the château de Montceaux-en-Brie. Margot was delighted, for she loved to ride, and would each morning join the hunt with her mother and brothers. It felt good to have the sun on her face, the wind streaming through her dark hair; to remind herself that she was fourteen years old, and still free.

The question of her marriage had not been discussed for a year or more, but then everyone was too concerned with the fact that the religious wars had broken out again. Last year Alva had been responsible for slaughtering thousands of innocents in the Netherlands. Since then, monks and Catholics had been killed by Protestants in retaliation; religious statues destroyed or desecrated, churches burned, with much barbarity on both sides. Neighbour once more distrusted neighbour, brother turned against brother.

Perhaps sickened by the scourge of killings, things had quietened down in recent months and the Queen Mother had decided that an autumn holiday would be the very thing for the King's increasingly fragile health.

'Country food and fresh air will do us all good,' she had declared. There was nothing Catherine loved more than a display of family unity.

It was as they were returning from a morning's hunt that a rider appeared at full gallop. Skittering to a halt in a cloud of dust, he proved to be one of Catherine's grooms and blurted out a warning of a plot by the Huguenots to kidnap the royal party.

Catherine reined in her horse with a cry of vexation, her eyes cold as they settled on the poor beleaguered messenger. 'They wouldn't dare! Tis all bluster and hot air.'

'But Madame, there are reports of soldiers massing at Rosay-en-Brie. I beg you move to Meaux, which is better fortified.'

The Queen Mother took some persuading, irritated at having her holiday interrupted, and convinced that peace was at last secure. Finally, she agreed to the change of quarters, although with strict orders that the family holiday should proceed as before. Fortified or not, she had no intention of confining herself to the house, and continued to ride out every morning. Margot felt nought but admiration for her mother's courage.

But then who would dare beard the she-wolf in her den, let alone when she was holidaying with her cubs?

It was barely three o'clock in the morning, with dawn not yet broken, when Margot was shaken awake by Madame de Curton. 'Hurry, my lady. You must dress quickly. The castle is under attack.'

Margot was out of bed in a second, reaching for her linen even as she rubbed the sleep from her eyes. 'What is happening?'

The governess let out a frantic moan. 'We are in danger of being murdered in our beds.'

The pair embraced, close to tears, finding some comfort in being together, as always, but there was no time to linger. Mayhem had broken out. Maids of honour were screaming, dogs barking, servants, dukes and princes running about in equal panic, the entire royal household out on the road, fleeing for their lives.

Margot and Madame de Curton travelled in the Queen Mother's chariot with the King and other family members, protected by Swiss guards within a square of pikes. Senior courtiers followed close behind in the fastest, lightest carriages. The rest were obliged to walk, or run if they could. The procession was hotly pursued, and never had Margot known such fear. Her heart was pounding, expecting at any moment to be apprehended by the enemy and her throat slit. It took twice as long as normal to journey to Paris so that they arrived close to collapse and weeping with shock and horror.

Charles at once fell into one of his tantrums. He wept and raged, vowing he never wished to be frightened like that ever again. 'I swear I will pursue the culprits to their deaths.'

It was left to Margot to calm him, a skill at which she had become adept. The young king, feeling lonely and sick, trusted no one, and his sister had become his solace and dearest friend, although Margot grew ever wary of upsetting him.

'Do not let this incident distress you, dear brother,' she soothed. 'See how well protected we are here in the Louvre. They can do us no further harm.'

'I am no coward to hide away, Margot. I will not be treated so rudely!' Charles cried, chewing on his fingernails as he moved about his privy chamber in great agitation.

'Of course you are not; no one has accused you of such.'

'I shall gather my men and fight. I must kill whoever has the effrontery to rise against us.'

'Sire, you must leave that task to others. You are too important to the realm.'

Madame de Curton added her own pleas for calm, and called for his nurse. The old woman came quickly and warmed a decoction of camomile tea, then held the young king warm and safe against her breast till he fell sleep. Margot watched with sorrow in her heart. Charles did so need to be a child again sometimes.

The danger remained strong, despite the relative safety of the Louvre, as the Huguenot rebels prepared to besiege the city. All entry into Paris was blocked, even the Seine, and the people soon grew hungry for lack of supplies. It was exactly as Catherine had feared: the Huguenots suspected her of being in league with Philip, and yet the Catholics didn't trust her either.

'This attack is the greatest wickedness in the world. I will pacify and conciliate no longer.'

She went to her desk, took up a sharpened quill and penned a furious letter to Philip of Spain. '*You may imagine with what distress I see the kingdom returning to the troubles and afflictions from which I laboured to deliver it.*'

It was almost two months before the siege finally ended with the death of the Lord High Constable at the Battle of Saint-Denis. Whereupon, blinded by her passion for Anjou, Catherine appointed her favourite son Lieutenant-General and put him in full command of the army. He was sixteen years old.

Anjou strutted with arrogance at the honour, confident he could make a good leader. Charles was less happy by the appointment, wishing that he could be the one to lead his men to war, and made no attempt to disguise his displeasure.

'I only agree to this because my brother will have great soldiers to advise him: the Duke of Nemours, Montpensier, and the Marechal de Tavannes.'

Catherine soothed the King's hurt pride, disguising her own reservations with a manufactured smile. The state of the treasury gave little prospect of a swift conclusion to their difficulties. And led by an effeminate fop who had been cosseted and petted throughout his life, was unused to the hardships of soldiering, there seemed little prospect of an easy victory. Yet Anjou was the love of her life and she must give him this chance to prove himself.

A bitter winter followed, and Coligny at Châtillon grew increasingly uneasy, particularly when a stranger, an Italian, came to live close to his chateau. He was being quietly surrounded by his enemies. Word had filtered through that Catherine had ordered the Admiral and Condé to be seized. She wanted the latter's '*tête si chère*'. His head, however, was far more valuable to the Huguenots still attached to his neck, not least to Condé himself.

Coligny swiftly moved his family to Noyers in Burgundy, together with the Prince de Condé, and they began to gather supporters. Still grieving over the recent death of his wife, yet he rallied sufficiently to write to Catherine in protest, accusing the Queen Mother of plotting to kill them. '*God will not leave unpunished the shedding of so much innocent blood.*'

It was the end of August, and without waiting for a reply the Huguenot leaders, along with their followers, slipped quietly away from Noyers that same night, and set out for La Rochelle, finding strength in being together. There was little time for mourning as Coligny led the way, his four young children by his side. Condé carried a babe in his arms, his wife the Marquise ill and fretting, the couple's children straggling along beside her. The rest of the company marched in almost biblical procession behind.

The numbers grew as many more joined them en route till they were likened to the flight from Egypt of God's chosen people: like children of Israel hopeful of a new land and redemption.

As they approached the Loire they saw that the river ran high. Panic rippled through them as they felt certain their pursuers must be closing in, but just as with the children of Israel, the floods subsided at an opportune moment and they crossed in safety. Yet they knew that their enemies would be waiting for them on the opposite bank, and with one accord fell to their knees and sang a psalm.

'Lord save us and be with us in the hour of our need,' Coligny prayed, and all who were with him found comfort in his calm.

Refreshed and invigorated from their prayers they travelled on with renewed hope, despite the perils that lay ahead, the crying children, and the hunger that cramped their bellies. In the first days of September, Condé and Coligny entered La Rochelle at the head of their followers.

Henry of Navarre lay in the summer meadows at Nérac savouring the charms of Fleurette, the gardener's daughter, the wars of religion the last thing on his mind. Following his visit with his mother towards the end of the royal progress in 1565, he'd returned to the French Court. But in recent months Jeanne had again secured his release for a visit, once more appealing directly to the King to bypass the Queen Mother's objections.

He was busy with the fastenings of Fleurette's bodice, her plump breasts spilling out of the low neck of her print gown, when the pretty young maid excitedly informed him that he was to be a father. Arrested by this startling news, all passion instantly deserted him. Throughout this long, delightful dalliance, any possible consequences of the pleasures they enjoyed together had never troubled him.

'Are you pleased?' the girl asked, giggling, and he had to smile because she was so very delightful. The dimples in her cheeks, her soulful eyes and the comeliness of her figure were really quite exquisite. Was it any wonder if he could hardly keep his hands off her, or that she had fallen? 'I shall give you a son,' she proudly announced, as if she could easily arrange such matters. 'And he shall be a fine Prince of Navarre, like his father.'

Henry removed her clinging arms from about his neck. Young as he was, she was by no means his first amourette and marriage was the last thing on his mind, certainly not to a gardener's daughter. But it was no fault of hers if she was generous and loving. He kissed her full red lips and regretfully tugged her bodice back into place. 'I trust he will be the image of his pretty mother. But how could we wed, my sweet? I love you dearly,' he lied, 'but my mother would never agree to the match.'

Fleurette pouted. 'My father would expect you to do the honourable thing. He would not have me ruined. He was very angry when I told him.'

Henry paled slightly, hiding his alarm as always with that merry laugh of his while his mind rapidly sought some excuse to escape. His mother might well hear of this scandal before he had time to break the news gently to her himself. She would not be pleased. Jeanne d'Albret put great store by high moral behaviour, and making the gardener's daughter *enceinte* certainly did not come into that category. Yet it was done now, so he must accept it. He would not be the first Prince of the Blood to produce a by-blow, and he accurately surmised that this child would not be the last of his born on the wrong side of the blanket.

He was on his feet now, still kissing Fleurette's hands and swearing his undying love. 'Do not fret, my sweet. I will not abandon you, and shall always recognize the boy, or girl, as my own. You will be well taken care of.'

'Of course I shall, as your wife,' the girl insisted, pressing her eager young body against his.

'Ah, there now, I believe my mother is calling me. We will talk of this later.' And with a last, lingering kiss, Henry left her.

One glance at his mother's face was sufficient to assure him that she had already heard the news. Henry gave a resigned shrug, smiling sheepishly. 'What can I say? These things happen. She can be properly taken care of, I trust? I would not see her in distress.'

Jeanne's expression was unforgiving. 'You distress me, your mother, by this unseemly behaviour. But I will speak to the maid's father and see that all due consideration is given to her when it comes to her lying-in. You must try to set a better example, Enric, and curb these rapacious appetites of yours.'

Should he remind her that they were but natural, certainly so far as he was concerned? Perhaps not. He had long since learned that dallying with servants and peasant girls was a sensitive subject to his mother. He was undoubtedly following in his father's, and his grandfather's footsteps. Perhaps that was why she wasted no further time in chastising him now, knowing it to be useless.

'We have other, far more important matters to concern ourselves with today than dallying in the rose arbour with servant girls.

If you are old enough to take a mistress, then it is time you began to practise the skills of soldiering. Condé and Coligny will be your mentors.'

Henry's expression was rueful, but he could see that something was afoot. The whole castle was abuzz, preparations clearly being made for their departure, and before the end of September, Jeanne d'Albret, the leader of the Huguenots, and her son, the fifteen-year-old Bourbon Prince, Henry of Navarre, rode into La Rochelle to join their followers.

The Queen Mother was at Saint-Maur, recovering from one of her periodic gastric attacks. Margot dutifully tended to her, and to the King who grew increasingly frail and thin, and was presently recovering from an abscess. She never raised any objection to helping to ease their ills, although she always felt rather nervous of Charles. His beautiful, golden-brown eyes and sympathetic expression hid a fatal flaw of insanity. If she carried out a task less efficiently than he pettishly demanded, or failed to answer his every beck and call, then he would lash out at her, pinch her arm, or fall into a fit, as if she were the naughty child and not he. Apart from his old nurse, no one but herself and his mistress Marie Touchet could keep him calm. Certainly not his mother, who had quite the opposite effect. He was remarkably obedient and dutiful to the Queen Mother's wishes, which was her intention of course, but if Catherine pressed him too far he would fall into a rage. Even Margot, who was fond of him, could not deny that he was an odd boy.

He often struck up inappropriate friendships with lute players or servants, and would sit with these unlikely companions listening to music or poetry readings by candlelight till well past midnight. To be fair, their mother never objected as the sessions seemed to bring Charles some sort of contentment.

At other times he would sink into worrying moods of deep melancholy, stay in bed all day, or worse, be gripped by a mad frenzy when he would don a mask, waken some of his wilder friends, and, taking lighted torches, would go on a rampage around the darkened streets of Paris. They'd call on some poor unfortunate, drag him from his bed and beat him senseless, purely for the pleasure of it. Or he might turn on his dogs or horses and thrash them instead. When the lust for violence came upon him, there was nothing anyone could do to stop it. The mere sight of blood seemed to both terrify and excite him.

There were certainly times when he frightened her, and Margot was careful always to do as she was bid, and thereby avoid a beating.

One afternoon, despite the risk of upsetting the King, Margot couldn't resist creeping away to see Guise, simply for the bliss of falling into his arms, and to savour the thrill of his demanding kisses. Soon he would be off to war with her brother Anjou, and Margot dreaded his going. She would not know a moment's peace while he was away, fearful he might be wounded, or worse.

'You will write to me every day,' she begged, as they sat together in a secret arbour.

'Of course, my love.'

He only had to look at her, or smile, and a quiver of longing would ripple through her. She gasped as he traced his lips over the curve of her throat, slid his fingers beneath the bodice of her gown to tease the dark bud of her nipple. She needed him so much. They belonged together. Why could her mother not see this and understand?

'I must go; the King will be wanting me.'

But he pulled her closer into his arms. 'Just one more kiss. Stay a little longer.' His mouth was hot on hers, the urgent trembling in his young body irresistible, his hand on her silky thigh beneath her skirts tempting her to taste unknown dangers.

Margot stayed with him till her hair was tumbled and her cheeks were hectic with passion, and when she finally raced through the rooms in answer to the King's call, she found him in a fine temper.

Catching Marie Touchet's warning glance, Margot sank into a deep curtsey then quickly reached to kiss his hand. Charles snatched it away and smacked her hard across the face.

'There, now you will be sorry for defying me. I have been calling for you this hour past.'

'I'm sorry, Your Majesty.' Margot was trembling, her face stinging, but she offered no excuses, no lies. Charles would not have believed them, and any dispute would only inflame his temper still further. She was grateful for Marie's presence, otherwise he may well have set about her with his whip. Fortunately, his mistress deftly distracted the King with a glass of warm cinnamon milk, and the moment passed. Until the next time.

Henri, duc de Guise, had grown even more handsome at eighteen than Margot's fond memories of him in that playful joust as a boy. His blond hair had darkened somewhat, but, like his father before him, he possessed genuine charisma and an engaging personality. The Parisians loved him; he was their hero. They would call to him as he rode by, or touch his cloak if he walked amongst them. They would call out '*Vive Guise*' and he would sweep off his great plumed hat and bow to them, grinning broadly.

He was a young man with a passion to emulate his father, the old warlord and military hero. Henri had been but thirteen years old when his father, Francis, the second duke, had been murdered, dispatched because of his opposition to appeasement with the Huguenots. Known as *Le Balafré* from a scar he'd received in battle, he'd been head of the House of Lorraine and an ardent Catholic. The blood feud born out of tragedy on that fateful day existed still, the Guise family convinced that the killing had been instigated by the admiral, Gaspard de Coligny. And the young duke was ardent in his desire for revenge.

But none of that was on his mind today as he stood before his uncle, the immensely powerful Cardinal de Lorraine. Tall and regal in his scarlet robes, the ecclesiastic exuded an awesome presence, known for his extreme Catholic views as well as the fact that his family's interests were of paramount importance to him. Guise was curious to know what scheme the old man was planning now, for he'd been summoned to his apartments to discuss his future.

A manservant brought wine as they sat in the window embrasure, looking out over the gardens of the Louvre, talking of the time Henri had hoped to gain military experience by fighting the Turks, but had been disappointed not to be involved in any action.

'Which was why I returned home to take part in the wars of religion, as they are again raging.'

'Nevertheless, I hear that by demonstrating immense courage, you have won over the love of the people. It appears to be a trait of yours. Haven't you already won Princess Marguerite's heart? She is growing into a great beauty.'

'She is indeed.'

'And you are fond of the girl?'

Guise paused before answering, scenting a purpose behind this apparently superficial enquiry, and wary of revealing his feelings too easily. 'We enjoy a mild flirtation,' he agreed with a wry smile.

The Cardinal laughed. 'I understand it has progressed far beyond that, although I see no wrong in it, I assure you.'

Guise frowned. 'I doubt her mother would agree.'

The man who had successfully installed his family close to the throne, as well as acquiring himself one of the finest suite of rooms in the Louvre on the old King's death, had no intention of being blighted by an ambitious mother, even if she were a queen. Catherine's second daughter, the Princess Claude, had already married the head of his house. He had once nursed hopes of a union between their girl Mary, Queen of Scots, and Charles or Anjou, but that was impossible now she was effectively being held prisoner in England. Guise was his last hope, and what better way to strengthen the ties between the two houses than by marrying his handsome nephew to the delectable Marguerite de Valois.

'You would not be against the idea of marriage? She is a prize worth winning, as I'm sure you'll agree. I would be willing to finance such an alliance, under certain conditions.'

Guise considered his uncle with undisguised interest. There was no disputing that he loved Margot. Who could not fail to love her, since she was so utterly irresistible? She had fire and a strong streak of independence, as well as rare beauty. But he was also ambitious. With royal blood in his veins, and a weak king who held on to the throne only through his mother's skills, Guise had every confidence that he could one day win the crown.

There were the two younger brothers, of course, but they too were sickly. He envied Anjou his position as Lieutenant-General of the army, a role Guise felt he could carry out with much greater skill, since he was now the accepted leader of the Catholic faction. But, inexperienced as Anjou was, the boy who was heir to the throne could easily be killed in battle. Alençon he dismissed without thought.

Henry of Navarre was the most serious contender as a Bourbon Prince, but he was a Huguenot, therefore Guise considered he possessed the greater right to succeed.

The wars of religion were far more than a battle between Catholic and Protestant. They were a fight for power, one the House of Guise meant to win. And, as his uncle indicated, did he not also have the love of Paris?

Aware of the Queen Mother's suspicion of the Guises, he had never considered a match between himself and Margot a serious possibility. Now he did so, and very much approved of the notion. 'What kind of conditions?'

'You would need to play your hand very carefully. The way you are behaving at the moment, like a love-sick puppy in the throes of first love, is attracting unwelcome attention and you will soon be the talk of the court. You must counter it by spreading your favours a little wider.'

The young man stiffened. 'I have no wish to do so. My feelings for Margot are neither light nor frivolous. I love her.'

'Indeed, and she adores you, only a blind fool would doubt it.' The old man leaned closer, the scent of the incense that always lingered about his person suddenly overpowering, making Guise feel slightly sick. 'Catherine de Cleves, the Princess de Porcien, has always favoured you.'

'She is married.'

'Not for much longer. Her husband is in his death throes. Besides, there are advantages in taking a married woman as your mistress.' The old lecher, who had never kept his own vows of chastity too strictly, leered mockingly at the young boy.

Guise flushed with anger. 'I have no wish for any other mistress.'

'But you wish for a crown?'

Silence hung between them as Guise fought with his principles. As great-grandson of Louis XII through his maternal line he saw no reason why he should not pursue his claim. He was not only a Prince of the Blood but also had access to an enormous revenue. And soon he would add his own heroic achievements to those of his father's.

Satisfied that he'd scored a point, the Cardinal continued, 'That being the case, we need to keep the scandal-mongers off the scent until we are certain of our quarry.'

Guise said, 'The Queen Mother is more serpent than fox; she will not easily be cornered. She is busy making all manner of marriage proposals for Margot. How would you ever hope to win her round?'

'Leave Her Majesty to me. I am richer even than the monarch himself, and, in my experience, a vast fortune is a great softener of prejudice. Besides, marriage negotiations rarely run smoothly, and I will choose my moment to put our proposition to her. Meanwhile, you must do what you enjoy most, continue to make yourself agreeable to our delectable princess, but also make political court to Catherine of Cleves.'

'And if Margot should hear of it and grow jealous, would that not ruin my chances with her?'

'You must judge how much attention needs to be paid to each,' the old man laughed. 'A challenge you will no doubt enjoy.'

'And how far should I go? As far as she will allow? That may be some distance, Uncle. Margot is near a grown woman and hot for love.'

The Cardinal growled. 'Don't test my patience, you young pup. Too much dalliance with the lady and you'll be facing a charge of high treason.'

'Treason? Surely you jest.'

'She is a Daughter of France, a Princess of the Blood. Deflower her, and the wrath of the House of Valois will put your head on the block. Remember that when you go a-courting.'

Angered by the biblical allusion which soon reached her ears, Catherine reiterated that her sole aim was to run the Huguenots to earth, defeat and destroy them.

She blamed everyone for failing to capture the leaders, and her mood for conciliation was long past. Anjou was kicking his heels, impatiently waiting to lead his army to victory while Charles jealously longed to prove himself. Catherine reassured her eldest son of the importance in his remaining quietly at home so that he could properly perform his duties as King. She knew that he did not obey her out of love, but from fear.

Of all her six children, only Anjou was not afraid of her, which was exactly how she liked it. She cared only for him, her favourite. Henri did not fall into a frenzy at the slightest thing. Nor was he overly sensitive. He was brilliant and handsome, audacious and daring. One day he would make a better king than this puny son who was feeble in both mind and body, tainted by the sins of his fathers.

Margot had grown more beautiful as the years passed, and was now quite the shining star of the court. The people of Paris had marvelled at her beauty as she passed by in the Easter procession, her face pale and serene, revealed for all to admire as she rarely wore a mask. She would adorn her dark hair, which she wore naturally curled down her back, with quantities of pearls and brilliant diamonds in the form of stars. Her figure, tall and elegant despite her youth, clothed in a gown of cloth of gold, the richest and most beautiful ever seen in France. Who could fail to love her?

Catherine saw how all eyes followed her daughter, including those of Henri of Guise. The pair were far too close for comfort, and the sooner the girl was found a husband, the better.

When the time came for Anjou to depart for Étampes, she kissed her most adored son a loving farewell, promising to join him the moment she could. Her daughter's embraces for her soldier lover were far more affectionate, and Catherine watched with displeasure as Margot had great difficulty in hiding her tears.

Mother and daughter returned to Paris and Catherine at once set about assembling the necessary supplies for the army, raising funds from whatever sources she could. The treasury was running low and she willingly pawned her jewellery, stopping at nothing to finance this most vital enterprise. She also issued a decree ordering all Protestant ministers to leave the kingdom within fifteen days on pain of death.

Despite her undoubted skill at manipulating events to suit herself, Catherine was riddled with uncertainties and superstitions, and would frequently consult wizards or astrologers, very much believing that the dead had more to say of relevance than the living. She was never without her talisman bracelet with its links of devil's hieroglyphs and engraved human skulls. Now, in accordance with these superstitions, Catherine visited a magician and had him read the star signs of the Huguenot leaders. She ordered him to make replica figures of each, jointed with screws that she could turn and turn.

One way or another, she would have their heads.

Catherine's frustration and fury were soon overwhelmed by other emotions as a messenger came clattering into the courtyard one morning, his horse in a lather as he'd ridden long and hard from Spain. Madame de Curton was the one deputed to relay the news to the Queen Mother, which she did with tears streaming down her face.

'Our precious child, our sweet young queen, has been taken from us. Our beloved Elisabeth has died giving birth to a barely formed girl child, who, I understand, likewise did not survive.'

Catherine's grief was dreadful to behold. She remembered those precious few days they'd enjoyed together in Bayonne when for the first time she'd begun to get to know this daughter of hers. How cruel fate was to snatch her away so young. She forgot the accusations of suspicion, the frequent quarrels and tears, her annoyance that Elisabeth had become the mouthpiece of her sombre husband, Catherine's most feared enemy. Since then their new-found intimacy had continued by letter, and strangely it was only in the written word that Catherine had found herself able properly to express her feelings. Now she hid in her privy chamber and wept as any mother would for a lost child.

Yet within hours she'd rallied sufficiently to appear before her council declaring she would offer Margot, now fifteen, as a replacement. Margot herself, when she heard this news, was horrified. To marry her sister's widowed husband was abhorrent to her.

Fortunately, distraught at losing his lovely young Queen whom he'd adored, Philip promptly declined Catherine's generous offer, and the ties between Spain and France fell loose once again.

Madame de Curton felt only relief that her precious charge was to be spared from becoming that stern monarch's fourth wife. The governess wished her little lady nought but happiness, if only a suitable husband could be found for her. So far, fortune had not smiled upon this quest.

A memorial service was held for Elisabeth, in which Charles stood in tears beside his black-veiled mother. He presented a sorrowful, desolate figure in violet satin, somewhat unprepossessing with his slightly crooked neck and a face gaunt from long periods of sickness.

But little time was allowed for mourning as Catherine sought a new marriage proposal for Margot, this time to Philip's nephew, the young King of Portugal, who largely ignored Catherine's request. The poor demented Don Carlos had died earlier in the summer, allegedly having caught pneumonia because of a predilection for sleeping on ice in order to avoid the intense summer heat. Catherine next pursued the King of Hungary, but that too came to nothing. If Margot was indeed a political pawn, she seemed to be of little appeal to anyone, her beauty apparently immaterial.

In a rare moment of sympathy, Catherine told her, 'My child, you were born in an unhappy age.'

But she remained determined to use this last unmarried daughter to bring another crown to the House of Valois, as well as peace to the realm, no matter at what cost to her own happiness.

Until then, it would be Madame de Curton's responsibility to keep the girl chaste. Considering Margot's growing fascination for a certain *chevalier*, it was a task no one in their right mind would envy.

Margot was thrilled when they received an invitation to visit her brother at the front, which meant she would also be able to see a certain *chevalier*. She guessed that Anjou was finding army life difficult. No doubt he missed his silken sheets, his warm, scented bedchamber, the court luxuries to which he was accustomed. He was not a natural soldier. He might enjoy the glory of victory but as lieutenant-general he was only in nominal command; Biron and Tavannes were the ones really responsible for the campaign.

She easily persuaded her mother to accept and the necessary preparations were made, Catherine arranging to meet her favourite son at the Castle of Plessis-les-Tours, because the camp was some long distance from Paris. The court reached Tours in less than three days, where the King met his brother with cool indifference, making caustic remarks about where the true glory lay.

Margot felt saddened to see her two brothers so at odds through foolish jealousy, but her concerns were of a more personal nature. She lived in fear of yet more marriage proposals as her love for the handsome Henri duc de Guise was stronger than ever. At least they were together again, albeit meeting in secret, and their lovemaking grew ever more dangerous and exciting.

'Oh, how I have missed you,' she cried, responding eagerly to his kisses.

'And I you, my darling. Every day we are apart is a torment. Let me hold you, caress you. You are so very beautiful.'

There was a desperation in their embraces as passion quickly ignited. How far dare she let him go? Margot wanted him badly, knew that he wanted her, but as always she drew back from the ultimate conclusion. His groan when she curbed his advances cut to the heart of her.

'I cannot, I cannot. The risk is too great. They scour Christendom for a husband for me, and you are not even on the list.'

'Then you must have Her Majesty rewrite the list, and set me at the top of it.'

'What makes you imagine I would ever take you as a husband?' she teased, looking up at him through her lashes. 'Even if the Queen Mother approved, which you know she does not.'

'You would have me tomorrow, Margot, and you know it. We are meant for each other, you and I.'

'Oh, it is true,' she cried, kissing him with great fervour. 'I do still hope to win the Queen round to a marriage between us.'

'Despite her plans to win you a crown?' His gaze was both concerned and adoring, the trail of his fingers against her skin bewitching. How could she resist him?

'Every failed proposal is a cause for jubilation, but we must at all times be discreet.'

Keeping up appearances before the court was an endless concern for them both, as well as a source of some amusement. They might politely converse if others were present, or take part in some group sport, such as the crossbow, at which Margot excelled. But they were ever circumspect, anxious not to reveal their love by the smallest hint of a stray glance.

Should their paths accidentally cross, she would feel his eyes upon her as she innocently walked by, pressing her lips together so that she would not laugh out loud and give the game away. Once or twice she risked lifting her eyes boldly to meet his gaze, and her cheeks would flame with the daring of it. Innocent as she still was, some instinct told her she could not hold back for much longer. She wanted him too much.

Oh, how she loved simply to look at him.

His dark eyes would crease softly at the corners whenever he smiled, and he would charmingly arch one brow as he teased her. His fair hair grew to a peak on his brow, and there was nothing she loved more than to run her fingers through those tousled curls. Margot adored his sharp little beard, so masculine and sexy, and, tall as she was, yet he towered over her now that he was grown into a man. The breadth of his shoulders, his very strength and vigour excited her.

Margot couldn't ever remember feeling quite so deliciously happy. Had the birds ever sung so sweetly, the sunshine radiated so much warmth? She was in love, and she wished she could share her joy with the whole world, but dare not. Their feelings for each other must remain a precious secret, for now.

Yet she refused to give up hope. Who knew what the future might hold for them both? And then one afternoon she spotted Guise on the terrace, saw how he lingered in conversation with the Princess de Porcien, and now it was Margot's turn to be jealous. Was he playing some game, some trick to divert attention, or could he truly be fascinated by this woman? If the latter, and she was certainly fawning over him while he smiled and simpered like some love-sick fool, then it was not in Margot's nature to take such matters lightly. She longed to slap the woman's face but her pride was too great, her fear of discovery too strong. Even so, she had no intention of sharing her lover with anyone, and she meant to punish him for his apparent betrayal.

Margot had instigated dancing each evening after supper, in order to enliven these few days of escape from camp life for the men, and tonight, as had become the custom, Anjou led her out in the first dance to commence the evening's entertainment. In view of her dismay over a certain *chevalier's* apparent betrayal, she was even more aware of what a stylish couple they made as they performed the steps with grace and majesty.

Sometimes they might dance the Italian pazzemeno, the grave pavan or, as now, the more lively galliard. Anjou looked remarkably handsome in his scented elegance, and herself radiant.

Margot's opinion of her elder brother had warmed over the years as the petty differences of childhood had slipped from them. Now that she was sixteen she had come to admire him greatly for he had proved himself to be a brave soldier and a fine orator.

She was also flattered by his sudden attention to her, for all he rarely spoke two words throughout the dance.

Tonight she was wearing a gown the colour of a Spanish carnation, one of her favourites, and a white gauze veil which would surely bewitch Guise, since it became her so well. She'd grown conscious of late of her own dazzling beauty for she saw it reflected in his eyes as he hungrily watched her every move. This evening she wished to see him burn, as she had done earlier when she'd spied him drooling over that woman. Even now he was dancing with her, and Margot yearned to scratch the harlot's eyes out. Was she not a married woman? Why could she not be content with her own husband? Or was she widowed now? She couldn't quite recall. Why did Guise feel the need for any other woman but herself?

Did he not ache for her, as she ached for him?

Later, with feigned indifference, she allowed him to lead her out in a dance, Guise's hand upon hers sending shivers of excitement down her spine, despite all her efforts to be unaffected by his touch. Margot was painfully conscious of every movement of his body, the scent of his warm skin making her inwardly moan with ecstasy. She'd worn her lowest cut gown to entice him, and fought to calm her breathlessness as his gaze lingered upon the rise and fall of her breasts.

Pointing her toe and taking the required leaps and steps in the dance, she occasionally cast him sly glances from beneath her lashes. But she offered none of her secret little smiles, no adoring gaze, only a chilly coolness, which Guise did not fail to notice.

'You seem distant tonight.'

'Indeed? No one could accuse you of being so with a certain lady I saw you with earlier.'

'Ah, I can explain . . .'

'I'm sure you can.'

'Margot, pray do not be angry with me; there is a reason.'

'I see the reason. You no longer love me. Do not trouble to make excuses; I care not what lights of love take your fancy.' They both knew she lied.

He lowered his voice to a whisper as the dance drew to a close. 'May I speak with you later, or tomorrow when we meet?'

'You presume too much, sir,' she replied and, holding her head high, she walked away, leaving him in his misery.

The following day, having taken Mass at the Church of the Minimes, Margot was dawdling in the park at Plessis. She was reading a note Guise had slipped to her under cover of the dancing, and was anxious not to catch up with the Queen Mother who was walking ahead with the Princes. She needed to be alone so that she could read the letter again, although she almost knew the words by heart.

Guise claimed to be distraught at their estrangement and wished to meet with her, in secret, of course. She was to tell no one, not even Madame de Curton, as there was something particular he wished to say. Was it an apology? Did he beg her forgiveness? Her heart skipped a beat with longing. She dared hardly hope that he loved her still. But then how could he not? They were meant for each other.

Pressing her lips to the letter she recalled their latest kiss, the one he had stolen when he'd waylaid her in the passage on her way to her bedchamber last evening when the dancing was done, dearest Lottie keeping careful watch while they embraced. She'd allowed it only against her better judgement, quite unable to resist, and the fire and thrill of his lips had scorched her, the memory keeping her from her sleep for quite some time afterwards. Now Margot attempted to recapture the very essence of her would-be lover, simply from the scratches he'd made on the parchment with his quill pen.

How strong he was, how powerful, how handsome! Did he really love another? She thought her heart might break if that were true.

Margot read the letter through yet again, carefully noting every word, planning her reply, which would be suitably encouraging without appearing too wanton. Lottie would somehow manage to deliver the message in the same way she had brought this letter to her.

A voice from behind made her start, and Margot quickly tucked the precious missive up her sleeve as she turned with a smile to her brother Anjou, hoping and praying he had not noticed.

'Dear sister, you grow prettier every day, your beauty outshining the flowers in the entire garden,' Anjou said, stroking her cheek with long slender fingers.

Margot found herself flushing with pleasure at this rare compliment, for he rarely praised her, treating her largely with indifference or, as in the dancing, as a prop to show off his own elegance.

'I marvel that such a court treasure can be my own little sister.' He took her hand and placed it upon his arm. 'I would have you walk with me. We will take a different avenue from that of our mother, as there are issues I wish to discuss with you.'

She was touched and deeply flattered, enchanted by this un-expected attention. It was barely a year since she'd been allowed to leave Amboise and come permanently to court, but every day there was some new discovery, some fresh excitement, which suited her nature entirely. Margot disliked idleness and dull routine, and whether they were visiting one of the chateaux along the Loire, entertaining the leaders of the royal army as they were now, or remained in Paris, she loved every second of court life.

She thought her elegant brother cut an impressive figure in his fashionable clothes edged with gold embroidery, precious stones and pearls. His linen was always of the finest quality, and his hair elaborately styled. His noble, graceful bearing often earned him praise, as did his refined manners, and he seemed somehow to give off an air of distinction quite at odds with his youth. Their mother called him a flower among princes, but then no one could love him as did Catherine.

They strolled along a leafy avenue beneath the poplar, lime, maple and white mulberry. 'Did you enjoy my speech the other day, telling of my great victory?' he asked.

Anjou had described with no small degree of satisfaction how the Prince de Condé had been shot in the back at Jarnac, his body dragged around the Catholic camp in an orgy of murderous delight. It was not a tale Margot could savour, unused as she was to the ways of warfare, though she took care to give no indication of such sensitivity as she smilingly responded, 'I am proud to call myself your sister.'

He squeezed her hand and drew her closer. Although he liked to think of himself as a man of courage, and relished parading the glory, he was content to leave the detail to his generals. Anjou far preferred to dally with a pretty woman, or better still, a pretty boy. His sister, he'd discovered, was a delight, and he meant to make full use of her obvious admiration for him. There was nothing he loved more than to be adored.

'I doubt our brother the King would share that sentiment. I should think he greatly resents my success.'

Margot could not deny it. When Charles had received the news of Condé's death, he'd fallen to his knees in a state of high nervous excitement. The thought of blood being spilled always sent him demented, and it had taken all of Marie Touchet's skill to calm him. Now, jealous of how this victory gloried Anjou and not himself, the young king had refused his brother the usual trophies of war, presenting the laurels of the campaign to Biron and Tavannes. Charles rightly suspected Anjou of coveting his throne, and would do anything in his power to curb those ambitions, the distrust between the two siblings growing daily.

Having no wish to exacerbate the ill feelings between them, Margot made no reply. Besides, she felt some sympathy for Charles since as king he was not permitted to take any risks to his person.

Anjou lifted her hand and kissed her fingers, a gleam in his eyes. 'Dear sister, it is because of this great destiny to which God has called me that I wish to beg your assistance in a most important matter.'

'My assistance?' Margot was astonished. Never, in all her life, had her elder brother asked for her help before.

'You already know how much I love you, and I perceive the same attachment in you for me. But we are no longer children and you have it in your power to do me a service. I am fearful that whilst I am away fighting in the wars, the King my brother will seek to insinuate himself into my mother's good graces and turn her against me. I need a faithful friend to support my cause and I know no one better suited for that task than yourself. You have wit, discretion, and loyalty. If you would be so kind as to undertake such an office, I would beg you to attend each day her *lever* and *coucher*. Be the first at her side every morning and the last to leave each evening.'

Margot was startled by this request, nervous of what it might entail. 'But you know how much I am in awe of the Queen Mother. She has but to look my way and I tremble with fear that I may have done something to displease her. Besides, I doubt she would accept me.'

'I shall commend your good sense and understanding. Do not be afraid to speak to her with the same confidence as you do to me, and she will approve. You may also be assured of my supreme gratitude.'

Margot felt overwhelmed by his faith in her. Young, impressionable, and new to court life, she was innocent of the world of political intrigue. Her handsome brother carried an aura of victory about him and, delighted to have his trust, she readily agreed to his request.

'You may rely on me. There is no one that honours or regards you more than I, and you may be assured that I shall act for you with the Queen our mother as zealously as you would for yourself.'

'Dear sister, I knew that I would always come first in your eyes.'

Later that same afternoon Margot met with Guise, as arranged, in one of the green bowers in a far corner of the park. Unable to help herself, she flew into his arms, eager for his kisses, and only when some of their passion was sated did she find the breath to scold him.

'You have betrayed me,' she cried, tears streaming down her pale cheeks.

He kissed them away, dried them with the heel of his thumb. 'Never, my darling.' He told her then of his uncle's clever plan. Margot listened without interrupting and, when he was done, burst out laughing.

'So this is all a ploy, a clever deception? Oh, how I do love intrigue. You kiss this other woman because you wish to have me as your wife?' There was a teasing note in her voice, but Guise answered with caution.

'In order to throw the scandal-mongers off the scent. I do it because I love *you*, not the Princess de Porcien. My uncle believes he can win the Queen Mother round to the idea of a union between us.'

'Then he is either a fool or an optimist,' she sulked, before flinging herself into Guise's arms once more. 'I do hope that he is right. I shall forgive you, but only if you promise that for every kiss you give her, you must give me two, three, a hundred.'

And laughing, he attempted to comply.

Later, as they sat in the bower with their arms about each other, she told him of the interview with Anjou. 'Why would he choose me for this task? I am no favourite of our mother.'

Henri of Guise frowned. 'He is up to some mischief, I'll warrant. I'm sorry to say it, but the duke your brother is two-faced. Even on the battlefield he is one moment claiming my valour inspires courage in him, the next he is jealous of my military achievements.'

'He is jealous of everyone, even of his own brother the King.'

'I do not wonder at it,' Guise laughed, 'since Anjou covets the throne.' He was no stranger to ambition himself, yet chose not to remind Margot of that fact just now, not when she had so generously forgiven him for his apparent betrayal. 'Every moment his enchanting sister spends with anyone but himself he must feel deprived, but then your person is so very beguiling,' Guise teased, pulling her once more into his arms.

She slapped his eager hands away, even as she showered his handsome face with kisses. 'But what must I do? Advise me. I am ignorant of court politics. How do I go about this task?'

'Exactly as he says. Be attentive to the Queen Mother. It can do no harm, and may well help our cause, which is another reason that I needed to speak with you . . .' He kissed her noble Valois nose. 'My uncle, the Cardinal, begs an audience with you, my love. He wishes to offer his advice and support, and I feel it would be in our best interests were you to grant it, at your convenience.'

Margot giggled. 'My mother calls him the old lecher. Is that why he is so sympathetic of lovers?'

'What matters his motive?' Guise carefully replied. 'He is a great man in possession of immense power and influence, and has come up with a plan to help us.'

'I would not hesitate to listen to such a man, if he could indeed bring us together.'

'Then I believe we may hope for a good outcome.'

And as Guise pushed her down into the sweet-smelling grasses to explore the secret delights of her pliant body beneath the heavy skirts, all thought of politics vanished from her mind.

★   ★   ★

When the army returned to battle and the royal party to court, the Queen summoned Margot to her *cabinet*. She hurried to obey, anxious to fulfil her promise to her brother, and sank into a deep curtsey, heart racing.

'Did I not see you walking in the avenues at Plessis with Guise?'

'Only briefly, Madame, merely passing the time of day.'

Catherine gave her raucous laugh. 'You exchanged more than a few pleasantries with that *chevalier*, I think. Enjoy him while you may, but take care, child. Pretty flirtations and nothing more. Have I not warned you that he is not for you?'

'Yes, Your Majesty.'

Margot stood before the formidable woman who was the Queen of this great realm, with a reputation that made great men tremble, let alone young girls like herself. This was, after all, no ordinary woman, and no ordinary Queen. Margot believed there were unexplained mysteries about her mother. She had an uncanny facility for seeing all and knowing all, even when matters were meant to be a secret. She could almost read Margot's very thoughts, and seemed to possess a discomfiting foresight or prescience of momentous events before they actually happened.

On the night before her husband, King Henri, Margot's beloved father, had fought in the tournament which had proved fatal to him, Catherine had dreamed that she saw him wounded in the eye and begged him not to fight. He had apparently laughed off her fears, but that was exactly what had happened. During her most recent illness, only days before Anjou was to fight at the battle of Jarnac, Catherine had lain sick unto death at Metz where she had gone to visit the convents, Margot herself nursing her mother, when she was again visited by a premonition.

She was heard to cry out, 'Look, see how they flee! Ah, my son falls. Oh, my God, save him!'

The episode had sent chills down her spine, and Margot believed that her mother possessed the power to use her black arts in order to predict, or even manipulate the future. Today she was all sweetness, speaking to her with kindness, and for the first time in her life Margot felt at ease in her presence.

'Anjou your brother tells me that he no longer considers you a child. In future, neither shall I. It will be a great comfort to me to converse with you as I would with him. Render yourself, therefore, assiduous in your attendance upon me, and fear not to speak freely, for such is my desire.'

The Queen's words filled Margot with joy. It felt like a turning point in her life, a new beginning. It had ever been her wish to please her brother and her mother; now she could serve both.

Condé's death was a bitter blow to the Huguenots. Louis de Bourbon, the hunchback Prince of Condé, had carried the charisma of having royal blood in his veins, and was a great loss to them. Coligny now stood alone beside his Queen; his wisdom and courage, his integrity and moral strength, and his skill at military strategy should make him appear well nigh invincible. But morale was low. The men were dispirited and battle weary, wanting an end to the strife, anxious to return home to their loved ones. Fighting an enemy so huge, so powerful as the Catholics had been daunting enough, but without Condé it seemed impossible.

Jeanne was an excellent statesman, but knew that she now faced her biggest challenge. The rabble-rousers, and those who relished a fight simply for the joy of it, had fled, yet the true believers remained. In the Queen of Navarre's opinion, these stalwarts needed something extra, someone special to inspire them. They needed a Prince.

She looked at her son with his glossy black Gascon hair and bright, youthful good looks, and tried not to recall the glitter of speculation which always came into those fine eyes whenever they rested upon a woman. Any woman. He was already a philanderer like his father. Little Fleurette, whom he'd so casually abandoned to bear her child alone, had been found drowned in the river, her heart broken by his rejection. Poor girl, it was indeed a tragedy to love a Prince.

Without doubt the boy was frivolous and light-minded, and in her heart Jeanne had little faith he could rise to the challenge which now faced him. Yet he looked good, sat upon his horse well, and there was pride in his bearing, courage in that young face. The question was, could he inspire loyalty and worship in the troops?

She ordered Henry to dismount and then, grasping him by the hand, she held it high, punching the air with their joined fists as they stepped forward to face the assembled troops.

'Friends and comrades, I give you my son!'

A ragged cheer went up and she smiled upon them all, glad to see they had some spirit in them still. Then she brought forward her nephew, son of the fallen Condé. A hand on each of them, there was great sadness in her voice as she addressed the men with a moving eloquence, and the battle-hardened soldiers who stood before her in their bloodstained weariness fell into a respectful silence to listen to her words.

'Children of God and of France, Condé is dead; but is all therefore lost? No, the God who gave him courage and strength to fight for this cause has raised up others worthy to succeed him. To those brave warriors I add my son. Make proof of his valour. Soldiers, I offer you everything I have to give: my dominions, my treasures, my life, and what is dearer to me than all: my children. I swear to defend to my last sigh the holy cause that now unites us!'

They lifted their heads as if to the sun, taking in every word as she breathed new spirit into them.

'It is a sad truth that we have suffered appalling atrocities, many of our best men slaughtered, our fine leader killed before our eyes, but we have others. We still have Coligny, and his brother Andelot. We have Rochefoucauld, Rohan and Montgomery. Condé may be no more. Our enemies may have destroyed the man but they cannot destroy our faith. We who loved him must fight on, as Condé himself would wish. We still have all to play for in this bloody battle, and cannot abandon the fight so easily. In his place, we have his son, Henri de Bourbon, the second Prince de Condé.'

She urged the young man to step forward. 'And my own beloved son, the future King of Navarre. It is time now for these boys to grasp manhood and realize their destiny. Condé was a fine Prince and our cousin, but his son, and mine, will stand beside you in his stead. I have every faith they are ready for the task.'

The cheer that went up now was rich with hope, a new fire lit within the troops.

Henry was feeling close to panic, at a loss to fully understand what was expected of him, although equally stirred by his mother's words. He wasn't sure he could ever match their zeal, or agree that any particular form of religion was better than another, let alone worth dying for. His dear friend and cousin, young Condé, was a fervent Huguenot, and appeared flushed with pride, eager to take on the mantle of his father. Yet Henry felt unequal for the role demanded of him.

He heard a few sniggers from the young soldiers, quiet snorts of derision from the older men, both of whom knew him for what he truly was: a licentious womanizer who loved to quaff beer and tell crude jokes in the barrack room. He might be a Prince of the Blood who would one day be a King, but could he lead this army?

Coligny stepped forward to be the first to swear fealty to the young man hovering on the brink of manhood, and would one day be his king. 'They ask only for you to have faith in them, Sire, and courage, if you can find it.'

'I am not without courage,' Henry quickly responded, thinking of the boar and stag hunts he relished, how he killed wolf and bear in the mountains of the Pyrenees. He loved to climb, and would scramble barefoot over rocks to reach the peaks. 'I would expect no concessions for . . . for being who I am.'

'And none will be granted,' Coligny agreed. 'What say you? Are you man enough for the task?'

Fired by the light in the older man's eye, and by his mother's faith in him, Henry grinned, excited suddenly by the promise of a new adventure. 'I am!' Then he turned to the raggle-taggle army of men before him and, addressing them in a strong, clear voice, made them a vow. 'I give you my solemn oath never to desert the cause. My life is yours till we achieve the freedom you deserve. I will stand by you unto death.'

An almighty roar greeted these words. The men threw up their caps and helmets, slapped each other on the back, laughed, and cheered, as fresh hope and vigour was returned to them. Condé grabbed his friend in a soldierly embrace, while Jeanne wept with quiet pride.

From the day Anjou begged for her support, Margot devoted herself to the Queen's pleasure. She abandoned her friends, her favourite pursuits of dancing and hunting, and even the crossbow, to give herself up to waiting upon her mother. Every morning she would present herself early at Her Majesty's *lever* and be the last to leave at night, exactly as Anjou had instructed. She felt confident she was giving satisfaction as Catherine frequently sang her praises to the beautiful ladies she gathered about her, *L'escadron de la Royne mère*, more usually known as her Flying Squadron.

Margot was thrilled when her mother allowed her into conferences, or did her the honour of talking to her for an hour or more. She played her part with assiduous care by speaking often of her brother's affairs, and again nursed Catherine during one of her bouts of ill health. Margot dared to hope that her mother might begin to regard her with some degree of affection after all.

Anxious also to keep in her brother's good graces, she made it her business to write to him regularly while he was away fighting, keeping him fully informed of her progress in order to prove how very much she had his interests in mind. Notes and letters also flew back and forth between herself and Guise, courtesy of the contacts made available through the trusted Lottie, and their love for each other continued unabated.

Life was suddenly rich and exciting, filled with new promise. Relations continued on these excellent terms for some weeks and Margot often accompanied her mother when she went to the front to review the troops and restore morale. Now they were at St Jean d'Angely with the King.

The Catholics had proved too formidable an army under the command of Tavannes, and had decimated the Huguenots. Charles had greeted this latest victory by Anjou with a cold and terrible silence. He told the Queen that he had no wish to see his brother usurp the power of *maire du palais*, and he would lead his own armies into the field in future, as did his grandfather, Francis I.

When Catherine blocked this plan, his mood became so terrifying that she thought it wise not to oppose him further. His knowledge of military matters was as feeble as his skill in government, yet he was determined to at least have a say in the battle and take a share of the glory enjoyed by his brother. Against all advice the King decided to besiege each town the Huguenots had fortified before attacking La Rochelle. Tavannes warned against this tactic, as it would split the Royal Armies, but the thirst for blood and glory was too strong, and Charles refused to listen.

Margot found living in the primitive conditions at camp both difficult and unpleasant yet did so gladly, if only because it afforded her the opportunity once more to be with Guise.

One evening as she prepared herself to meet him, Madame de Curton came to her, deeply troubled. 'You should be wary of a new favourite of your brother's,' her governess warned. 'He is Louis de Beranger, baron du Guast, of noble descent, arrogant, ambitious and highly political. He has so ingratiated himself into the Duke's confidence that he dictates all his daily affairs, even controls his purse.'

Margot giggled. 'Considering my brother's profligacy, some control would be no bad thing.'

Madame pursed her lips. 'I do not trust the man; his evil little eyes flick everywhere, and I believe him to be spying for his master. You must have care, my lady, when meeting with your own favourites.'

The two women looked at each other, Margot aware Madame was referring to her liaison with Guise, but at seventeen was too much in love to think clearly. Planting a consoling kiss on her governess's cheek, she laughed off her concern. 'Lottie, do you trust no one?'

'Not if I think they may harm you, my precious.'

'Surely I can trust my own brother?'

'I have heard du Guast tell the Duke that one should never love nor trust anyone save oneself, nor rely on them, neither sister nor brother. I believe him to be a great student of Machiavelli. Pardon my frankness, but this jealousy that is souring relations between the King and the duke d'Anjou seems to be growing daily more bitter. You must take care, my lady, not to be caught up in their squabbles.'

'A foolish nonsense!' Margot said dismissively, paying little attention to her mentor's warning as she perfumed her hair with musk, and smoothed her gown in readiness for a secret meeting with Guise.

She was tired of this ongoing rivalry between her brothers, weary of Charles constantly seeking her company so that he could issue a litany of complaints about Anjou's latest boasts and triumphs. Margot would listen sympathetically, agree with everything he said in a desperate attempt to soothe the King's fraught nerves, so that he didn't fall into one of his tantrums. Anjou was equally demanding, asking for endless reassurance that she did indeed love him, and didn't favour either of her other brothers, or anyone, above him.

Oh, but she was worn out with it all. She wanted some fun, someone to love her for herself, and not for what she could do for them!

'You worry too much, darling Lottie. Hasn't Anjou made it plain how he trusts me to be his mouthpiece with the Queen Mother?'

Charlotte de Curton bit her lip and managed, with some difficulty, to keep to herself any private views she might hold on Anjou's tendency to be hypocritical.

Margot tweaked a curl into place. 'Now, will I do?'

'You look beautiful, as always, my lady. But is this wise, agreeing to see the Duke of Guise alone? And the King will notice if you again miss supper.'

As a royal princess Margot was rarely alone, and the only truly secure place for them to pursue their friendship in anything like privacy was in the tent which she shared with Madame and her most favoured ladies-in-waiting. This evening, as so often during these weeks at St Jean d'Angely, Lottie would smuggle in the young lord while everyone was at supper, before quietly withdrawing to keep watch outside. The secrecy only added to the piquancy of their meetings.

Now she laughed as she hugged her beloved governess with warm affection. 'Beg His Majesty's forgiveness and tell him I have a headache. Do stop fretting, dear Lottie; it is barely dusk, and sadly our meetings must needs be short. How can we be in any danger when I have you to guard me, and not only my brother's favour, but that of my mother too?'

Guise swept a bow, then taking Margot's hand, brought it to his lips, the warmth of his breath at once igniting a fire in the pit of her belly. She lifted her chin and addressed him with a calm firmness. 'Have you just left your mistress, the Princess de Porcien, to come to me?'

'I have no mistress but you, as you well know. She is but a political foil. You possess my heart.'

Margot tossed her head, biting back a spurt of jealousy. 'You must still be mad to come to me here.'

'I am mad *for* you, that is certain. Admit it, you feel the same.'

'You flatter yourself.' Even as she pretended resistance, her chestnut eyes flashed quite a different meaning altogether. 'You amuse me, that is all.'

'I think I do more than that, Margot my sweet.' He laughed, and, flinging himself into a chair, pulled her unceremoniously on to his lap, silencing her mock squeals of protest with a long, hard kiss.

His kisses quickly grew more bold and, far from protesting, Margot returned his embrace with equal passion, a wanton desire burning within. She gave no further thought to her squabbling, jealous brothers, to Lottie keeping guard outside, or even the woman who was an alleged rival for his affections. All that mattered was his mouth hungry upon her own, his hands caressing and fondling her breasts.

It was some long moments before her senses returned to anything like normal, and when she finally broke free of his hold her eyes were glazed and her breathing rapid. 'What if one of my ladies should march in? We would be undone. The King would beat me.'

Guise grinned. 'He would never risk bruising a skin so fine as yours. More likely he'd have my head on the block, or so my uncle informs me.'

Margot gave a little cry of distress before running to peep through the tent flap in a panic. 'You must leave at once. Someone is coming, I'm sure of it. I heard a rustling in the bushes.' She pressed a hand to her breast. 'I can feel my heart racing with fear.'

'You're too brave to feel fear, my sweet. Your heart races only for love of me,' he said, laughing, as he pulled her back into his arms and began to kiss her with renewed passion. 'There is no one coming, my sweet, else your faithful companion would have warned us.'

She almost pushed him away, but then thought of her beloved Lottie guarding the entrance, and burst out laughing too. 'You are right, it is but the wind. Yet we must take care.'

'Naturally.' He kissed each fluttering eyelid, the enticing curve of her lips, the soft mound of each breast above her gown. 'Would you give yourself to me, if I asked?'

'You are bold, sir.' Margot slipped from his grasp to pour them both a goblet of wine. Handing one to him, she smiled, instantly negating her protest even as she urged him to drink and be gone. 'My mother must never learn of these visits. These are dangerous times, and she is not an easy woman.'

'Indeed, you speak true. I would not be the first to die at the hands of the Black Queen.'

'Don't call her that. Do not say such terrible things.' Margot tossed her head, offended by this slur upon her mother.

'I do not exaggerate, I swear.' Guise set his wine down on a low table, dropping his voice to a throaty whisper. 'Did you not hear that she put a price on the heads of Coligny, his brother d'Andelot, and La Rochefoucauld, all Protestant nobles? I was almost tempted myself by the 50,000 écus for Coligny, though I might have done it for half the sum to be rid of the man who killed my father.'

Margot turned away in disgust. 'You talk wild.'

'Do not fret, my sweet; several attempts have already been made on the old fool's life, but mine was not among them, so do not scowl at me.' All levity vanished from his voice now as he tenderly stroked her slender throat, ran the heel of his thumb over her full rosy lips. 'But I was never more serious. We must tread carefully. You surely heard of d'Andelot's death at Saintes in May.'

'I heard.' Margot struggled to repress a shudder, as if a goose had walked over her grave.

'Coligny and La Rochefoucauld both fell ill at the same time. A remarkable coincidence, do you not think?'

'That does not prove my mother was the one responsible.'

'Who else would dare? In any case, Her Majesty openly rejoiced at the news, claiming that God would mete out to the other leaders the treatment they deserve. She has been denounced by those implicated in the crime, and by members of Coligny's own family, although no one hangs around long enough to press home the charge. Catherine de Medici is a woman who breeds fear as well as respect. There is much talk of poison, of the Queen Mother's notorious *parfumier* René being involved; of a man claiming to be a servant of Coligny's being found with a sachet of poison in his pocket; a dog which instantly dropped dead when fed a slice of apple.'

Margot laughed. 'You have read too many fairy stories about wicked queens. Enough of these tales. I refuse to listen to any more of your nonsense.'

'It is not nonsense, Margot. Watch your back, and have your darling Lottie guard you well.'

By way of reply Margot tugged his head down to hers and captured his mouth with her own in a long, demanding kiss, tasting him, bruising him, taunting him with her passion. 'I fear no one, certainly not my mother. I am a Princess of the Blood!' Yet there was a tremor in her voice as she issued these words, and Guise felt it.

Tenderly he asked, 'Then why do you tremble? From love of me?'

'Goodness, you have far too high an opinion of yourself, my lord.'

Margot's anxiety to have him gone from her quarters was increasing by the minute for, despite her brave bluster, she was suddenly afraid, for her lover if not herself. Only a fool would not be. The tales of unexplained deaths and the possible role played in them by the Queen her mother were too commonplace to dismiss lightly.

Conceding to her anxiety, Guise pulled aside the tent flap to check the way was clear to make his escape, before returning swiftly to her embrace. 'Would that I had the entire night to prove my love to you. Although now that you have the Queen's ear, you could perhaps take the opportunity to persuade her to view me with a little more trust and benevolence.'

Margot pressed herself against his hard body as she kissed him farewell. 'You overstate my influence. My power is not so great as you might imagine.'

'That you hold over me could not be stronger. I am ever yours to command.' As if to prove this, he captured her in his arms one last time, making her shiver with fresh desire.

'You must go now. Quickly!'

It was several more long and dangerous moments before she could bear to let him go and Guise slipped away into the dusk.

So absorbed were they in their love that neither noticed a slight movement among the sheltering trees beyond.

Later that evening, du Guast was combing and curling his master's hair as the duke lounged on the great bed that almost filled his tent. Anjou insisted on looking his best, terrified of falling prey to the lice which were rife among the men. It was during these intimate moments when they were largely alone, save for a trusted few, that his favourite was able to exert most influence.

Du Guast would urge his royal master to be more forceful and less indolent, and frequently alert him to those who might wish to take advantage of his generosity. His arrogance was such that he sought to further his own ambitions as much as the duke's, and observed the increasing resentment between the monarch and the heir to the throne with studied attention. He knew his master to be jealous of Guise, and fearful of his rival threat to the throne.

Tonight he suggested that the reason for the King's presence at St Jean d'Angely was all the fault of Guise. 'He is the one responsible for encouraging Charles to intrude upon your glory, by means of the love letters he writes to the Princess.'

Anjou did not doubt it. He succumbed readily to the charm of his favourites, and found this new friend particularly delightful. He was elegant and beautiful, intelligent and an aristocrat of distinction.

'Are you suggesting that my sister has betrayed me to that knave? She has told him of my business, my private thoughts, and become his instrument?'

Du Guast feigned regret, knowing he must tread carefully around princely sensitivities. 'I tremble to risk offence, for I know how you treasure your sister's goodwill. And worship her beauty,' he added, rather winsomely. 'But I fear that may be so.'

'Then I have been made a fool of by them both!'

'Have you not noticed,' du Guast slyly remarked, 'how it is always the duc de Guise who begs leave to protect and escort the Princess whenever she wishes to ride out and escape for a while the pestilential atmosphere of the camp?'

'I know well enough how the man covets the throne.'

'Ah, that may be so, Sire, and . . . no . . . I cannot say it. I may be entirely wrong.'

'Speak your mind; you know that I trust you. You are my eyes and ears.'

Du Guast hid a satisfied smile. One of the pages he employed as a spy had spotted a visitor to the Princess's royal quarters this very evening, though it was too dark by the time he left to see his face clearly. Du Guast suspected it would have been Guise.

'The gossips say that they may have ventured beyond pretty letters, that they are not only lovers but plan to wed.' He put up a hand to affect reluctance. 'I can say no more at this juncture without proof, but is it not also true that Guise has an uncle with the funds and power to assist with such an ambition?'

Anjou met the adoring gaze of his favourite in shocked surprise as he pondered these words. Guise was already his rival on the battlefield; now it seemed that he competed for his sister's affections as well. Anjou hated his commanding presence, his athletic skills, and the way the people of Paris held him in such high esteem. If Margot was in love with the fellow, then the pair of them could make a formidable alliance that could threaten his own ambitions. Curbing his impatience for the King to die was bad enough, but he would tolerate no challenge to his own rightful succession.

'Then it has gone much further than I feared. We must find proof. It is time we put an end to his mischief.'

'Unfortunately, the King adores his sister. His Majesty spends an hour every afternoon in her company and won't hear a word said against her. As for the Queen Mother, she is well known for her broad mind in these matters. They both believe the Princess's reputation to be impeccable.'

'Then we must give them reason to question it.'

Margot came to the Queen Mother's *lever* as usual the next morning, and at once sensed a change in her attitude. Catherine ordered her to return to her own quarters, repeating this command several times when Margot stood paralysed, numb with surprise. The other maids of honour avoided her questioning gaze, clacking quietly to each other like a gaggle of gossiping geese. Puzzled and hurt at being thus banished, Margot quietly withdrew, but not to her own quarters. She waited close by until all was quiet, then, gathering her courage, she again presented herself to the Queen.

'May I know in what way I have offended you, Madame?' she asked, sinking into a deep curtsey.

At first it seemed that her mother might decline to answer, but then all the snarling bitterness she still harboured against the House of Guise came pouring out. Catherine deeply resented them for the power they had held over her during the reign of François II. How many times she had regretted the folly of her husband, Henri II, in allowing their daughter Claude to marry the Prince of Lorraine, thereby linking them with that despised family. Were they not determined to overthrow the royal dynasty of the Valois?

'I hear you have been intimate with the Duke of Guise.'

'Madame,' Margot replied, shocked by these accusations, 'that is untrue. Who told you this?'

'You have betrayed and offended your brother whose confidence you have held in low regard.'

So it was Anjou, or no doubt this new favourite of his. 'My brother praised me. Does he now wish to deprive me of those privileges, for some imagined fault?'

The Queen Mother's face darkened with fury. 'Do not treat me as a fool. Did I not see you walking with Guise in the green alleys at Plessis with my own eyes? Do I not see how he lusts after you? Now that I know how far this fancy has gone, you will put an end to it, at once. You are a Princess of the Blood and he is not for you.'

Margot was near to tears, desperate to prove her innocence. 'I swear on my mortal soul it is not true. We have not been intimate! I am still pure.'

Catherine considered her daughter with careful scrutiny. 'I am minded to think that if you speak so earnestly then I must believe you. There, there, do not weep. We'll have done with this discussion, for now.'

'Thank you, Your Majesty, I am most obliged.' Another deep curtsey, one of humble gratitude this time, even as she trembled. 'But as long as I live I will remember this evil thing that my brother has done.'

'You will do no such thing! You will treat the duke with all respect due to his station.' Then she banished her wayward daughter from the royal presence, and this time Margot did run to her tent, where she fell on her bed in a storm of tears.

In the ensuing days Margot kept a careful distance from the duc d'Anjou, who made no attempt at a reconciliation. Far from obeying the Queen Mother's orders, she rebelliously continued to favour her alleged lover, allowing Guise access to her private quarters and openly conversing with him in public.

'Do you appreciate the risks you run?' her frightened governess warned.

'I am not afraid of my brother, for all the lies he might tell about me. I mean to remain true to my *chevalier*.'

She was young and in love, with fire and spirit in her heart, developing an independent mind of her own, and stubbornly refused to be bullied by a jealous elder brother, or the contemptible du Guast, who was busily spreading libellous mischief against her. Besides claiming that the Princess Marguerite had so far forgotten her royal status that she had become Guise's paramour, he accused her of being without shame, demonstrated by the flightiness of her manner. She was, he said, one of the new breed of French women who, while claiming to be devout, were actually far too independent and free-thinking for their own good. They were nought but a trouble to their husbands, were they fortunate enough to find one.

The slurs upon her name grew worse as dark whispers began to circulate of notorious conduct with two officers of the King's bodyguard while she was at Bayonne as a young girl.

Anjou, while affecting to maintain his belief in her, yet claimed the slander was true to any who cared to listen.

Guise was incensed by this defamation of his lady. 'We must refute this slander. I'll not allow such calumny to be spoken against you.'

'Say nothing. The more we protest, the more they will believe in my guilt.'

He considered the surprising wisdom of her words. 'Yet what of your reputation? It could be damaged beyond redemption.'

The gossip partly infuriated and partly amused her, yet she smiled. 'It may well be to our advantage. If I am viewed as soiled goods, what foreign King would have me then? My mother the Queen might have fewer scruples in bestowing my hand on one previously considered unworthy.'

And if Guise found himself thinking of his own ambitions as he joined in her ready laughter, a part of him still feared for his beloved's safety. Following her lead, he treated the slander with silent contempt, taking out his fury by displaying even greater prowess on the battlefield, his accomplishments as a *chevalier* enraging his rival still further.

St Jean d'Angely finally surrendered to the siege ordered by the King after two months, but by the following spring morale was at an all-time low. Catherine was facing difficulties paying her army, the Catholics had lost ten thousand troops and one of their best generals, and her only recourse was to reopen the peace talks. They did not go well, as Jeanne remained distrustful of her old enemy.

'A peace made of snow this winter will not last the summer's heat.' She was certainly not prepared to deny her religion, which she believed was what Catherine demanded. 'My God,' she said, 'is as meat and drink to me.'

Distrust filled the air and difficulties continued to hinder any meaningful negotiations. It seemed likely they would lumber on all summer, so it was that the Queen Mother decided to play her most important card.

A marriage between her daughter and the Bourbon Prince of Navarre might achieve the solution they all craved. The girl was growing too wilful to be left free for much longer, and what better way to win peace for the country, and quash the power of the Guises once and for all?

While Jeanne hesitated and the peace talks stalled, the match with Portugal suddenly took on a new impetus. One afternoon Catherine summoned Margot to her *cabinet* to inform her that ambassadors from the Portuguese Court had arrived to see for themselves whether or not she was worthy of their King.

'Wear your most magnificent attire for a banquet which is to be held this evening by way of welcome. You will be expected to entertain them and make yourself agreeable, do you understand?'

Margot took in the import of her mother's words in silent horror, struck dumb by the suddenness of it. 'Your will is mine,' was all she managed by way of response, attempting to disguise the tremor in her voice.

'Can I believe you to be sincere, when I know how you favour that young scoundrel Guise? I am reliably informed that he still has designs on you.'

Margot rightly guessed that the Queen Mother's informant would be Anjou, slyly undermining her yet again. She swallowed, judging her answer carefully. 'We are but childhood friends. I would do nought to offend Your Majesty.' She dare not admit that she had sworn to love Guise and no other, that she would forever be faithful to him, whilst there remained any hope they could be wed.

'I am aware that old lecher the Cardinal of Lorraine is anxious for you to accept his nephew, even though I have made it abundantly clear a marriage between you shall never take place!'

Margot stiffened her spine, and recklessly responded, 'Pray bring the Portuguese negotiations forward then, so that you can have proof of my obedience.'

With that she begged leave to withdraw, and fled to her apartments and the security of her governess's love.

Madame de Curton was quietly working on her embroidery when her young charge burst into the room, hair awry, and eyes dark with panic.

'Oh, Lottie, my mother has ordered me to wear my richest gown and my finest jewels this evening for the Portuguese ambassadors. I am to charm them so that they see me as a fit bride for their king.' Moaning with despair, she fell to her knees. 'What am I to do? I cannot bear it. I had dared to hope – dream – that Guise or his uncle would save me, despite, or even because of the scandal about me. When I spoke with the Cardinal some months ago, he was optimistic, filled with certainty that he could help. Now his protestations of support seem like sand in the wind beside the tenacity of my mother.'

Madame de Curton looked with sadness upon her charge. The girl was highly intelligent, shrewd and clever, capable of making a far better monarch than any of her brothers. Yet she was betrayed always by her soft heart. 'The King of Portugal is young, my lady, of an age to yourself, and not at all like Don Carlos. He is, I believe, quite good-looking, being tall and slim and blond, and would bring you a crown.'

'But I do not love him. I have never even met him.'

'You cannot hope for love in a marriage, my precious. It is your duty to marry where the Queen your mother decrees, as I have told you many times before. You cannot escape your destiny.'

'I know it, I know it!' Margot said, still raging. She was on her feet, striding about the room, railing against her fate. Swinging about, she stamped her foot in fury. 'I shall wear my plainest gown, my dullest jewels. I will not smile at the envoys that King Sebastian has sent, but scowl and sulk. I will not laugh at their jokes, or listen to their boring chatter, and I will fawn over every word Guise utters. We'll see what they think of that!'

Madame de Curton couldn't help but laugh. 'If you behave badly you will put yourself in a poor light, it is true, but whatever you wear, my dear one, your beauty will shine through. Nothing could prevent that, even were you to attend the banquet dressed in sack-cloth and ashes.'

Margot ran to her governess to bury her head in her lap and weep, partly from despair and fear, and partly from fury at her own impotence. 'Don't you understand? If they decide I am suitable, I could be married and in his bed within a few short weeks, days perhaps. How could I bear that when it is Henri of Guise that I love?'

'Because you must. Because you are a Princess of France.'

Margot was silent for a long time while Madame tenderly stroked her hair, her mind spinning. Taking a breath, she continued more calmly. 'If my opinion counts for nothing, and my mother and brother can marry me off to whoever brings them the greatest political reward, then my body is no longer my own.'

'I'm afraid not, my sweet.'

Margot's eyes lit with a sparkle of mischief. 'But I can at least choose who shall have my maidenhead, can I not?'

'Oh, my lady!' Madame gasped, putting a hand to her mouth. 'Do not speak so.'

But Margot was already at her desk penning a hasty note. In it she poured out her love for Guise, telling him of the banquet that very evening, and the fate that awaited her. Then she begged him to meet her afterwards in a certain apartment on the stroke of midnight. She signed it with a flourish, knowing he would understand. They had enjoyed many secret meetings, but none so late, or in such a private setting. Sanding and folding it carefully, she gave the letter to her governess. 'See that you hand it to him personally, and do not attempt to dissuade me. I must see him one more time in complete privacy before they sell me off to the highest bidder.'

Pride and fear of the Queen Mother ensured that Margot look her best for the ambassadors. She bathed in warm scented rose oil, and Madame de Curton patted her dry before smoothing more fragrant unguents over her soft skin. The law strictly forbade any artisan or common bourgeoise to wear silk, which was permitted only for those of noble birth as it signified social prominence and power. Margot's own chemise and petticoats were of the finest, costing more than some people earned in an entire year, as was her boned corset that cinched in her tiny waist, and the high lace-edged collar that framed her beautiful face and her lovely bosom, so firm and white it billowed delightfully above the neck of her gown. The mere sight of it was meant to entice Guise to kiss it.

It was for him that she dressed this evening, her would-be lover whom she wished to impress, not the Portuguese ambassadors.

Margot had a natural talent for style and was already becoming a leader of fashion at her brother's court. She knew how to adapt a gown, a dainty cap or ornament into something charming and desirable. The ladies and maids of honour would emulate the design, hoping to borrow some of the wearer's beauty.

Her gown was of cloth of crinkled gold tissue, the richest and most costly in her wardrobe. Diamond pendants in the shape of stars hung at her ears and adorned her throat. Her hair, which was dark and not considered to be a fashionable colour, suited her perfectly, enhancing her chestnut eyes. She had Madame de Curton twist and curl and arrange it high upon her head in the style favoured by her beloved late sister, the Queen of Spain. A touch of colour to her cheeks and lips and lashes, and she was ready.

Now Madame de Curton stood back to admire the results of her labours, love and pride all too evident in her old face, for tonight her charge had excelled herself, some inner radiance causing her to look even more beautiful than usual.

'Your grace and charm will win the heart of any king, and his courtiers.'

'What need I of kings when I have the love of my *chevalier*?'

Margot was very nearly eclipsed by the dazzling magnificence of her own brother. Anjou was resplendent in a doublet and hose in a delicate leaf green, threaded with gold and silver, a white lace ruff of immense proportions about his slender neck. His dark hair was brushed up into curls behind his cap, and he smelled divinely of violet water. The Portuguese ambassadors marvelled at the sight of such a fop, seeming more Italian than French with his olive skin and long eyes, and so very effeminate. He had clearly taken as much trouble over his *toilette* as many of the ladies.

And indeed, the French ladies were a delight, particularly *les dames galantes*. Most of all they were bowled over by Margot's beauty, and saw at once that their young king would be a fool not to be enchanted by so delightful a princess. She would be an undoubted sensation at the Court of Lisbon.

Unfortunately, they had not been granted the power to conclude the union. Their task was to report back to His Majesty, King Sebastian, to confirm that she lived up to the extraordinary beauty that rumour described. They observed Margot's mannerisms, her eloquence and facility with language, and felt quite able to recommend her for the esteemed honour of being crowned Queen of their realm.

But then they began to notice a more disturbing trait. She sat beside them at table, as was expected of her, but her attention frequently wavered. She forgot all her usual good manners as hostess to her guests and failed to pass them the roast duck, pheasant, carp, lobster, custards, syllabubs, raspberries, and myriad other dishes with which the table was loaded. She did not refill their empty Venetian wine glasses, or ask if they wished to taste the spectacular towering confection of sugared pastry the cooks had prepared, leaving it all to the servants.

'I believe you love reading and often stay up half the night finishing a book?' one envoy politely enquired. 'Which will please my master the King, as he is a great reader himself. He is particularly fond of the great philosopher Thomas Aquinas.'

'I do love all manner of literature, although I read only to please myself, and not at the will of others,' Margot airily informed him, licking the sugar from her fingers.

The ambassador conceded this cutting remark with a polite head bow. 'And you ride, and are skilled with the crossbow, I hear?'

Margot put back her head and laughed, a deep throaty sound that brought heads swivelling in her direction, not least that of Guise. 'Ask my dear friend here how many times I have beaten him at the sport.'

She did, in fact, perversely allow her 'dear friend' to monopolize her attention throughout the evening. The Portuguese ambassadors noticed that the princess barely gave them more than a passing glance, or the courtesy of a single enquiry as to the health of *Don Sebastion*, their beloved monarch, let alone request any details of his person. At one point Charles was heard quietly to reproach his sister for her ill manners, but she was oblivious to all entreaties to behave.

And the enmity that clearly existed between herself and her brother the duc d'Anjou was equally worrying. The envoys were concerned. Could this most beautiful of princesses be flawed? Was she selfish and spoiled, or could it be that she was entirely disinterested in their suit?

So far as the ambassadors could ascertain, following a few judicious enquiries and careful observation, it became evident that the duc de Guise was the sole object of her devotion, and could yet win the hand of this royal beauty. Negotiations consequently faltered, a circumstance which was seized upon by Anjou to further slur his sister's reputation, and greatly incurred the wrath of the Queen Mother and the King.

Not that Margot paid any heed to either, as she had other delights to look forward to this evening. She certainly had no wish to enchant the Portuguese envoys, so felt perfectly free to behave as she wished. She enjoyed dance after dance with Guise, flirted most recklessly with him, laughed at the silliest joke or the simplest turn of phrase made by her lover. It was soon the opinion of the Portuguese ambassadors, who watched this performance with growing dismay, that the princess was deeply enamoured of the young lord.

Catherine pinched her daughter's arm, reprimanding her in furious undertones. 'You naughty minx, do you deliberately mean to undermine our plans? Can you not behave with more decorum?'

'I have already agreed to marry the King of Portugal, or King Nebuchadnezzar if it is your will. Whoever you choose for me. Until then, I believe I am free to dance and make merry with whomsoever I please.'

'Go to your room at once!' ordered the Queen. 'And present yourself on the morrow for a ride in the forest with the Portuguese envoys, only this time come with your manners intact.'

Margot scampered away, giggling with delight at the little storm she had created. What did she care, when she had a most delightful and secret appointment to keep.

Margot was in his arms the moment Guise came through the door. It was in the early hours of the morning that she'd crept unseen through the silent, shadowed passages of the Palace, her heart trembling with excitement and fear. There was nothing she loved more than an adventure. Now they were at last together in this deserted apartment in some far-flung corner of the Louvre where no one would ever think to look for them. The Princess hadn't even risked bringing Madame de Curton with her, in case the presence of the governess lurking in some alcove might attract attention.

But the loyal Lottie had done her work. The room was lit by a dozen candles set in golden sconces about the walls, sufficient to cast a roseate glow over the bed, ready made up with silken sheets. A flagon of wine stood waiting on a side table, and two silver goblets. It was a scene set for lovers, and Margot smiled at Guise through their kisses, laughing as he struggled to rid himself of coat and shirt without letting go of her for a second.

'I have waited so long for this moment,' he murmured.

'And I. See how I come to you with nothing but my love.'

She had already divested herself of the heavy gold gown and her jewels, of silk chemise, corset and hair ornaments. Her face bare of paint and artifice, she stood before him in her simplest nightgown, her feet bare.

Margot took his hand and kissed each of his fingertips, then gently placed it over her breast. He gave a low groan at the ripe softness of her body beneath the thin fabric.

'You need no ornament for such beauty to shine, and I believe you would look even more lovely naked.' Pushing the nightgown from her shoulders, he took a step back so that he could look at her as he smoothed trembling hands over her bare breasts, the curve of her ribcage, her flat belly. Margot shivered with delight.

His expression was one of quiet reverence as he studied every inch of her pale beauty: the fire in her eyes, the length of her long legs, the curve of her hips; a veritable Venus. And she too studied him, loving the breadth of his chest and shoulders, so strong, so powerful, the narrow hips and muscles bulging most gratifyingly beneath his hose. She touched a half-healed battle scar on his shoulder with her lips, and he gave a soft moan.

'Would that I could have you as my wife. I would spend my life loving you.'

She stepped into his arms, pulling his head down to hers to brush her lips lightly over his, teasing him, making him want her all the more. 'I still hold sway over my own body. For tonight at least.'

'My precious darling, do you know what you are saying, what you risk by this madness?'

'If it is madness, then it is the kind that I welcome with all my heart.' Tears glimmered in her eyes as she clung to him. 'Tomorrow they may command me to marry the King of Portugal, or Hungary, or some foreign madman. Who can say which king's bed I shall be in by next week, as duty demands? It matters only that tonight I can be in yours, that I can give my most precious gift, myself, to you first, my dearest love, and not some stranger.'

He kissed her then with a greater passion, lighting a fever within them both, and, as the kiss deepened, he lifted her in his arms and carried her to the bed, gently setting her down and arranging her now flaccid limbs so that he could lie beside her.

'Do I, oh soon-to-be-queen, have permission to kiss you here?' He kissed the hollow between her breasts, then brushed his mouth over each erect nipple, suckling each dark bud, and Margot groaned in agony. 'Or here?' He moved further down, to the smooth silk of her belly. 'And what about here?' He parted her legs and kissed her inner thigh.

His touch was honey sweet yet brought a pain of yearning she'd never before experienced, deep in her secret places.

And it was these parts his questing fingers had found now. Margot gasped with shock, but was soon purring with delight, stretching her arms above her head as sensation overwhelmed her. Never, in all her dreams and longing for Guise, had she imagined it would be like this. She was almost sobbing with need but still he made her wait.

'Not yet, not yet, my love. I want you to take the same pleasure from our first coupling as do I. Let me teach you the skills.' His voice was languorous, his breath warm against the pearly translucence of her skin, every movement he made transmitting a mesmeric power over her that could not be denied.

He parted her legs with his knee and was lying above her now, and oh, how she loved the weight of him. At some point he must have removed the rest of his clothes for his bare flesh felt wonderful against her own. She kissed his beloved face, traced his winged brows with a growing breathless wonder, stroked the strength of those high cheekbones, loving the crispness of that short, sharp beard, for she knew herself lost to all sensation but her need of him.

Margot discovered that taking pleasure with this man was a delight she had no difficulty in learning. Making love was instinctive to her, fulfilling that need which had burned for so long; relief at last from self-sacrifice and denial. There also emerged in her the flowering of a delicious rebellion, a selfishness that could never again be denied. Their coming together was the realization of a promise, the reaching and touching, however briefly, of a dream.

She was in a haze of desire, needing to touch the velvet hardness of him, taste him, prove to him her love.

His hands slipped beneath her, curving about her delightful rump as she instinctively lifted her hips. Nothing seemed more natural in that moment than that she should open herself to him and he slide inside her, just as if he were meant to be there. But nothing could have prepared her for the cataclysmic effect of this seemingly simple act. It was as if she had fallen into a world made only of sensation, where politics and intrigue, pain and rejection did not exist. She took him into the heart of her, into her soul, enveloping him with her own heat and desire.

And as he moved within her, she cried out against the half pain, half pleasure of it, before giving herself up to the blissful joy of him, instinctively adjusting her own movements to the rhythm of his as he thrust harder, again and again, deep inside her. He did not spare her now but rode her hard, fiercely, feverishly, arching above her, at last able to express his long-held passion, completely demanding as he made her entirely his, so that they both cried out with the joy of release.

'You will marry *me*, not some foreign king, is that understood?'

'Oh yes, yes, yes!'

It was at this moment that the door flew open and Madame de Curton burst in. 'My lady, my lady, we are discovered!'

There was no time to speak, or even think, as Madame was babbling about uproar in the King's apartment. Margot had never seen her loyal servant in such a state.

'His Majesty has been shown a letter by Anjou, no doubt intercepted by du Guast, as a page has divulged your presence here tonight. Make haste, my lady, make haste! They are coming for you; they'll be here at any moment. Get you gone, my lord, if you value your head.' Whereupon she snatched up Margot's nightgown to hastily dress her.

Madame de Curton had time only to add a little rouge to her charge's deathly pale cheeks before two guards entered to escort Margot to the Queen Mother's apartment. Guise had escaped through the window, with only seconds to spare.

Margot stood before her mother in a ferment of fear. The Queen had been waiting for her, stiff-backed with regal splendour despite being clothed only in her nightgown and velvet *robe de chambre*, her fury and impatience all too evident. The King was pacing back and forth in a temper, a fleck of foam at the corners of his mouth. As Margot had entered, Catherine quickly dismissed her ladies and Madame de Curton.

Margot thought she might expire of terror when Charles suddenly lashed out and struck her across the head. He began to beat and punch her in the stomach and knocked her to the ground where he set about furiously kicking her. For once Catherine made no effort to stop him, but rather joined in. She dragged Margot to her feet and ripped her nightgown from her, slapping her face this way and that, tearing at her hair, oblivious to her daughter's screams and cries for mercy.

'Whore! Harlot!'

What other names the Queen used as she set about her, Margot couldn't hear, or afterwards remember, but they were not pleasant.

No one came to her rescue – nobody would dare – as Margot was subjected to the most brutal attack. She was completely defenceless, unable to protect herself against their cruel spite and violent assault. No matter that she begged and sobbed and pleaded; they did not stop kicking and punching her until, fearing for her daughter's life, Catherine at last dragged the King off her. Margot lay curled on the floor covered in cuts and bruises, her gown in shreds about her naked body, shaking with terror.

Dawn was breaking and Catherine's *lever* would take place very soon as the new day began. The Queen Mother steadied her breathing, wiped her brow, and quietly urged the King to return to his own room and rest.

'Go, I will see to this.'

'I want Guise next. I'll kill him! I'll kill him!'

'Rest first, my son, while we think on how best to proceed. We must keep this night's business to ourselves or we'll lose all hope of the Portuguese match, or any other for this trollop.'

When Charles had retired in a highly wrought state, still muttering furiously to himself, still wringing his hands and biting his fingernails to shreds, Catherine set about restoring some sort of order.

She personally bathed Margot's wounds and bruises, found one of her own gowns in place of her daughter's ruined one, dragged the knotted tangles from her hair. When finally the morning's *lever* took place, the sense of calm about the Queen and her daughter might have felt surreal to each of them, but it gave no hint of what had gone before. If the ladies of the robe had overheard the commotion, or knew of what had taken place, none acknowledged it. Appearances were kept, and the King's discipline administered.

The Queen had made it very clear that wayward, recalcitrant daughters would not be tolerated.

Margot's nerves were in tatters, her courage quite gone. By late morning, under strict orders from the Queen Mother, she was seated upon her best horse, pale-faced and drawn, sick to her stomach and still trembling with emotion, yet beautiful as ever in her burgundy riding costume. The cuts and bruises, the scratches from her mother's sharp nails, were hidden beneath her gown and her dignity. To all outward appearances, nothing untoward had occurred.

The chase through the royal forests was to go ahead as planned, even though the Portuguese envoys would not now be present. The Queen had spent hours closeted with the King in his privy chamber, the duc d'Anjou also present, along with the ambassadors, but now they had left court to return home to their own country, the question of the proposed marriage undecided.

The courtiers gathered for the ride without them. The King, who loved hunting and always rode with great gusto; Anjou, du Guast and his other favourites, various councillors and gentlemen; Margot's ladies, and her brother Alençon close by her side.

Guise was there too, doing his utmost to feign insouciance.

Acutely aware of the close proximity of her lover, of how others covertly watched them, and of the risk he ran simply by attending the hunt, Margot did not dare to look his way. Nevertheless, as the party set off into the forest where shafts of sunlight pierced the green gloom, perhaps out of rebellion, or loyalty, he stubbornly rode by her side. He placed his hand over the reins of her grey mare, leaning over to speak with her.

'Are you all right? You look woefully pale.'

Margot still dare not meet his gaze but gave her head a little shake, her lips trembling. 'I am perfectly well. Please, don't . . . it is all over for us.'

The sharp glare of the King silenced her. She could say no more, only cast her erstwhile lover an apologetic little grimace before spurring her horse to a canter.

Margot's hopes and dreams were at an end. Madame de Curton made it her business to go about the court, ears pricked, and discovered that on seeing a pair of hunting knives left lying on a table, the King swore to use them to kill Guise for presuming to aspire to the hand of his sister, and for compromising her reputation.

'You know how angry he gets, my lady. Further, the duc d'Anjou has also sworn that should Guise ever again attempt to approach your apartments, it will be his last visit.'

Margot was at once alarmed. 'Dear God, Lottie, he must not come. He must make his escape and leave court with all speed. What can I say to convince him?'

Madame grasped her beloved charge's hands, her old face wreathed in sadness. 'You must renounce him, my darling. It is the only way to save his life.'

Margot knew in her heart this was true. Suspicion and fear seemed to be everywhere, pressing down upon her like a great weight. Yet it wasn't so much fear for her own safety that made her tremble, but for her lover. They could have his head for despoiling a royal princess, and she would rather face the block herself than allow such a thing to happen.

Uncaring of his safety, that very same evening Guise appeared at the royal salon, ready to pay homage, as usual, to the King and the Queen Mother. He was prevented from entering by Charles, who imperiously demanded where he thought he was going.

'Sire, I am here to serve Your Gracious Majesty!'

'You would serve us best, Monsieur, were you to depart. You may leave at once, for I have no further need of your service.'

Guise bowed, judiciously making no reply and, on retiring to his chamber, discovered a note from Margot urging him to marry his alleged mistress, the Princess de Porcien, for the sake of his own safety, and for her own.

'Only when you are safely wed to another will our security be assured.'

At last acknowledging the danger, to her as much as to himself, he gave urgent orders for his servants to pack his belongings, and departed for the Hôtel de Nemours in Paris.

Margot felt utterly bereft, her lover not only gone from court but within days had married Catherine of Cleves, the widowed Princess de Porcien, in a grand wedding in Paris. She'd salvaged her reputation, put a stop to the calumny being whispered about her, but lost the one man she could ever love. A helpless panic overwhelmed her.

And the ripples and repercussions from one night of love proved to be far-reaching. There wasn't a single member of the House of Guise left at court. Banished in disgrace, they wisely chose to return to the family estates for a while. Thanks to the absence of the sly old Cardinal of Lorraine, the peace talks finally reached agreement, resulting in the Treaty of Saint-Germain. In this, discrimination against Huguenots was banned, and freedom of worship permitted in La Rochelle, Cognac, and certain other towns. In addition, goods and properties confiscated during the civil wars were restored to their owners.

Catherine thought the treaty far from perfect but believed it would at least buy time. With this in mind, she was able to turn her attention back to her favourite pursuit: that of marriages for Charles and her beloved Anjou, not forgetting the headstrong Margot.

These ambitions had very nearly been thwarted by her daughter's latest escapade. The proposed match with the King of Portugal seemed doomed, but Catherine was determined that Nostradamus's prophecy would be fulfilled. As part of the peace talks she reopened negotiations with Jeanne d'Albret for a marriage between her son, Henry of Navarre, and Margot. Navarre was a small kingdom but it nonetheless came with the required crown. As well as consolidating the peace, the union would lure the Huguenots out of their stronghold where they'd hidden away for far too long.

The wedding of Charles and Elisabeth of Austria took place on 25 November 1570, a splendid occasion at which Catherine spared no expense, despite the parlous state of the treasury. As ever, she wanted to make the citizens of Paris gasp at the magnificence of it all.

The beautiful young bride was dressed in a gown of silver set with pearls, a cloak of purple embroidered with fleur-de-lys flowing from her slender shoulders, and with a jewelled crown upon her fair hair she looked enchanting. Even Catherine left off her customary black to display herself in a gown of gold brocade for this special occasion. Anjou and Alençon did their best to outshine everyone with their jewelled brilliance, but Paris fell in love with Elisabeth's fragile blonde beauty at first sight.

Margot was equally enraptured by the girl's sweetness and calm, and Elisabeth marvelled at her sister-in-law's exuberance and beauty. They were a perfect foil for each other and became firm friends. The Princess proved to be devout, fresh and unspoiled, and with a quiet, loving nature, content with her lot, she was smiling happily the morning after her wedding night.

Catherine sighed with relief, although aware that Charles had his gentle, sensitive side and none of his brother's perversions, one could never be absolutely certain of him. She now turned her attention to her beloved Anjou, offering him to Elizabeth I of England in place of Charles. Ever the consummate diplomat, Elizabeth pretended to give the matter her serious attention, for all their age difference was considerable, she being thirty-seven to his nineteen years.

Anjou himself was less enamoured of the proposal, seeing the virgin Queen not only as old but a heretic, and possibly illegitimate. His passion was still for Renée de Châteauneuf, whom he absolutely adored, albeit in a romantic, poetic fashion. But he was content to play the game and wrote many letters filled with flowery phrases and gushing compliments to the English Queen's beauty. When nothing came of them, he soon grew bored. In despair, Catherine offered her youngest son, François-Hercule, the Duke of Alençon, to the English Queen instead, and Elizabeth diplomatically considered him, too, despite the fact he was even younger and far less prepossessing.

Christmas at court passed with its customary merry-making and feasting, although Margot could not bring herself to appreciate its joys. She wept quietly at Midnight Mass on Christmas Eve as she remembered her lost love, nor did she have much appetite for the dinner of oysters, foie gras, and traditional *bûche de Noël* that followed. She kept thinking how much more fun it would have been had Guise been by her side, as he used to be, and dare not allow her mind to dwell on what he might at this moment be engaged in with his new bride.

The banquet seemed endless, dragging on for hour upon hour

until the moment when the entire court processed with great ceremony to a withdrawing room so that the servants and lower orders could partake of their own meal in the main hall.

While the courtiers enjoyed dessert, wafers, and spiced wine, known as the *void*, and were entertained with carols sung by the choir, in which the King himself took part, Margot escaped the hubbub to lie on her bed and weep into her pillow.

Twelve days of feasting followed and she hated every one of them. Catherine was as jovial as ever, laughing at the puppet shows and applauding the actors in the mystery plays. In normal times Margot herself might have acted in one, or written the lines, but this year she took no part, her heart too bruised for celebrating.

In the New Year she was called to the Queen Mother's *cabinet* and at last given news of her fate.

Margot was outraged. 'You mean to marry me to that oaf, to that clod-hopper of a provincial? A *Huguenot*? How can you ask that of me? Have you forgotten that I am a Catholic?'

'Would you defy me?'

'How could I, when your will is mine?' Margot instantly responded, her usual clever reply which irritated her mother rather than offering the obedience she demanded.

It did not trouble Catherine in the slightest that Navarre was the son of her old enemy, and a Huguenot. Metaphorically speaking, the Queen Mother would climb into bed with anyone, so long as it brought wealth and peace to the nation, and added to her own power.

The King had readily signed the Peace Treaty, the Queen Mother quietly reminding him that he would need her support to enforce it. For all his feebleness of mind and body, the boy was growing in independence, but Catherine had no intention of letting go the reins of her regency just yet. She had not forgotten the agreement she'd made with Alva in Bayonne all those years ago, and much as she needed peace for France, if the two religions could not co-exist peacefully side by side, then more drastic measures would indeed be called for.

She'd written to Jeanne twice in recent months, asking her to come to court to discuss the proposed match, and to bring her son with her. The Queen of Navarre, however, was proving to be highly suspicious, and so far had refused. Admittedly, it was not in the woman's nature to be greedy for a crown, however tempting the prospect.

Now Catherine made an attempt to reassure her daughter. 'You would not be obliged to embrace his faith; rather I hope the opposite will be the case, given time and the right degree of persuasion.'

Margot was close to tears remembering what she'd lost: her brave, handsome *chevalier*, so gallant, so exciting. 'Navarre doesn't wash enough, his hair sticks out like an old brush, and he stinks of sweat and garlic.'

'I shall ensure that when he arrives, he is cleansed, groomed and combed before being brought to you.'

'Nor do I relish a mother-in-law as austere and Puritan as Jeanne d'Albret.' Margot loved her life in the French Court, as well as being the subject of great admiration for her burgeoning beauty. She did not welcome the prospect of living in some far-flung rural backwater, let alone one ruled by thrift, modesty and sober piety. That was not the Valois way.

'The boy has turned seventeen, long past time he cut his mother's leading strings,' Catherine agreed, failing to see the irony of her own words. 'He's a good looking, amiable young man. I quite warmed to the boy when he lived with us here at court.'

'He is a fool! A nincompoop! Nothing but a capricious flirt, always chasing some light of love.'

'Then I should think the pair of you will suit each other well.'

Margot burst into tears.

'There, there, you know I wish only for your happiness, dear daughter,' Catherine soothed, with weary insincerity. 'You claim my will is yours in this issue of your marriage, and the union will bring much-needed peace.'

Margot dashed away her tears, furious at her own weakness. How many times had she heard her mother claim that this, that, or the other action would put an end to these dratted religious wars? '*Peace*, you say, when will France ever have that? And what of Philip of Spain? He would not welcome such a marriage.'

It was certainly true that King Philip had expressed extreme displeasure over the peace treaty, at what he judged to be complete surrender to the Protestant cause. Catherine still feared war with

Spain above everything, and could only hope that such a risk could be avoided, if she took proper care. She would also need a special dispensation from the Pope as the pair were third cousins. Catherine didn't see this as a problem either.

'I am sure we can circumnavigate any possible difficulties from that quarter. As things stand at present the Court of La Rochelle is being run almost as a separate country, within the bounds of our own great nation, heedless to our laws and the will of our monarch. This marriage would go a long way towards consolidating peace for our realm, child. It is your duty to the King, and to France, to bring it about.'

'And presumably you would also gain the Kingdom of Navarre,' Margot dryly remarked.

Catherine allowed herself a small smile. 'We would indeed. Now I'd quite forgotten that. Which might well prove to be a useful defence against Spain, since the territory sits upon the border between our two nations.'

Margot was fully aware that the strategic position of Navarre and Béarn had always been a part of the bargain, despite the Queen pretending otherwise. She loathed the very idea of this marriage, felt ill-used by her mother and brother, but was numb with grief over losing Guise, far too emotionally battered to resist any longer. There wasn't an ounce of fight left in her. Besides, it was impossible to defy her. Didn't Catherine of Medici always get her way in the end?

When the Queen of Navarre received an invitation to go to Blois and discuss the wedding of her son to the Princess Marguerite, she couldn't bring herself to accept. Much as she longed to see Henry happily settled and secure, and such a union would undoubtedly strengthen his claim to the throne of France, yet she held back. Jeanne still didn't trust her old enemy. She remembered too well how Catherine had led her own husband, Antoine, by the nose with one of her notorious Flying Squadron. Might she not do the same with her son?

On the same day that Elisabeth was crowned at Saint-Denis at the end of March, a rather more modest, typically Calvinist affair was taking place in La Rochelle. Coligny was marrying for a second time to a lovely new bride.

Jacqueline d'Entremonts was a young widow who had long admired the fifty-year-old Admiral, and, hearing that he had become sad and lonely after losing his wife and son, and brother Andelot, she'd let him know of her affection for him. He'd resisted her advances at first, because of their age difference, but she'd won him over in the end, and the pair had fallen in love. Now they were man and wife and none could be happier.

Jeanne wept to see their joy and, kissing them both, wished them many long years of happiness together. Following the ceremony, Coligny knelt before Henry and asked for his blessing. The young Prince took a drawn sword and dubbed him Knight. Téligny, who was about to become Coligny's son-in-law, buckled a pair of golden spurs on to the old warlord, and set a golden helmet on his head.

'Never had a man greater friends, or truer loyalty,' Coligny cried.

But the joy of the day was marred by news from England that his brother, Cardinal Odet, who had been intending to join them in their celebrations at La Rochelle, had died at the pilgrims' lodge in Canterbury in mysterious circumstances. Was this another case of death by poison? If so, then who was responsible? Surely not Catherine, now that they had the Peace Treaty and she was seeking a marriage for her daughter Marguerite. Would she take such a risk? Or was dispatching another member of his family her way of reminding Coligny of her power, should he refuse to lend his support to her wishes?

More likely the perpetrator was Guise. That family still possessed a strong desire for revenge over the death of the leader of their House, *Le Balafré*. But whoever was the perpetrator, there was every reason to take care.

Catherine was sitting sat at her writing table reading her correspondence when she was brusquely interrupted by Marie Touchet, who came running unannounced into her privy chamber. 'Your Majesty, forgive me, but I beg you to come to the King at once. He hides in terror in his bed, refusing to rise, convinced that the wrath of God is about to strike him dead at any moment.'

Catherine leaped to her feet in great alarm, knowing the King's mistress, inoffensive as the girl was, would never intrude upon her unless it were urgent. 'Why, what has happened?'

'He has received a missive from his Holiness the Pope, and it has struck the fear of God into him. I have never seen him in such a state. This time I truly fear for his sanity.'

Together, the two women hurried to Charles's bedchamber which they found in great disarray, chairs and tables stacked up against windows and doors as if to barricade it against some imagined demons. The young King himself was huddled shivering behind his bed curtains, his gaunt face ashen, his golden eyes like black coals in his head, flecks of foam at his mouth as he screamed at some poor page to bring him his bible and his rosary. 'And a priest. I must have a priest. I must be shriven.'

Catherine could never remember seeing the fragile young King in such a lather of terror. 'My son, my son. Calm yourself, I pray. See, Marie is here, and I, your mother. What has upset you so?'

Charles flung a crumpled letter at her. 'It is from His Holiness. Read it, read it! France is doomed! *I* am doomed! Is it because my nurse is Huguenot, and my beloved Marie the daughter of one? I have always tried to be more sympathetic of their cause than most. Is this the price I must pay?'

Catherine's heart sank as she read the letter, and saw at once why Charles was in such a dreadful state.

In it the Pope repeated his urge for strong action against the Huguenots, calling for their destruction. '*Let Your Majesty take for example, and never lose sight of, what happened to Saul, King of Israel. He had received the orders of God, by the mouth of the prophet Samuel, to fight and to exterminate the infidel Amalekites . . . But he did not obey the will and the voice of God . . . Therefore he was deprived of his throne and his life.*'

'You see how he likens me to Saul?' screamed the King, in great agitation. 'I could lose *my* throne, *my* crown, even *my* life! What am I to do? What does His Holiness ask of me?'

Catherine stifled a sigh. In her view, the words of Pius V could not have been more clear, although she privately wished that the Holy Father would confine such dramatic remarks to herself, who was robust enough to take them. His letters to her were far more plain speaking, to the point almost of callousness. He frequently chastised her for failing to curb the Huguenot advance, offering his assistance, and that of heaven, in order to root out the heretics. But then he understood her practical nature, as well as her power over her son.

The plan growing in her mind was becoming firmer by the hour, and the King must be brought round to it, little by little. Catherine calmly regarded her son as he chewed on his finger-nails, weeping and wailing like a demented child.

'We must do as the Pope commands, my son. We must rid the land of Huguenots, sparing no one. They are the ones at fault, not you. We cannot allow them to hide away in La Rochelle challenging our realm with their rival religion.'

And to make her point, she continued to read out loud from the Pope's letter. '*By this example, God has wished to teach all kings that to neglect the vengeance of outrages done to Him is to provoke His wrath and indignation against themselves.*'

Charles let out another wail of anguish and buried his head under his pillow. Marie was beside him in a second, her arms tight about her lover in protection.

Catherine was unmoved, her firm resolve all too apparent in the cool tone of her voice. What was it Alva had said? 'The head of one salmon is worth the heads of a thousand frogs.'

But it wasn't simply the head of the salmon she was after now; she wanted the frogs too.

She smiled upon her troubled son. 'Our previous efforts to be rid of these heretics failed miserably. Next time we must succeed. We must flush them from their murky pool and destroy them. We have the lure, now we must set the trap.'

When Coligny again received a summons from the Queen Mother, both his new wife Jacqueline and his Queen begged him not to go.

'You must not even think of attending,' Jacqueline tearfully protested.

'Dearest, why should I be concerned now we have the Peace Treaty? Moreover, the Queen Mother's letter is full of goodwill and she claims Charles is in great need of me.'

Coligny had ever been fond of the boy, as there was much to admire in the young king. Unlike his brother Anjou he was modest in his dress, hating the cosmetics and gewgaws favoured by the court dandies; was less perverted in every way, and undoubtedly the most decent of the three Valois brothers as well as the most affectionate, albeit with that fatal flaw of instability. He was also surprisingly thrifty, by comparison with the rest of his profligate family, and considerate. Coligny applauded such sensitivities, and felt no hesitation in returning to court.

'I have always enjoyed a good relationship with the King. Does he not call me father? What is there to fear?'

'Only that Catherine killed your brother Andelot, and now Odet.'

'Where is the proof? The attacks more likely came from the House of Guise, or the Jesuits.'

'I should think she wants you under her thumb,' Jeanne warned. 'Or to throw you in the dungeons for daring to challenge Spain.'

The old Admiral smiled and shook his head. 'Her Majesty assures me she's had the Spanish ambassador recalled. And there is still much work to be done.'

Coligny dreamed of French rule in the Netherlands, of ousting the Spanish from that land, and with the new Peace Treaty in place saw no reason to decline the invitation. Kissing his new wife farewell and promising to return with all speed, he set off to obey his monarch's summons.

The Admiral rode into Blois on a sunny September day, confident of a warm welcome, to find the Queen Mother confined to her bed with a fever, the King in attendance. The usual etiquette was performed, the bowing and kissing of hands, Charles clearly delighted to see his old friend again.

But then the King jokingly remarked, 'We have you now, *mon père*, we shall not let you go whenever you please.'

Coligny froze, unable to think of a suitable response, the underlying tension in the room all too evident. But then he remembered the wild carelessness of this young man; how he was a simple soul full of bad jokes and warm affections, and managed to acknowledge the jest with a smile. The awkward moment passed and everyone breathed again.

Coligny was very soon back in the King's good graces. Charles welcomed his old friend with affection, showered him with gifts, including one hundred thousand livres in compensation for losses suffered during the war, and an escort of nobles, equalled only by that allowed to princes.

In return, Coligny began to exert considerable influence over the young King. Charles proved to be greatly enthusiastic over the Admiral's plan to drive the Spanish out of the Netherlands, obsessed with leading an army to victory himself, in order to outshine his brother's military achievements.

'My mother so loves my brother that she steals for him the honour due to me. I only wish that we could take it in turn to reign, or at least that I might have his place for half the year.'

In Catherine's opinion Charles never could eclipse Anjou. He may now be married, his young Queen content in her marital bed, but she saw little hope of the pair ever producing a son. The King was far too feeble, too weak and sick. She had only to be patient . . .

Having brought Coligny to court, she now began to doubt the wisdom of her decision. He was here so that he could be controlled and used to further *her* plans, not to impose *his* will upon the young king.

Filling her son's head with impossible dreams of conquest in the Netherlands could be viewed as dangerous nonsense, but she was prepared to tolerate the fantasy, for now, as she never would allow it actually to happen. Not for a moment would Catherine risk upsetting her powerful neighbour, although she took great pains not to reveal her reservations by even the smallest degree.

It was worth a little dissembling, a pretence that she approved of the plan, if by this she could win Jeanne d'Albret over to the marriage between young Navarre and Marguerite. Once that was safely accomplished, she could neatly withdraw from any dangerous confrontation with Spain. All she needed was the Queen of Navarre's signature on the marriage contract.

It was February of the following year before the two queens came face to face at Chenonceaux and discussions could at last begin. Jeanne was clearly unwell, arriving in a coach large enough to accommodate a hot stove in the centre of it to keep her warm. When Catherine remarked upon the length of time it had taken to reach this point, Jeanne was dismissive.

'I do not suppose, as the saying goes, that you eat little children.' Even so, she had left her son safely at Béarn.

She knew that this was a brilliant match, that Henry would

gain the throne of France, and the opportunity to establish Protestantism. Yet she could not shake off a dreadful foreboding. The House of Valois was a family blighted by perversion, poison, and profligacy. Jeanne trembled for the principles and morals of her son.

There were the usual arguments over dowry and property, and towns currently occupied by the French Catholics which the Queen of Navarre insisted must be returned to her. Religion was the biggest stumbling block, Jeanne adamant that her son should not be required to take Mass, or even enter the Cathedral for the wedding.

In order to amuse her honoured guest, Catherine held masques and balls and entertainments. At one sumptuous banquet the guests were served by beautiful girls dressed as nymphs, their breasts fully exposed for anyone to ogle or fondle.

The Queen of Navarre was privately appalled by the sight of Anjou and his foppish friends with their painted faces and frizzed hair that stood up all around their velvet caps. Grotesquely outlandish in their huge ruffs, pleats and gold embroidery, with long dangling earrings, and rings on every finger, these scented creatures seemed to illustrate all that she despised most about the French Court.

Like peacocks they spent their days strutting and displaying their fine feathers, and at night turned into court monkeys, giving themselves up entirely to debauchery, to dancing, quarrelling, drinking, playing with dice and cards; committing every conceivable sin. These young cockscombs didn't give a fig for morals, modesty or thrift, being entirely profligate and worshipping nothing so much as excess. It was not uncommon for her to discover a pair of them engaged in a brawl or act of fornication beneath the royal table, or ravishing one of the young serving girls behind a curtain.

The Queen Mother remained supremely oblivious to this bacchanalian frenzy, concentrating entirely on her food, uncaring of whatever debauchery her sons got up to. Even the King, as mischievous as anyone, might don a saddle and gallop about pretending to be a horse, feed his new bride sweetmeats, or creep away to visit with his mistress.

Jeanne was shocked to the core when Anjou came to a banquet

dressed as a woman in high heels and magnificent silk gown, his face even more rouged and painted than usual and his hair covered with a glorious blond peruke. Turning to her would-be daughter-in-law she asked in horrified tones if this was a common occurrence.

Struggling not to smile, Margot gravely agreed that it was. Relations with Anjou had not improved and she loved to see him despised and dishonoured. 'There is nothing my brother likes more than to dress up as a courtesan – except, that is, to behave like one.'

'And it is to this court that you would have me bring my son?'

Margot looked at the older woman with wide, innocent eyes. 'Madame, I ask for nothing in this world save for the will of the Queen my mother.' A lie both of them recognized and accepted as politic.

Jeanne was beginning to feel like a dowd beside the glamour of the Princess Marguerite. The girl was always superbly dressed, the complexion of her lovely face faultless, and her hair dressed with pearls, precious stones and rare diamonds shaped like stars. Jeanne felt ill and tired by comparison, and suspected she was seen as something of a laughing stock and a provincial. She wrote often to her son, sending him tips on how *not* to wear his hair in the style of Nérac, promising that she would call at Paris to buy him the latest fashions before returning home.

Margot considered her future mother-in-law to be plain in the extreme, a most stern and severe woman with no sense of humour, and when asked outright if she would change to her husband's religion, defiantly replied that she would not.

'If it pleased God that our marriage should take place, I would not fail to obey him, and Your Majesty, in all reason. But even if he were King of all the world I would not change my religion in which I have been brought up.'

At this point Jeanne lost patience and called the marriage off. She had grown increasingly paranoiac, convinced that holes had been drilled through the walls of her apartment, and that she was being spied upon. She was exhausted and desperate to return home, refusing to speak further on the match. It was the King who gently brought the discussions to a satisfactory conclusion by conceding to many of her requests, and finally, on 14 April, the Queen of Navarre signed the marriage contract.

She left Chenonceaux to travel to Paris in early May, and in June news reached the palace that despite taking time out to find a cure for her many ailments, she had sadly died. She was forty-four.

Her fellow Huguenot leaders were devastated by their Queen's sudden death, and deeply suspicious. There was much talk of a poisoned glove, since Jeanne had been seen to visit Catherine's Florentine *parfumier*, Monsieur René, before departing. No one could deny that the Queen had already been unwell, and even had they dared to do so, nothing could be proved.

Margot felt only a secret relief that she would not now have to deal with a difficult mother-in-law. And when she heard that the Princes of Lorraine were to return to court her heart skipped a beat at the prospect of seeing Guise again. Married or not, she would have no hesitation in restarting their affair, should he desire it. What would she have to lose? Guise was all that mattered to her, not some Bourbon cousin. Her one consolation in losing her gallant *chevalier* and marrying this malodorous provincial was that she would at least gain a crown. She would be Queen of the tiny Kingdom of Navarre, rural backwater though it might be, and she was Valois enough to appreciate the value of that. But would it be enough to bring her any happiness? Margot rather doubted it.

'Do not anyone say that marriages are made in heaven; the gods would not commit so great an injustice.'

Part Three

A BLOOD RED WEDDING

1572–1573

August 1572

'They are come. They are come!' Madame de Curton rushed into Margot's apartment all in a flurry to inform her mistress of this stupendous news. Pausing only long enough to catch her breath, she continued, 'The bridegroom comes riding into Paris, attended by the Prince de Condé and eight hundred Huguenot gentlemen. They are all in deep mourning for his late mother, the Queen of Navarre.'

Margot stared at her beloved companion, transfixed with horror, scarcely registering the excited gasps from her ladies-in-waiting. 'Then it is going to happen?'

'It would seem so. The Prince – or rather the *King* of Navarre – is even now being received with great honour by King Charles, and by the Queen your mother.'

Margot put her hands to her face and let out a low groan. 'Oh, Lottie, do they not believe that I am a sincere Catholic? Are they so determined to punish me for my transgression in loving Guise that they would force me to spend the remainder of my life in the most remote corner of France they can find? I feel as if I am being banished from my home.'

Margot was deeply afraid of the future with this man she cared nothing for, and of never seeing Guise again. She feared that this sacrifice could all be in vain, the much longed-for peace never attained. And if the wars broke out yet again, the people of Béarn would blame her. As might her mother and brother who seemed to take special pleasure in blaming her for every ill. Thus she could be despised by both sides, be unloved by the Court of Navarre and an exile from the French Court which she held so dear. It was a troubling prospect.

'There, there, do not fret, my lady.' Madame gathered the girl in her arms, holding her while she wept. 'We will find a way to make a good life in Béarn, with all the fun and gaiety that you desire.'

'And you will be with me? You will not allow them to separate us?'

'Only God can do that,' said the old governess, aware she was getting on in years.

'But what of the dispensation? Pope Pius V withheld his consent, but since he died in May, I thought – I hoped – that the newly elected pope might follow his lead and also refuse.'

Madame drew Margot to a window seat, away from the other women. 'I have heard it whispered abroad that a message has indeed come from Pope Gregory XIII. This missive is said to contain either the dispensation itself or the promise of one. We do not know which, as the nuncio Salviati presented it to the Queen Mother and she passed it on, without opening it, to the Cardinal de Bourbon who is to perform the ceremony. I understand that he too has refrained from opening the sealed package.'

Margot regarded her governess in dismay. 'Then how will we ever know if it is a yea or nay?'

'We won't.'

'This is the work of my mother. She fears the letter may be a refusal, not only because of our close kinship but the fact that the Holy Father will view Navarre as a heretic. She wants the deed done before the package is opened and the truth revealed.'

Madame de Curton did not presume to comment on this point, for all it was a shrewd assessment of the Queen Mother's fondness for devious practices. 'It is but a rumour, my lady, although I confess it is a certain fact that Her Majesty has given strict instructions in the form of a letter to the Governor of Lyon, that no further communication with Rome may take place until after Monday.'

'You mean until after the wedding has taken place.'

'It would seem that is the case, yes.'

Margot clasped ice cold fingers tightly together in her lap. 'So that if a dispatch should arrive saying no such dispensation can be granted, the King my brother will not receive it?'

Madame gazed upon her charge, sympathy softening the lines of her old face. 'He will not.'

There was a short silence in which Margot digested this distressing news. 'I hoped to the last for a reprieve, Lottie, but I see no help will come from any quarter. I am to be sacrificed for a hope, a flimsy dream of peace.'

After a long moment she stiffened her spine, and there was a new resolution in her voice when she spoke next. 'Then if no one is to save me from this offensive alliance, I must needs rely upon myself.'

They came into Paris from far and wide. First the Guises, who returned with a strangely muted triumph to the city from which they'd been banished, clearly unhappy with the turn of events. The Princes of Lorraine headed east to the Rue Saint Antoine and the Hôtel de Guise, accompanied by scores, if not hundreds of their followers; some were Catholic extremists, others a motley band of adventurers and vagabonds looking for trouble. They made sure they lodged round and about their leaders.

A day or two later came the Huguenots, flocking in from La Rochelle and from every corner of the kingdom. But because of the huge numbers, rooms were in short supply, and they found themselves widely scattered, obliged to seek lodgings as best they may. Those who got there first took up residence as close as possible to Faubourg Saint-Germain, or to Coligny at Rue de Béthisy, but the vast majority were disappointed. Many were driven to dossing down in a doorway or some dark corner among the twisting streets and alleys.

The city was an incongruous mix of malodorous, makeshift hovels huddled together in every available square and alleyway, seedy taverns, tall, narrow houses, and magnificent mansions. The glory of the Louvre and the still-unfinished Tuileries palace and gardens, the Gothic towers of the Sainte-Chapelle and Notre Dame, even the Palais de Justice, contrasted starkly with the fetid squalor which the citizens were obliged to inhabit. And in the intense August heat hung a miasma of filth and dust and flies over the congested streets; the enticing scents of excellent French cooking clashing with foul odours from the river.

Merchants, lawyers and bankers, shopkeepers and pâtissiers, smithies and city burghers alike watched the invasion with uneasy hearts. Much as they wished to rejoice on this special day for a very special Princess, the fear that trouble might at any moment break out between the two factions dampened their spirits considerably.

The worried citizens hastened to board up their shops and

businesses while setting out their market stalls to do a roaring trade in salted herrings, fruit, bread, and pastries. Barbers styled lice-infested hair for all those wishing to present themselves well, prostitutes plied their trade, and those with nimble fingers and no scruples made a fortune from easy pickings.

Catholic pulpits rang with dire predictions of doom, wise women told fortunes and spoke of ill omens that warned the wedding would run red with blood. And whenever they heard voices lifted in prayer or psalm singing, the Parisians defiantly sang their own ballads. They hung out their flags of celebration even as they cleaned and repaired their weapons.

The police and the Watch, who supposedly shared the task of keeping guard over this teeming city from their sentry boxes, abandoned all hope of controlling the hordes, giving more attention to protecting themselves and their own families.

The wedding took place on Monday 18 August, as planned. From the moment Madame de Curton woke her at dawn to begin her *toilette*, Margot felt sick to her stomach. She wanted to turn and run and keep on running, far from the Louvre, a million miles from this oaf of a husband she loathed.

She was nineteen years old and knew she should be thankful she'd not been wed long since to the mad Don Carlos, or someone equally revolting. Yet how she longed for Guise, her *chevalier*, and for what might have been.

Margot was bathed in milk to keep her skin soft and white, anointed with scented unguents, her hair washed and brushed and polished with silk till it shone. Dressing her took hours, each item of linen, stocking, corset and kirtle passed tenderly along the line by her ladies, then set in place, adjusted, pinned and tweaked until finally she was gowned and ready.

The Princess positively blazed with diamonds. Pendants hung in her ears, rings adorned her fingers, a brilliant necklace circled her throat, and gems were sewn on to her gown. With a crown upon her head, a regal *coet*, or close gown of spotted ermine, about her shoulders, and her blue robe bearing a train of four ells in length carried by three princesses, she looked like a Queen already.

Yet despite all of this magnificence, and dear Lottie's best efforts to cheer her, Margot felt filled with dread.

'I'm not sure I can face this.'

'You can because you must,' came her governess's not very reassuring reply. 'You are a Princess of the Blood. This is—'

'My duty, I know, Lottie.' Margot longed to fall into her nurse's arms and weep, to feel her loving arms about her, but the time for such weakness was past.

She stepped outside and saw, to her immense relief, that Navarre and his entourage had discarded their mourning and decked themselves in embroidered pale-yellow satin, brilliant with jewels. Were he anyone else, she might have thought him handsome. The entire court was likewise richly attired. King Charles's splendid outfit had cost upwards of five hundred thousand crowns, and Anjou, not to be outdone, was weighed down with over thirty costly pearls in his hat alone. Margot couldn't help but smile at her brother's vanity as he strutted, peacock-like, back and forth. Everyone was waiting to lead her, the sacrificial lamb, to the altar.

She was accompanied by a hundred and twenty ladies all dressed in gleaming gold of rich tissue, velvet, heavy brocade, silk or satin. Yet the Princess's beauty outshone them all, bringing gasps of admiration from all who gazed upon her.

A platform had been raised for her to walk on, leading from the Bishop's Palace to the Church of Notre Dame, hung with cloth of gold as was the custom for Daughters of France. Below it thronged the people, the Huguenots only too evident in their simple, plain attire, in sharp contrast to the more flamboyant Catholic nobles.

But followers of either faith seemed, for the moment at least, content to be packed in alongside each other like sardines in a barrel, willing to endure the suffocating August heat as they were all eager to view this magnificent royal parade. Wasn't this to be a day, a week of celebration? Even a medal had been struck to commemorate the event. What was there to fear on such a joyful occasion?

Yet Margot feared for them, and for herself.

She was led to the altar by her two brothers, the King and the duc d'Anjou, and was received on the steps of the great Western door of Notre Dame by the Cardinal de Bourbon. It had been agreed that the King of Navarre would not cross the threshold and that the bride would later enter the church alone to take the usual nuptial Mass.

Margot walked, stiff-backed, teeth clenched. She could feel the sweat gathering between her breasts, the weight of the heavy train dragging behind her despite the assistance of those who carried it. A pain had started up, throbbing somewhere behind her eyes, and she was deeply aware of the silent crowd pressing in on all sides. It felt more like a brooding resentment than reverence. They had wanted a Catholic husband for their princess. They had wanted Guise, the King of Paris. As, of course, had she.

Henri of Guise watched events unfold from a respectful distance, his heart aching as the bride was led to her fate. His beloved Margot. Never had he seen her look more beautiful. Did she feel his eyes upon her, burning into her proud, straight back? Would she turn and meet his hungry gaze? How he wished that he could have been the one to stand beside her. It should have been so. He felt he'd been deprived of his rights, of an opportunity not only to be happy with the woman of his choice, but also to be a good and true king of this realm. Others before him in his family had worn the crown, why not him?

The Cardinal de Bourbon pronounced the benediction and all proceeded exactly as had been rehearsed, until she was called upon to give the usual assent. Margot did not speak. She could not. Something inside of her turned stubborn and the words died in her throat. How many times in the past had she been asked if she agreed to this or that marriage proposal? Always she had answered that she would do as the Queen her mother willed. Now, for one moment of rebellion, she thought she might do as *she* pleased, and refuse. If she was not willing, how could they make her agree?

The entire assembly seemed to hold its collective breath while they waited for her response. She heard a sound behind her, and half turned, some instinct telling her that it was Guise.

He was on his feet, his gaze searing into hers.

Guise was astounded by her courage. Was she even at this late stage about to refuse? He wanted to run to her and gather her in his arms, to rescue her from this humiliation. As their gaze locked he felt as if he were looking deep into her soul, seeing not the beautiful, magnificent Queen but the vulnerable, uncertain woman within, whom he had loved since she was a girl.

For one mad moment Margot thought he might be about to shove his way through the ordered rows of seating, knock everyone aside and stride over to carry her off. She almost called out to him, but some spark of common sense prevailed and she bit down hard on her lip to prevent herself from such madness.

Her heart was pumping. Should she run? Could she escape?

And then a hand grasped her by the nape of her neck and pushed her head forward. The King, annoyed by her obstinacy, had forced her head to bob in a nod of assent. The Cardinal at once accepted this as agreement, hastily declared the couple united in marriage, and the deed was done.

She could hardly believe it. Without her speaking a word of assent, it was all over. Her mother and brothers had bullied and finally forced her into this marriage, the Cardinal a party to their scheme. How Margot hated them all, hated this husband standing so silent and sullen beside her. No doubt he thought he'd taken a step closer to the crown by marrying a Daughter of France. No good would come of this day, she was sure of it – although even Margot, in the very depths of her misery, could not have predicted the catastrophe that was to follow.

Wishing to avoid the service, Coligny remained within doors, walking with the Constable's Huguenot son, Damville. The pair spent the time admiring the banners of Jarnac and Moncontour which were hung on the walls of the nave.

'In a short while these will be torn down and replaced by others, better to see,' the Admiral said, still dreaming of expelling the Spanish from the Netherlands and taking it for France.

At the conclusion of the service the wedding party walked along the platform before the hushed multitude of watchful citizens, as far as the pulpit where the bride and groom parted and went their separate ways. The bride was led up the choir to the high altar and the duc d'Anjou, as the representative of the bridegroom, stood beside Margot beneath the canopy to receive Mass. Navarre left the church and met with Coligny at the Bishop's Palace where they paced up and down the court with several of his gentlemen.

At last the moment came when the entire cavalcade must process back to the Louvre. As Margot waved and smiled to the onlookers, the cheers of the suspicious Parisians for this new Huguenot husband of their Princess were lacklustre and grudging. Only when Guise passed by did they let out a loud and hearty cheer: *Vive le Guise!*

The young lord responded, as always, by sweeping off his plumed hat and saluting them. And if the Huguenots resented this apparent snub to their King, Margot herself laughed with pleasure to see her beloved so adored.

The wedding party dined with typical extravagance. When Catherine first came to France as a young bride, she had brought with her the traditions and foods of her homeland, chefs and bakers, and that most prized tool of all, the fork. With this implement she ate her favourite pasta, and the natives of her adopted country followed her lead. The dish was served today at her daughter's wedding banquet, a feast for a Queen indeed.

For the first course there was a selection of soups sprinkled with aromatic herbs, roast beef, goose, pork and veal, capon, chickens, venison, quails and a variety of pies. Salads came next, followed by the small round cheeses from the Auvergne, and the soft creamy variety which the palace cooks bought from the peasant women of Montreuil and Vincennes who sold them in the Paris markets in small wickerwork baskets. There were sweetmeats and pastries of every description, decorated to a fine art by the pastry cooks, along with candied raisins, figs, prunes, almonds and dates, and the finest wines poured from huge silver flagons.

After the feasting came the dancing, as musicians played for hour upon hour. The guests were royally entertained by the brilliance of the ballet, the merry jests of the masques and dramas, and the young King of Navarre did not fail to appreciate the charms of the court beauties.

The Duke of Guise, having congratulated the bride, studiously avoided her for the rest of the day, willing himself not to glance in Margot's direction. He noticed, however, as did everyone else, that she danced very little and an air of sadness seemed to hang upon her. When he felt he'd carried out all that duty and courtesy required, he approached the King and begged leave to retire early, which caused much muttering behind hands as he strode from the banqueting hall.

Margot watched him go with a physical ache in her heart. So proud, so handsome, and hurting badly, as was she. This day could have been so different, could have been the epitome of all they had once desired, had her mother found one ounce of compassion in her heart – assuming she even possessed one.

All too soon the moment came for the bride to be escorted to her bedchamber and Margot was deeply thankful to find Madame de Curton waiting for her, as always.

'What am I to do?' she wailed. 'How am I to endure this?'

'With your usual courage and good spirit,' the old woman told her. 'Your husband is a fine looking man; perhaps it will not prove quite so unpleasant as you fear.'

When Lottie had divested her mistress of her wedding garments, scented and dressed her in a silken nightgown, the Queen Mother and Margot's three brothers, Charles the King, Anjou, and François-Hercule the Duke of Alençon, together with as many of her ladies-in-waiting and gentlemen courtiers who could squash into the bedchamber, saw her safely into bed with her husband.

'You can safely leave the rest to me,' Navarre told them with a laugh, and a wicked gleam in his eye.

Thankfully the court agreed, and with many ribald jokes and jests they returned to their drinking and merrymaking, leaving the young couple at last alone.

'Would you like me to leave with them?' Henry quietly asked.

Margot was startled. 'Why? Do you wish to leave?'

'I believe I wish to be in this bed as much as you do. Neither of us chose this marriage.'

They regarded each other in silence for a moment, judging a new frankness between them. But then feeling very slightly piqued by his wish to abandon her marriage bed so soon, Margot slanted a sly glance up at him. 'Yet here we are.'

'Indeed.' He settled himself more comfortably upon the big square pillows. 'So what can I tell you about myself? I believe you are fond of reading, and so am I. My taste for poetry was fostered by the Queen Mother, who taught me to appreciate the verse of Dante, her own countryman. For my own choice I prefer the chivalrous romance of the troubadours.'

'I can imagine,' Margot dryly remarked.

'My disposition is generous and I am known to be magnanimous. Nor will I curb your purse, so I do not see how you can fault me.'

'I'm sure I'll think of something.'

'Then if you see no good in me, what do we do about this most piquant situation? I would have you know that I have never yet taken a woman who wasn't willing, and do not intend to change that habit with my own wife.'

Wife! The word had a terrifying sound to it, ringing out in her head like the toll of a doleful bell. Margot blotted it out and manufactured a small smile. 'I am aware of your fondness for the softer sex. I've seen you chasing after them often enough, have I not?'

Navarre gave a low rumble of laughter deep in his throat. 'Do I assume by that judgemental remark you are an innocent still? If so, then Guise is not the man I took him for.'

'Do you mean to insult me?' she snapped, which made him laugh all the more.

'I mean you to see that we are not so unalike, you and I.'

'Oh!'

'Perhaps we may come to terms, to some sort of agreeable compromise? Now that we are man and wife, and will, I trust, be left to our own devices.'

His nose was a touch too long perhaps, but then so was hers, and his was narrower. His mouth was full and red and smiled a great deal. For once he smelled of soap and fresh air, of good wine and something else that was not altogether unpleasing. The Queen her mother had once promised to have him scrubbed and combed before sending him to her, but Margot rather thought he'd made the effort on his own account. 'I was grateful that, despite your being still in mourning, you really looked very fine today.'

He inclined his head in a brief acknowledgement of the compliment, but his eyes, she noticed, were on her breasts. 'They told me you had grown into a court beauty, and I see that you have.'

'Thank you.' Margot was suddenly finding difficulty with her breathing. There was something so innately sensual about this man that she could not help but flush charmingly at his words.

He gave an idle shrug. 'I did not entirely mean to flatter you.

Sadly, the paints and powders of courtly artifice are not to my taste. I prefer the blush of a maiden's cheek to come from the sun and the wind rather than out of a pot. Or else from too much loving,' he smirked.

She wanted to slap him for his impudence but his finger and thumb had captured her chin, tilting it slightly so that he could better see her face in the lamplight. His fingers were caressing her cheek in a most beguiling manner, and Margot struggled to resist a soporific need growing in her that really had nothing to do with tiredness at all.

'You seemed enchanted enough by my mother's women, the *Escadron Volant*. I saw you eyeing them at the wedding feast. Perhaps you may come to see things differently and be less interested in your peasant girls, now that you are at court.'

'Ah, I may say that the peasant girls of Béarn are a particular delight, but there are none here right now, and yet I cannot claim to be too disappointed by what I find.'

Now it was Margot's turn to laugh. She suddenly saw the ludicrousness of their situation, almost farcical in a way. Here they were in bed together, quite against their wishes. Despite their protests, each had been obliged, for whatever political purpose, to go through with this marriage. They were now man and wife. An undeniable fact.

He had somehow drawn nearer and Margot found herself transfixed by the wicked gleam in his eyes. They were dark and mysterious, almost mesmeric. Perhaps Lottie might be right. He was not entirely unpleasant, and if not as handsome as Guise, really quite a fine looking man. She could never feel anything for him that could remotely be described as love, but there were other delights to savour. She feigned a sigh of resignation. 'And we are expected to do our duty, I suppose.'

He was untying the ribbons of her nightgown, and she saw no reason to stop him. 'I dare say we must.'

'I can only hope it will not be too onerous.' She sighed again, rather theatrically.

He moved closer, pulling her down in the bed beside him. 'Let us hope not.'

And to her great surprise, Margot did not find it in the least onerous. Henry proved to be a skilled and accomplished lover, and they each found pleasure in their coupling. Margot discovered that she was not dissatisfied with the night's business. Perhaps some sort of agreement might be reached in this marriage, after all.

On the evening of Wednesday 20 August, the King held a masque in honour of his sister's nuptials. Dramas were performed in which Navarre and his cousin Condé dressed as knights entering paradise, only to find themselves driven back into hell by the King and Anjou. In another the Huguenot Princes were cast as Turks, who had recently been beaten at Lepanto, and were conquered again to the great joy of the enthralled courtiers. If there was a darker meaning to these dramas, a hidden message being made, for the sake of good relations Navarre and his friends pretended not to see it.

A sense of nervousness and unease was spreading. Beneath all the merriment there was a growing feeling of hostility, people choosing to move about in groups as if needing to feel safe, muttering quietly together. The kind of rumbling before a storm breaks.

Coligny escaped from the celebrations at the first opportunity and retired to his chamber to write to his beloved wife, promising he would leave within a day or two. His time at home had been far too brief, particularly now that Jacqueline was expecting a child. He'd slept soundly, ate a frugal diet, savoured the daily *prêches* and the singing of psalms at a twice-weekly family service. Most of all he'd enjoyed supper each evening where family and servants gathered together to share the food and talk of their day. There would be his sons, his daughter Louise, newly married to Téligny, perhaps a minister, old comrade or humble soldier or two. He saw this meal as an act of fellowship, in remembrance of his Saviour, and many had followed his lead and taken up the custom.

Despite his weariness, he'd continued to hold council with church and military leaders each morning, working on plans to help the Prince of Orange chase the Spanish out of the Netherlands. Tragically, when the proposed invasion had taken place in July, the Huguenots had been decimated, with only a few hundred weary survivors returning home. It was a savage blow to his hopes.

Charles had been equally distraught that he was not, after all, to have his moment of glory, terrified that Spain might declare war upon France. The young king's efforts to creep from under the shadow of his mother had proved to be a miserable failure.

Coligny had viewed that first expedition as merely the opening foray and still strived to convince the King that they must not give up but send more men, and greater armies. Sadly, Charles was no longer pliable and would not agree.

The Admiral had returned to court for the wedding at Catherine's insistence, but there had been no warm welcome this time, not even any bad jokes. The King had been cool towards him, the Catholic nobles and the Queen Mother actively hostile, and he'd found only opposition to his grand plan to win the Netherlands for France.

The old Admiral was deeply disappointed, which was perhaps why he'd spoken so unwisely to the Queen Mother. 'Madame, the King refuses to adventure the war. God grant that he be not overtaken by another from which he will have no power to retreat.'

Catherine had glared at him, seeing in this remark a deliberate threat. Perhaps he should have guarded his tongue, as Téligny was constantly urging him to do. The trouble was he still grieved for the loss of his Queen, missing her common sense and wise counsel.

His hopes for an early release from duty proved to be over-optimistic as the banquets, ballets and pageants continued with relentless magnificence throughout the week. Coligny had a strong suspicion that the King was avoiding him.

'*Mon père*, I pray you grant me yet four or five days of pleasure, and after that I promise you, on the faith of a king, to give you and those of your religion content!'

Quite certain that he could win Charles round, the Admiral had already issued orders for troops to be quietly mustered, before even setting out for the capital. Now he waited impatiently for the celebrations to be over so that a day could finally be agreed for the next invasion.

When Catherine received a furious message from the Duke of Alva demanding to know why a huge force of Huguenots were gathering in Flanders, she took it at once to the King. She would have liked someone to relieve her of the burden of what to do

about Coligny, but that was not to be. Charles was riddled with
fears, deeply afraid that because of his tolerance for the Huguenots,
and for allowing his sister to marry one, the Pope might excom-
municate him, or the Guises turn on him. He'd sought the support
of his old mentor as protection, which Coligny had gladly given.

Now when his mother informed him of Coligny's secret plans,
he fell into his customary panic. The prospect of war with Spain
was terrifying, even to Charles. There was no hope of support
from England, as Elizabeth had no desire to take on her powerful
Catholic rival. Without question, war would be a calamity.

'What is to be done?'

Catherine's resentment had grown and soured with each passing
day as she'd watched them together, the old man and the boy
she had once so easily controlled. Now she would be the one to
decide.

'You can safely leave this matter in my hands.'

The plotters gathered: Guise, his mother Anne d'Este, widow of
Francis of Guise and now the Duchess of Nemours, and her former
brother-in-law the Duke of Aumale. The Cardinal of Lorraine
remained in Rome, where he'd been since the banishment. Tavannes,
Nevers, Retz and others of Catherine's trusted circle were also
present, and it was a matter of moments to draw up a plan to deal
with Coligny.

The Duchess herself offered to do the deed, since she had the
greatest grievance against him. The entire family remained eager
for vengeance for the murder of her husband, *Le Balafré*. In the
end, Maurevert was the chosen assassin, as he would be a more reli-
able shot. The candidate was called and informed that if he valued
his safety, he would not refuse.

The Duchess suggested that the shot be fired from the ground-
floor window of a house on Rue des Fossés, owned by her family,
and conveniently located on the route Coligny would take on
his way home.

Catherine was very much in favour of this plan, as suspicion
would naturally fall upon the Guises and not on herself, or the
King. And if the Huguenots rose against the Princes of Lorraine,
she might well be rid of both troublesome factions.

                              ★   ★   ★

At the usual council meeting the next morning, the duc d'Anjou presided in the absence of the King, who had risen late. On leaving the *cabinet* Coligny met Charles coming out of the chapel, having heard matins with the Queen Mother. The pair talked quite amicably together and the old Admiral accompanied His Majesty to the tennis court, where the King, the Duke of Guise, and Teligny were to play.

Coligny politely declined joining them in a game and continued on to his apartments at Rue de Béthisy, accompanied by his friends. They strolled through the Rue des Fossés, Saint-Germain, discussing the latest dispatches he'd received from the troops. Coligny was about to hand one over to his comrade when a shot rang out and his arm fell uselessly to his side.

He sank to his knees in agony as pandemonium broke out, his friends instantly distraught that their beloved leader had been shot.

'Tell the King,' Coligny implored. 'But take care not to alarm him.'

Some forced the door and rushed into the house to seek the perpetrator, but the assassin had made his escape by the cloister of the Church of Saint-Germain l'Auxerrois and they found only a smoking arquebus. Others ran to the stables behind the house, which they realized belonged to the Guises. Téligny called a doctor, and had his father-in-law carried inside so that he could be properly attended to.

Charles was still playing tennis when news of the attack reached him. He threw down his racquet in a fit of temper and let out a string of oaths. 'Shall I never have a moment's peace?' he cried, then ran in terror to his apartments and locked himself in, fearing he might be next.

Anjou too trembled at the prospect of the Huguenot chieftains deciding to retaliate. Catherine received the news with her usual equable calm, just as she was about to sit down to dinner. She regally ordered that the Royal Surgeon, Ambroise Paré, be called. Fortunately, as a Huguenot himself, he was above suspicion so far as the Admiral was concerned.

At first it seemed as if Coligny might lose the entire arm, as fears were expressed that the bullet could have been poisoned. But thanks to the surgeon's skill, and the old man's courage and tenacity to withstand the amputation of a wounded finger, and much painful probing to extract the bullet which had then lodged in the arm, the limb was saved. Those about him showed less patience, striding about and furiously speculating on the identity of his assailant.

'I have no enemy but the Guises,' Coligny calmly insisted, and when his friends angrily cried for blood, he forbade them to retaliate. 'But I do not assert that it was they who struck the blow.'

Old soldier that he was, he seemed unperturbed by the attack and received several callers during the course of the morning, Navarre and young Condé among them. Following this visit the cousins went straight to the King, threatening to leave Paris forthwith unless immediate guarantees were given for the safety of their men. They also demanded that the Princes of Lorraine be banished from the city.

Charles flew into a frenzy of distress, crying out that it was himself who was most wounded by this attack on *mon père*.

'It is the whole of France. They will soon come and attack the King in his own bed,' Catherine cried, which did little to reassure her son, serving only to exacerbate his anxieties still further.

The streets became thronged with noisy crowds, the people suspicious that something serious had occurred, exactly as they'd feared. They filled every avenue and, at around eleven o'clock, an hour or so after the shot had been fired, the King gave orders for the Catholics living by the Rue de Béthisy to be moved out, and Huguenots be allowed to replace them. This went some way towards calming nerves but groups of Protestants could still be found huddled together whispering at every corner, and the sense of dread grew hourly.

Coligny asked to see the King. 'For I have certain things to tell him which concern his person and the State.'

Charles came with all speed, although not alone. Catherine had no intention of allowing him such freedom. She brought with her Anjou and Alençon, and the Admiral's most bitter enemies: Tavannes, Montpensier, Retz and Nevers.

Crowded into every room of Coligny's house gathered the

Huguenots and, as she walked through to his bedchamber, Catherine could feel their sullen silence, their simmering rage.

Charles, clearly moved by the plight of his beloved mentor, began to weep. '*Mon père,* you have the wound but I have the pain.' As always the smell and sight of blood had a disturbing effect upon him. 'Is that then the blood of the famous Admiral?' he sobbed. Head nodding and twitching on his crooked neck, he began to get excited and started to rant about vengeance and salvation.

Catherine judiciously stepped forward to place a calming hand on her son's arm. 'We all bleed for you,' she told Coligny, her smile cold.

The Admiral spoke of his long fidelity to the crown and of his ambitions for the Low Countries. 'I implore you, with all the urgency I have, not to lose the present opportunity from which France may reap great advantage.' He was becoming more agitated, determined to have his say. 'My only regret is that my wound should deprive me of the happiness of working for Your Majesty.'

'I will avenge this outrage in so signal a manner that the memory of the penalty shall be eternal,' cried the King.

'Your Majesty need not seek far for the culprit. Let Monsieur de Guise be questioned, Sire. He will confess through whose benevolence I lie here. I rely on your justice to avenge this crime.'

'*Par le mort Dieu!* I promise that I will do you justice.'

'Is it not a disgrace that your desire for peace has been violated in this way?' he told Charles. 'All because fifty thousand crowns was offered to any man who brings my head.'

Téligny put up a hand, as if in an attempt to halt this alarming tirade against their Sovereign. 'Father, I beg you, have a care for your health.'

Catherine added her own warning. 'Pay heed to your son-in-law's wise counsel, Monsieur, else we might start asking questions concerning certain matters regarding the assembly of troops.'

In the ensuing silence, perhaps out of morbid curiosity, or oblivious to the tension growing around him, Charles asked if he might examine the bullet that had wounded him.

Catherine snatched it from his hand. 'I am very glad,' she dryly remarked, 'that the bullet was not left inside you, for I remember that when Francis of Guise was murdered near Orléans, the doctors told me that if the bullet had been got out of him, even though it was poisoned, there would have been no danger of his death.'

Meeting the old man's shrewd gaze, Catherine realized she may well have condemned herself out of her own mouth. She glanced anxiously at her son but he was too absorbed with the bloodstains on the sheets, and hadn't heard her. She quickly rose, urging him to make his farewells and leave the patient to rest. Charles obediently complied, and they were almost at the door when Coligny called out and he hurried back alone to the bed.

'Reign by yourself, Sire,' Coligny whispered to the King beneath the rasp of his breath. 'Trust no one, not even the Queen your mother. Only evil will come of it.'

Catherine grew suspicious as she stood impatiently tapping her toe, Anjou beside her, itching to interrupt what seemed an unnecessarily prolonged conversation. Must the fellow always stir up trouble, even in the hour of his death? Although he was taking an unconscionable time to reach it. She knew then that he would survive, and that Coligny meant to use this attempted assassination to strengthen his position with the King.

But surrounded as she was by a dozen Huguenots, many more filling adjacent rooms and the street below, she dare make no move. Their distrust was all too evident. Some whispered in corners, others strolled insolently about, showing none of the respect due to her station, making her feel decidedly uneasy.

Losing patience she marched back to her son's side, a fraction too late to hear what had been said. 'Come, the Admiral has talked enough. Too much excitement will be bad for him.'

'What did he say to you?' she sharply enquired of her son as they were driven back to the Louvre in her coach.

'Nothing of any importance,' Charles sulkily responded, turning his face away.

But Catherine was having none of his moods today, and throughout the journey back to the Palace she subjected him to an inquisition that gradually wore down his resistance. Confined with his mother and brother alone in the carriage Charles could find no escape, and at length his nerves snapped and he blurted it all out.

'He said that you were a malign influence over me, that

everything had gone to pieces in your hands, and that only evil would come of it.'

Following this outburst he fled to the sanctity of his privy chamber, to his darling Marie Touchet and his beloved nurse.

Catherine privately resolved that next time she would find someone who was a better shot.

When news reached Margot that an attempt had been made on the life of the Admiral, she was thrown into a panic. She hastily dispatched a message to Guise via Madame de Curton, warning him to lie low, as he was being implicated in the plot.

'The King may arrest you. The Huguenots are baying for Guise blood, and I greatly fear for your life.'

Guise and his uncle, the Duke of Aumale, begged the King for protection so that they might leave the city for their own safety.

'You can go to the devil if you wish, but I shall know how to find you if I need to,' was Charles's brusque response.

Guise and his men slipped quietly out of Paris, but retreated only part way to Porte Saint-Antoine before returning to the comparative security of the Hôtel de Guise. Charles, entirely hood-winked by this subterfuge, and fearful of reprisals, applied himself to writing letters of assurance to the Queen of England, among others. He laid the blame entirely upon 'the evil enmity between the House of Châtillon and the House of Guise'.

The Queen Mother attempted to persuade him that if Guise had indeed been involved in this attempt upon the Admiral's life it was surely excusable. 'He is a son who has been denied justice, and has no other means of avenging his father's death.'

'He cannot take the law into his own hands,' Charles shouted. '*I* am the King, not Guise. He should be brought back and punished!'

The sense of dread in the city was palpable, and Navarre demanded instant protection for the Protestants. The King placed a guard of fifty arquebusiers outside Coligny's lodgings, militiamen were stationed at strategic points about the city with the orders to keep the populace calm and prevent looting, yet the Huguenots were still not reassured. They anxiously considered their options. Some were for leaving Paris forthwith, but Coligny was against

the idea, and his son-in-law Téligny, Navarre and Condé all agreed
that it would be an insult to the King. Charles had swiftly ordered
an enquiry, and convinced them by his genuine concern of his
own innocence in the affair.

They were less trustful of the Queen Mother but had no proof
that she was involved. The most likely suspects were still the
Guises. Téligny would have moved the Admiral to the Louvre
but others thought this a bad idea. The surgeon too agreed that
in his weakened state, the old man might not survive the move.

This decision was reported back to Catherine by one of her
spies, who reported everything, even the most wild and radical
comments. He told her that the Huguenots were quietly arming
themselves in defence, but that he did not rule out the possibility they might instigate an attack.

Catherine was enraged, not only by the truculence of the
Reformationists, but also by the independent action of the King,
who seemed to be more and more on their side. Time was of
the essence, and she said as much to Anjou.

'They couldn't resist the lure of the wedding, and are now
caught like rats in a trap. But the Admiral could at any moment
decide to leave and a valuable opportunity will be lost, perhaps
for ever. The man is not only stirring up trouble in France with
this new faith he clings to so tenaciously, but planning a war
against the Spanish in the Netherlands.'

'And setting the King, your own son, against you,' agreed Anjou.
'His folly is too great to be ignored.'

Death was the only solution.

Catherine once more met with her collaborators in the quiet
privacy of the Tuileries gardens where they could walk in the
cool green alleys without fear of being overheard. As before, in
addition to Anjou, these included Tavannes, Nevers and Retz,
plus two Florentines and Guise, his mother Anne d'Este, and his
uncle the Duke of Aumale.

'Several arrests have already been made,' the Duchess informed
them. 'Mainly servants believed to be involved in the plot.'

'A horse was recovered which led to the identity of the assassin,'
Aumale added. 'Thankfully, they have not captured Maurevert
himself.'

'Excellent!' Catherine's expression was thoughtful. 'Despite these minor difficulties all seems to be proceeding according to plan. The King remains entirely unaware of the plot, although he cannot be kept in ignorance for much longer.'

Charles's fear was centred upon the Guises, and in bringing justice for the Admiral. If he succeeded and Coligny lived, the senseless young king would take them all into a war with Spain, and the Huguenots would be stronger than ever. Was ever a woman more blighted than she? Catherine knew that she had to win Charles round to her way of thinking, to somehow get him to see that the blame for this situation lay not with the Guises, but entirely with the Huguenots. More importantly, not with her.

'Whatever we decide,' she told her fellow conspirators, 'the King must agree.'

Heads nodded gravely. The collaborators were all too aware of the risks involved in what they now planned; that a second and more successful attempt on the Admiral's life was likely to produce an uprising.

Tavannes was most insistent that any ensuing conflict be confined within the city walls, and not allowed to spread nation-wide.

Anjou, thinking of his hopes for winning the Polish crown since the king in that country was said to be failing, and with less appetite for military glory these days, agreed that another civil war should be prevented at all cost. 'We must act with all due speed.'

'There are Huguenots clad in armour even now patrolling the streets outside our own house,' Guise warned. 'The Louvre could indeed be their next target.'

Dismay and anger simmered amongst them.

Catherine stifled a shudder. She had once laughed as loud as any when her enemy had named a cannon after her, *La Reine la Mère*, because of its huge size. Now she wished she had blown them all to smithereens.

'I have long thought that we need more than the head of one salmon to effectively decapitate this religion. We need several of their fellow frogs as well.'

There were murmurs of assent, and the conspirators at once began to devise a list of the most prominent Huguenot leaders, many of whom lodged with or were adjacent to the Admiral. They huddled together beneath the tall poplar and lime to make their plans, sweating in the August heat despite the shade. It was agreed by all that they would finish the task which Maurevert had begun.

'We must warn the King of this likely attack upon his person, and of the plans we have made here today. Once Charles has learned this truth, I will bring him round to understanding the extent of our alarm. He will be with us in this, I am certain of it.'

This plan met with entire agreement as none could dispute that although the King was more than ever under the influence of the Admiral, no one could instil terror in him better than his own mother.

It proved a more difficult task than the Queen Mother had expected. Charles refused to believe this indictment against his dear friend, the man who called him son.

'Coligny would never harm me. He loves me.'

'He cares nought for you; he loves only his religion.'

With consummate skill she pursued her argument. She let her spy describe what he had heard at the lodgings, including the mutterings of the most unwise fanatics, never mentioning how Coligny had quieted their worst ravings.

'I cannot break my word, my tryst of friendship. I love the Admiral; I do not wish him hurt.'

'Yet he would have *you* hurt.' Catherine calmly reminded her son of Meaux, the night the Protestants had come to kidnap, perhaps even kill the royal family. 'Remember how they pursued us throughout the night to Paris. Did you not swear that you would never again allow them to put our lives in such peril?'

Charles had never forgotten that night, had suffered nightmares as a consequence for weeks afterwards.

She described the blood spilled during the following siege of Paris, including the death of the Constable. 'Would you go through that again?'

'No, no!' His distress was pitiful.

He never looked people in the face when he spoke to them, perhaps because he had always desperately avoided the fierce, condemning glare of his own mother. He'd hunch his shoulders, lower his head and sullenly stare at the floor. Now Catherine grasped his shoulders and forced him to look her in the eye, an experience which set him shaking with renewed terror.

'We must put a stop to their evil plotting. It is vital that we take out all the Huguenot leaders, before they have the chance to act.'

Still he hesitated, so Catherine turned the screw one more notch. 'The Huguenots will tear you limb from limb, put you to the rack, shred the skin from your bones. You cannot begin to imagine the pain they will inflict upon you. They are planning to kill us all. Not only Your Majesty and your two brothers, but also your own mother and sister, even your beautiful wife the Queen. Would you have them take your beloved Elisabeth and put her to the rack? See them pluck her pretty pink fingernails out one by one?'

Charles cried out in his agony. He was exhausted, his fragile mind no match for his mother's clever manipulation, her relentless mental bullying. He cowered in a corner sobbing, begging her to protect him, unable to shut out the sound of her voice as her vile descriptions of torture and violence crawled like maggots into his ears, defiling him, filling his tormented mind with new horrors, bringing him to a manic rage. His limbs jerked, flecks of foam formed upon his lips as his frail hold upon sanity dissolved before her onslaught.

At length he cried out, '*Par la mort Dieu!* Since you choose to kill the Admiral, then none must be left to reproach me after it is done. Kill them. Kill them all!'

Then he fled from the closet, leaving the conspirators quietly to finalize their plans.

It took the rest of that night. Names and addresses were checked, plans hatched, times fixed, the Eve of St Bartholomew being the chosen date. The Duke of Guise and his men, together with his uncle, were allotted the task of going to the Rue de Béthisy and disposing of the Admiral. The city gates were ordered to be locked, all boats on the Seine to be moored along the Quai des Celestins, while chains would be stretched across the river at intervals, out of sight below the water line until the moment came. The Queen Mother commanded that a Watch be placed over the powder magazine, and guns mounted opposite the Hôtel de Ville.

Strategies were set in place to protect their own people, each to wear a white sash upon their right arm to identify them. Arms were issued to the Catholic nobles, and armed guards made available to protect their properties. Every conceivable angle was considered. Nevers, Tavannes, and the rest would deal with Rochefoucauld and the other Huguenot leaders. The signal for the start of the attack would be the bell of the Palais de Justice when it tolled three in the morning.

Catherine was well satisfied. It had been a good night's work.

Any reservations Charles experienced in the following two days were easily dealt with. From being an unwilling participant he became zealous in their cause, the blood lust upon him. He wanted his beloved wife and his old Huguenot nurse protected, as well as the surgeon Ambroise Paré.

Catherine made no objection. Once taken into the Louvre in her keeping, they would not be at liberty to offer any warning to others. There would be no further difficulties with the King, so long as she kept him closely watched.

And there could be no delay. Speed was of the essence.

Two nights later on Saint Bartholomew's Eve, the 23 August, Margot went to her mother's *coucher* as usual. There seemed to be more persons present than she expected, both Huguenot and Catholic, whispering together in their separate groups. No one spoke to her, but then she did not expect them to. She knew the Protestants to be suspicious of her because she had insisted on remaining a devout Catholic. Margot was also distrusted by the Catholics because of her marriage to the King of Navarre, a Huguenot. Not for a moment did it occur to her that the Queen Mother's bedchamber might actually be a hive of conspiracy.

Margot sat on a coffer and chatted with her sister. 'Why do you look so sad?'

'No reason,' Claude protested. 'You are imagining it.'

The Queen Mother was talking to her ladies when she seemed suddenly to notice her. 'Daughter, what are you doing here? Go at once to your bed.'

Margot felt an immediate urge to rebel, to say that she was a married lady now and could surely retire when she wished, but she did not possess the courage to pick a quarrel with her mother. She rose, made a curtsey and turned to take her leave.

Claude at once burst into floods of tears and, seizing her by the hand, prevented her from leaving. '*Mon Dieu*, my sister, for the love of God, do not stir out of this chamber!'

Margot was greatly alarmed. 'Why? What is it? What's wrong?'

The Queen Mother clicked her tongue in annoyance and called Claude over to her. Margot watched in puzzled silence as the pair exchanged heated words, but she caught only a few scraps of what was being said.

'There is no reason for her to be sacrificed,' Claude cried.

'She will not be!' Catherine spat the words from under her breath.

'But if any discovery should be made, she would be the first victim of their revenge.'

'If it please God, she will not suffer any hurt. It is necessary she should go to bed as normal, to prevent any suspicion that might arise from her staying.' Turning upon Margot, the Queen Mother again ordered her to bed.

Claude tried to smile, the tears still standing proud in her eyes. 'Goodnight, dear sister.'

'Goodnight,' Margot softly replied, mystified by their behaviour, and departed the Queen's bedchamber deeply troubled. She'd already been sacrificed in this marriage; what more were they asking of her? In what way was she a victim? And from what further hurt must she be protected? Something was clearly afoot, but what?

The moment she reached her closet, Margot threw herself upon her knees and prayed to God to take her into His protection and save her, although from whom or what, she had no idea.

By the time she had changed into her nightgown and went to her bed, she found Navarre already there, surrounded by thirty or forty of his comrades, all Huguenots.

'What is this? My bedchamber has been invaded by strangers?'

Nobody answered. But then no one was listening. Margot almost stamped her foot with annoyance but instinct warned her such an action would only make her look foolish, as no one was paying her the least attention. She climbed disconsolately into bed beside Navarre, anxiously wondering what was troubling them all, and if they would ever leave. It wasn't that she was particularly anxious to make love with her new husband, although the act was never without its pleasure, but she was weary and ready for sleep.

There was little chance of that as the men talked throughout the night, much of it about the attack upon the Admiral. They resolved to demand justice of the King, to call for the Duke of Guise to be arrested. And if the King refused to comply then they would take him themselves, with their own swords at his throat.

Margot listened to all of this with increasing dismay. She kept well snuggled down beneath the sheets, her eyes tight shut, hoping they would not realize that she listened, for they all knew Guise had been her lover. Sleep was quite impossible, however, and Margot could not get the thought of her sister's distress out of her mind. What was it exactly that was troubling her? Why were Claude and her mother arguing?

The instant Margot left her mother's *coucher*, even as Huguenots and Catholics still mingled together in the same room, Guise was summoned and Catherine quietly issued her final orders. Everything was now in place, and so secretly had they made their plans, with only a handful of trusted people, that no suspicion had leaked out.

Charles ran to his chamber in no fit state to object, once more in the thrall of his mother. He was convinced the Huguenots intended to destroy both the Catholic religion and himself, but deeply regretted that he had not the power to save Téligny or La Rochefoucauld. He made a feeble attempt to save the latter when he came to bid the King goodnight.

'Do not go, Foucauld,' he begged. 'Stay here and sleep with my *valets de chambre*.'

La Rochefoucauld, young and hot blooded, and with a pre-arranged assignation with a court beauty, laughingly told the King that he had a better offer and begged to be released. He drew the King's bed curtains and departed.

Charles found no peace that night. He barely closed his eyes, and when in the early hours his mother came to him, as she had promised, he was waiting for her fully dressed.

The Queen Mother, Anjou, and the King stood together in a window embrasure, the shutters open to let in the cool of the night as they waited for the toll of the bell, the signal for the killing to begin. It was to come in the hour before daybreak with the bell of the Palais de Justice, but Charles's courage was fast slipping away.

'We cannot do this terrible thing. Have we all run mad?' he cried. 'God will punish us.' He was in a state of indescribable fear, but panic was spreading amongst all three conspirators.

The Louvre seemed to glow with a strange light, cast upon it by royal messengers carrying flaming torches as they moved about their secret business in the streets below. Catherine could hear raised voices as people demanded to know why extra guards had been placed there, and what was causing this stir of unrest. She heard shouts and the exchange of blows, the numbers gathering in front of the Palace a warning that if the enterprise was to succeed, it could not long be delayed.

Catherine had by now convinced herself that all her exaggerated claims of Huguenot conspiracy were in fact true. She was more than ready to twist the facts in order to devise a policy to suit herself. She heard only what she wished to hear, believed what she wished to believe, and would always have her own way in the end.

In any case, they had come too far to back down now. How many times before had they tried and failed to rid themselves of Coligny and cripple this new religion he so zealously guarded? Too many to count, it seemed, and always he had escaped them. This was surely her last chance to honour that promise made so many years ago at Bayonne.

But Catherine very much feared the King might retract his agreement and spare his dear friend at the last moment. He could easily call off the plan, and she dare not contemplate the consequences of such an action. The entire royal family would be slaughtered in their beds once word spread of what they had been about this night. She searched for a way forward, for the right words to persuade him, and while she hesitated, a single pistol shot rang out. They all three started as if they themselves had been shot. Catherine was the first to recover.

'There, it is too late,' she cried. 'They are coming for us already.'

The King fell to his knees in a state of abject terror, his hands clasped tightly in prayer.

'We cannot wait for daybreak,' she announced, and ordered Anjou to send word that the signal was to be changed. They would act when the tocsin of Saint-Germain l'Auxerrois, the church opposite the Louvre, sounded, as that would be the first to ring. As her favourite son hurried to do her bidding, Catherine thought she might even have it moved forward an hour.

In another bedchamber in the Rue de Béthisy, the old Admiral lay quietly dozing, making a slow but steady recovery. Sleep wasn't easy because of the pain and discomfort in his arm and hand. The surgeon Ambroise Paré had earlier tended to his wounds and remained by his side, as did Téligny, Carnaton, and Coligny's faithful old servant, Nicolas Muss.

Sometime in the early hours he heard the sound of the tocsin of Saint-Germain l'Auxerrois, followed by horses' hooves in the street, but he was untroubled, accustomed as he was to these sounds. Outside his door stood a guard posted there by the King, so he felt no alarm when he first heard the sound of raised voices, one insisting they needed a word with the Admiral, that he bore an urgent message from the King.

'Let the fellow in,' the Admiral ordered with weary resignation, and his *maître d'hôtel* faithfully obeyed. Going downstairs, the unsuspecting servant opened the door only to be stabbed through the heart. Men at once flooded into the courtyard, killing one of Coligny's own Swiss guards. The other managed to escape and rushed up the stairs, slamming shut doors and barricading each as best he could as he passed through.

Startled by the sudden fracas Coligny struggled to sit up, realizing in an instant that the moment he had long dreaded had finally arrived. Showing no sign of fear he got out of bed and pulled on his *robe de chambre* before turning to his chaplain. 'Let us pray together, Monsieur Merlin. I fear we may have need of His strength this night.'

As the two men knelt to pray, they heard the pounding of fists on the door below. One of his colleagues, Cornaton, cried, 'They are knocking down the inner door.'

Paré said, 'God summons us to His holy rest. The house is forced, and we have no means of resistance.'

Téligny turned in a panic to the Admiral. 'Go quickly, Father-in-law. If you hurry, you can make an escape through the window and over the rooftops.'

But Coligny remained on his knees. 'For a long while now I have been preparing for death. You, my friends, if you still can, must save yourselves, for you cannot save me. I do not wish those who hold you dear to be able to reproach me with your death. I commend my soul to God's Mercy.'

'If you stay, Father, then so shall I. I would not desert you now.'

Coligny shook his head. 'No, save yourself, boy. Think of my daughter, think of Louise. Is it not enough that she loses her father this night? Let her not lose a husband as well. Go now; there is not a moment to lose.'

Even as he spoke they all heard the door below give way, followed by the sound of heavy footsteps on the stair.

The men clambered quickly out through the window, Téligny's thoughts on his beloved wife. Only his pastor, the surgeon Paré, and Nicolas Muss, Coligny's old servant, remained by his side, refusing to leave. There was a loud shout as the door to the outer chamber was breached. The Swiss guard fought valiantly, but, greatly outnumbered, fell dead before the onslaught.

The bedroom door was flung open and the assassins barged in: Bême, Tosinghi, and others. They were startled by the sight of the white-haired old Admiral on his knees praying with a quiet dignity, his pastor beside him, and paused, suddenly indecisive.

Bême pointed his sword at Coligny's breast, causing a prick of blood to form. 'Are you the Admiral?'

'I am indeed, young man. You should have pity on my age, but do what you will. My life is almost done; *you* have no power to shorten it.'

'Have I not?' the man asked as he ran him through with the sword. 'Traitor! Take this for the blood of my late lord and master Francis of Guise, whom you didst so perfidiously slay. Die!'

Coligny was knocked to the floor and the rest of the assassins fell upon him like a pack of ravenous wolves, all wanting a share of the kill. The faithful Nicolas was likewise dispatched, the Admiral's belongings looted. Merlin, the loyal chaplain, was spared, perhaps because he was a man of the cloth, and he escaped through the window and over the rooftops in the wake of Téligny. Ambroise Paré, the surgeon, was apprehended by a group of archers to be taken back to the Louvre, under instructions from the King.

Guise had not even dismounted from his horse, and called from below in the street. 'Is it done? Bême, have you finished?'

'It is done,' he called through the window.

'Well then, throw him down here, so that we may see for ourselves.'

They lifted the old man, who, in his last gasps of life clung desperately to the windowsill for a second before being hurled into the street below.

As he lay crumpled on the cobbles, Angoulême insolently wiped the blood from his face to check he was indeed Coligny. 'Yes, it is he.'

Guise, still on his horse, having taken no part in the murders, watched in silence as the old Admiral was kicked and sword whipped, his head cut off to carry it to the Louvre, from whence it would later be taken in solemn state to Rome. His body was then dragged through the streets to be further savaged by the mob before being hung on the common gallows of Montfaucon, and left to be picked at by the crows.

By this time houses blazed with light as the people rose from their beds to see what all the disturbance was about. They found men clad in the livery of the city carrying lanterns at the end of long poles, soldiers prowling the streets, mingling with the growing masses.

Pursued across the rooftops, Carnaton was the first to be shot, swiftly followed by Téligny, who fell to the street below with the name of his beloved Louise on his lips. Merlin remained in hiding.

And having dealt with this most pressing of tasks, the assassins remounted and moved on in search of fresh prey.

Margot must have slept eventually, for when she woke, daylight was creeping in around the bed curtains. She pulled them back to discover it was daybreak, and that both the bed and the bedchamber were empty. The King of Navarre and his men had gone.

She sat up, wondering if it was too early to call Lottie, who was growing old and could be a slug-a-bed in the morning these days, when Madame smilingly appeared, as fresh and serene as ever.

'Did you sleep well, my lady?'

Margot pouted. 'No, I did not. My husband and his chattering comrades kept me awake half the night.' At least whatever danger her sister had feared must now be past. Claude seemed to be flinching at shadows these days.

Madame looked around. 'And where is your good lord, might I ask? It is barely dawn.'

'I know not and care even less. Make fast the door, Lottie. Having suffered such a disturbed night I mean to catch up on some lost sleep.' And, flopping back upon the pillows, Margot turned over and fell instantly asleep again.

It must have been an hour later when she was wakened by a violent banging at the door. It sounded very much as if someone were hammering on it with both hands and feet, a voice calling out, 'Navarre! Navarre!'

'Ah, that must be your good husband now,' Madame said. 'All right, all right, no need to shout, my lord, I am coming,' and the old lady hurried to let him in.

The room was instantly filled with men, none of them Navarre. One young man, badly wounded with a gash on his arm from a sword or pike, ran in hotly pursued by four archers. He threw himself upon the bed in terror, begging for the Queen of Navarre's protection. Margot screamed, struggled desperately to get out of his way, but the man grabbed her by the waist, holding her fast so that her body shielded him from his attackers. He too was screaming, both of them utterly terrified, while the archers strove to take aim upon their victim.

Margot was convinced they were both about to be shot when Nançay, Captain of the Guard, strode in, and on seeing the Princess thus surrounded, the intended victim clinging to her like a limpet, he actually laughed out loud at the sight.

Margot was incensed. 'I see nothing to amuse you, good sir. These men would kill us both, me and this poor quivering fool wrapped about my waist.'

'Begging your pardon, Madame.' Somewhat chastened, the Captain ordered his archers to stand down, severely admonishing them for their indiscretion, and ordered them out of the chamber.

The man was still shivering in her arms, making no attempt to move, and Margot cradled him to her breast. 'Your men attacked this poor fellow, hunted him down like a wild animal. I refuse to release him to you. I order you to spare his life.'

The Captain graciously bowed. 'I concede his life to you, my lady, and I apologize for the over-enthusiasm of my archers.'

Margot imperiously called for Madame de Curton, who crept shakily forward, as shocked by the invasion as was her mistress.

'Please see to his wounds, dear Lottie. Let him lie down in my dressing room for a while to recover.'

'My lady.'

While Madame helped the injured man into the closet, Margot demanded to know what was going on. De Nançay's expression was sour as he told her swiftly and calmly what was taking place that night within the walls of the Louvre.

Margot was stunned, shocked to the core, quite unable to take in what he was telling her. 'Dear God, and my husband?'

'Safe, in the King's bedchamber.'

'But, I . . . I don't understand. Coligny and his fellow leaders again attacked, you say? Who would do such a vile thing?'

'There is no time to explain further. With your permission, Madame, I would escort you to your sister's bedchamber. Perhaps you should dress.'

It was then that Margot thought to examine her gown, her eyes opening wide with horror as she saw the state of it. All down the front of the young bride's silken nightgown was a dark red stain. It was covered in blood.

This was indeed her *Noce Vermeil*, or Blood Red Wedding, as it would ever after be called.

Paris was in uproar. False rumours were spread in every quarter that the Huguenots had attacked the King in the Louvre.

The cry went up. 'Kill! Kill!'

But it did not stop with the leaders. The streets of the city were soon thick with corpses, with children riffling through their pockets for treasures, or playing amongst them out of sheer daring. Men armed themselves with pistols, cutlasses, pikes, poniards, whatever they could find, and prowled the streets ransacking houses, cruelly killing without respect to sex or age. Tavannes and his men rode through the streets urging people to commit the most outrageous atrocities. Throats were slit, heads lopped off, entrails disembowelled. Private vengeance was swiftly acted upon, old enemies disposed of, every petty jealousy or squabble viciously settled. Debts, family feuds, betraying husbands and expensive lawsuits alike were dealt with by sword or dagger, whatever the victim's religion, under the pretence that it was at the orders of the King.

Catholics also perished, sometimes by accident or mistaken identity, more often through an act of vengeance by their enemies.

Carts rumbled through the streets, sometimes filled with items from the looted houses, others laden with mutilated bodies which were then cast into the Seine. The gutters soon ran with blood, and the rats crept up from the sewers to taste the spoils of the night.

And there was no way out for those who ran for their lives. Chains were drawn across each street, all chance of escape blocked, every exit barred, even the river. Men and women were pulled from their houses and slaughtered without ceremony; babies stolen from their mothers, ostensibly to save their souls with Catholic baptism, but butchered whether the deed were done or no.

Throughout the night Catherine and her sons kept vigil within the Louvre, the King continually raving, roaring and cursing; by turns enthralled and revolted by the smell and sight of blood. Alençon sat nursing a silent resentment over having been kept out of the secret plotting, a slight he found hard to forgive.

Rochefoucauld, alone in his own bed in the early hours when the masked murderers came for him, thought he'd been invaded by the King in disguise. He was familiar with how Charles loved to play this game of thrashing his friends for sport.

'You won't take me in,' he called out, laughing as they approached. 'See, I have got my clothes on.' Without troubling to respond, they brutally stabbed him to death, showing no mercy.

By morning the followers of Condé and Navarre were summoned to the courtyard, only to be mown down, one by one. Charles watched from his window, grotesquely entranced by the whole performance. Catherine stood beside him, perhaps to ensure that he did not escape or weaken when the hapless victims called up to him for mercy. Seeing the King standing there, in apparent charge, they could not then blame her.

All was chaos, a dozen or more dispatched in very short time.

Some Protestants, believing the massacre to be the work of the Guises, arrived at the Louvre seeking protection from their Sovereign. They came on foot and by river, but what they found there soon had them turning tail and running for their lives. Seeing them run, the King, inflamed by what he had just witnessed, snatched up an arquebus and fired after them. His shots failed to reach the fleeing mob, but the guards proved more skilled, and Charles laughed with macabre satisfaction when he saw their dead bodies floating upon the water.

'Have I not played the game cleverly?' he cried.

Catherine, as composed and cold as ever, calmly discussed with her *Escadron Volant* which Huguenot was the most handsome, or had died the most heroic death, and even who should be next, rather as they might discuss the most favoured colour for a new gown. That night her ladies disposed of several gentlemen who had long been an irritation to them.

As dawn was breaking, wrapped in the Captain's cloak, Margot was led along the passages of the Louvre by Nançay. She'd quickly changed her nightgown but not troubled to dress, and was half fainting with dread at what she might find.

'You say my husband is in the King's apartment, and quite safe?'

'He is, Your Majesty. Would you have me take you to him?'

'No, I will go to my sister, as you suggest. I believe I can manage now.'

But the Captain insisted on accompanying her, which proved to be wise, for, as they entered the antechamber of her sister Claude, another gentleman came running in, fleeing from the very same archers who had so recently invaded her bedchamber. They charged and ran the poor man through with a pike, leaving him dead at her feet.

Margot screamed and fell into a dead faint. Caught by the Captain, he half carried her into her sister's apartment, other Huguenots fleeing with her. Navarre's First Gentleman of the Bedchamber, and

Armagnac, his First *Valet de chambre*, all begged their new Queen to save their lives. Right at that moment she doubted she could even save her own.

Margot threw herself on her knees before the King and Queen Mother and begged for the life of her husband, and of Condé, his much loved cousin. Catherine agreed without argument. Not out of the goodness of her heart, but because she dare not destroy all the Bourbons as that would place too much power in the hands of the Guises. She needed to have some form of insurance.

Unaware of the workings of her mother's mind on this matter, Margot simply praised God that they were to be spared.

'There will be conditions,' Catherine insisted. 'They will be forced to convert to the Catholic faith.'

The King had the Huguenot princes brought before him, and made his wishes plain. 'Let it be understood that I wish for one religion only in my Kingdom. Choose now – the Mass or death!'

'It would be difficult,' Navarre calmly remarked, 'to abjure the religion in which I have been nurtured.'

'I would never take the Mass,' Condé cried, ever the fervent believer.

'Then it is decided,' cried Charles. 'Take them.'

Navarre stepped quickly forward and, slapping his cousin on the back, remarked in his usual merry tone, 'But then again, coz, where is the value in dying for a religion? Can we not perhaps agree to worship God in some other way?'

'Indeed, *I* cannot. I must be faithful to my creed, or die for it.'

A part of Navarre envied his cousin for his courage, yet he saw little point in becoming a dead hero. While inside he trembled more with rage than fear, he smiled equably, managing to maintain his image of the easy-going fool, ready to compromise in a way which would have grieved his mother sorely, had she been present.

'Ah, but let us pause and consider this matter for a moment. Your Majesty would not, I take it, tamper with our conscience?' He did not quite explain what it was his conscience might demand.

'I would have you declare yourself of the true Faith.'

'Quite so, and there has been enough killing this night, has there not? What benefit is there in adding to it? I may well find it in me to agree to your demands.'

Condé was outraged. 'I have five hundred gentlemen ready to avenge this lamentable massacre.'

'Do you wish to feel the point of my dagger?' roared the King. 'As for you, brother Navarre, only show good faith and I will show you good cheer.'

'Will you allow us a few hours to ponder on our choice, Sire?'

He was so far out of his mind with blood lust that Charles might not have agreed to even this period of delay, had not his beloved Queen added her own pleas to those of Margot's. Elisabeth fell to her knees before him and, weeping openly, begged the King to be generous, as he was known to be. She had hardly stopped crying since the atrocities had begun – when she wasn't on her knees praying for her husband's salvation, that is.

At length, the entreaties of both Elisabeth and Margot won the day, and Navarre was allowed three days in which to make up his mind, and to talk his fanatical cousin round to his way of thinking. He knew it would be nowhere near long enough.

Charles seemed almost relieved by this decision. Close to exhaustion, he wanted an end to the slaughter, but with the killings now spreading far beyond the city walls, what had been easy to start was going to be far less easy to stop.

Margot discovered that sparing the lives of her husband and Condé did not resolve all their difficulties. They were made virtual prisoners in the Louvre, herself included, kept strictly within its four walls. There was also a bitter resentment in those who believed that being Princes of the Blood should not have saved them. Without question Navarre owed his life to her, and to the fact that he was willing to at least consider taking the Mass. To the dismay of all who loathed even the idea of a Huguenot ascending the throne of France, it was clear that no further attempt could be made upon Navarre's life while he remained the Princess's husband.

A day or two later, while helping the Queen Mother to dress for chapel at her morning *lever*, Catherine drew Margot close for a private discussion.

'Tell me, daughter, is your husband virile? Is he like other men?'

Margot looked at her mother askance. What kind of question was that? She really had no wish to discuss the intimacy of her marriage bed with her own mother. Nor was this the place. There were a dozen people gathered in the chamber: the Queen's physician, her secretary, various ladies-in-waiting, and even a few noblemen.

Playing for time, Margot carefully tied the ribbons of the Queen's petticoat about her plump waist. It was a task she loathed, her mother's sweat, mingled with the stale perfume from her underwear, always making her nauseous. 'Madame, how would I know? I have no knowledge of other men.'

Catherine met her daughter's innocent gaze, knowing she lied. But then it was a family trait, and she did it well. Thoughtfully, she sipped her coffee. 'I think you are unduly coy.'

Margot blushed. 'I can only reply as did the Roman lady when her husband chided her for not informing him of his stinking breath, that never having approached any other man quite so close, she thought all men were alike in that respect.'

Catherine let out a rumble of laughter, enjoying the joke, for Navarre had a reputation for not being attentive to his toilette. 'I only ask,' she continued, 'because if he is not virile, I can easily procure you a divorce from him.'

Margot took the kirtle handed to her by the next lady in line, welcoming the distraction as she steadied her breathing. 'Divorce? Why so? Less than a week ago you were insistent upon this marriage.'

'Ah, but the situation has changed. It is no longer politic. If you are still intact I could have it set aside.'

Margot was speechless, quite unable to take in what her mother was suggesting. This marriage, which had been forced upon her, and performed at great cost to the treasury, not to mention the loss of thousands of innocent lives, was to be dissolved, simply because it was no longer *politic*? Was then the only reason for the wedding to lure the Huguenots to the capital? She shuddered at the thought.

Catherine continued, 'You could have Guise for a husband, if you so wished.'

'Guise?'

'Didn't you once favour him? Rampant for him, I seem to remember.'

'But you were against the match, and now he is married. We both are.'

'I am not against the match *now*,' Catherine snapped, growing irritated by her daughter's obstinacy. 'It may well serve, after all. And he could gain his freedom as easily as you can yours.'

Margot realized she was being offered what she had always dreamed of: marriage with the man of her heart. It seemed too good to be true. Perhaps it was. Nothing Madame Serpent did was ever as straightforward as it seemed. And what of her husband? However reluctant they had both been for this marriage, country bumpkin in need of a good scrub though he may be, yet Navarre did not deserve what had been meted out to him and his followers. Nor did she deserve to be treated like some pawn on a political chess board, or made to choose between having her husband killed or divorcing him. Margot was suddenly filled with anger.

'And were I to divorce him, would he still be safe?'

Catherine slipped her bracelets on to her arm, the bone skulls jangling against each other as she did so. 'Why would he not be? He is a Bourbon Prince of the Blood.'

Margot met her mother's gaze with one equally steady. 'Since you put the question to me, then I can only declare that I am content to remain as I am. You wished me to be married to the King of Navarre, and I have done your will. I suspect the design of separating me from my husband is in order to work some mischief against him. How would I live with myself if that were so, and something dreadful were to happen to him?'

'We must all learn to live with the consequences of our actions,' Catherine answered dryly.

On the evening of the 25 August Catherine led her sons the King, Anjou and Alençon through the streets of the blood-soaked city, going first to visit a miraculous thorn bush. Paris was eagerly seeking a sign of approval from God to justify the events of Saint Bartholomew's Eve, and the Almighty, or someone, had supplied it in the surprise flowering of a hawthorn at a season when blossom was never normally seen. Surely this must be the very portent they needed. Catherine posted guards to protect this precious bush from the fervour of the people, or else to conceal the fraud.

Bells were rung in joy, and some claimed to have seen a new star near Cassiopeia, surely a symbol of salvation? The Huguenots said it marked the slaughter of the innocents.

Festivals were held, with much celebrating and rejoicing all over the city, people grasping at any opportunity to dress up, play, dance, and distract themselves from the grim reality of what had taken place. The city stank, suffering from a plague of rats since every cemetery was full to overflowing, and those corpses whose relatives could not afford to pay the twenty livres for a burial were left to rot in the streets.

A thanksgiving was held in the Louvre, although neither Navarre nor Condé were permitted to attend. Margot stayed away with them, out of defiance. Alençon didn't attend either, still sulking over having been excluded from the whole business, and feeling horribly snubbed as a result.

'Be thankful, dear brother,' Margot consoled him, 'that the carnage is not on your conscience.'

The two Huguenot princes were strictly confined to their apartments within the Louvre, not permitted to communicate with each other. Margot was allowed access to their chambers in the hope of seducing her husband to change his faith. She begged him, and Condé, with all her heart to do so, for only she understood the danger of crossing the Queen her mother. The Prince de Condé remained silent and uncommunicative, brooding over the loss of so many of his dear friends.

The King of Navarre remained valiantly good tempered, joking and feigning indifference to the doctrines of either creed, studiously refusing to convert unless or until his cousin likewise agreed to do so. He did, however, make clear his abhorrence of the acts perpetrated on St Bartholomew's Eve. And when Charles commanded him to accompany himself and his mother on their progress through the streets of Paris, he bluntly refused. No one could deny that he lacked courage.

Margot remained firm in her intention to remain loyal to her husband, and Catherine was obliged to accept it. No doubt the girl had been eager enough to consummate the marriage, wanton hussy that she was. The Queen Mother still had mixed feelings towards her son-in-law, which very much blew hot and cold, sometimes very cold. At other times she couldn't resist laughing at his jests as much as ever she did, often amused by his merry wit. Nonetheless, being forced to drop her plans for an annulment was irritating. Had she known how useful Guise could be, she might never have set herself so against him in the first place. Although who could say she wasn't right to do so, knowing the strength of that arrogant young man's ambitions?

Charles was the one causing her the greatest concern. The events of last week seemed to have changed him, even while he claimed to have no recollection of them. He was so deathly pale he looked like a walking ghost, frequently crying out that ghosts in fact visited him in his sleep. He suffered horrendous nightmares in which he would leave blood on his pillow from biting his own tongue in agitation, or he would wake screaming that bodies were falling on him. His periods of gloom were growing darker, his excitable moments all the more manic, his demented mind seeming to slip further into an abyss from which she could not save him.

He'd even taken to travelling to every execution, once attending a hanging where he'd reportedly held a lighted torch close enough to see the agonized expressions of the victims. It was as if, once awakened, his lust for blood could never be quenched.

Nor had it been satisfied in the country at large, as the massacre spread and the atrocities accelerated, rather than diminished. The carnage, pillage, rape, and brutal murder continued unabated. Catherine never enquired how many thousands died, or whether they were Catholic or Huguenot, for both factions suffered appalling losses. She really had no wish to know. It was said that in Paris the number killed amounted to more than two thousand, and there would no doubt be many thousands more in the cities around France in the coming days and weeks.

It was perhaps unfortunate that the events of Saint Bartholomew's Eve had got so out of hand, that more 'frogs' had been killed than she had quite bargained for. But many of these people were little more than peasants, and so of no consequence.

Catholics had been of the firm belief that permitting heresy to live in their midst was like nurturing a disease in the body of Christ, and had grasped the opportunity to purge the infection. They believed in one religion for France, that society would collapse if cobblers and women could debate the meaning of the Bible.

Those in the lower classes had adopted a more prosaic view. The price of food, fuel, and shelter were now so high that it was difficult for the populous to make ends meet. Homelessness and poverty were increasing, and they had been ready enough to take their hostility and resentment out against any who seemed more comfortable than themselves, seeking scapegoats for their misery.

Yet Catherine was strangely content. She had never felt so at ease with herself. The relief that she'd finally achieved her goal was a deep and abiding satisfaction.

Coligny was no more, and his wife, the wonderful Jacqueline, was now held in prison. The woman could stay there till she rotted, so far as the Queen Mother was concerned. The Admiral's estates had been razed to the ground, his goods and chattels confiscated, everything he owned destroyed.

'Coligny's sons went to view his body on the gibbet, at least what remained of it,' Charles told his mother over supper one evening, the massacre being the one topic of conversation.

'Indeed?'

'The fifteen-year-old sobbed, apparently, while the seven-year-old stood frozen, too shocked even to cry.'

Catherine reached for another chicken leg, and shrugged. 'Children are very adaptable.'

Margot said, 'Word has it that some of the Huguenot leaders escaped. Guise pursued one on his horse but had to abandon the chase, the other man's mount being faster. Yet he hotly denies being responsible for the massacre. Can that be so, Mother?' she guilelessly enquired, eyes wide with innocence.

Catherine did not trouble to answer.

Charles was still obsessed with the blood and gore. '*I* heard of a young boy being discovered beneath the rotting corpses of his parents and siblings. Someone passing by heard his cry and released him. What must it have been like for him, lying in all that blood and pus, perhaps being nibbled by rats?'

'It is a story to warm the heart, dear brother, not to dwell on its more unsavoury aspects,' Margot gently scolded him. 'I believe that Merlin, Coligny's chaplain, also lived,' she announced, earning herself a glare of disapproval. 'They say he escaped over the rooftops and then hid in a barn where he was nurtured by a hen who laid an egg into his hand.'

'What nonsense you do prate,' Catherine snapped. 'Enough of this chatter; I have work to do.' And with that she abruptly left the table.

A day or two later while the court was at dinner there came a terrible sound – a deep-throated kacking and screeching from above – and the whole room darkened. Many of the ladies cried out in terror, and even the gentlemen felt the hairs at the back of their neck lift.

Margot hurried to the window, the King and Queen, and the rest of the courtiers, quickly followed, and what they saw left them speechless with fright.

The sky was black with ravens, their four-foot wingspan seeming to touch tip to tip as they wheeled and dived, their shaggy jet feathers and hooked bills bringing a chill to every person present. They hung in the air like an ominous cloud of doom before settling in huge, squawking numbers upon every rooftop and pedestal of the Louvre.

'Dear God, they come as predators, to scavenge in this city of the dead.'

'It is an evil omen,' groaned Charles, completely unhinged by the sight.

That night the King suffered his worst nightmare yet. Little more than two hours after he'd retired, he came running from his room to rouse Navarre and the gentlemen of his bedchamber. 'Can you hear them?' he cried. 'Can you hear them crying and groaning, howling and blaspheming? They have risen from the dead to come and extract their vengeance upon me.'

It took all three of his favourite ladies – Margot, Elisabeth and his nurse – to settle him that night.

Part Four

LOVERS AND LIARS

1573–1574

Margot was walking along the passage from her husband's apartments to her own chamber when an arm suddenly hooked about her waist, and with a small squeal of alarm she found herself pulled behind an arras into an ante room. Before she could draw breath to protest, a mouth had closed over hers in a long, demanding kiss. Quite unable to move, being trapped between the unforgiving door and the powerful breadth of a man's chest, she succumbed completely to the pleasure of it. But then it was a truly wonderful kiss.

When she was finally released, she gave the perpetrator of this outrage a sharp slap across his handsome face, even though she'd known instantly that it was Henri of Guise. How could she not, having savoured the delicious taste of his lips more times than were quite proper in a young girl?

Entirely unconcerned by her reaction, he put back his fine head with its cut of close-cropped curls, and laughed. 'I thought you'd avoided me long enough, my pretty, and that it was time we got re-acquainted.'

Margot straightened her gown, flustered by the warm flush of excitement on her cheeks. 'And you thought that was the way to go about it, did you?'

He smiled at her, a molten power in his liquid, dark-eyed gaze. 'I needed to gain your attention.'

'You have most certainly achieved that.' She laughed suddenly, tremulous, nervous, and as delighted as he by the encounter. But then, instantly ashamed of herself for this apparent betrayal, Margot scowled crossly at him. 'I should not, by rights, even be speaking to you. I will admit that I do not believe all the rumours I hear about the Princes of Lorraine, but nevertheless we are enemies now, you and I.'

'Never!'

''Tis true. You not only perpetrated that vile deed upon the

Admiral and God knows how many other unfortunates, but seem set to treat my husband in a like manner.'

'I have done nothing to make you think so, nor is it my choice that Navarre has been incarcerated, though perhaps it may be for his own good while tensions still run high. In any case, I wish the man no harm, I swear it.'

She considered his expression with serious appraisal, wondering if he spoke the truth. 'Would that I could believe you.'

He grinned as he reached for her, his hands instinctively capturing her neat waist, before daringly brushing the tips of his fingers over the silken smoothness of her deliciously white breasts above the low neckline of her gown. 'I hope we are not about to have one of our squabbles. That would be tiresome. I have always valued you as a woman of opinion, Margot, but it is so long since I held you in my arms that I can hardly bear to look at you without wanting to possess you.'

She felt half giddy with desire, her need for him so strong it was almost a physical pain in her heart. Even so, she slapped his hands away. 'I *do* believe you innocent of at least some of the crimes charged against you.'

Guise leaned both hands upon the door, trapping her between it and himself. 'Only some? And if I swear I never laid a finger on your husband's precious leader, for all I welcomed his death as my father's murderer, would you believe that?'

Margot looked him straight in the eyes. 'I might.'

He pushed himself off and half turned from her. 'Let me tell you, darling Margot, that following the massacre, the position of the Princes of Lorraine has become increasingly hazardous. Ever wary of the designs of the Queen your mother, I asked the King to vindicate the House of Guise in the sight of the people, begging him not to shrink from his responsibility in the bloody mischief of that night. And Charles, in the presence of his parliament, has acknowledged that we were the instruments and not the originators of the massacre.'

Her brown eyes upon him softened somewhat at these words, her voice barely above a whisper when she spoke. 'I am glad to hear it, and suspected that may well be the case, knowing my mother, and my brother Anjou, as I do. Nevertheless, we are on opposite sides now. You cannot deny it.'

His brow puckered with concern. 'I never thought to hear you say such a thing. You and I, Margot, are trapped by our own destiny, pawns in a much greater game, of which we have but limited control. I do not deny that I am a faithful adherent of the Roman Catholic Church, devoted to my faith. It is also true that I consider the dogmas of Luther and Calvin to be too radical and revolutionary for my taste. A positive curse upon society. The death of the Reformationist leaders was unfortunate but necessary. They had presumed to revolt against the established church.'

Margot's eyes opened wide. 'You think it was lawful therefore to have them killed?'

'I do, since they were likewise traitors to the State, but the killing was never intended to accelerate as it did.'

'How could it not when the oppressed grow hungry for vengeance?'

'The Queen Mother believed the danger could be contained.'

'My mother is fond of convincing herself of facts that are indisputably flawed. And is it not true that your own maternal grandmother, Renée of France, was a Huguenot?'

Guise had the grace to flush. 'She did show leanings in that direction, it is true.'

'Leanings? Do not dismiss me as some light-minded fool, Henri. I know she was a firm friend of Calvin all of his life, and of my own late mother-in-law, Jeanne d'Albret, and Gaspard Coligny.'

The Duke was looking increasingly uncomfortable. 'I believe she was a friend of Coligny's mother; that may be so.'

Margot set her hands on her hips. 'And still surrounds herself with Huguenot friends, I am told. Come, admit it, your own *grandmother* is a Reformationist to her very soul, so much so that her husband once charged her with heresy and dispatched her to a convent to think on her sins. I have heard the tales. And did not your father Francis, her own son-in-law, so strongly disapprove of her "leanings" that he once laid siege to her in her château? Is *that* not so?'

He was irritated now, annoyed that she dared to challenge him on this personal family matter. 'A man cannot be held responsible for the choices made by his forebears, whether Protestant or Catholic. I am responsible only for my own.'

'And you choose an extreme rather than a tolerant viewpoint?'

'You may well think so.'

'My very tolerant husband certainly does.'

He suddenly pulled her into his arms. 'Margot, my love, why do we quarrel about doctrine and religion? Navarre would be the first to see the folly in that. I wish to hear you tell me that you have missed me, that you have pined for me these last two years while we've been apart. Did you think of me when that new husband of yours bedded you? Was he the great lover he claims to be, or did he pale by comparison?'

Margot was laughing again, their quarrel forgotten. How could she not be amused and entranced by him, even when she was infuriated by his intransigence. Did she not understand him, heart and soul? Ambitious and arrogant he may be, but not for a moment did she believe Guise to be cruel, or heartless. And she loved him still, she could not deny it.

'But how can we ever now be friends?' There was a wistfulness in her voice as his lips tracked a delightful progress along her throat and behind her ear. As for his hands . . . Oh dear, she dare not even consider what his hands were doing.

'I was hoping,' he murmured, as he began to unlace and untie various ribbons and bows, 'that we could be very much more than friends, now that we are both safely wed. Whether or not my grandmother or your husband are Huguenot needn't be too much of a barrier, need it?'

Margot pursed her lips, feigning anger, before lifting them to be kissed. Even so, when the kiss was over she gathered his invading hands between her own and pushed them away with a small sigh of reluctance.

'Would you have me break my wedding vows, and so soon?'

Guise could not suppress a grin. 'You must know that *noste Enric* is unlikely to make a faithful husband.'

Margot stiffened, gathering her pride about her. 'I have no reason not to believe that his fancy for chasing lightskirts is over, now that we are wed. Our marriage is turning out rather better than I had hoped, as a matter of fact.'

He gave a scornful bark of laughter. 'You say I must not treat you as a fool, yet surely you, more than anyone, Margot, must be aware that marriage is about politics, not love.'

'Can I not hope for both?' she snapped with haughty grandeur.

'If you do, then you are bound to be disappointed. When your new husband grows bored and reveals his true colours, and you are ready to be loved as you deserve, I will be waiting.'

He pulled open the door, about to depart, but she halted him with a flash of temper. 'And why would I turn to my husband's enemy for love?'

Guise regarded her with barely restrained patience. 'Because you know me better than that, Margot. I do not deny my flaws of pride and a degree of ambition. I own to having the insensitivities of a hardened soldier. I am also a devout Catholic. But I swear before God I am no murderer. Remember that, my love, when your marriage turns sour.'

Margot remained steadfast in her support of her husband. She visited Navarre every day in his apartment, often spending her nights with him. He was allowed some freedom of movement, but only within the confines of the Louvre, and with an escort. The King expected her to urge him to convert, and she did so willingly in order to save his life, as she was doing now.

'*Enric,*' she pleaded. 'Why will you not? Why lay yourself open to danger? You have never claimed to be a zealot in the matter of religion.'

'I am not quite without scruples, Margot. They killed my people. Besides, I cannot abandon my cousin Condé. He is a man of great integrity if somewhat rigid in his morals. He still bears a grievance against your brother Anjou for having killed his father at Jarnac, and is adamant that he will not take the Mass.'

'I can only sympathize, yet I hear that his wife has readily agreed.'

'Dear Lord, does he know?'

'Not yet, and I have no wish to be the one to tell him.'

'Indeed, I would not advise that you did. Marie was never a strong advocate of the reformed faith, having accepted it only on their marriage, but he will hear no word against her. He adores the silly minx.'

Condé had married Marie de Cleves only a few days before Margot and Navarre's own marriage. She was a captivating beauty with a lively, flirtatious personality, and the young Prince de Condé had fallen entirely under her spell. Unfortunately, he was not the only one to do so.

Margot hesitated before relating the rest of her tale. 'I'm afraid your cousin's resentment against my brother can only increase. Anjou is apparently besotted with the Princess, and has paid excessive court to her, visiting the Hôtel de Nevers, where she took refuge, for many hours each day. They say that the young bride finds her new husband alarmingly severe and reserved, constantly chastising her. Anjou, on the other hand, is all charm and flattery. She is apparently ready to declare herself a penitent, anxious to be returned to the bosom of the Holy Mother Church. Devout Catholic though I may be, I cannot but suspect that her ardour has a more earthly root.'

Navarre was deeply disturbed by this news, for the sake of his beloved cousin if not for himself. But Margot proved to be entirely correct and a ceremony did indeed take place early in September, with the lovely new bride kneeling on a velvet cushion and tear-fully renouncing the religion she had so recently embraced. The Cardinal de Bourbon pronounced the absolution, and afterwards Marie partook of the Holy Eucharist.

Catherine herself informed Condé of his wife's defection. Even then he might have remained firm in his resolve had not the Duke of Nevers revealed the attentions being paid to his beautiful new wife by the Duke of Anjou.

Obstinacy dissolved in the face of passion. Condé agreed to take instruction in the Catholic faith at the monastery of Saint-Germain des Pres, where his uncle, the Cardinal de Bourbon, was abbot. The ceremony was performed the following day, and his freedom granted by the King.

Navarre held out for only a few days longer. Weary of confinement and desperate to return to Béarn, he finally accepted the Mass. Why should he not? Did he not believe in tolerance?

In the weeks following, gossip at court concerning Anjou and the Princess de Condé was rife, as was that regarding Margot and Guise, for all the new Queen of Navarre declared her innocence. Margot longed for Guise, ached for him with every fibre of her being, yet felt her new husband deserved her loyalty more, and her distrust of Anjou remained obdurate.

But then the prospect of a Polish crown for Anjou came into view, and the court had a new source of tittle-tattle.

The people of Paris had never seen anything like it. They watched, open-mouthed with astonishment, as the Polish ambassadors made their entry into the city one hot August day in 1573. A cortège of fifty carriages, each drawn by eight horses, along with several dozen more men on horseback, entered the capital in a long, stately procession to parade through the city streets so that they might be seen by all. The tall, stately Poles were a sight to behold with their shaven heads and long beards, robes of gold cloth trimmed with a deep border of sable, wide boots studded with spikes of iron, and caps sparkling with rare gems. They were both majestic and fierce with their scimitars, swords, and jewelled quivers filled with arrows. Even their horses were richly caparisoned in gold, and decked out with plumes and bells which jingled as they rode by, bearskins flung across their saddles.

The next day a group of them attended the Louvre to present themselves to Anjou. It had taken months of discussion and legal argument to reach this point, plus a considerable sum of money paid willingly enough by Charles, who was more than anxious to see the back of his brother.

The Polish envoys approached, and if Anjou found their appearance strange, he could tell by their confused expressions that they didn't quite know what to make of him either. He stood before a canopied throne in all his magnificence: elegant, scented and pomaded, diamond pendants swinging from each ear, his hair curled and back-combed, topped off with a toque he considered to be suitably Polish in style, and decorated with huge clusters of pearls.

Anjou guessed they thought him frail and weak by comparison with the tough-looking warriors among their own party. They might well be right. Even now one of his headaches was beginning to pound behind his temple. But he meant to show them that he had strength of will, which they would soon discover was not so easily governed by others.

The following day, the ambassadors again repaired to the Louvre, this time to pay homage to the King and Queen of Navarre, to the Prince and Princess de Condé, and the Cardinal of Bourbon.

They were instantly entranced by the beauty of their new King's sister, and indeed Margot was exquisitely dressed in a velvet gown of Spanish rose, covered with spangles. Her naturally dark hair was hidden beneath a glorious blonde peruke, which she'd taken to wearing on grand occasions such as this, and upon which she wore a cap of the same rose velvet, adorned with plumes and jewels. Not a soul in the room could deny that she looked utterly ravishing.

The Polish nobles were lost in admiration, likening her to Aurora, who comes at dawn with her fair white face surrounded with rosy tints.

It was not the first time Margot had been the subject of such accolades. The soldiers in her brother's army had often declared that the conquest of such beauty would be better than that of any kingdom. Even great nobles would gaze upon her in silent awe, and the Polish ambassadors were likewise rendered speechless.

Lasqui, the head of the Polish embassy, overcome by the sight of her, was heard to remark, 'Never do I wish to see such beauty again, as nothing could be as fine.'

Sadly, Margot's own husband appeared indifferent to her courtly charms, his own attention, as ever, busily assessing the relative beauty of various members of the *Escadron Volant*.

When the ambassadors had concluded their carefully prepared speech in fluent Latin, Margot stepped forward and replied on behalf of herself and her husband, the King of Navarre, in the same language, speaking with eloquence and fluency, vivacity and charming grace, and without the assistance of a single note.

She sent silent thanks to her beloved Madame de Curton, who had been responsible for arranging her education and teaching her so well. She presented her hand to be kissed, and proceeded to chat with each of the envoys in whatever language seemed appropriate; to the Pope's representative in Italian, Latin or German to the Poles, and in French to her own people.

'What a divine woman,' they cried, highly impressed by her language skills, as well as by her beauty and charm.

The ceremonies continued, day after day, the Polish lords revelling in the opulence, as did their wives, who went everywhere with an entourage of pages, dwarfs, and torch-bearers.

The Queen Mother held a magnificent ball at the newly completed Tuileries Palace to celebrate her favourite son's new status. It was magnificent, as were all her extravaganzas. The guests dined on whole roasted peacocks richly stuffed, their tails spread wide; guinea fowl and venison; mullet, plaice, and bream; tarts and pastries garnished with sugar and rosewater; custards and candied fruit. And when the tables were cleared, the *Escadron Volant*, dressed as nymphs, entertained the assembled company with dancing and ballet, songs and poems to commemorate the glories of the life of the new King of Poland, and the realm of his beloved France.

Anjou hated every moment, dreading the day when he would be forced to leave this court which he loved so much. He viewed the acceptance of the Polish throne as little more than a form of exile, and felt thoroughly piqued by his brother's determination to banish him from the realm.

Not only that, but he would be forced to leave his beloved Marie and required to marry some Polish princess. His mother had shown him a portrait of a severe-looking woman of small stature, more than twice his age, dressed entirely in black as she was still in mourning for her brother. She apparently waited for him at Krakow with great excitement.

How will I endure it? He felt as though his heart was bleeding. His love for the Princess de Condé may still be platonic in the strict sense of the word, but he adored her, wanted no other woman as his wife, and he had nurtured hopes to make her so very soon, once he'd freed her from marriage with his enemy.

Catherine drew closer, instinctively able to read the gloomy thoughts of this, her most precious child. 'Do not fret, my son. Your exile will not be for long. Charles is failing; any fool with eyes in his head can see that. You will wear a far more splendid crown sooner than you might imagine.'

'And Alençon will grab it while I am gone,' he groaned.

Catherine smiled. 'No, you can trust me to guard your heritage well, my darling. I will ensure that no one shall take it from you.'

The entire court was to accompany the new King of Poland on the first stage of his journey as far as Blamont – Margot, Navarre, and Alençon among them. Not that Anjou was paying much attention to the preparations being made on his behalf, being too caught up in his love affair.

Margot watched with wry amusement as her brother cheated, lied, bribed, and flagrantly flattered the silly Princess de Condé

in order to win her, oblivious to her marital status or her finer
feelings. He was like a greedy child, always wanting what another
had, particularly if the object of his desire belonged to his sworn
enemy. There was a ruthlessness beneath his gallant charm, and
Margot feared for how things might turn out. The fair lady's
husband must surely be aware that if he declined to consent to
a divorce, in order for his wife to marry her new lover, Anjou
could dispatch him as easily as he had his father at Jarnac.

Margot herself made a point of keeping well out of his way.

And then one evening as they savoured a delicious bouilla-
baisse at supper, he asked, 'Are we to be friends again? I would
have us reconciled before I depart upon my new life. You know
how I shall depend upon your goodwill in my absence from
court.'

'It was not I who marred our friendship,' was her cautious
response. Margot was not so easily flattered these days, nor so
inclined to believe her brother's vows and promises. Having seen
the leaders of the Huguenot faction cut down so savagely on
Saint Bartholomew's Eve, she recognized the lengths the Queen
Mother and her favourite son were prepared to go to rid themselves of obstinate opponents. She was now infinitely more wary
of them both.

Anjou passed her a dish of sugared almonds, which she declined.
'I would not have you work against me. Can we not reseal our
pact?'

'So far as I am aware I never did work against you, brother.
The malicious rumours that were spread about my behaviour
were simply that, with no truth to them. But you must understand that my first loyalty now is to my husband. And I have
other siblings, and friends, who all deserve my love.'

He stroked her cheek with the backs of his fingers, causing a
cold shiver to run down her spine. 'Ah, but far better to ally
yourself with a future King of France than a husband who is still
Huguenot at heart, and a weakling malcontent. I'd advise you to
think carefully before bestowing your favour, sister dear.'

Margot's heartbeat quickened. Was that a threat? Did Henri
believe that she should be exclusively his creature? Was she allowed
to love no one but him?

She felt no guilt for no longer loving this brother with his twisted, scheming mind and his selfish demands. Love had been banished by caution, and by fear.

She realized that Anjou's behaviour was greatly influenced by their mother. The Queen's passion for this favourite son of hers, her longing to see him on the throne of France, was a major factor in the formation of his character, almost compelling him to practise deceit, to conspire and to plot. Catherine had instilled into his young mind that it was perfectly reasonable to use whatever means necessary to achieve his heart's desire. He was now not only self-obsessed and hypocritical, but entirely unscrupulous.

Margot had no wish to be his friend, but feared making him her enemy.

As a consequence of her distrust of Anjou, Margot found herself turning more and more to her younger brother. Alençon seemed to be making every effort to win her affections, using whatever means at his disposal to make himself agreeable to her. He too had been deeply affected by the events of that terrible night, but somehow had not been corrupted by them. Left out of the entire business he expressed increasing sympathy for the persecuted. He was not a fanatic, had no strong feelings for either religion, nor had any immediate hope of ascending to the throne of France, although he certainly coveted it.

'They see me as being of no consequence,' he mourned to Margot as they strolled in the gardens one lovely autumn day.

'I'm sure you exaggerate,' she consoled him, her heart filling with affectionate sympathy for this, the least prepossessing of Catherine's sons.

They had never had the opportunity to get to know each other well as their mother had largely ignored him and the poor boy had spent much of his childhood and adolescence alone in various country palaces, having little contact with his other siblings. Now she saw that he was every bit as ambitious as them.

'I mean to prove myself. I dream of a future every bit as brilliant as my brothers'. I too want a crown.'

Margot laughed. 'The Valois obsession. Take care what you wish for, dear François. Crowns sometimes come with more problems attached than you bargain for.'

Alençon pouted. 'I still have hopes it might be achieved through marriage with Elizabeth of England, but that isn't certain, despite our mother's efforts. Therefore, I must look elsewhere to make my mark and gain influence.'

Margot suggested they rest for a moment on a garden bench, realizing he needed to talk, that something was preying on his mind. 'And do you have any particular solution in mind?'

Seeing him nervously glance over his shoulder, she smiled re-assuringly and squeezed his hand. 'It's all right, we are quite alone. Anjou, or the King of Poland as we must now learn to address him, is talking with the Queen Mother in her privy chamber. You can speak freely.'

Alençon continued, although carefully keeping his voice low. 'I am as delighted as Charles by the imminent departure of Henri to Poland, and have already put in a request to take over the post of Lieutenant-General when he leaves.'

'I'm not sure that will be granted,' Margot tactfully warned, all too aware of Anjou's duplicity in assuring the boy of his support in this request, whilst urging Charles to the contrary.

An excitement now crept into Alençon's voice. 'There's talk of a new party being formed, a league which goes by the name of *Les Politiques*, who believe in toleration and religious freedom rather than following the strict tenets of the reformed church. They are not yet very strong, but when they are, I hope they will accept me as their leader, which would improve my standing in this ongoing conflict that afflicts our family, as well as on the wider political stage.'

Margot frowned as she considered this startling news. 'I have no problem with tolerance and moderation, but what is your plan?'

'I am already engaged in secret talks with the Huguenots, who are desperately in need of more leaders. They believe, with the help of the German Reiters, they can conquer the Netherlands.'

'Coligny tried and failed.'

'We may be more successful next time. This would be my first step towards independence, which would ultimately lead to my being declared King of Flanders.'

Margot was momentarily lost for words. It sounded a highly dangerous undertaking, yet never able to resist an adventure herself she did not blame him for dreaming of a crown. This neglected young man deserved something of his own. Even his name, François-Hercule, was an echo of his elder brother, François II. He was eighteen years old and surely had a right to some independence, and a future that was not despoiled by a manic King or the perverted tastes of Anjou.

'You think it a hopeless task,' he said, reading her silence as a condemnation.

'No, no, I would not presume to comment on the possible success of your mission, and I do most certainly wish you well in it.' Whereupon, she put her arms about this young brother of hers with his pock-marked face, so often referred to as the runt of the litter, and hugged him close. 'Be assured that so long as you bring no harm to our brother the King, whom I also love, you have my full support.'

'I knew you would understand, Margot. I need to prove myself, to get out from under our mother's thumb and escape the claustrophobic confines of the Louvre. Together with the rest of the court we will shortly be escorting the new King of Poland on the start of his journey, and I may never find a better opportunity to make my escape. The Huguenots have troops waiting at Champagne and I wish to join them.'

'As does Enric.' Their gazes locked, Margot's eyes bright at the prospect of fresh intrigue. Seconds later she was on her feet. 'Come, let us talk to Navarre. He may have a plan.'

Catherine could hardly bear to consider the prospect of parting with her adored son. Delighted as she was for him to be elected as King of Poland and gain a crown, she would have welcomed any delay in the hope that a better one might soon present itself.

Having accepted the burden of responsibility for the massacre, as Sovereign of the realm, Charles seemed to be dying, piece by piece, before her very eyes. His depression and state of health gave Catherine grave cause for concern. She might not love him as she did Anjou, but she had stood by his side as regent since first he became King at the age of ten, and cared for him in her way.

The events of that terrible week had affected him badly. Many involved in the massacre had gone mad, fallen into a deep melancholy, or taken their own lives. The people of Paris blamed her, naturally. They said the Italian woman had sought revenge for her continued unpopularity. Not that their hatred troubled Catherine in the slightest. She was used to it.

'All the evils of the Kingdom are imputed upon me,' she would say to her ladies, as if it were a merry jape.

A book had been published claiming to tell the story of her life, listing all the murders and vile deeds for which she was deemed responsible. The author was a Huguenot, and Catherine had one of her women read it to her each evening, enjoying it hugely.

'If they'd given me notice I could have told them so much more,' she chortled with her easy humour, rattling the stone devils on her bracelet.

'Even the Catholics are reading it and believing it,' warned her ladies.

'Let them, I care nought for public opinion.'

Another of her lies. The great Catherine de Medici cared very much what the world thought of her.

She knew Charles was still frantically writing letters, almost as a means of seeking absolution for the crimes, although the response he received was not encouraging. The views of foreign monarchs on what had taken place on St Bartholomew's Eve were mixed. Philip of Spain, still fighting a religious war in the Low Countries, applauded the vile deeds perpetrated, as did the Vatican, which had no quarrel with exterminating those who refused obedience to the authority of the Holy See.

Maximilian II, father of Charles's young Queen, took a rather different stance. Officially he maintained a marked silence on the matter, although Elisabeth had admitted that in private he described the act as the most abominable that could have been committed.

England had been appalled by the news, so much so that Queen Elizabeth had apparently refused to receive the ambassador sent by the French Court to explain and apologize for the massacre. When at length the man was finally admitted to her presence, Elizabeth had received him dressed in full mourning.

The woman was a consummate actress, Catherine thought, with venom in her heart.

Charles seemed to grow weaker by the day. There had been moments when she'd feared that the end was nigh, but the imminent departure of his brother appeared to have quite lifted his flagging spirit. The bad feeling that still existed between her sons had grown ever more poisonous, the jealous rivalry now turning to bitter hatred.

Catherine was at least thankful that the King did not possess an heir, his infant son having died and the new child Elisabeth had recently borne him was a girl, to be named after herself. The way was clear for her beloved Anjou to return and claim his rightful inheritance, when the moment came, as it surely would.

Yet despite everything, she had failed to quash the Huguenots, who seemed to be growing bolder, continuing to make outrageous demands. They had defeated Anjou by holding La Rochelle, his military desire for glory apparently a thing of the past. Even the women had fought alongside the men, pouring boiling pitch from the battlements down upon the royal troops, and bombarding them with stones. A form of peace had finally come early this summer, and liberty of worship was allowed in La Rochelle, Nîmes and Montauban, plus a few other small concessions. More than enough, in Catherine's opinion.

As for Navarre, who knew what went on in that young man's head? Although he loved pleasure and dalliance as much as did her own darling Anjou, Catherine could not help but admire the fact that he never brought shame upon his status, nor took part in the more frivolous and depraved revelries which so appealed to her favourite son. Navarre loved to play the fool but no one could be entirely sure what private thoughts went on behind the mischievous glint of those Gascon eyes. Could she trust him? Only time would tell.

Henry, King of Navarre, was in torment. He felt entirely responsible for the deaths of his friends and comrades. He should never have come to Paris, never have agreed to this marriage in the first place. He had given them his word that no harm would come to them, believing the assurances he had received from Catherine and from the King. How could he have been so naïve, so stupid?

It was hard to guess how much of the massacre had been

pre-planned, but he suspected that even if the Queen Mother
had never intended for it to spread quite so rapidly and terribly
as it had, she'd planned the death of Coligny in advance, and
possibly those of the other leaders as well. Navarre was devastated by the atrocities, by the losses inflicted upon the Protestants
that night. His cousin Condé was likewise in a sorry state, sunk
deep in a fit of melancholy, not even certain he could hold on
to the wife he so worshipped and adored.

Yet not for a moment did Henry allow his panic, his abiding
fear for his own safety to reveal itself either in his manner or
his expression. He remained resolutely cheerful, full of vitality
and good humour, and kept up the façade of affable fool, the
merry, good-natured chap, which indeed he was at heart. A
card he now played for all it was worth, for his very life depended
upon it.

Let them imagine that he was too stupid to recognize the
danger. Let them think he was like the Queen Mother with no
heart, caring for no one but himself. Yet, unlike her, he had
no real desire for power, only his freedom. He remained alert
to every nuance, for any possibility of a way out of this disaster.
He obligingly accepted the Mass, made an official apology to
the Pope and, most difficult of all, conceded that his home
kingdom of Béarn must return to Catholicism. It was a bitter
pill to swallow.

So when Margot came to him with Alençon to discuss their
future, he was more than ready to listen, and join in their plans.

A day or two later Margot was shocked to discover from one of
her ladies that word of their plan had leaked out. She went straight
to Charles, and the Queen Mother. Falling on her knees, she
begged them not to punish the persons she was about to name;
otherwise she could not reveal what she knew. 'No harm must
come to them. You can easily put a stop to this folly without
revealing how you came by the knowledge of it.'

Catherine exchanged a speaking glance with her son, who
seemed confused and indecisive, as always. 'We agree. Speak, child.
What is it you have learned?'

Margot told all, again begging her mother to excuse their folly.
'My brother is desperate for an adventure, and my husband is

simply anxious to return to his homeland. They cannot be blamed, and they meant no harm to the King.'

For once Catherine kept her word, and without ever informing either her son-in-law or her troublesome younger son how she had come to hear of their plot, she simply informed them that they would not, after all, be accompanying the royal party to Blamont. They would remain in the Louvre, where they would be 'safe'. And since the Queen Mother's word could not be disputed, they were obliged to accept that their plan had failed.

Margot was relieved that they never did hear her part in the failure of their scheme, and at least she'd been successful in ensuring that no harm came to them. What she didn't foresee, and perhaps should have allowed for, considering her own personal experience, was the devious nature of her mother's mind.

Catherine was furious, not only by the sheer audacity of the plot, but the fact that no word of it had reached her ears. Had Margot not panicked and revealed all to her, she might never have heard of the plan, which could well have succeeded. Such an occurrence must never be allowed to happen again. Consequently, she sent for one of her *Escadron Volant*, whom she received alone in her privy chamber.

The Queen Mother was seated in her most comfortable chair, veiled and gowned in her usual regal black as the young woman stood quivering before her. She did not invite her to sit.

Charlotte de Sauves was not only young but very beautiful and, some might say, a rather silly member of that delightful bevy of ladies of the robes and maids of honour whom Catherine employed to further her schemes. Now just twenty-three years old, at the age of seventeen she had become the wife of Simon de Fizes, Baron de Sauves, who had been secretary at different times both to the King and later to Catherine herself. Soon after their marriage in 1567 he had been appointed Secretary of State and if the Baron disliked the tasks his wife was sometimes called upon to fulfil for the Queen Mother, he had more sense than to express his displeasure. He at least had the consolation that she performed these duties out of patriotism towards France, although no one could deny that Charlotte enjoyed her work, and was vain enough to like being so admired.

'My daughter,' Catherine explained now, 'seems determined to remain loyal to this new husband of hers. Navarre is likewise behaving in an exemplary fashion towards her. Most extraordinary.'

'Perhaps they are in love,' murmured the romantic Charlotte.

Catherine gave the girl a quelling look. 'The chit is also growing exceedingly close to her brother Alençon. The three are remarkably cosy, which was not at all in the plan. Yet I believe she still hankers after Guise.'

Charlotte experienced a thrill of anticipation. There wasn't a lady-in-waiting not fascinated by the handsome young duke, and she would be more than willing to enjoy an *affaire* with Guise herself. Misunderstanding completely the direction of the Queen Mother's thoughts, she burst out excitedly, 'You wish me to steal Guise from her, so that she remains true to her new husband?'

'No, you silly minx, I mean quite the opposite,' Catherine snapped. 'It is of vital importance that I keep a close eye on that young man's activities, for all he has agreed to take the Mass, and those of my youngest son.'

Charlotte frowned, cleverness not being one of her skills, which were largely of a more erotic nature. 'Then what is it, exactly, Madame, that you want from me?'

Catherine spelled out her demands with barely constrained patience. 'I wish to know what they do with their time, and who they consort with. What their plans and schemes are. While Margot has told me much of her husband's activities, I need to be sure that she is not relating only what she wishes me to hear. It is essential that I am kept fully informed of all that goes on in those apartments. And I need their friendship squashed.'

'Between Queen Margot and her husband, you mean?'

'I mean between them all! You can most effectively sever any budding friendship between Navarre and my younger son by using the skills at which you are most adept.' Catherine actually managed to smile at the blank look of horror in the young woman's eyes. 'My son is surely not so ugly that you couldn't take him to your bed?'

Charlotte swallowed, disguising her dismay with some difficulty as she thought of Alençon's dwarf-like appearance and pock-marked face. 'Of c—course not, Your Majesty, if that is your command.'

'It *is* my command. I wish you to seduce them both. There is nothing like jealousy over a woman to spoil a friendship. Love affairs cause more squabbles in this court than anything else. Once you've captured both their hearts, or at least their lust, and my daughter has discovered her husband's defection, she will cease to feel quite the same affection for him. A simple mission, Charlotte, quite within the bounds of your ability.'

The girl thought wistfully of Guise, stifled a regretful sigh, and remembering who it was who issued these instructions, smiled. 'Of course, Your Majesty.'

'They say my son-in-law was quite the young stud before his marriage. I'm sure it won't be difficult to turn his head with a few of your tantalizing smiles.'

Charlotte almost shuddered at the prospect. If there were women who lusted after this provincial country bumpkin who ate raw garlic, loved to walk about barefoot and rarely washed his feet, she wasn't among them. She had rather sympathized with the Princess Margot for being obliged to marry the man and share his bed. Now *she* was expected to steal him from her so that she could enjoy this pleasure for herself. It was hard to believe.

The Queen Mother was glaring at her, awaiting an obedient response. Charlotte sank into a deep curtsey. 'Your wish is my command, Madame. I will do as you ask.'

'You most certainly will, and report to me daily. Daily, do you understand, girl?'

'Yes, Your Majesty.' And Charlotte withdrew to her room to stamp and rail, and contemplate with horror the prospect of sleeping with both an ugly dwarf, and an oaf with bad breath.

Once she had calmed down somewhat, it occurred to her that she might reward herself by seducing Guise as well. The Queen Mother hadn't exactly said that she couldn't. And she would most certainly deserve such a reward. What cared she if the Queen of Navarre's nose was thereby put very slightly out of joint? Smiling, she called for her maid to fetch her prettiest gown. 'We have work to do.'

The entire court, save for Margot and the two Huguenot princes, who remained confined to the Louvre, escorted the new King of Poland as far as Vitry-sur-Marne, where they halted when the

King became unwell. Charles was left behind with Elisabeth and his nurse, while Catherine continued on the journey with the new King of Poland as far as Blamont. Here she made a reluctant farewell, imposing many tearful embraces upon her son, which he valiantly endured.

'Go, but you will not stay long,' she recklessly told him. And since they both knew that Charles was already hovering at death's door, it made the parting easier.

Henri, accompanied by the Polish ambassadors, was obliged to continue along roads lined with French Huguenot refugees who booed and hissed, hurling insults and stones with equal measure. Catherine returned to court, to check on the progress Charlotte might have made.

Navarre was not slow to respond to the delightful charms and seductive technique of Madame de Sauves, and they quickly became lovers. He would visit her most afternoons, and sometimes evenings as well in her little apartment in a quiet corner of the Louvre, where he could savour her beauty in private. She was an imaginative, ardent mistress, making no fuss about his toilette, never insisting that he scrub his teeth or bathe before he came to her bed.

But then one afternoon when he arrived a little earlier than expected, Henry was in time to see his brother-in-law, Alençon, about to scratch on the door of the lady's room to announce his own furtive arrival.

Navarre set his fists on his narrow hips and laughed out loud. 'Well, well, so she has been entertaining us both, has she? What a clever minx she is.'

Startled and scarlet-cheeked, Alençon was suddenly terrified that this fine, brave soldier might call him out. A duel with such a hero would surely lead to almost certain death. 'This is my m–mother's doing, not m–mine,' he stammered, ever the coward. 'I beg your pardon, Sire, I was completely unaware of your own attachment to the lady.'

Grinning broadly, Navarre slapped the young man on the back, and began to walk him a little way along the passage. Only a year or two younger than himself, yet he was so lacking in experience. 'You'll learn much from her, Alençon, so pay heed to your lessons.'

'Does this mean we can no longer be friends?' the younger man enquired, still trembling, nervous that the King of Navarre might be walking him out to the courtyard where he would then draw a sword on him. He couldn't quite believe this show of bonhomie to be genuine, although many claimed that Navarre was the embodiment of *l'esprit Gaulois*.

Henry laughed all the louder. 'We're men of the world, you and I, why should we not remain friends? Let us only ensure that we do not double-book the lady again, eh?' And they both laughed at the joke, if rather awkwardly on Alençon's part. 'Shall we throw a coin or roll a dice for this afternoon's slot?'

'No, no, you take it, by all means,' Alençon quickly agreed, relieved he had escaped punishment so lightly.

When Charlotte next reported to the Queen Mother of her progress, she was obliged to confess that she had easily succeeded in seducing both men, but that setting one against the other was proving more difficult.

'They remain firm friends, Madame, and seem content to share me.'

This did not please Catherine one bit. Never fully able to understand the workings of human nature, she was always puzzled when people didn't behave according to her plans for them. 'And is my daughter aware of this *ménage a trois*?'

'No, Your Majesty.'

Catherine's full lips curved into a smile, although it did not reach her dark, shrewd eyes. 'Then see she is made aware of it.' Surely Margot could be relied upon to react with passion to the seeming betrayal of her new husband, which might very nicely upset the apple cart.

The moment Margot discovered that Navarre was involved in a liaison with Charlotte de Sauves, she reacted with characteristic fury. The information was brought to her by her good friend Henriette, the Duchess of Nevers, who thought she would rather know that her new husband was playing her false, than be left in ignorance.

'Rumour has it that the lady is also entertaining your brother.'

Margot gasped. 'Charles?'

'Heavens, no. The King is devoted to Marie Touchet, and his

lovely young Queen, of course. No, no, I mean the Duke of Alençon.'

Margot was astonished. 'I don't believe it.'

'It is true. They only discovered it themselves when they both arrived at the same moment to service the lady.' Henriette burst into a fit of giggles. 'How I would have loved to see that encounter.' But then, seeing her friend's scowl, she quickly changed her tone. 'I'm not suggesting that the circumstances aren't irritating, highly galling in fact. Nevertheless, you may prefer to hold on to your pride and not reveal that you are aware of his philandering,' the Duchess urged. 'At least the knowledge of it will help you decide how you wish to respond.'

'Respond?'

The Duchess of Nevers smiled conspiratorially. 'Most women would treat the matter with the utmost discretion while embarking upon an *affaire* of their own.'

Margot had never in her life practised discretion, and she certainly had no intention of starting now. She left her friend, and her women, to their gossip and went at once to confront her straying husband.

One glance at her face told Navarre the reason for her visit, and he instantly cleared the chamber of his gentleman. Margot barely waited for the doors to close before giving vent to her anger.

'How dare you behave thus? We have scarcely been married twelve months! What can this woman give you that I cannot? I have long been aware of your fancy for peasant girls, but de Sauves is a court beauty, as fond of the powder and rouge that you claim to so dislike in me.'

Navarre shrugged, good-naturedly smiling at his own folly, yet wisely remaining silent, hoping she might blow off steam then calm down. But Margot was a long way from calming down yet.

'She is no more beautiful than I; many would say less so. Am I so lacking in charm that you can put aside our marriage vows and be tempted by one of my mother's harlots?'

'Strong words, Margot, not comely on a lady's lips.'

'But you clearly dislike my lips, since you seek another's. What is so special about de Sauves that you would rather taste hers? Have I not performed my conjugal duties with sufficient diligence and attention?'

He dared to laugh at this. 'My dear, there is nothing amiss with either your lips, or your diligence in the business of the bedchamber. I am sure any number of gentlemen would give their souls to savour your delights, and I will continue to enjoy them myself, should you so permit. But, Margot, my dear, you and I both know that we neither of us sought this marriage. It was a political necessity. I believed we understood each other on that score. Need our marriage vows be taken quite so seriously, in the circumstances?'

Margot's pride was too bruised to see any logic in this way of thinking, not in the heat of her rage. She thought of how her mother had offered to procure her a divorce, only a few days after the ceremony had taken place. Yet out of foolish loyalty to Navarre, and perhaps as a consequence of her own pride, she had declined. Had she agreed, she might now be married to Guise, and free of all this misery.

'Have I not done all that could be expected of a loyal wife?' she railed at him. 'Did I not save your life, and that of your cousin?'

He looked suitably humbled. 'Indeed you did, and I am most grateful.'

Margot stamped her foot. 'I don't ask for your gratitude, but your loyalty.'

'Not my love then?' he teased.

'Will you please try to take this matter more seriously? My mother the Queen cleverly set up this whole little charade. Do you imagine that de Sauves would ever have looked your way had she not been ordered to do so, let alone favour my poor dear Alençon? That is what my mother does: dabbles, schemes, and interferes in other people's lives in order to pry into their affairs. Are you such a fool that you cannot see this?'

He was not smiling now, and it was some moments before he chose to answer. 'Many people make the mistake of seeing me as such. Has it not occurred to *you* that it may be because I allow them to?'

Margot fell silent. What was he saying? There was so much more to this infuriating man than she had bargained for.

He came and gathered her hands between his own to give them a comforting squeeze. 'Come, Margot, let us not squabble over trifles. We need all our wits about us for far more important matters.

I shall certainly keep mine about me while I enjoy Madame de Sauves' charms. And I would have no quarrel with you taking similar license.'

She stared at him in stunned surprise. 'Would you not?'

He shrugged and grinned, again at his most engaging. 'What's sauce for the gander . . .?'

Margot considered him with haughty disdain, but there was a thread of hope starting up somewhere deep inside. 'Well,' she huffed, 'all I can say is that at least your new mistress will spare me the necessity of suffering your presence any further in my bed. Good day to you, Sire.' And, storming out of his privy chamber, she slammed the door behind her and went straight to Guise.

She found him throwing dice with a rabble of friends in the courtyard. There was much noisy laughter and manly repartee as they placed their bets. Margot paused, framed in the doorway, a light breeze lifting tendrils of her dark hair which tumbled to her shoulders, as she wore no wig today. Some instinct warned Guise of her presence and he glanced up, eyes narrowing with speculation as he considered her lovely face.

Margot knew that she looked eminently desirable in her amber gown with its saffron kirtle, and lifting her chin slightly she met his gaze with a challenge in her own: one filled with promise.

She strolled over to the men, her movements slow and languorous, ostensibly watching the game as she circled the group. But she could tell by the way he edgily moved his body that Guise was intensely aware of her closeness. She could smell the tantalizing warmth of his skin as she brushed past him; could see the way his thick curls grew in a whorl at the nape of his neck. How she longed to reach out and run her fingers through it.

'Tonight,' she whispered, and then, swivelling on her polished red heels, sauntered casually away without a backward glance.

Guise came to her privy chamber at midnight, as she had known that he would. Madame de Curton let him in, casting one last anxious glance at Margot before slipping out and softly closing the door behind her. Margot locked it, then turned to face him. She meant there to be no interruptions this night.

He grinned. 'I see that the gossip has reached you.'

Margot did not trouble to deny it, since the answer was perfectly plain. Understanding her as he did, he would appreciate that she no longer felt obliged to remain loyal to a husband who had betrayed her, even had Navarre not effectively given her permission to ignore their wedding vows. Much as Margot was a dutiful Daughter of France, she was still a woman, needing to be loved.

This time there was no hesitation, no verbal banter or playful teasing. Pulling her into his arms, he began to kiss her with demanding, searching, evocative kisses. Margot responded with equal passion as he impatiently stripped off her gown and silk petticoats, peeled off each stocking, his fingers clumsy in his haste, although she helped him with stubborn laces and to shrug off his own attire.

They made love as if hungry to abate the raging need inside, as if they had longed for this moment for years, as indeed they had. They cared nothing for the consequences: for the disapproving presence of Madame de Curton in the room beyond, for how the Queen Mother might react if news of their encounter leaked out. They closed their minds to the memory of that other time when the King's men had discovered them, Guise barely escaping with his life, and Margot beaten to within an inch of hers. Margot thought this night might be worth dying for.

'You love me still?' she asked.

'How could I not?'

A shaft of moonlight illuminated their naked bodies on the silken sheets, but they did not notice. They gloried in the pleasure each gave to the other, the triumph of finally coming together with the familiarity of long-term lovers, and yet with a new edge to their passion; one acknowledging a love reunited.

Afterwards, she lay in the crook of his arm and smiled as she slept.

The second time was more leisurely. Margot thought he might still be asleep, but she had only to tickle the inside of his thigh with her toes for him to waken, pull her beneath him and begin loving her all over again, more slowly this time. There was much touching and tasting, nibbling and nuzzling. Margot arched her back as she pressed herself against his lean hard body, making little mewing sounds as he caressed her, then crying out in ecstasy at the climax, oblivious to who might hear her. Seconds later he let out a groan and sank against her.

They lay for some hours entwined together in complete contentment, sleeping a little, loving a little more. Guise did not stir until the first shades of an apricot dawn crept over the horizon.

'I must go.'

'You will come again?'

He leaned over to kiss her softly on the lips. 'You have only to beckon me with your little finger, with your entrancing smile, and I will come.'

They met frequently after that, and it felt so good to have him as her lover again. Margot felt safe in his arms, as if she belonged there. Secure, cherished, and loved, as she so longed to be. She would almost purr with happiness whenever he held her, returning his kisses with eager abandonment. And this time there was surely no danger. They were both married, so what possible harm could come of their liaison now?

Charles was ill, Anjou far away in Poland, and even the Queen Mother no longer seemed interested in calling her to account for her indiscretions.

Margot was no fool, quite certain that Catherine would soon be made aware of their new relationship, if only through the antics of de Sauves in her husband's bed. Fortunately, Margot managed to avoid being in it herself, sending Navarre on his way whenever he came calling. Not that her rejection seemed to concern him in the slightest, as he would only chuckle, assuring her that he could find a welcome elsewhere.

'Then do so, and see if I care!' she cried, flinging her slipper after him as he backed away, laughing.

'Ah, but we must repeat the exercise at some point, my love, else how are you to provide me with an heir?'

A charge to which she could find no answer.

The fact that after more than a year of marriage she still hadn't fallen pregnant troubled Margot at times, but then she would shrug the worry aside, too busy enjoying life. Why would she want all that messy business of having babies anyway, when there were so many more interesting ways to spend her time? Like deciding what she should wear to delight Guise tonight. How could she surprise and fascinate him even more? Her love for him was all-consuming. She had no thought for the future.

And then Madame de Curton came to her one evening in her privy chamber and Margot saw instantly, by the older woman's expression, that she brought bad news.

'What is it? Is my brother the King ill again?'

'His Majesty continues sickly, my lady, but no worse than yesterday, or the day before. No, it is other news I bring you. Would that it were not I who must break it to you.'

Margot felt a stab of fear. 'What is it? Tell me quickly.'

The governess sighed, suddenly feeling her age in this hotbed of gossip and intrigue. 'Madame de Sauves has a new conquest.'

'You mean she has tired of *noste Enric* already?' Margot let out a peal of mocking laughter. 'Why am I not surprised? It's probably those smelly feet of his.'

'No, no, she still sees your husband, and your brother.' A slight pause for a steadying breath before Madame continued. 'But she now entertains Guise as well.'

The silence following this disclosure was deep and profound. Margot felt the pain slowly spread from her heart across her chest, expanding ever outwards as if it might consume her entirely. Was it not bad enough that she was forced to tolerate the fact he still slept with his wife, who seemed to have a knack for producing children as easily as shelling peas from a pod. But this – this was too much. For the first time in her life she turned her back on her faithful companion.

'Leave me.'

'My lady, I beg you . . .'

'Leave me, Lottie. Please. I need to be alone.'

Madame de Curton quietly withdrew, her heart bleeding for love of her mistress. Margot sat on the edge of her bed, hands clenched tightly in her lap, paralysed by despair. She felt desolate, utterly bereft. What had she done to deserve such treatment? And from the one man she had trusted, the one man she could truly love for life, and whom she had believed loved her. But he had lied, and betrayed her like all the rest.

'Why?' She was standing before him, tall, proud, defiant. They were in a quiet bower, shielded from prying eyes by a bay hedge;

the kind of place lovers might meet, where just yesterday she had sat on his lap and let him caress her.

Guise gave his easy laugh. 'It is of no consequence. There is nothing in our coupling, I do assure you.'

'Nothing but lust? You mean you do not love her as you do me, yet you still want to put your cock in her, simply for the hell of it?'

Guise winced, not liking her tone, or her coarse language. 'Don't make too much of this, Margot. She offered herself to me and . . .'

'. . . she was too tempting to resist.'

'There really is no need for you to be jealous. I was amused by her, that is all.' He held out his arms in a helpless gesture towards her but she stepped back, out of his reach.

'I forgave you when you married so quickly and stayed away so long.'

'My love, you ordered me to wed, in order to save both our skins.'

'I know,' Margot conceded, a tremor in her voice. 'There seemed no alternative at the time. I believed you when you said you took no active part in the murder of the Admiral, or the other leaders.'

'And that is so; I never touched the man, though I was glad enough of his demise.'

'But this, this is a betrayal I cannot forgive. A marriage may be political, at least for such as ourselves, but a love affair is a choice, a pledge of love and honour between two people.'

His expression was growing troubled, a doubt creeping into it. 'She is a silly chit, good for nothing but a tumble in the hay. Whereas you and I do indeed have something special. You are my one true love.' He pulled her into his arms, grinning his mischievous grin, but Margot slapped at him, shoving him roughly away.

'We are done here, Monsieur Guise. You may leave.'

'Margot,' he groaned, a wry pleading in his voice. 'I thought a liaison with her might prove useful.'

'You thought nothing of the sort. Pray leave me.' The hurt he had inflicted cut too deep, was so painful that she could not find it in herself to weaken or respond to his wheedling. She felt not the slightest urge to relent and forgive. Margot drew herself up to her full height, and in that moment she had never looked more like a Queen. 'Good day, my lord.'

Realizing he had no alternative but to obey, Guise stifled a furious sigh, sketched a bow, and strode purposefully away. But he called back to her over his shoulder. 'Remember that I will still be here, waiting, when you are in a better temper.'

'You can wait till hell freezes over,' she shouted. 'I'll have no more of you.'

Navarre was puzzled by all the fuss. 'Margot has hardly spoken to me in weeks, and will not let me near her,' he confided to Condé as they rode back from the hunt one morning, having bagged several brace of pheasant. It was early in 1574 and the King and Queen of Navarre were still virtual prisoners in the Louvre. They were obliged to tolerate the guards regularly searching their apartments, even looking under their beds to check that no intriguer was lurking there. Today, they had been permitted to accompany Charles and his court to Saint-Germain, although as always they were never without an escort.

Navarre watched Margot riding ahead, studiously ignoring him. 'Does she seriously imagine that I could be a faithful and true husband to her, even unto death?' He almost laughed out loud at the thought. Impossible! It simply wasn't in his nature, not when there were so many beautiful women to enjoy. De Sauves fascinated him, and was considerably more tolerant of his foibles than his dear wife, so why should he not savour the delights she had to offer? 'I'm quite certain Margot still holds a candle for Guise, she cannot deny it.'

'Wives seem to imagine there is one law for them, and another for their husbands,' Condé grumbled, the bitterness he felt at his own wife's defection all too evident in his tone.

Navarre cast his cousin a sidelong glance, noting how he slumped dispiritedly in the saddle. 'How is the lovely Marie?'

'Not too well at present. She is *enceinte*.'

Navarre reined in his horse. 'Dear God, you do not think she carries Anjou's child?'

'Indeed I do not! Is the man even capable of siring a child?'

'There's no evidence to the contrary. Even if he does prefer pretty boys, he's not averse to dallying with a woman now and then, so how can you be sure?'

It was clear by his cousin's grim expression that he couldn't.

Nevertheless, Condé seemed determined to remain loyal to his beloved Marie. 'She tells me their love affair was purely platonic.'

Navarre kicked his heels into the flanks of his horse to spur it on. If that was what Condé chose to believe, then who was he to dispute it?

His cousin was proving to be a source of great irritation to the Queen Mother by ostentatiously parading his new religion. He would make the sign of the cross even if he was about to do nothing more taxing than peel an orange, or cross the Palace courtyard, as if to say, 'see what a good Catholic I am?' The performance was as insincere as it was flippant and insulting.

On one occasion Catherine had said as much, rebuking him for his sacrilege.

Condé had sarcastically retorted, 'Ah, Madame, the Princess my wife initiates me well in the use of that sign! Have you received any letters from your son this week? If not, I can tell you that he is well. Every other day brings couriers from Krakow bearing letters of a most passionate nature addressed to her. They are filled with protestations of fidelity, signed with his own blood. Can anyone doubt his sincerity? And my darling Marie weeps constantly over his absence.'

Now he told Navarre, 'I am driven near demented by jealousy.'

'Then let us hope we are allowed out on another hunt soon. The day has been kind to us, perfect for hunting,' Navarre airily remarked, considering it wise to change the subject. 'No wind, no rain, and the birds falling as they should. Although they are a somewhat tame prey for my tastes. Do you remember that time in Pau when we invited the ladies to join us on a hunt? Just as well they didn't as their nerves would have been in shreds. Two of the horses killed by bears, and a bowman hugged to death by another. Then one ferocious beast charged that group of men stationed on the top of a precipice, and the whole lot of them, bear and all, fell and were dashed to pieces on the rocks below.'

Condé smiled ruefully at the memory. 'We've enjoyed some good hunts together, but perhaps that one was a touch too adventurous, Enric, even by your standards.'

Navarre sighed. 'You speak true.'

They dismounted, leaving the stable lads to tend to the horses, and walked together across the courtyard, heads still bent in quiet conversation.

'You'll need to take excessive care with de Sauves,' Condé warned, returning to their earlier topic.

'I do assure you, coz, that I exercise extreme caution in any post-coital conversations with the lady. It would be reckless in the extreme to indulge in indiscreet pillow talk with a spy of the Queen Mother's, and I am under no illusions that that is what she is.'

'Catherine would snatch at any excuse or opportunity to persecute you,' Condé agreed.

'I will not give her the chance.'

'So you'll take care?'

'I'll take every care.'

Margot was feeling ill-used and neglected. She had endured many betrayals in her short life: by her brother Anjou, and by her own mother. Now, it seemed, she must accept treachery from the two men who should be the most loyal to her: her husband and her lover. Guise's infidelity was the worst to stomach. If she couldn't trust her beloved *chevalier*, the one man she truly loved and who claimed to love her, then who could she trust?

She sat impatiently tapping her toe, paying scant attention to the skipping and leaping of the dancers taking part in the evening's entertainment. It irritated her slightly that everyone else seemed to be enjoying themselves, while she felt dispirited and low.

Navarre was stepping out with his accustomed clumsiness, while Guise was lounging in a corner talking to his friends. Margot steadfastly averted her gaze and idly watched a rather handsome fellow expertly lead his partner through the lively steps of the tourdion.

How the ladies of Catherine's court did love to dance. They made the excuse that the exercise was good for their health, as well as for their amusement. Although the real motive was to seek any opportunity to get close to whichever young man had currently taken their fancy. Often, at the end of a dance, the gentlemen would be permitted to kiss their partner, which always elicited much giggling and delight. Margot rather thought there was no country in the world that danced with more grace and elegance, more devotion, than they did here in France. They had even danced at the Château of the Tuileries the day after St Bartholomew's Eve.

Later would come the ballets, for which the Queen Mother had her *Escadron Volant* specially trained by a dancing master. Margot would often join in, as there was nothing she loved more than taking part in a performance of dance or drama. But tonight she meant to retire early to her bed, in which she would be sleeping alone.

The Duchess of Nevers, who was seated beside her, whispered in her ear. 'Are you watching le Comte?'

Unaware that her eyes had indeed been following the pair of dancers, now performing the Galliard, Margot shook her head. 'I know not to whom you refer, Henriette.'

Her friend squeezed her hand. 'Yes, you do. See how he watches you. He may be dancing with that strumpet, but his eyes have rarely moved from your face. He is dying from love of you.'

Startled, Margot glanced at her friend, then back at the gentleman in question. 'Who is he again?'

'Hyacynthe Joseph de Boniface, le Comte de la Molle, known simply as La Molle by his friends. He is the younger son of an aristocratic family from Provence, one of your brother Alençon's gentlemen, although quite low down in the pecking order, I have to admit. He is forty-four years old, experienced, charming, gallant and, as you see, exceedingly handsome.'

The Duchess cast Margot a sly, sideways look from beneath her lashes, noting how her doleful expression had suddenly changed into one of keen interest. Feeling that her mistress was in dire need of a distraction, she pressed his suit still further.

'He made quite an impression upon Elizabeth of England when he was sent to prepare the way for the duc d'Alençon. Although not successful in winning the Queen for your brother, he certainly won the hearts of the ladies of the English Court, and Her Majesty apparently considered him one of the finest dancers she had ever seen.'

'He is certainly skilled in the art,' Margot murmured, becoming increasingly fascinated as she studied his lithe grace, his natural elegance, his handsome figure.

The Duchess of Nevers giggled. 'He is skilled in other arts too, I am told, and has quite set his mind to winning you. But he dare not approach Your Majesty for fear of seeming impertinent or above his station, and although he is well thought of by his master, the Queen your mother seems less enamoured of him.'

'Indeed? That is almost a recommendation.'

'Perhaps, Ma'am, you would allow me to introduce you to him?' the Duchess finished, with an air of unconcern. 'Or mayhap choose to invite him up yourself?'

Not fooled for a moment, Margot turned laughing eyes upon her friend. 'Henriette, you are wicked, utterly outrageous.'

By way of reply the other woman shrugged her pretty shoulders. 'Where is the value in chastity? No one else practises it, and certainly not our husbands. My own is in Poland with your brother, so heaven knows what mischief he gets up to. Did I mention that La Molle has a charming friend, Coconnas, with whom I confess I am already acquainted? He is a Piedmontese nobleman and captain of the guard to the duc d'Alençon. I should warn you, darling Margot, that La Molle arouses a fierce discontent amongst the husbands of the wives he pursues. He is reputed to be an enthusiastic and lively lover, but does not neglect his sacred duties either, being deeply religious.'

Margot looked askance at the alleged libertine in wide-eyed disbelief. 'He does not appear to me to be the religious type.' She noticed how he had somehow managed to dance closer to her, and was by now shamelessly ignoring his partner, who was growing quite frantic with jealousy as his adoring gaze fastened firmly upon the Queen of Navarre.

The Duchess cupped a hand to Margot's ear as she whispered, 'Your brother the King has been known to remark that anyone who wishes to keep a record of La Molle's conquests need only count the number of daily Masses he attends.'

Margot burst out laughing, thoroughly intrigued by this time, fascinated by the description her friend was giving her, and by the wicked gleam in the eye of the man himself. The gentleman in question had now parted company with his dancing partner and repaired to sit upon a chair, recently vacated by another. He even sat most elegantly, Margot noted, both feet and knees close together, not crossed or sprawled in a careless fashion.

He was a fine-looking man who seemed perfectly at ease with himself. He wore a short cream jacket lined with crimson satin,

matching velvet cap trimmed with a white ostrich plume; a pearl
hung from his left ear, and the hip-length cloak fell from his
shoulder with draped perfection. Even his gloves were of scented
leather. Without question he was a dandy, although not quite the
fop as was her brother Anjou.

'Despite his apparent devotion to the faith, he is also said to
be deeply superstitious,' Henriette continued. 'Coconnas tells me
that he has begged Cosimo Ruggieri, the Queen Mother's own
sorcerer, to make a spell for the purpose of winning Your Majesty's
heart.'

Margot was helpless with laughter, despite feigning horror at
such whimsical nonsense. 'Enough, Henriette, you win. I shall
meet the fellow. But spare me your introductions.'

As Margot approached the row of chairs, several young gentlemen
sat up very straight, gazing upon the Queen of Navarre with
hopeful adoration that she might invite them up to dance. One
or two even stretched out a hand to her, which she politely
pretended not to notice. Margot did not keep her gaze lowered,
as was sometimes the case with more timorous young ladies. Nor
did she wear a mask, as it was not her custom to do so, but fixed
her gaze firmly upon her alleged admirer. She did not speak,
merely sketched a slight curtsey and waited.

La Molle scrambled swiftly to his feet, doffed his cap, and
described a perfect bow, left foot elegantly extended, making the
accepted reverence from the side wherein lay his heart.

'I am humbled by your invitation, Your Majesty.'

'So I should hope,' Margot laughed.

He kissed his hand to her, allowing his lips to touch his fingers
in a slow and seductive fashion, his eyes never leaving hers. Margot
responded by daringly offering her own hand for him to kiss, an
honour he accepted with alacrity.

She thought that his manners were sublime, true and correct,
that he did not fawn, although he was no doubt filled with vanity,
all too aware of his own handsome good looks and his attraction to the ladies.

'The question is, can you amuse or entertain me for the length
of an entire dance, for I am not in good humour this night,' she
said, thinking to discomfit him.

'A dance is but a moment in time. Only allow me sufficient access to your person, Madame, and I could do both.' While his words were daring to the point of reckless, his expression was serious, and so confident that it was Margot who felt vaguely discomfited.

When the dance was over she returned to her chair, only to find that the moment the musicians started up again, he was beside her in an instant.

'A gentleman always returns a lady's invitation,' he remarked.

Margot couldn't help but chuckle, her usual good humour returning. 'I think you are a shameless rake, Monsieur le Comte.'

'I think you might be correct,' said he with a smile.

And they did indeed quite shamelessly exploit the rules by continuously inviting each other up to dance for the rest of the evening. Not a soul in the room could fail to notice the growing attraction between them, which was not only openly displayed, but positively flagrant. It pleased Margot to see how Guise's gimlet gaze followed their every move, every step in the dance, every glance and hold. She prayed that he might grow jealous, wanting him to storm over and come between the pair of them as they sat with their heads together, gossiping and giggling, almost as if they were lovers already. Unfortunately, he wasn't the sort of man to do anything quite so dramatic.

Navarre was simply amused, accosting her on the subject the very next day. 'I see you have a new fancy, wife; a handsome friend to become your devoted slave, and indeed your own devotion to him is clearly evident.'

'In view of your own *affaire*, I do not see how it can be any business of yours with whom I dance.'

Navarre shrugged. 'I have to say that I do not like the fellow. He is an upstart who thinks too well of himself. I feel you could do better, but if he amuses you, who am I to judge? You must do as you choose, dear lady, I will not stand in your way.'

'Why would you care?'

'Why indeed?'

Before leaving for Poland, Anjou had made his dislike of the Comte well known, not only because he was a favourite of Alençon, but because he had dared to flirt with his darling Marie.

Charles had stoutly defended the man, but now, on hearing the gossip of what had gone on at the dance, he too was infuriated by his impertinence.

Walking in the gardens with his Queen and Marie Touchet, each lady now happily reconciled to the other, he watched in dismay as his sister continued to make an exhibition of herself.

'The fellow is little more than a commoner, a mere servant, however well connected.' Charles was reduced to the same state of rage he had once experienced when she had flirted with Guise before her marriage. 'The girl is incorrigible, a wanton. Does she not appreciate that only gentlemen are allowed to flirt and play games of love with those of a lower rank? Certainly not Princesses of the Blood.'

'I dislike this too close a friendship between Navarre and Alençon,' Catherine told him. 'And talk of your sister's behaviour is rippling through the palace like a forest fire.'

'I will deal with this. Madame, you are the cause of everything. *Everything!*' he screamed at her.

Charles was tired, exhausted, frequently ailing, but still needing to prove, to himself at least, that he was in charge of the Kingdom. He constantly rejected Catherine's advice, hated and feared her, haunted as he still was by the demons of the massacre. Yet in this she might be right. He too was terrified of the influential friend-ships his younger brother was acquiring, the intrigue which was undoubtedly bubbling between Alençon and Navarre. Now his own beloved sister was behaving like a wanton.

'I will make her sorry, and teach that lout to regret his impu-dence.'

Rippling with rage, Charles gathered about him a few of his most loyal gentlemen, including a secretly amused Guise, and they hid themselves at the foot of the staircase leading to the Duchess of Nevers' chamber. They had been informed that La Molle was attending a supper party that evening, and impatiently awaited his departure. Charles carried a cord and was visibly jittery, frantic for the moment the libertine would come clattering down the stairs, when he intended to strangle him.

An hour slipped by, and another, Charles's highly emotional state worsening by the minute. When La Molle still hadn't appeared on the stroke of midnight, he began to shiver, although whether from frustration, fury, or simply cold, wasn't clear. At length Guise ventured to suggest to His Majesty that the miscreant may not appear at all.

'Why would he not?' roared the King, setting off a fit of coughing.

'I suspect,' said Guise, 'that he may have paid a call upon another lady, following supper with the Duchess. He may not come down these stairs until morning.'

Charles reacted with horror. 'If you are referring to my sister, then think carefully on what you impute.' He was turning purple with rage, and then almost as quickly lost all colour completely as he began to cough up blood.

Guise was instantly alarmed. 'Sire, allow me to help you to your rooms. We can do no more this night.' Taking Charles gently by the arm, he half carried the King of France back to the care of his nurse.

Margot lay upon the black satin sheets she'd had made specially to show off her white skin, her new lover beside her. 'I would say that you fulfilled your part of the bargain splendidly, for you did indeed both amuse and entertain me.'

'And for longer than the length of a dance. Would you care for a reprise?'

Margot laughed. 'You are incorrigible, sir. See, it is nearly morning, and long past time you left.'

Their night of love making had gone some way towards appeasing the sense of loss and rejection she harboured as a result of her husband's casual betrayal and the defection by Guise. The excitement of discovering new thrills had acted as a solace to her bruised pride. La Molle had proved to be an experienced lover and, despite his maturity, his body was lean and hard, and quite beautiful. Margot could quite see why he was a favourite with all the ladies.

Not that she could ever compare the emotions he inspired in her with those of Guise, the man she truly loved. Yet surely it was better to enjoy the attentions of this handsome fellow, rather than spend endless sleepless nights alone? Wasn't she a woman who needed to be loved?

Le Comte was preparing to leave, pulling on his breeches,

fastening his cloak in place, when something dropped from an
inner pocket. Margot picked it up.

'What is this?' She was frowning, for it was a small waxen doll
with a pin stuck through the heart.

'Madame, you make me blush. I had the Queen Mother's
astrologer, Cosimo Ruggieri, make that for me. As you can see
it wears a crown and is meant to be in your likeness. It was
intended to make you fall in love with me.'

Margot's eyes widened. 'I suppose this pin piercing the heart
is supposed to represent your love for me?'

His smile was mischievous, and beguiling. 'Have I not pierced
your heart, Madame, with my unwavering devotion, and my attention to your needs this night?'

'Be gone, fool. This is no more than superstitious trickery,' and
she tossed the doll to him, laughing all the while.

Grinning, he tucked it away again in that secret pocket. 'Ah,
but it worked, Your Majesty, you cannot deny it. I swear I shall
never now be parted from the doll, hoping that it may keep me
in your good favour.'

'You need only love me to achieve that,' she smiled. 'Not
depend upon trickery.'

'The King is gravely ill, and this time they fear for his life,' Navarre
announced to Condé one morning. 'The lung disease has
progressed and his condition is worsening. Nor will the February
chill help to sustain him.'

The pair were waiting in Alençon's ante-chamber for the start
of one of their secret meetings, kicking their heels and pacing
back and forth with impatience. They were always edgy and on
their guard on these occasions, for were the Queen Mother to
discover how they met privately with Huguenots within the walls
of the Louvre, she would spare no one. And the Bastille was a
far less pleasant prison than this one.

'And with Anjou in Poland, the Queen Mother grows ever
more suspicious of the ambitions of her youngest son, whom she
fears may attempt to usurp the throne intended for her beloved
favourite. Having rid himself of one brother, His Majesty now
appears to be harassed by the other,' Condé dryly remarked.

'Indeed, particularly since he refused to grant Alençon the post of Lieutenant-General. Charles is considering offering it to his sister Claude's husband, the Duke of Lorraine, instead.'

Condé raised his brows in surprise, then sadly shook his head. 'Had Alençon been granted such a high office, he could have done much for our cause.'

'By bowing to his brother and the Queen Mother's wishes in this matter, Charles has forged a new enemy,' Navarre agreed. 'It does not surprise me in the slightest that Alençon is bitter. How could he not be when his own mother has made it very evident by the way in which she has largely ignored him all his life, that he is of no account. She pours all her love and attention into Anjou. If Charles is jealous of her favourite, how much more so is Alençon? And Good Queen Bess seems resolutely unwilling to take her little frog, as she calls him, for a husband.'

'He grows increasingly restless, a born intriguer. I'm not sure I can trust him.'

A dwarf entered with a flagon of wine and proceeded to pour a goblet for each of them. Condé watched with a thoughtful frown as he was followed by La Molle and Coconnas, who were laughing and preening themselves like the fops they were as they took their seats at the table.

'This little court he keeps, think you not it's an odd mix? Sober Protestants and roués, pretty women, alchemists and adventurers. Most of whom have linked themselves to him in order to further their own interests. Although I believe Alençon himself is equally guilty of that crime. He is far more concerned with his own selfish glory, rather than the good of France.'

Henry gave his cousin a playful punch. 'Not all men are as unselfish or as devoted to God as are you, coz.'

Other gentlemen began to arrive: Damville and his brother Montmorency, along with Turenne and Thore, slipped quietly into their places, shuffling papers and conversing together in a relaxed fashion as the dwarf attended to their needs, pouring more wine.

'Unlike you, my good friend, your brother-in-law is not a natural leader. Men would not follow him to their deaths, or women fall at his feet as they do yours. Nevertheless, this rival court of his seems to have persuaded the Duke that Spain, the Pope, and his mother are all in league against him.'

Navarre gave a wry smile. 'They might well be right. We may

differ in many respects, Alençon and I, not least in our nature, but we both live in fear for our lives within these grim walls.'

Condé readily conceded this. 'If the fellow has the desire to be a leader of our party, then let him. We're in dire need of such at present, and he might make a fine statesman one day, if he could but rid himself of this obsession over sibling rivalry.'

'I doubt he will remain a Huguenot for long. It is no more than a passing fad.' Dropping his voice to a whisper, Navarre continued, 'He means to join the *Politiques*, once they have grown sufficiently to require a leader. Alençon seems to have a need to be independent, to be his own man, and they will readily accept him since he took no part in the massacre of St Bartholomew's Eve. What better way to prove the honour of their campaign than to have a Son of France as their leader? Alençon's aims, however, are less altruistic. He wants a crown, perhaps at any price.'

The door opened and the Duke himself came in, an odd mix of self-importance and diffidence warring for supremacy on his ugly face. 'Pray, gentlemen, be seated, I beg you.'

He began with an assessment of the situation in the Low Countries: the successes achieved in Normandy, of twelve hundred brave Béarnais troops gathering near Fontenay, towns opening their gates to the Huguenots. He then moved on to the health of his brother, his tone slightly mocking.

'My mother the Queen fears that if the King dies, we will make moves to prevent her favourite son from leaving Poland to take up his rightful succession.'

Condé whispered behind his hand, 'And he does so like to spread disaffection and stir up mischief.'

Navarre grimaced. 'The mischief is stirred mainly by the King of Poland and his mother.'

Montmorency was speaking now, urging the Duke not to enter into conspiracy against the King. 'I counsel you, Sire, loudly to proclaim your tolerant principles. You can place yourself at the head of this great faction without offending your brother the King. Once your position is secure, you can begin to oppose the over-whelming influence of the Princes of Lorraine, who are in league with the Queen Mother.'

The discussions continued as Navarre again whispered under

his breath to his cousin. 'It is not for me to judge. Margot wishes me to offer this youngest brother of hers my full support in this venture to become King of Flanders. I enjoy his company, and see no reason not to help a young man make his way in the world, so am happy to do so. It might at least serve to take his mind off stealing his brother's crown.'

'So be it,' Condé agreed with a sigh. 'If that is what you wish, then we should proceed to get the matter settled here and now, although I confess I am growing tired of secret meetings and intrigues. I nurse a desire to retire to my estates and spend time with my wife.'

'And I mean to return to my homeland, to rid myself forever of Catherine's shackles. If he and I can assist each other to achieve our freedom from what has effectively become a prison, then our friendship may well prove to be mutually rewarding.'

A plan was devised whereby Alençon and Navarre affected their escape from court under cover of darkness. The night of the Carnival on Shrove Tuesday, the 23 February, seemed the most propitious, as the court would be alive with laughter and merriment, with dancing and feasting, the courtiers too raucous in their drunkenness to notice anything untoward. Two hundred cavalry were expected to arrive at Saint-Germain that night, under the leadership of one Captain Chaumont-Guitry, who would meet with Navarre and Alençon, and quietly spirit them away while the celebrations were still in progress. Their intention was to flee north to join the rest of the Huguenot forces, ready to embark on the planned invasion of the Low Countries.

As the day drew near, tension amongst the conspirators was palpable, and Alençon's nerves began to crack. A born coward, weak and selfish, he lived in fear of imminent discovery. His fears were fulfilled when there was some mix-up over the time and Guitry arrived at Saint-Germain with his men much earlier than the day agreed. Worse, the detachment under his command was smaller than expected, large enough to attract attention, but too small properly to protect the two princes. The whole enterprise suddenly seemed perilous.

He at once fell into a panic and became utterly paralysed with terror. Navarre, Turenne and the others urged him to hold fast to his nerve and the agreed plan, but Alençon fled, weeping, to his sister. 'How dare I risk this dangerous enterprise now?' he cried. 'What should I do?'

Margot attempted to calm him. 'You should continue exactly as we have planned. We must behave as if everything were perfectly normal.'

'I cannot go through with it, I cannot, I cannot,' he kept repeating, feverish in his desperation. 'The Queen Mother will discover all. De Sauves may well have warned her of the plot already.'

Margot accepted that the woman would be certain to pass on to the Queen Mother any whispers she might overhear while in Navarre's or her brother's bedchamber. She could only hope that had not been the case, but it was obvious that her younger brother was incapable of behaving normally. He was a quivering wreck. The danger was that his very behaviour might alert suspicion, and the plan revealed before it could properly be carried out, thus endangering other lives, including that of her own husband.

News of the arrival of a detachment of Huguenot soldiers in the vicinity of Saint-Germain did indeed reach the ears of the Queen Mother, and the court was soon buzzing with the rumour that they intended to slaughter the King, his mother, and all members of the court.

Margot begged Alençon, now out of his mind with terror, to make his escape amidst the mayhem. 'If it is to be successful, it must be now.' But he refused to budge.

In despair, Margot sent for La Molle, hoping he could help to calm him. The Comte had acted as go-between in making these arrangements, together with Coconnas, the lover of the Duchess of Nevers, but he too was alarmed by the high nervous state of his master, and by the way news of the detachment of soldiers had leaked out so quickly. Could Captain Guitry even be trusted?

'It may well be too dangerous, Sire, for you to risk flight.'

'It certainly will be if my brother does not have the stomach for it, and has been indiscreet with his mistress,' Margot murmured, torn between pity and exasperation for the ineffectual François-Hercule.

'I must throw myself upon the King's mercy. Ah, but then

I would have to face my mother.' The young prince wrung his
hands in fear, whimpering piteously, trembling at the prospect.
If he did not have the stomach to risk flight from the Louvre,
he certainly couldn't find the courage to face the Queen Mother's
wrath. 'La Molle, you must do it for me. You must go to the
Queen and speak on my behalf. Confess all and beg her to
forgive me.'

'But Sire, is that wise?'

'It is if I wish to save my neck,' screamed Alençon, too far
gone in his distress to think rationally. 'Tell no one – not Navarre,
not Condé. No one!'

'That would be wrong,' Margot protested, alarmed by the way
their simple plan was suddenly falling apart. 'They have a right
to know what is happening, that there will be no attempt to
escape tonight.'

'All right, all right, tell them the plan has been aborted if you
must, but do not on any account reveal my confession.'

La Molle and Margot exchanged a glance of desperation. She
recalled that previous occasion when she had confessed how the
princes had planned an escape on their return from escorting her
brother Anjou to Poland, and how she had begged for them not
to be punished. She'd sought and won Charles and her mother's
compassion, successfully securing forgiveness. Perhaps it could
work again, and her brother was certainly in no condition to
continue with the plan.

'Are you willing to try this?' she asked La Molle.

'I am.'

She sighed. 'Then I will speak to my husband and tell him we
have decided it is too dangerous to proceed and he should lie
low for a while.'

It seemed the wisest course of action.

Catherine listened in stony silence as La Molle waxed almost
lyrical over his master's loyal devotion to the King and Her
Majesty, how she could ever rely upon his good services, before
frankly confessing the entire plot: how the King of Navarre and
the Duke of Alençon had planned to make their escape and join
the Huguenot army.

'That was the true reason for Guitry's advance,' he informed her.

Pale with fury, Catherine instantly despatched the officer on guard to command the presence of the two princes. Concerned not only for the safety of the King, but for the throne of France itself, she meant to make an example of these two young men. She had no fears that, well guarded as it was, the security of the Palace could be breached, or that her runt of a son could ever succeed in such a venture, despite his love of intrigue. But she had every intention of using the evidence of this plot to bring him down, if only to ensure it was never repeated.

Whatever happened, the people of Paris must see that this miscreant had endangered the life of their Sovereign, as well as the succession for her favourite son. It was a sin tantamount to treason, and one she would not tolerate.

During the next few hours there was complete uproar as courtiers rushed about making arrangements for a hasty departure, some planning to leave by coach and litter, others by boat. The Palace guards were doubled, extra patrols of Swiss Guards set up, and the King urged to flee at once to Paris. It felt like the Surprise de Meaux all over again. Once more the royal family were forced to flee in the middle of the night to Paris, carrying the poor dying King with them on a litter.

Navarre and Alençon were placed in the Queen Mother's coach, although not for their greater comfort. Catherine had not done with them yet. Once the King and his court were safe, the reckoning would come. Even Madam de Sauves was also included in the royal party, in order to entertain the Queen Mother and her two lovers with her bright chatter.

Charles cried, 'If only they had waited at least for my death.' For the entire length of the perilous journey that night he kept repeating, 'Too much malice! Too much malice!'

'A fitting way to describe my mother's regency, wouldn't you say?' Margot whispered to her husband.

Navarre, fearing this may be the end for him, made no reply. It seemed inevitable that he would be charged and executed as a traitor.

The court settled at the Castle of Vincennes, the chateau being well fortified and able to withstand a possible attack. In any case, the King could go no further as he was in a high fever, haemorrhaging so badly that his devoted nurse and Queen were constantly changing his blood-soaked sheets.

The confession had not attracted the beneficial result that Margot's had done on that previous occasion, and the Queen Mother remained terrified that the throne itself was under serious threat. Even more so when on having the conspirators' belongings searched, a waxen image wearing a crown with a pin piercing its heart was found among La Molle's goods and chattels. She had the man brought before her.

'What is this? You have conjured spells to slay the King?'

La Molle was horrified. 'Indeed, I would never do such a thing, Your Majesty.'

Try as he might to beg the Queen Mother to believe that the image was not that of the King but of Margot, whose heart he'd wished to capture, Catherine remained unconvinced. She was far too credulous of the black arts, of ill-wishing and evil omens, having performed many such rites herself over the years. His pleas fell upon deaf ears. Further investigation revealed that it was her own favourite astrologer, the swarthy Italian, Cosimo Ruggieri, who had made the doll.

He too was arrested, and, when questioned, the frightened man insisted that La Molle spoke true, that the doll was indeed a likeness of the Princess, her heart pierced by love. Catherine refused to accept even his word. How could she when her son the King was sick unto death?

Ruggieri did not help himself by showing concern for his Sovereign. 'Is the King vomiting?' he asked. 'Does he have pains in his head?'

'Why do you ask? Have you put them there? You must tell us the exact truth of the King's illness,' Catherine demanded. 'You must remove the spell.'

'There is no spell,' the astrologer cried, fiercely protesting his innocence, but the Queen Mother remained stonily unmoved. 'You have even worked your magic to make my younger son follow La Molle, your co-conspirator. You must undo that magic as well.'

Cosimo was flung into prison. Catherine hated to be cheated by those she had trusted most.

When all of this was later related to Margot, the Queen of

Navarre almost fainted from fear. Her dear friend Henriette, the Duchess of Nevers, was likewise in a state of terror. If both their lovers, and even Cosimo Ruggieri the Queen Mother's favourite, had been arrested, Navarre and Alençon were also in serious danger, not to mention the women themselves. Margot dreaded to think what might happen next.

The two princes were held under close house arrest, and then the questioning began. Alençon's version changed each time as he desperately sought to defend himself, vehemently protesting his innocence. He blamed everyone but himself, swore there had been no intention to attack the King, although he could not satisfactorily explain his motivation in wishing to join the Huguenots or the *Politiques*.

Catherine considered him with open contempt as he stood quivering before her. 'What have you done, my son? Will you kindly hasten to disavow all that has been planned in your name?'

In the end he readily agreed to write and sign any document she presented in order to declare his innocence. '*We, son and brother of the King of France, having heard that some impostor has sown and spread false reports against us . . .*' All lies, but a way out for both mother and son. Alençon scarcely paid any heed to the words; he simply signed.

Margot made the decision to do all in her power to save her husband. No matter what their differences, and even if he meant less to her than Guise, or even La Molle at this precise moment, she felt bound by her wifely duty to do all she could to help him. She was afraid for him, terrified at what the Queen Mother might do. She had no wish to see his head on the block.

She wrote an impassioned and articulate defence, as carefully reasoned as that of any lawyer. It began, 'The King my husband, having none of his councillors available, charged me to put his defence in writing, so that his evidence would harm neither himself nor anyone else.'

She begged for royal clemency, and Navarre himself read the plea directing it at the Queen Mother, not to his inquisitors. He reminded Catherine of his boyhood spent under her care, how she had educated him in the ways of the French Court, and of his loyalty to the crown since that date. It mentioned how he had fought alongside his mother when threatened by the Princes of Lorraine, and how, once peace had been declared, he had agreed to this 'very happy' marriage with her daughter Margot. Despite what had occurred since – losing his friends and comrades in the massacre only days later; the humiliation of being held virtually a prisoner in the Louvre, and having spurned the Huguenot faith – he had never ceased in his loyalty to the King.

'I have endured many petty persecutions and tribulations, partly from the King of Poland's favourite, du Guast, and others of the Catholic faction, who plot against me to blacken my name. I am kept under armed guard, my apartments searched daily, even my servants subjected to harassment and dismissal. I have frequently asked to speak to the King to assure him of my good service, only to be told that His Majesty has no wish to receive me. All I wish is to return to my realm where I can live in peace with my people. That is all, Madam, that I know,' he concluded. 'I very humbly beg you to consider whether I did not have just and sufficient reasons for going away.'

He spoke with passion and sincerity, but it was Margot's cleverness which really won the day. Moved by the power of her daughter's words, and her carefully contrived argument, Catherine agreed to spare both princes from execution. They were still, however, to be denied liberty of person or any opportunity for Navarre to return to his own kingdom.

La Molle and Coconnas stood trial next, and were less fortunate. Whether or not anyone believed in the black arts, other than Catherine, they were quickly found guilty of plotting against the King. They were taken into the bowels of the castle where La Molle was the first to be put to torture, his fingernails ripped out one by one by red-hot pincers, the beautifully elegant body that Margot had so adored and loved splintered and broken on the rack.

Yet he remained loyal, not implicating her, or anyone else, in the conspiracy. Coconnas was less brave and named several co-conspirators who were also arrested and sent to the Bastille.

The Queen of Navarre and Henriette, the Duchess of Nevers, had scarcely stopped weeping since the arrest of their lovers. The fear that their beautiful young men might be executed any day was too dreadful to comprehend. How had it all gone so terribly wrong? Margot visited the prison every day to see La Molle, accompanied by her dear friend, who likewise wished to see Coconnas. They took food and small comforts, doing what they could to alleviate their suffering.

Broken men, they were held in a subterranean cell with little in the way of fresh air or light, so constructed that they did not allow the prisoners either to stand, sit or lie with any degree of comfort. They were obliged to pay their gaolers if they wished to be fed, but no amount of bribing would secure their release. The two men, once so loved and worshipped by their admirers, could do nothing but await their fate.

Margot discovered that she was allowed to travel back and forth with her women right into the prison courtyard. Her coach was never searched, the guards paying her little attention once they grew accustomed to her visits. They never looked inside, nor made any of her ladies take off their masks.

'All we have to do is smuggle in some women's clothing, and one of the prisoners could then make his escape by leaving with us, disguised as a woman.'

'Only one?' the Duchess asked.

'There is always the danger that the guards will take a careful count of how many of us go in, and how many come out. We must mingle with the crowd to confuse them, but to attempt to bring out both men would be far too dangerous.'

Henriette was horrified. 'Yet they are closely watched, even if we are not, so once it is discovered that one is missing, the other will be in far greater danger.'

Margot knew in her heart which man she would rather save, but then the Duchess too had her favourite. 'We must allow them to decide. Only they can make such a decision. We can but offer to save one.'

'Even so it would be highly dangerous to ourselves. Dare you take the risk?'

'La Molle does not deserve to die for such a paltry conspiracy.'

'Nor does my Coconnas, but you would risk losing the King's good graces if the scheme fails, Margot. He would never forgive you. Your reputation and your good relations with him would be ruined for all time, if not your own life put in danger.'

Margot was sombre. 'That is indeed a serious risk, I do concede it. And what of you, Henriette? You would be running the same risk. Think of the Duke, your husband. Think of your children. Yet we must decide soon. Time is of the essence. If we do nothing, then tomorrow, or the next day, both men will lose their heads.'

The two women looked at each other, and in silent accord an agreement was reached. Whatever the risks, they had to try.

The two friends set about making careful preparations that very afternoon as there was no time to be lost. Margot put on a second gown, Henriette an extra petticoat, before they each wrapped themselves in their cloaks, Margot wearing two. She pulled the hood up to hide her face.

'I swear I must look as fat as a pig, and I'm sweating like one too. Does it look obvious that I am overdressed?' she asked, anxious suddenly.

'No, no, my lady. You are as slender as a willow wand.'

'Don't forget to tuck a spare mask into your pocket, Henriette. No lady is ever seen out and about without her mask, save for myself on occasions, and whichever one of them is chosen, he must needs hide his face.'

'And his beard,' her friend agreed, hiccupping on a hysterical giggle.

All went perfectly smoothly. The ladies settled themselves comfortably against the cushions of the Queen of Navarre's coach, which was waved through the gates into the prison yard by the guards without being apprehended.

Margot climbed out of it on legs that felt decidedly shaky. She could hear Henriette at her side almost whimpering with fear. 'Hold your head high and look confident. Let us mingle with that group of wives over there. Quickly, while no one is watching.'

The Queen, the Duchess, and a maid, each carrying a basket of food, hurried across to join the line of women already queuing at a small side door. As always, the stench of the prison almost overwhelmed them as they entered, and the ladies quickly held their pomanders to their noses.

'I swear I shall faint clean away from the stink of it one of these days,' moaned the Duchess.

'There are no days left,' Margot grimly reminded her. 'This is

the last. We must put the plan into action at once. Delay could
be fatal for us all.'

With fast-beating heart, Margot led the way down a stairway
slippy with moss and fungi, and something far less pleasant. The
sound of feet scampering away into the darkness made her shudder
with revulsion. They reached the prison cell in what felt like the
bowels of the earth, and the turning of the huge rusty key in
the lock by the gaoler grated loudly in her ear, causing her to
tremble with a new fear. If the plan failed, she may well be hearing
that sound locking her into such a cell.

Margot held up her lamp, struggling to adjust her vision in the
gloom. La Molle lay curled in a corner, his eyes fixed and glazed.
Coconnas was huddled beside him, the cell barely big enough to
accommodate the two prisoners, let alone their visitors. There was
no other light but the lamps they carried with them and, as always,
Margot was shocked by the sight of her lover. He looked like a
bundle of filthy rags, half dead already. She fleetingly recalled his
crimson-lined, cream satin cloak, the glorious elegance of the man
as he danced, and the way his enigmatic smile would melt her
heart. Tears ran down her cheeks at the thought of this lost beauty.

For the first time she began to question the wisdom of her
scheme. Could he even get up, let alone walk out of this place
disguised as a lady-in-waiting?

She kissed him on the mouth, trying not to mind the foul
stink that emanated from it, or the lice that moved in his hair.
Nor did she allow herself to recall how scented and smooth this
skin, now so grey and rough, had been when last they'd made
love beneath her satin sheets.

She wasted no time in asking after his health, an irrelevant
question in the circumstances. Margot let him sip from the flask
of wine she had brought, gave him a hunk of cheese to eat, but
he turned his head away.

'Where is the point in eating? I shall need no more food from
tomorrow.'

'It is vital that you keep up your strength.'

She rapidly outlined her plan, and as she saw hope dawn in
his loving gaze, hastened to explain how they could only risk
taking one of them out. 'You must decide quickly. Which of you
is it to be?'

But they could not decide. The two men fell to quarrelling, knowing that whoever was left would undoubtedly suffer further torture before the blessed relief of death finally overtook them. How could one friend leave the other to such a torment? They clasped each other in terror and regret.

'We will die together, as we lived together,' La Molle finally announced. 'There is no other way.'

Margot was forced to accept the futility of her plan. But she was shocked and devastated by their decision, tried desperately to make them change their mind while the Duchess wept, adding her own pathetic pleadings. But no amount of tears or persuasion would alter their decision.

Then came the rattle of a key. The gaoler was at the cell door. It was time to go, and reluctantly the two ladies kissed their lovers goodbye and departed.

The following morning, 30 April, Margot and the Duchess watched in horrified disbelief as their lovers were executed on the Place de Grève. From the safety of the Queen of Navarre's coach, they saw how La Molle showed remarkable strength and courage, walking unaided to the scaffold. His last words were, 'God have mercy on my soul, and the Blessed Virgin. Commend me well to the good graces of the Queen of Navarre and the ladies.'

And how the ladies wept, all of them, for the tragic loss of such beauty.

The head of Coconnas was the next to roll, and was equally mourned.

Following an execution, according to custom, the heads were placed on public exhibition in the square, as a warning to the populace. Later that night, Margot sent her chamberlain to collect the heads of both their lovers, giving instructions for them to be embalmed and buried in the Chapel of St Martin at Montmartre.

She could not bear to go herself. For days Margot couldn't even bring herself to leave her room. The two friends were distraught, inconsolable in their loss, weeping and sobbing together, offering each other what comfort they could in their grief. The Duchess of Nevers ventured out only to call for a maid to bring them some sustenance, although persuading Margot to eat was difficult.

Margot felt responsible for La Molle's death. If she had not encouraged Alençon in his ambitions, and her husband in his bid to escape, none of this would have happened, and these two innocent men might have been alive to this day. It was a bitter lesson.

One morning, Henriette came running into the privy chamber in a highly nervous state. 'You won't believe what I have heard. It has been noticed that the heads are gone, and it is being whispered that we have them here, that you keep La Molle's head in a silver casket under your bed, so that you can kiss his lips whenever you wish.'

Margot looked at her friend in horror. 'Dear God, can I not even mourn my lover in peace? When will the rumour-mongers let me be?'

The King was dying. As the scents of spring and May blossom drifted over the Palace gardens where the courtiers strolled, the windows of the royal bedchamber remained fast shut against any inclement chill. The threatened plot, the rush to Vincennes, had all been too much for Charles's weakened state. He lay swamped in apathy and despair, unable to summon the strength to rise, uncaring of day or hour, or of what was going on around him.

Relieved as Catherine was that she'd successfully quelled this latest plot, yet she still saw dangerous waters ahead. Her beloved Anjou was many miles distant in Poland, far from the throne he was about to inherit. Alençon, on the other hand, was dangerously close, as was Navarre. She didn't trust either, and, secretly calling her most trusted messenger, urged him to ride with all speed to Poland to warn her son that the King's death was imminent.

Charles looked so frail and thin. He was but a month from his twenty-fourth birthday yet he looked like a wizened old man with scarcely any hair left on his head, his cheeks hollowed, the skin grey and pallid. It was as if the death mask were already upon him.

Elisabeth of Austria, Charles's Queen, sat opposite her husband, weeping and never taking her eyes from his face. She had always loved him, and he returned her adoring gaze with gratitude, but also sent for his beloved Marie Touchet. His mistress came at once to make her farewells and sit by his side, holding his hand.

Nearby hovered his loyal old nurse, constantly wiping his brow or changing the bed sheets as he continued to cough up blood. He gazed up into her face, looking with love upon this woman who had brought him up, been as a mother to him, and, since she was Huguenot, whose life he had saved.

He cried out in his despair. 'What blood and what murders! What an evil counsel was given me. Oh, my God, forgive me all that, and have mercy upon me. What will become of this country, and what will become of me, into whose hands God commended it? I am lost! Full well I know it.'

His nurse leaned close to whisper to Charles under her breath, loyal to her beloved charge to the last. 'May the murders and the bloodshed be upon the head of those who compelled you to them, and upon your evil counsellors.'

The King's confession was heard and the last rites given. Charles asked for the prayer of Sainte Geneviève, the patron saint of Paris, to be said to him, as if by this means he could gain absolution for the atrocities he'd sanctioned against the capital.

The next day he slept fitfully and, when he woke, cried out, 'Call my brother.'

But when Alençon was summoned and came to stand by the bed, Charles shook his head, and said again, 'No, no, let my brother be fetched.'

'It is Navarre he wants,' Catherine murmured with dismay. 'Well, let him be brought. He and my younger son can act as witnesses for this document.'

Navarre came in fear and trembling. Under strict orders from the Queen Mother he was taken to the King's bedchamber not through the open passages or via the other Palace apartments, but up a secret staircase lined with arquebusiers. He trod with extreme caution, keeping a wary eye on the guards who accompanied him, half expecting at any moment that one might turn and stab him through the heart, or finish him off with a bullet in the head.

By the time he reached the King he could hardly believe he'd been spared, and almost fell to his knees at the foot of the bed in gratitude, so great had been the strain.

Catherine presented the dying King with a document to sign, one which placed the regency in her safe hands until Anjou arrived from Poland to take his rightful place on the throne. She insisted that Navarre and Alençon act as witnesses, and that they agree it had been drawn up at their request, and not hers.

Charles then called for Navarre to come close, whereupon he embraced him.

'Brother, you are losing a good friend.' Charles's voice was so feeble it was barely above a whisper, and he was obliged to pause frequently in order to catch his breath. 'Had I believed all that I was told, you would not be alive. But I always loved you. Do not trust—'

Catherine stepped hastily forward to interrupt. 'Do not say that!'

'Madame, I do say it, for it is the truth.' A fit of coughing took him and his nurse hurried forward to soothe him and wipe the blood and spittle from his mouth. But even in the hour of his death, Charles found the strength to rail against his mother, still determined to hold on to some small degree of independence.

He gathered his failing strength and again addressed Navarre. 'Believe me, brother, and love me. I trust in you alone to look after my wife and daughter. Pray God for me. Farewell. I rejoice that I leave no male child to wear the crown after me.'

And on these last words, poor mad Charles IX finally escaped his mother and found peace with his maker.

Before the end of the day Catherine dispatched a second messenger in the wake of the first, calling for her favourite son to come and claim his crown.

Part Five

ESCAPE

1574–1578

August 1574

Margot waited with something like dread for the arrival home of her brother, the King of Poland. Where once she had been flattered by his attention, now she felt only loathing and fear. Knowing the sorry state of their relationship, of his petty jealousies and the way he had always tried to control her, she could not imagine his becoming King of France would improve relations between them. On the contrary, she rather thought all the worst excesses of his nature would come to the fore once he held the reins of power in his hands.

Having learned of the death of his brother, Charles IX, from the Emperor Maximilian, whose messenger reached him before those of Catherine, he'd been so anxious to escape Poland that he'd apparently galloped off in the dead of night.

'Not only that, but he took with him the Polish crown jewels: pearls, rubies and diamonds,' Henriette said, savouring the telling of this convoluted tale to Margot.

'He's like a greedy jackdaw,' Margot scathingly remarked.

'Lost in the forests and pursued by the ambassadors of his court, Henri's men forced a poor woodcutter at sword point to lead them safely to the frontier.'

'He must have thought he was the hero in some romantic ballad.' The scorn she felt for her elder brother was all too evident in her tone.

Madame de Curton pursed her mouth in that disapproving way she had when one of her charges had displeased her. 'Why must Henri forever over-dramatize?'

They were once more travelling in Margot's coach, a capacious, handsome vehicle lined with beautiful yellow velvet trimmed with silver brocade; large enough to accommodate not only Madame, who was always with her, but her friend the Duchess of Nevers, the Duchess of Retz and Madame de Thorigny. The journey was again taking place in the heat of August, but this time she was not heading for Bayonne and a possible betrothal to a madman, but to Lyon to herald the arrival of a new King.

'And did the courtiers catch up with him?'

'Apparently so. They begged him to return to Krakow but Henri swore that he must first save France from the Huguenots, promising to return at the very first opportunity. All lies! Once back home, we all know that he will never set so much as a toe out of France ever again.'

'Am I the only one who mourns my brother's death?' Margot asked on a sigh.

Madame de Curton put an arm about her young mistress to hold her close, as she always did when this rebellious, over-affectionate girl was suffering. 'His little Queen still weeps for him.'

'Oh, Elisabeth is my dearest friend. I love her dearly and hope it will ever be so between us.'

'Charles is in a better place now, my lady. Do not weep for him. The burden of his distress and pain has been lifted.'

'And he is safe from my mother at last,' Margot agreed, drying her eyes with a silk kerchief, a useful fashion accessory imported from Italy by Catherine when she first came to France as a young girl. 'I cannot see Henri bowing to our mother's whims, as did poor Charles. The battle of wills between those two might prove to be most entertaining,' she said, smiling suddenly with mischievous delight.

'The Queen Mother will ever indulge his fantasies.'

'My mother has been making herself quite ill, continually celebrating this momentous event by gorging herself on all sorts of delicacies, like cockscombs and artichokes, which do her no good at all.'

'It is the rheumatism which plagues Her Majesty that drives her to such folly, my lady. Have some sympathy for her ageing years.'

'Why do you always see the best in everyone, Lottie?'

'Only where appropriate, my lady. I see no malice in overeating. The Queen Mother harms only herself with such indulgence.'

'Well, that makes a change. Her malice has done enough harm already.'

'The weakness of over-indulgence is in us all,' scolded Madame, ever the stern governess.

'It is certainly a fault in Henri, together with indolence and pure selfishness,' Margot sharply responded. She had no intention of defending her own weakness, although she was only too aware of the silent accusation that she had indulged in an inappropriate love affair, one which had resulted in dreadful consequences.

She met the Duchess of Nevers' troubled gaze with a poignant smile, both ladies still haunted by the tragic loss of their lovers. Anxious to protect her friend from further scolding, Henriette leaned forward to continue her story in hushed tones.

'But having left Poland, the King did not rush straight home to France. Tales have reached us of His Majesty being feted in Vienna, and while in Venice, when he should have been attending a state banquet held at great expense for his benefit, he was lounging in a gondola decked out in gold. The rumour-mongers have it that he roamed abroad at night visiting certain ladies of disrepute, and that he spent his time buying perfume and jewels, which he showered upon everyone he met, along with cash and other gifts. He is said to have spent thousands of écus and is already in debt.'

Margot rolled her eyes heavenwards in despair. 'Can France afford such munificence? It is long past time he came home and took up his responsibilities, before he bankrupts us all. Why has he delayed so long? It is months since Charles died.'

'Because he likes the idea of the glory of a crown, but not the work or the responsibility that goes with it,' Madame dryly remarked. 'Yet he is here now, and you will see him soon enough, my lady. The Queen Mother is eager to welcome home her . . .'

'. . . favourite son and see him fulfil her long-held ambition for him,' Margot finished for her, a bitterness creeping into her voice. 'I know that full well. Would I not make a better king than all of my brothers?'

'Indeed you would, my lady, were it not for Salic law.'

'And a better quean than the King of Poland,' giggled Henriette.

The tension in the carriage eased as all the ladies indulged in merry laughter at the joke.

Margot said, 'Come, we must not be too gloomy. There will be balls for us to enjoy in Lyon, Henriette; parties and entertainments. Perhaps the bitterness and the rivalry will end, and we can be free again, free to enjoy a new reign, a new beginning. Life may take a turn for the better, do you not think?'

Her friend looked doubtful. 'We can but hope so.'

Madame de Curton said, 'Do not forget, my lady, that the King's favourites – his mignons, including Louis du Guast – will also be present, and if he can find some way to make trouble for you, he will.'

Margot looked at her trusted governess, wide-eyed with dismay, all her natural frivolity dissolving in a second. 'Oh, I had quite forgotten du Guast. Then perhaps we should urge Henri to stay away forever.'

The reunion between mother and son took place at Bourgoin near Lyon on 5 September. It was a most moving scene, with both parties weeping and playing up to the high drama of the occasion, even if the courtiers watched with a more jaundiced eye. Henri threw himself into his mother's arms in an extravagant display of affection, before kneeling to kiss her hand.

'I owe my life to you, Madame and most dear mother, and now, moreover, liberty and my crown.'

Catherine had dispatched dozens of letters and money to her son in the months he had taken meandering home from Poland via Habsburg and Italy, a route she had recommended for safety's sake. Henri must have found several missives waiting for him when he'd arrived at the home of the Emperor, and again in Venice, but not troubled to reply to any of them, no doubt being far too busy enjoying himself. Yet so pleased was she to have him in her arms at last, she could not bring herself to chastise him.

'I have so long waited for your homecoming, my son. I know how well you loved Venice with its mystical, artistic ambience, which does not surprise me. You have always been more Italian than French, taking after your mother rather than your father. But now you are home at last.'

'There is no country in the world to equal this Kingdom.'

'My one consolation is to see you here in good health. You are my life, my all. If I were to lose you I would wish to be buried alive.'

Henri took a step back, his patience for effusive displays

of maternal affection being strictly limited. Catherine smiled affectionately at her darling boy and summoned the Duke of Alençon and the King of Navarre to present them formally to the new King of France.

'Sire,' she said, addressing her son in low, soft tones, 'pray deign to receive these two prisoners, whom I now resign to Your Majesty's pleasure. I have informed you of their caprices and misdemeanours. It is for Your Majesty to decree their fate.'

They had been made to ride in the Queen Mother's coach like naughty schoolboys – although even that had made a welcome change from being cooped up and constantly under guard, either in Vincennes or in the Louvre where their rooms were searched every day.

Catherine had done a great deal more than that. Following the princes' pardon, grudgingly given, the security surrounding them had been strengthened. The windows of the Louvre, all strongly barred, looked out over the river, taunting them with the reality of their confinement. It had been made clear to the King of Navarre and Alençon that they would not be permitted to leave without a pass signed by the Queen Mother, which she had no intention of ever granting. Swiss guards were posted at every entrance, and any visitor who passed over the drawbridge must sign their name upon a list, which was delivered to Catherine each morning by the officer in command. She even insisted that both ends of the Place du Louvre be walled up, leaving only one exit across the Rue des Poulies.

They had been constantly on the alert listening for the approach of her heavy footsteps, the sound of her master key turning in the lock. At any hour of the day or night she would march through Margot's apartments, then on to those of Navarre and her youngest son, simply to reassure herself that they were not engaged in secret plotting.

'By the help of God I know how to keep this kingdom safe and tranquil, and to rule all so well, that on the arrival of my son the King he will find everyone obedient and peaceable.'

They had had no choice but to be peaceable, Navarre thought, locked up as they all were with nothing to distract them. Now Alençon eagerly grasped his brother's proffered hand, and burst forth with a litany of excuses to justify the enterprise – how they had been shamefully treated by Charles, forced, to their very great regret, to plot an escape for their own protection.

'But since his death, we have no other desire than to live and die your faithful subjects.'

'Preferably live,' added Navarre with dry good humour.

Henri pretended to laugh at the jest, and with carefully contrived graciousness embraced both princes. 'Be it so, *mes frères*; the past is forgotten. I restore you both to liberty, and ask only in return that you will give me your love and fealty. If you cannot love me, love yourselves sufficiently to abstain from plots and intrigues which cannot but harm you, and which are unworthy of the dignity of your birth.'

Catherine stood fanning herself in the heat, watching this display of filial affection with pleasure. She did so like to see family unity.

It was Margot's turn next to step forward and greet the King her brother, a chill of foreboding in her heart, remembering how, as the Duke of Anjou, Henri had made her life a complete misery by allowing his favourites to manufacture malicious lies against her. She thought he looked thinner than ever, deathly pale, and the fistula on his eye seemed worse. There was something in the way he stared so fixedly at her which caused all the fear she had so carefully suppressed to surge up again, block her throat and threaten to choke her. For once Margot was rendered speechless, quite unable to utter a single word of her practised welcome.

The occasion was made worse by the fact that not far behind him stood his favourites: Villequier, Cheverny, and the notorious du Guast. Margot guessed they had kept him fully informed of her own part in the La Molle scandal, of her alleged plotting against her beloved brother Charles, even though that was untrue. She had wanted only for her husband's safe return to his homeland, and some independence for Alençon. She had made it plain from the start that she would do nothing to hurt Charles.

Henri embraced her warmly, murmuring extravagant compliments over her appearance and beauty, and, despite the stifling heat, a shiver of fear trickled down her spine at his touch, which she had great difficulty in suppressing. She could tell by the shocked expression that crossed her governess's face that she had momentarily allowed these emotions to show. She could only pray that Henri, in his self-absorbed arrogance, had not noticed.

Fortunately, he'd half turned away to greet his erstwhile mistress, Mademoiselle de Chateauneuf, who remained stubbornly single, and seemed still to be making sheep's eyes at him, constantly giving him longing looks. Henri offered the lady his hand with a curl of distaste to his lips, paying her scant attention as he glanced over her head, seeking another, more beloved face.

'Where is Marie, my Princess and future Queen?'

Catherine hastily stepped forward to explain that the Princess de Condé, whom Henri most longed to see, was too far advanced in her pregnancy to risk the journey.

'She eagerly awaits your arrival in Paris,' his mother assured him.

It did not seem to trouble him in the slightest that his intended bride was still married, and carrying her husband's child.

Margot, not knowing whether she'd been granted leave to depart, and longing to do so, cast an anguished glance towards her own husband. Navarre answered her with a broad wink, almost causing her to disgrace herself yet again, this time by giggling. It was strange how they had come to be on such good terms, yet friends were rare and much needed in this court.

Margot's marriage with the King of Navarre may not have been a love match, yet he had proved remarkably easy to live with. Accustomed as she was to the mad melodramas and machinations of her siblings, this even-tempered, pragmatic man seemed benign by comparison. He abhorred cruelty and intolerance, possessed a quick wit, liked to play the fool and yet possessed more intelligence than he was given credit for. Margot remained loyal to him.

Nor did he ask anything more of her than this. He certainly did not demand fidelity, but then he wasn't capable of that himself. He was as fickle now as he had been as a young boy chasing his first love. Nevertheless, Margot had allowed him back into her bed. An heir was still needed, and she didn't have a lover at present, a fact she noted with some regret.

She had lost Guise, her one and only true love, and now La Molle, who had at least amused and entertained her. Yet she was a woman who needed affection, not an empty bed and a lonely heart. She glanced about her at the handsome young courtiers, wondering if there were any likely candidate amongst them. She might ask Henriette for a recommendation.

The following day Henri entered Lyon to rousing cheers from an enthusiastic crowd. His entourage was meant to impress. He rode in a magnificent chariot draped with black velvet, the Queen Mother at his right hand, Alençon opposite. The King and Queen of Navarre rode on horseback beside the carriage, followed by the three Cardinals of Bourbon, Guise, and Lorraine, and the usual train of courtiers. The entire royal party were dressed in robes of violet satin and velvet, being in semi-mourning, a display of such splendour the local people would never forget.

Henri endured the procession and celebrations, the seemingly endless prayers and speeches with a modicum of good grace, but it was the first and last public function he deigned to carry out while in Lyon. He ate sparingly at the banquets as his digestion was not good, and like Charles before him drank nothing but water.

The abscess under his arm was troubling him greatly and he'd developed another sore on his foot, but he told no one of these nuisances, nor how a nightly cough plagued him. He had the intelligence to realize that a king, particularly one not yet crowned, must show no sign of weakness, nor any of the health problems that had so beset all of the Valois brothers.

For that reason he avoided excessive exercise such as tennis, riding or hunting, tournaments or jousts, and his earlier passion for military glory was now quite dead.

Instead, he spent his mornings in bed and his afternoons reclining in a golden barge on the Rhone with his favourites. Henri intended to enjoy some lazy days in the sun, as he so liked to be warm. He had done no work of kingship in Poland, and although he intended this to change once he reached Paris and took on the crown of his beloved France, he felt he deserved a little respite for the exile he'd been forced to endure in what he had considered to be a cold, bleak land.

Catherine looked on with fond affection. She was more than content to allow his indulgences while she maintained a firm hold on the reins of power, as she had done throughout her years as regent for Charles. She was filled with pride in her certainty that Henri would make a fine king, and happy to spend her days engaged in state business and planning his coronation while he rested. Nevertheless, she carefully outlined what would be expected of him, and how he should conduct himself: dealing with matters of state in the morning, eating at set hours, taking regular exercise and spending time with his family every afternoon. She warned him always to make himself available to the people, to hear their petitions personally and allow them access to his person.

Henri had no intention of doing any such thing. He disliked having the common people leering at him, or the noble gentlemen of court drawing their chairs too close when he dined, much preferring they keep their distance and leave him in peace. If he felt moved to perform any paperwork at all while he rested in Lyon, it was to rearrange the regulations and ceremonial for how court life must be lived in future. Henri would never allow himself to be under her thumb as Charles had been.

'You can do everything,' she told him. 'But you must have the will.'

She paid little heed to the young ambitious men who gathered about him, thinking them vain and foolish, fops and dandies all, failing to credit them with the intelligence to direct or influence the King. She did not take them seriously, or anticipate their ever having any actual control over affairs of state. Nor did she appreciate that a day might come when this vain, capricious son of hers might ever consider her a hindrance. How could he possibly not need her, after all she had done in his name?

Margot dazzled the court, as always, when she opened the dancing at the first ball, partnered by her brother Alençon. She was almost twenty-two years old and still at the height of her beauty. Lord North, an emissary sent by Elizabeth of England to greet the new King Henri Trois, was enchanted by her, as was a certain gallant among the courtiers.

Louis de Clermont, Seigneur de Bussy d'Amboise, known simply as Bussy, fell head over heels in love with the Queen of Navarre at first sight. Before the evening was over, he had danced several pavans and galliards with her, and Margot was equally enraptured by him. To have a man's adoring gaze upon her made her feel gloriously happy, and did she not deserve a little happiness after all the recent trauma?

'Is he not the most handsome man you ever saw?' she whispered to her dear friend, Henriette. 'Who is he?'

'He comes from a noble family. I believe his great-uncle is a cardinal. But take care,' warned the Duchess. 'An elegant dandy he may be, but he is also an insolent rascal with a reputation for daring duels and amorous conquests. A scandal is already circulating concerning a quarrel over a lady, and how he insisted on calling his rival out. The King forbade the duel but Bussy defied His Majesty and arrived with two score of gentlemen as support. Fortunately, he suffered nothing more serious than a wounded finger, but that behaviour is typical of him. He is highly audacious and impudent.'

Margot laughed. 'I do so like a man with the power of his own convictions, one not afraid to take a risk.'

Henriette smiled at her friend, even as she gently scolded her. 'He is hugely ambitious, holds the keys of your brother's coffers, and helps himself to funds if he has an account to settle, or so I am told. Take care, my lady. Remember what happened the last time you were tempted into a little light dalliance.'

'Am I expected to live like a nun, or a chaste obedient housewife, while my husband spreads his favours as he chooses? I think not. I deserve a little fun too, and to find love where I can. Or at least enjoy a mild flirtation.'

'Flirt as much as you wish in public, Margot, but do not allow yourself ever to be alone with him. Promise?'

'I promise I will never be alone with him,' Margot parroted, then quietly added, 'at least until I am more sure of him.'

A frown puckered the Duchess's brow. 'Tread warily. I want no harm to come to you, dear friend.'

'What possible harm can come of a little mild flirtation?'

One Sunday afternoon in early September, Margot decided on a visit to the convent of St Pierre of Lyon. It was said to be beautiful, and as one Mademoiselle de Montigny had an aunt there, the necessary admission could easily be gained. The genteel nuns, some incarcerated there by heartless families, were always appreciative of company from the nobility.

There would be seven in the party: Margot herself, attended by the said Mademoiselle de Montigny; the Duchess of Nevers; Madame de Rais, and two maids of honour, plus her lady of the bedchamber, Madame de Curton. The coach was somewhat crowded but as the vehicle left the courtyard, two of Henri's favourites, de Liancourt and Camille, sprang on to the step. Clinging on as best they could, they merrily asked if they too could come along to see the handsome nuns, and the ladies laughingly agreed.

On their arrival, Margot ordered the driver to wait with the coach in the square where various gentlemen of the court had lodgings, while they went to view the convent.

They had no sooner gone than Henri's coach drew up. The King was ostensibly visiting a sick friend, but it was no coincidence that he arrived in the same square only moments after Margot and her ladies. He had with him several gentlemen, including the King of Navarre.

'Is that not your wife's coach?' Henri asked.

There was no denying it, as the Queen's gilt carriage was easily recognizable with its yellow velvet lining edged with silver. Navarre said nothing.

'And is that not the house where her lover lodges? I swear she has gone to see him.' To prove his point, Henri sent one of his men to check if she was indeed there.

Sadly he was disappointed, as his emissary found no sign of either Margot or her alleged lover. Turning again to Navarre, he said, 'The birds have flown.'

When Margot arrived back at court, having enjoyed a most pleasant afternoon with the ladies of the convent and entirely ignorant of what had taken place, she called upon her husband, as was her custom.

Navarre met her with a rueful smile. 'I am ordered to tell you that you must go and see the Queen your mother. But I promise you will not be very well pleased.'

'Why will I not? What have I done now?'

'It is better if I say nothing, but be assured, Margot, I do not give the least credit to the story, which I believe was fabricated in order to stir up a difference between us, and spoil the friendship between your brother and me.'

Annoyed that he would not tell her what was happening, Margot flounced off. As she reached the door of her mother's apartment, she found Guise waiting for her. Taking her firmly by the arm, he drew her to one side.

'The Queen Mother is in a terrible rage, I would strongly advise you not see her today.'

'But why? What has happened? What is it I'm supposed to have done?'

Guise quickly explained how the King had followed her to the square at the suggestion of du Guast, and accused her of visiting a lover. 'He means to damage you, as he did before.'

Margot was appalled. 'But that is not true. I am innocent. I was visiting the convent with my ladies. I must see the Queen Mother and explain.'

'It would not be wise. I urge you not to do so.'

'But I must!'

Guise put his hands gently upon her waist and kissed her brow. 'May God go with you then, my love.'

Once more Margot was obliged to face the full power of her mother's wrath. She recalled all the times in the past when the Queen Mother had railed at her, had pinched her or slapped her about the head, and on that awful occasion assaulting her with both feet and fists, ripping her nightgown to shreds for having discovered her with Guise. Her brother Charles too had frequently attacked her when in a fit of rage, and had near killed her on that occasion. Margot shivered now at the memory. Could that happen again, even though she was a married woman, and the punishment, were she to deserve such, should rightly come from her own husband?

Navarre and Guise's warning proved to be entirely justified. Margot had barely entered the Queen Mother's privy chamber when Catherine flew into a furious temper, shouting at her and accusing her of all manner of wanton behaviour. Margot defended herself as stoutly as she could, calmly explaining the purpose of her outing, and listing the names of those who had accompanied her.

'These ladies were with me the entire afternoon. Ask Mademoiselle de Montigny; her aunt lives at the convent and helped us gain access. Ask Liancourt and Camille, who are the King's servants. They begged a lift and stayed with us, joining in the fun.'

Catherine refused to believe her. Her favourite son had given her the facts as he saw them, and she would far rather take his word than that of a wayward daughter.

'Why do you see only wrong in me?' Margot cried, her heart starting to pound.

'How can we not when your younger brother is proving to be at odds with the King, and a threat to his crown? And you and Navarre are his supporters in this.'

'You read too much into that, Madame. How can a perfectly normal friendship be seen as a threat to the King?'

'You know perfectly well why,' Catherine roared, her rage now incandescent. 'The two princes were fortunate to keep their heads.'

Margot swallowed, realizing she trod on dangerous ground, but could not allow this to go entirely unchallenged. 'Yet you declared them innocent of such a calumny, Madame. This is not the first time Henri has done me ill service by listening to the malice of his favourites. He finds faults in others when he would more likely find them in himself. Why do you listen to such nonsense? Why do you believe every corrupt word he utters?'

The Queen Mother was incensed by this criticism not only of her own good judgement, but also of her precious darling. 'I have my spies who keep me fully informed of all that goes on in this court. Think you I am not aware of your flirting with a certain gallant? My *valet de chambre* saw you in that square, visiting with your lover. I have his word on it.'

Margot knew that she lied, that she was covering up for Henri. 'Then you have been misinformed, Madame. I was not there! I was in the convent, visiting with the nuns, as I have already explained.'

Arguing her case, however just and right it might seem, only served to inflame the Queen Mother's rage all the more. Moreover, Margot was painfully aware that every word of their quarrel was clearly audible by her *Escadron Volant*, whose ears would be wagging at the other side of the partition.

Realizing it was hopeless to defend herself further, and still fearing her mother might physically attack her, Margot fled from the privy chamber almost in tears, back to her husband's apartment.

Navarre was waiting for her, anxiously pacing the floor. As soon as she entered, he went to take her hands. 'Was it not just as I told you?' he laughed, and then seeing her face, softened his tone. 'Do not grieve or torment yourself. I'm sure it can all be put to right. Liancourt and Camille will be at the King's *coucher* and will inform him of the wrong that he has done you.' Henry put his arms about his wife, awkwardly patting her shoulder as if to offer comfort. 'I am sure that tomorrow the Queen Mother will receive you in a very different manner.'

'I have suffered too gross an affront in public to forgive those who caused it, by which I mean du Guast, and the King my brother. Nor can I tolerate this vicious attempt to set us against each other.'

Navarre grinned. 'Ah, but, God be thanked, they have failed in that, have they not?'

She smiled then, feeling the warmth emanating from him which made him so very likeable, despite his failings as a husband. 'I believe any thanks are owed more to your amiable disposition than any divine intervention. However, we must interpret this little episode as a warning to be on our guard against the King's stratagems. I'm sure he means to bring about dissension between yourself and Alençon by causing a rupture between you and me.'

As if on cue, the Duke of Alençon at that moment entered, and Margot ran to grasp her younger brother's hands and bring him over to Navarre. 'I wish you two to renew your friendship, to swear you will allow none to cause friction between you.'

Laughing off her anxiety, they shook hands and slapped each other on the back in brotherly fashion, quite at ease in their comradeship.

'There,' Margot said, well pleased as she kissed each of them on the cheek. 'No one can do us harm so long as we remain united.'

Satisfied perhaps that he'd successfully stirred up trouble, and despite the Queen Mother's continued disapproval, Margot's other brother Henri turned contrite, perversely wishing to smooth relations between them.

'I am more than ready to offer you a thousand apologies, dear sister. I never believed a single word against you.'

He was positively effusive in his apologies and excuses, blaming others, showering affection and goodwill upon her with not a shred of sincerity, quite unable to recognize his own hypocrisy. First he'd accused her of seeing a lover, and now claimed he'd never believed in her guilt.

The experience of this superficially trivial incident chilled Margot to the bone and increased her fear of the new King. How could she ever trust him?

A day or two later Catherine was shattered to receive the tragic news that the Princess de Condé had died. She had successfully given birth to a healthy daughter, but Marie herself had never properly recovered from the birth. There had been rumours that the child might be Henri's, but generally it was believed that their love affair had been entirely platonic and romantic. Some even doubted her son's ability to produce an heir. Catherine hoped and prayed they were wrong. But now, in view of the hopes he had built up for their eventual marriage, she was at a loss to know how to break these dreadful tidings to her precious boy.

He spent every free hour writing passionate letters to his beloved, had stubbornly refused to accept the old spinster bride they'd planned for him in Poland, remaining faithful to his darling Princess. He constantly reaffirmed his promise of the crown of France, begging her to take the necessary steps to obtain a divorce the moment her accouchement was passed.

Now that romantic dream was as dust.

Fearing his reaction, Catherine left the letter strewn upon his writing table amongst his other messages. Later that day, and quite by chance, Henri picked it up, and read it without warning. He cried out in shock then fell to the ground in a dead faint.

Catherine was immediately called as his *mignons* carried the King to his bed where he lay for days in a stupor, refusing either to eat or drink. Much to her alarm, his condition deteriorated into a high fever as he gave himself up to grief.

Consequently, the court remained in Lyon for two more months until Henri was sufficiently recovered to sail down the Rhone to Avignon. Despite his mother's exhortations that he should seek an alternative bride, he remained in deep mourning which manifested itself in another bout of religious fervour. He joined the brotherhood of the *battus*, who indulged in ascetic extravagances. They dressed in sackcloth, wore masks, walked barefoot in torch-light processions and thrashed themselves with a whip or switch.

Henri had first been inspired to take part in these dangerous habits years ago by one of his favourites, Lignerolles, to whom Catherine had taken a dislike and who had been found mysteriously murdered in a dark alley quite close to the Louvre. Now he again eagerly adopted these practices, hung a rosary of small ivory skulls on his girdle, and even had tiny skulls embroidered in white silk on to his funereal black clothes, shoes and stockings. He prayed constantly to the Blessed Virgin for his beloved Princess de Condé's soul and bullied and persuaded others among the courtiers to join him in his pilgrimages.

Navarre refused to take the matter seriously. 'This show of penitence is more to my taste when viewed at a distance rather than close at hand,' he joked.

Among these devoted followers was Guise's uncle, the Cardinal of Lorraine, anxious not to be left out of the pious displays. Tragically, walking barefoot through the streets on a snowy night in December brought on a chill which turned to pneumonia, and a few days later he died. That night there was a terrible storm. The Jesuits claimed that *le tigre de la France* had died a fine death, taken from a nation who had never properly appreciated him, and would go straight to heaven. The Huguenots said the storm proved the witches were holding their Sabbath, and had come to spirit away his soul to hell.

Catherine privately gloried in the death of her hated rival. 'Now we shall have peace,' she said, as she calmly sat down to dinner that night. 'The Cardinal de Lorraine is dead and he was the one person that prevented it.' Perhaps realizing that a little caution would be wise, she added, 'He was a great prelate and a wise one, and France – and ourselves, also – have suffered a grievous loss in his death.'

But beneath her breath, she added, 'Today has died the wickedest of men,' and, lifting her glass to her lips, she suddenly began to tremble; the glass fell from her hand to smash on the tiled floor.

'*Jésus!*' she cried. 'There is Monsieur le Cardinal! I see him, I see him before me.'

Margot felt the hairs rise at the nape of her neck, as they had done many times before when faced with evidence of what seemed like her mother's second sight.

Seconds later Catherine pulled herself together, laughing the whole thing off by saying that she'd seen the good man on his way to Paradise. But she suffered nightmares that night and, like her daughter, those who had witnessed the Queen Mother experiencing visions on previous occasions did not hesitate to believe that she saw him in very truth.

Henri ignored his mother's efforts to find him a bride, having set his heart on Louise de Vaudémont whom he had met at Nancy when returning from Poland. Although not beautiful, her figure was slender and he'd found her to be gentle, elegant and kind. Most of all she reminded him of his adored Marie. He'd discovered that the young girl was not treated well by her family, her father being somewhat neglectful and her stepmother unkind. She'd spent her days alone in prayer, reading and needlework, and Henri had felt great pity for the way she was persecuted. He'd generously tried to rectify this neglect by asking her to dance, and taking her with him whenever he drove about the countryside. Now he announced his intention of marrying her.

Catherine was appalled. 'But she is of the House of Lorraine, a girl of no consequence who possesses no fortune.'

'Nonetheless I have already dispatched the Marquis du Guast with a request for her hand.'

The matter, it seemed, was settled, and Catherine was once more obliged to accept the inevitable. Much to her dismay, her son already seemed to be exercising his new power and independence rather sooner than she had expected.

Henri was crowned at Rheims, but it was not the joyous occasion he had hoped for. The Huguenots were making substantial gains under the leadership of Damville. On his way to his coronation, those whose towns were under siege by the King's armies lined the streets to curse him, shouting that he would not murder them as he had the Admiral, which made Henri shudder with foreboding.

On the day itself he found the ceremony so long and tiring that Henri demanded constant rests. He complained the crown was too heavy and hurt his head, and during the sacrament it almost fell off, which was looked upon as a bad omen – as was the fact that those upon whom he'd touched for the King's evil were not in fact cured of their ills. But then he had barely been able to bring himself to lay so much as a fingertip upon their unclean skin.

The following day was his wedding day, and Henri welcomed this with much greater enthusiasm. He insisted upon dressing Princess Louise's hair himself, prinking her gown and making up her face, spending so many hours on the task that the service had to be postponed until late evening.

Later the people would chant, 'Henri de Valois, King of Poland and France by the grace of God and his mother, concierge of the Louvre, hairdresser-in-ordinary to his wife!'

The decision to marry had been made so quickly that there had been no time to collect the usual gifts of money from the populous, although he meant to make up for this lack later. The state of the treasury was parlous but his mother had spared nothing in providing a magnificent state occasion. Neither had Henri exercised any thrift when designing the gown and jewels for his young bride, or for himself and his favourites. He'd handed over vast sums of money to du Guast for this very purpose.

He meant to squeeze yet more taxes out of the people in order to pay for it all, and for the pageants, balls and masques he would hold.

Madame de Curton, Margot's faithful old governess and lady of her bedchamber, came to her one morning and asked if she had any livres in her purse, so that she might purchase some new silks. 'We are quite out of several colours and the ladies are working on new hassocks for the Priory. I wouldn't trouble you, my lady, only the merchant from whom I attempted to order them has politely pointed out that a long standing account for fabrics, garments, hats, ribbons and gewgaws has still not been settled since the wedding and coronation, which was many months ago.'

Margot shook her head in despair. 'I learned the other day, Lottie, that the treasury is so low the King cannot afford to journey home to the capital. The people are saying he cannot even afford the price of a dinner.'

'It is certainly true that the court pages have been obliged to pawn their cloaks in order to fund their own travel expenses.'

Margot let out a growl of fury. 'Yet Henri hands out gold to his favourite, du Guast, along with fat bishoprics which the odious man sells on at a profit. How have we come to this? I have asked my mother time and again for money to pay my ladies-in-waiting but she fobs me off with endless excuses.'

'I understand Her Majesty is seeking a loan, and you needn't fret about my own wages, my lady. My needs are small. A few silks are all we require.'

'Oh, Lottie, but you shouldn't have to come begging for them like this,' Margot railed, riffling through her purse and pockets in the hope of finding a few coins. 'But what can you expect when a knave such as my brother occupies the throne? He is taxing the people so much they can barely afford to eat. Yet he frizzes his hair, plays with his lap dogs, parrots and monkeys, enjoying his frivolities so much he can barely find the time to attend council meetings.'

Sufficient funds were finally collected to enable the court to return to Paris, but even as they arrived they learned that Margot's sister, Claude, the Duchess of Lorraine, had died. Catherine could hardly bear it and took to her bed. Claude had never been her favourite, but visiting this happy family, her daughter and grandchildren, had been one of the few joys in her life. Now she was gone, yet another lost child.

Margot, too, was distraught, for she had ever been fond of her sister, remembering how Claude had wept and tried to warn her of the St Bartholemew's Eve massacre. She would be sorely missed.

As if being plunged once more into mourning was not enough hardship, yet another malicious rumour began circulating that one of Margot's ladies, a Madame de Thorigny, was said to be exercising an evil influence over her. The King issued an order that she must be dismissed.

'What sort of influence? What is it he accuses her of?' Margot wearily asked Madame de Curton when her companion broke this unpleasant news to her.

'I do not know how to explain it, or what words to use,' the poor woman said, her cheeks flushed bright crimson with embarrassment.

Margot sighed. 'Say it quickly, Lottie. However unpleasant, be assured no blame will be attached to you. I know the root of this mischief.'

'Well, they are saying that you and she are engaged in . . . are excessively fond of . . . that you hold a particular affection for her and . . .'

'Stop!' Margot was aghast. 'Are you saying that I am now being accused of having a love affair with one of my ladies-in-waiting?' She did not need to wait for Lottie's nod of agreement; she saw the answer in the flame of scarlet in the old woman's usually pale, faded cheeks.

Margot burst out laughing. It seemed essential to see the funny side, or she might well go mad with fury. But really it was no laughing matter, as she could not bear to lose such a good friend. She went at once to her husband, but sadly, on this occasion, he was unable to help her.

'I agree it is all a nonsense, Margot, but Henri is the King. If he says that I must dismiss Madame de Thorigny, then I have no choice but to obey. Let us be glad that is all he demands. Be thankful it is no worse. If du Guast ever convinces him we are plotting against him, then he'll be calling for our heads.'

It was not a comforting prospect.

Henri watched with sullen disapproval the strong friendship that was evident between the King and Queen of Navarre and the Duke of Alençon. He saw it as an attempt to undermine his power, was deeply afraid of where it might lead, and therefore sought any opportunity to divide the parties.

'Your mother suggests we use Madame de Sauves,' du Guast quietly remarked one day, as he massaged his master's elegant hands with perfumed oil.

'My sister is the cement that holds it together,' Henri railed. 'I hoped to create a coolness between Margot and Navarre; then we might start to get somewhere. Unfortunately, they remain good friends, not in the least jealous of each other.'

Du Guast's lips curled upward in the parody of a smile. 'I could urge Madame de Sauves to strive harder at creating jealousy and dispute between this triumvirate, to convince Navarre that his wife is not only jealous, but plotting against him. Neither Navarre nor Alençon have been faithful to the lady. We need her to inflame their passions afresh so that they can think of nought but her, desire her to such an extent that they become violently jealous of each other. Trust me, Sire, I will speak to de Sauves, and ensure she uses every artifice at her disposal to bring this about.'

'Oh, I do trust you, Louis, with my life. Pray stroke my head, I swear it aches from all of this worry.' And Henri lay prostrate on the bed while his favourite tended to his needs.

Henry of Navarre lay contentedly in his bed, his mistress, Charlotte de Sauves, curled seductively by his side. He met her each morning at the Queen Mother's *lever*, due to her role as a lady of the robes, and spent as much of the rest of the day with her as he possibly could, only returning to the matrimonial bed very late at night.

The courtesan was draped across the bed in a silk *robe de chambre* that was very nearly transparent, and in Henry's view she looked absolutely delicious. He kissed her full generous mouth and told her so.

'How would I tolerate being penned up in this royal prison were it not for you? For years I have barely been allowed to go out, hunt, joust, or take part in any of the pursuits which keep a gentleman amused without a guard by my side. And even now that the King has granted me liberty, or so he claims, I am still closely watched.' He grinned wickedly. 'But here, with you, I am not under scrutiny. With you I can be myself.' He fondled her breasts, the peak of each nipple excitingly erect beneath her filmy gown.

Charlotte arched her back, moaning softly as he pushed the thin fabric aside and began to caress the soft mound of her belly and the delightful triangle beneath. She nipped at his shoulder with her pretty teeth, raked her fingernails across his back as he mounted her, and gasped with joy as he penetrated her yet again.

His energy always astonished her, even if his foreplay might leave something to be desired. Guise was a more imaginative lover, but his visits were rare. He too had a wife, and still yearned after Queen Margot, much to Charlotte's irritation.

Now, as she bucked and churned beneath Margot's husband, attempting to ignite him to greater passion, as du Guast had instructed, she gazed up at the ceiling, idly tracing the swirling patterns painted in Italian fashion on the wooden beams. Even as she gave a sterling performance in the art of love, Charlotte was secretly bored, mentally assessing how soon she could escape and if she could lure Guise into her bed later.

Yet she smiled to herself, knowing that so skilled was she in artifice that Navarre believed she preferred him above all her other lovers, and never felt neglected. Men were so easy to please, so long as you had the sophistication and the experience.

His hands were cupping her buttocks, smoothing up and down the silky planes of her back, lifting her against him. She offered him her mouth and he claimed it with almost brutal force, as if all the demons of hell were clamouring for his soul. The poor man was highly charged with frustration, having been penned up, as he called it, so long between these four walls.

She sighed with a mix of relief and pleasure when finally he reached his climax, shifted his weight from her and lay sweating by her side.

'Does your darling wife give you half so much pleasure?' Charlotte teased, and Navarre gave a throaty chuckle.

'I never compare my women. They all have their own individual charms.'

Charlotte rolled over on to her side, pretending to pout as she trailed a finger down his naked chest. 'Are you saying that you have other mistresses, besides me? How ungallant! Tell me, I want to know.'

'If I have, they would never match your fire, my sweet. There, does that satisfy you? And do not you also have other lovers? Who do you lie with, my brother-in-law?'

Charlotte languorously rose from the bed and went over to admire her reflection in the Venetian looking glass, her gown slipping from her silken shoulders. She tweaked a curl into place, smoothed a caressing hand over the firmness of her breasts, the trim line of her slender body. 'Perhaps I prefer him to you? What do you say to that?' She pivoted on her heel, swirling about to cast him a teasing glance and, with a rumble of barely restrained fury, Navarre reached out, grabbed the hem of her gown and dragged her squealing back into bed.

'You vixen, I hate to be bested, but then the Duke is a friend, so I will forgive him.'

Charlotte almost ground her teeth in fury, even as she smiled. Why was he not even the slightest bit jealous of the time she spent with Alençon? The King of Navarre was far too casual in his approach to love, and she had been instructed that it was her task to change that in him.

'It does not surprise me if you feel the need to have other women in your bed, as your wife neglects you shamefully. Not only that, but she cuckolds you with her many lovers.'

Navarre laughed, stretching his limbs, feeling relaxed and sated. 'Not so many as her enemies claim, and I have no objection to Margot finding pleasure and affection where she will. As do I.'

De Sauves gazed at him out of wide innocent eyes. 'And you do not even mind that she betrays your confidences, that she tells all your business to her brother the King?'

Navarre became very still. 'What are you saying?'

Charlotte put a delicate hand to her mouth in feigned dismay. 'Oh, dear, perhaps I have spoken out of turn.'

'How do you know this?'

'I'm sorry, but the ladies of the robe do so love to chatter. Word gets about.'

'The entire court is a hothouse of gossip,' Navarre growled. 'What is it they are saying?'

'That Queen Margot is duplicitous and has betrayed all your private business, your *amourettes*, your plans for the future and hopes of returning to your homeland. She is very much in her brother's pocket.'

Navarre's eyes narrowed, trying to follow this, which didn't sound at all like his wife. 'Nonsense, Margot has no fondness for the King.'

'But he holds sway over her. Are you quite certain you can trust her?'

Seeing the doubt in his face Charlotte at once burst into tears.

'Oh, dear, it is all because she is jealous of me, isn't it? She told me that you no longer love me, that she means to poison your mind against me. I believe she wants to oust me from your life, and I swear I could not bear it if she succeeded.'

Navarre, ever the perfect knight who hated to see a woman cry, was devastated to see his delightful mistress so upset, and must needs console her and make love to her all over again.

But he thought a good deal on what she had told him, and as she repeated the claim each and every time they met over the next few days, he began to think that there might well be some truth in the rumour after all. Certainly no harm would be done by exercising a little more caution.

Margot was alarmed to discover that, quite out of the blue, her husband suddenly stopped speaking to her. He became distant and reserved. Instead of being his usual open and friendly self, happily confiding his conquests to her as if with a much-loved sister, he began studiously to avoid her company. He stopped coming to her bed, which infuriated her all the more, despite the number of occasions she had complained about his unwashed feet, or the odour of his garlic-tainted breath.

When she tackled him on this odd behaviour he coldly informed her that she no longer held his trust.

'I have been reliably informed that you have betrayed my confidences to the King, and to the Queen your mother, relating all that has passed between us.'

'Reliably informed by whom?'

'It will not do, Margot.'

'It is a wicked lie!' She fervently denied the accusation but he simply walked away.

The following morning as she left the Queen's *lever*, Charlotte de Sauves smilingly whispered her condolences to Margot for the loss of her husband's favour.

'These lies are du Guast's doing, and yours.'

Charlotte put back her elegant head and let out a trill of laughter, although the merry sound of it was tinged with acid. 'Rumour is rife. Do you imagine your husband isn't fully aware why you pay such frequent visits to your brother's apartments? You're entranced by a certain gallant by the name of Bussy.'

The sheer effrontery of the woman struck Margot dumb. Not for a moment would she admit the truth to this malicious, manipulative strumpet. Since coming to Paris she had indeed seen more of Bussy d'Amboise. Her excuse was that she could hardly avoid him, since he was First Gentleman to Alençon, and she was in and out of her younger brother's apartments all day. But even had he not been so accessible, she would have sought him out. He was handsome, daring, audacious, master of the sword fight, and, most of all, fun!

Margot lifted her chin high. 'Bussy formerly worked for the King, and His Majesty is annoyed that he's chosen to leave his service and devote himself to my brother, who regards him highly. Which does not surprise me for there is none to compare with Bussy d'Amboise for valour, reputation, grace and wit. Du Guast would seek any way to hurt him, and me, out of pure vengeance. Yet I have spread no lies or mischief against my husband.'

Charlotte coolly smiled. 'But is it any wonder that he believes you have? He is convinced you are less innocent than you profess, when you willingly flaunt this relationship, causing him great distress.'

Margot couldn't help but laugh. 'I believe it would take someone with more skills than I to cause my husband any distress over my supposed intimacies with "a certain gallant", whether the rumours be true or false. We have a measure of agreement, he and I, which suits us both very well. Nor should you imagine that I feel any jealousy over your own dalliance with *noste Enric*. I suggest you'll find it a waste of your valuable time to attempt to cause dissension between us on that score.'

Charlotte's tone was now that of a spitting cat. 'I suggest to you, Madame, that you concern yourself with your own affairs, and keep your long Valois nose out of mine.'

'No, indeed, you are the one who must take care,' Margot snapped, and quitted the Queen's ante-chamber, slamming the door behind her.

She went at once to her brother, for it was very evident that where once they'd taken their rivalry in good part, now they were increasingly at loggerheads. De Sauves had cleverly made each of the men think they were of first importance to her, and had created dissent between them.

Alençon, however, refused to listen.

'On all other matters you heed my advice, why not this?' Margot cried.

'I will not be ruled by my sister on who I choose to be my mistress.'

Margot wondered if he was perhaps becoming rather full of his own importance, now that he was next in line to the throne. As heir he should properly be addressed as Monsieur, although most of his friends continued to call him Alençon, herself included.

'Can you not see that you are both being used? She is creating disaffection as a means to ruin the friendship between you and Enric, a fact you have long sworn never to let happen.'

But no matter what she said, Alençon remained unmoved by her pleas. It was clear that he was utterly besotted, the fascination too strong, and all Margot's arguments proved useless.

Navarre was sitting at his desk about to write to a friend, chewing on the end of his quill pen and wondering how to describe his concerns. There was increasing tension at court, and dissension between the different factions seemed to be growing ever more dangerous. Nerves were tested, which frequently led to sword fights and skirmishes.

One evening, aware that Alençon was with Madame de Sauves, Navarre had waited for him, and when Alençon had emerged from her apartment, he'd pretended to be just passing by and had 'accidentally' knocked the Duke in the eye with the hilt of his sword, leaving it badly bruised.

When they'd met the following morning, Navarre had attempted to look sympathetic. 'Why, *mon dieu*, what is the matter with your eye? What a bruise! How did you come by it?'

'It is nothing,' the Duke had brusquely responded, and brandishing his sword dangerously close to Navarre's throat, had hissed furiously at him, 'If anybody says that I got it where you think I did, I will make him deny it.'

It had taken several courtiers, who happened to be present, to prevent a fight which might well have ended in the death of one of them. And this despite their pledge to Margot to remain united.

Navarre was beginning to sense that he may have misjudged his wife and was rather regretting his coldness towards her. He had no idea whether she was currently engaged in an *affaire*, nor did he greatly care. Generally speaking, they rubbed along surprisingly well, and she'd shown little sign of jealousy over his own notorious infidelity, beyond bruised pride. She'd gently bullied him into improving his manners and etiquette, and taught him much about how to survive in the French Court, not least how to keep his head on his shoulders.

Despite their petty squabbles, he did not believe she would ever betray him to the King, whom she despised. Did she not have every reason to want to keep their triumvirate strong, if only to protect her precious young brother?

She believed that du Guast and Henri were guilty of plotting unfounded mischief, and of using de Sauves to bring them all down. It was certainly true that Charlotte, who was a born coquette, loved nothing better than to play off one lover against the other. There had been several occasions lately when she'd annoyed him by fawning over Alençon in his presence. Could Margot be right? Was that a deliberate ploy? Not that he'd been any more faithful to the delectable Charlotte than she was with him. Perhaps he was growing bored with her, and she seemed to be less available these days.

Navarre began to write: '*This court is the strangest place on earth. We are nearly always ready to cut each other's throats. We carry daggers, wear coats of mail and often a cuirass beneath a cape . . . All the band you know wants my death on account of my love for the Duke . . . They say they will kill me, and I want to be one jump ahead of them.*'

But it was not in fact Navarre who they attempted to kill.

Margot was resting in her apartment at the Louvre when news reached her that her lover had been attacked. One of her brother's gentlemen, an Italian, who was one of the party, came running for help, dripping blood from an open wound in his shoulder.

'Bussy is attacked!' he shouted, and Margot went white with shock. 'We were set upon by a score of armed guards, the sword fight fast and furious. I know not if he is safe.'

Alençon joined Margot and was all for setting out there and then to defend his First Gentleman, but the Queen Mother, who had also responded to the call, urged him not to risk his life.

'It is full dark, and you are ignorant of where the attack took place, or the nature of it. Your life is too precious to me, my son. See how many children I have lost already, and you are the heir apparent. You must not go.'

'But if we do nothing Bussy may lose his life. I cannot stand by and let him die.'

Alençon was all for ignoring her orders, even though Margot added her own pleas to those of her mother. But Catherine was so determined to protect her son that she had all the doors securely barred, refusing to allow him to leave. The Duke had to be content with sending a contingent of his men, who returned some hours later to report that Bussy had thankfully escaped unscathed.

'Hampered as he was with an injured right arm tied up in a silvery-grey scarf loaned to him by yourself, good lady, he nevertheless stood his ground and fought hard, defending himself with commendable skill. "Would you fight a fellow with only one arm?" he cried, unable to believe, even as he parried and thrust, that this could be a serious attack. But when one of his colleagues, who wore a similar scarf, took a sword thrust through the stomach that killed him instantly, Bussy realized the assault did indeed have mortal intent. Unable to defend himself properly, he took refuge in a doorway, found it to be unlocked, and slipped quietly inside to escape by a back entrance.'

'Praise God for providence,' Margot breathed.

Next morning, the intended victim came striding into the Louvre, his usual daredevil self, grinning from ear to ear as if he had endured nothing more taxing than a joust at a tournament. He was eager to prove by his solid presence that he had indeed defeated his enemies.

Margot almost fainted with relief. 'This is the work of du Guast,' she cried, longing to enfold him in her arms but dare not to do so before the curious gaze of her brother and his entourage. Normally she snapped her fingers at public opinion, cared not a jot what anyone might think of her, but today, with Bussy having come within a whisker of death, discretion seemed the better part of valour. 'At least you are safe,' she said, her smile radiant.

But she spoke too soon, for moments later the room filled with armed guards and he was arrested. She cried out in his defence but her lover was marched away, as was her brother. In fear, trembling, she waited anxiously for what might happen next. Was this to be a repeat of that earlier incident? Would she soon be seeing poor Bussy's head roll as La Molle's and Coconnas's had done? How would she endure it?

The pair were held in prison for several days before Catherine, who was weary of the foolish squabble, finally persuaded Henri that there was no plot, no intrigue against him, merely foolish jealousy, and that he should settle for dismissing the miscreant from court.

The pair were released and Bussy banished to his estates. The dashing young courtier left on a note of defiance, flaunting Margot's favour in his hat, accompanied on his journey by the highest noblemen in her brother's service.

The Queen Mother, who harboured no bourgeois principles or moralistic disapproval, caring only that a love affair not turn into political intrigue against the crown, ordered her daughter to be more discreet in future. And although Margot would miss her lover, she sighed with relief that at least this way he would keep his head.

But the incident proved that she might never be free to have friends, or a lover, simply because of the King's paranoia over possible intrigue against him.

Only days later, Navarre fell ill. Fearing for her husband's life, Margot painstakingly nursed him back to health, just as she had done once before. Terrified of the *morceau Italianizé*, she personally prepared his food, bringing him warm possets and beef broth to tempt his appetite, allowing no one but herself to feed him.

'I did not realize you cared so much,' he joked.

'There is nothing wrong with you except that you have exhausted yourself with too much love-making,' she scolded. 'I should have let you suffer.' And they smiled at each other, once again in perfect accord.

They both knew that with no one to trust in this pernicious court, they must needs rely upon each other. Margot had no more wish than Navarre to be constantly at the King or Queen Mother's mercy. The recent attack on Bussy, and Navarre's sudden illness, served as a sharp lesson to them all.

The two princes quickly reconciled their differences and began to plan their escape in earnest. They were now both of the opinion that they faced as much danger in staying as they risked in attempting to break free of their imprisonment.

Tensions between the two royal brothers remained edgy and Henri was constantly threatening to put Alençon in the Bastille. Since Henri's accession to the throne both he and Navarre had been allowed a little more freedom in that they could now join the hunt, or visit friends nearby, although every move they made was kept under close scrutiny by du Guast and his guards.

Alençon resolved to escape and join the *Politiques*. As always, he sought his sister's help, and between them they devised a plan.

One afternoon Alençon decided to visit his latest mistress in the Rue Saint-Marceau, not de Sauves on this occasion. Muffled in the folds of his cloak, and with a hat pulled down to his nose, he slipped quietly out of a side door of the Louvre, sauntered past the guards without being apprehended, and walked to her house. Once safely inside, he thanked her with a hasty kiss before exiting by a back door where his men were waiting with horses. Alençon quickly mounted and rode out of Paris without a backward glance. Somewhere along the road he met up with Bussy and a mounted escort, and together they made their way to Meudon and finally Dreux, which was in the Duke's apanage. He had found a safe haven at last.

Knowing that the arrangements she'd so painstakingly put in place had gone smoothly, Margot took care to keep out of the way of the King and the Queen Mother. She walked in the gardens, visited friends, even challenged Guise to a match with their crossbows as they had done in the old days, and said not a word to anyone. No one noticed Alençon was missing until past nine o'clock when her mother asked why her youngest son had not come in to supper.

'Is he unwell?'

'I know not,' Margot blithely replied. 'I haven't seen him since early afternoon.'

The Queen Mother sent word to his room, enquiring after his health, and when the report came back that he was not in his apartments, utter mayhem broke out. The Duke of Alençon was missing from court. He had vanished. Where could he be?

Catherine sent pages scurrying here, there and everywhere, shouting at them to search every nook and cranny of the Louvre. Henri ordered the courtiers to scour every corner of the gardens, nearby streets and squares, and houses of his brother's friends, but no trace of him was found.

Yet again they sent for Margot and cross-examined her closely, firing a volley of questions at her.

'When did you last see him?'

'Early this afternoon, as I said.'

'Did he say where he was going?'

'No.'

'Has he gone to join the Huguenots?'

'I know not.'

'Did you help him to escape?'

'How would I dare after all that has happened?'

Somehow Margot held her nerve and maintained a wide-eyed innocence throughout. Henri lost his temper completely, screamed and shouted, stormed back and forth, and finally summoned all the princes, lords and nobles of the court and barked orders at them. 'I want my brother found and brought back here, dead or alive.'

No one moved.

'Are you deaf? Did you not hear what I said? He means to make war against me.'

'Sire, we would lay down our lives for you, but the Duke is a Prince of the Blood,' said one brave soul. 'None would wish to pursue a prince to his death. He is the heir apparent.'

'He will be a dead one if ever I get my hands on his neck. I will teach him the folly of threatening a monarch as powerful as myself.'

But the ensuing silence told Henri that none would wish to be involved in so hazardous a business. Why would they risk attacking a royal personage, when Alençon or his retainers could as easily turn upon them once they came into power? Henri was furious. His brother was free. There was no way to bring him back, and God knows what mischief he would wreak against the crown now.

In the following few days Margot was in agony, constantly glancing over her shoulder, starting at shadows, fearful for her brother's life, and her own. The Queen Mother sent out half a dozen of her most trusted agents to locate her recalcitrant son. 'Offer him every assistance, and then arrest him. Bring him home in whatever state you find him.'

But they too failed.

Margot wept, terrified lest he be captured and put to the sword, or brought back to court and executed. Why had she been so reckless as to help him to escape? Would she live to regret getting involved in his schemes, if she lived at all? She loved intrigue, was always willing to face danger, but it was the waiting that unnerved her, the not knowing what was happening. And the King was in such a black temper, she feared what he might decide to do next.

She made a desperate bid for calm. 'I dare say he will be at his estates. Go there yourself, Madame. I beg you don't arrest him, but talk to him. Try to understand his motives.'

Catherine agreed to consider the suggestion.

As if she did not feel bad enough, Margot was then laid low with a bad cold, and after a week of misery the Queen Mother came to her bedchamber one morning to see how she was faring. Margot had hardly slept, her eyes were red raw and swollen with her cold and with tears. Now she trembled, as she always did when in the presence of her mother.

'I come to inform you that a letter has arrived, in which the Duke writes that he has escaped for the sake of his liberty and because he has been in daily expectation of the ultimate resolution. The *morceau Italianizé*.' Catherine laughed, as if highly amused by the notion of her youngest son being in mortal fear of his own mother. 'What a coward that boy is. He says that on more than one occasion he has been made sick by drinking a certain wine, when we all know that he simply drinks too much. The danger is all in his head.'

Margot was unconvinced, but attempted to smile. 'Will the King send his forgiveness?'

'I am to set out within the next few days to find and meet with the young absconder as you suggest, and hope to knock some sense into that silly noddle of his. While I am gone, you, Madame, are to remain in your room, strictly confined until he is found.'

'I – I don't understand. He is innocent!'

'If so, then why does he run?'

Margot could find no answer to this.

Catherine's lips curved into a cold grimace that might pass for a smile. 'Do not fear, I shall find him, but until I do you will remain as a hostage for him. You will regain your freedom only when he has relinquished his threats to the crown and the Catholic Church, and returned to the Louvre.'

Margot listened in dawning dismay. Her beloved younger brother may be free at last, but she was to be held captive in his place.

Catherine doggedly pursued Alençon until they at last met up towards the end of September near Chambord, where they spent a tearful day of reconciliation.

Word had reached her that young Condé was gathering men in Germany and heading for the French frontier to join forces with Damville. She dreaded the threat of invasion, which would be certain to strengthen the Huguenots still further. Their demands were already growing more audacious. It felt almost as if the Admiral and their leaders were not dead, as if they had 50,000 men still at their beck and call.

And Alençon, her own son, saw himself as King of the Low Countries, set to be her enemy in yet further warfare, and confident of victory.

She cared little that people were starving due to extortionate food prices, but France could not support another war, nor wanted one. Morale was low, and the populous less willing to pay for more bloodshed, or to obey a profligate King whom they treated with open contempt. Even their interest in religion was taking second place to the need to put food on the table. Yet even as Catherine negotiated with her youngest son and his fellow leaders for peace, she sent a message to the other to start preparing for war, just in case it became necessary. As ever, Catherine was in two minds on what was the best way to proceed.

Fighting did indeed break out again, and in one of the bitter battles on 11 October, during which the Duke of Guise won a fine victory at Dormans against the German Reiters, he was wounded in the face, which resulted in a scar very like that

suffered by his father. He was now given the same nickname of
Le Balafré.

On 31 October, on All Hallows' Eve, du Guast was found
murdered in his bed, killed by a musket shot while recuperating
from a venereal disease. There was much speculation over the
perpetrator of this deed, some laying the blame upon Alençon,
while others whispered that the Queen of Navarre herself was
involved.

Margot, innocent of the charge, nonetheless received the news
with joy. She was ill in bed herself at the time, and regretted only
that she was not fit enough to dance on his grave.

Catherine returned to Paris in January 1576 to meet with a storm
of distrust and anger from the King. Henri was gravely dissatisfied with what she had achieved, believing she had made too
many concessions, and mother and son had yet another of their
disagreements, which were becoming distressingly frequent.

Nerves were just beginning to steady and tempers cool when
one day a rumour spread like wildfire around court that the King
of Navarre had not been seen for more than twenty-four hours.
Henry had come to be on friendly terms with the King, obediently taking Mass and doing all that was expected of a good
Catholic, and they had foolishly thought he could be trusted.
Now he too had gone.

Catherine flew into a rage and blamed the King, while Henri
indignantly shouted that it was no failure on his part. The next
day, while they were at worship at Sainte-Chapelle, Navarre
suddenly appeared before them, booted and spurred, and grinning from ear to ear.

Catherine almost gaped at him. 'Son, we thought you gone.'

Navarre kissed her on each cheek, trying not to turn up his
nose at the stale odour of white lead that she used to keep her
face pale. 'I was out hunting, as I believe I am now permitted to
do. I suppose it would have been easy to run away, had I so wished,
but the thought never entered my head.'

'I dare say it would not,' she agreed quite equably, thinking
him a great fool.

'Besides, I heard you were fretting for me, so here I am, at
your service.'

'A pretty little scene,' Margot murmured as he moved away. 'I might almost believe you myself, did I not know you to have more wit than you let on. You are not quite the idiot you pretend.'

'Nor quite so relaxed in my southern ways as people imagine,' he agreed. 'Did I not play the fool well?'

'Indeed, very well, and with a light heart.'

'Yet the game is deadly serious.' He was not laughing now.

'Were they taken in? That is the question.'

He smiled lazily at her. 'We shall see, my dear. We shall see.'

When, a day or two later, on 3 February, Navarre did indeed go missing, nobody paid the slightest attention. He rode out to hunt in the forests beyond Paris with Guise, stopping at the great Fair of Saint-Germain on the way, where the pair of them strolled, arms about each other's shoulders in brotherly fashion.

'Now we'll go on to Senlis,' Navarre urged. 'Come, we'll have good sport.'

Guise agreed, but once in the forest it was easy to give him the slip and for Navarre to ride ahead and take a different path with his men. Once out of sight of Guise and the guards, he dug his heels into the flanks of his horse and rode hard, not stopping until they had crossed the Loire.

Here he reigned in his tired horse, lifted his eyes to the heavens and cried, 'Thanks be to God for my deliverance. They were the death of my mother at Paris; they murdered the Admiral and all my noblest servants. And they would not have done much better by me if God had not preserved me. I would not return there if they dragged me.'

But at this poignant moment, when he was at last a free man, Henry of Navarre added in his usual jocular fashion, 'I only regret Paris for the sake of two things I left behind. The one is the Mass, the other is my wife. As for the first, I must try to do without it. But as for the latter, I cannot do without her, and would wish to see her again.'

'He has gone without saying goodbye,' Margot mourned to Madame de Curton. 'Did he say farewell to his mistress?'

'I know not, my lady.'

'I did not even hear him go, but then we occupy separate beds, although in the same room.'

Margot was deeply thankful that he was safe, yet oddly sorrowful at his departure. With both brother and husband now gone, she was quite alone.

The next day the King strode into Margot's privy chamber in a rage such as she'd never seen in him before. She'd grown used to Charles's tantrums, but lazy, indolent Henri could rarely summon the energy to disagree with anyone, let alone lose his temper. The King spent hours each day lying on a divan, lazily drinking sherbets, since he never touched wine, fondling or teasing his lapdogs into a frantic excitement. Lately, though, his behaviour had been growing ever more erratic, and now he was beside himself with rage, shouting and abusing her, calling her all manner of names.

He was quite convinced that she had played a major part in the Princes' disappearance. 'My own sister has betrayed me!' he roared. 'It would give me great pleasure to kill you here and now.'

Margot cowered before him, shaking with terror, expecting the blow to fall at any moment. It might well have done so had not the Queen Mother intervened. Catherine had always balked at murdering the nobility, and certainly stopped short of disposing of her own family. Now she urged her son to be calm.

'Let us take a moment to consider, my son. You might well have occasion for your sister's services at some time in the future. Just as it is prudent not to put too much confidence in friends, lest they should one day become our enemies, so it is equally advisable to conduct ourselves in like manner towards our enemies, if we hope they may one day become our friends. It will be punishment enough to lock the girl in her room. Post guards at the doors of her apartments by all means. Hold her hostage, as she deserves.'

Margot attempted a protest at this indignity. 'I have not spoken with my husband. He did not visit me when I was recently indisposed, nor did he even take leave of me when he left court.'

'That is nothing,' Catherine scoffed. 'It is merely a trifling difference between man and wife which a few sweet words conveyed in a letter would set to rights. Once he has regained your affections, he has only to write and beg you to come to him, and you would set off at the first opportunity. This is what the King my son wishes to prevent.'

Henri grudgingly allowed himself to be soothed and calmed, and to accept these less radical measures. But his anger simmered on beneath the surface as he glared at Margot, his long Italian eyes hard and unforgiving.

By way of retaliation he ordered the murder of her former lady-in-waiting Madame de Thorigny, whom he had earlier had dismissed from her household for an alleged unseemly relationship with her mistress. He sent a party of men to kidnap the poor woman. They took her from her house, bound her arms and legs, and carried her to the Seine where they were about to throw her in the surging river when a troop of soldiers came upon them and rescued her. She would live to tell the tale, but it was a salutary warning to Margot, filling her with fresh fear.

'The King will not be satisfied till he has my head on the block,' she sobbed to Madame de Curton. 'I am done for. There will be no peace for me here. They will hold me as hostage until I can follow my husband to freedom.'

Life for Margot fell to a new low, far worse than the years of incarceration she'd endured when they'd all three been held in the Louvre following the St Bartholomew's Eve massacre. She was confined to her own apartment with guards posted at the door to prevent her from leaving, and apart from the ever faithful Madame de Curton, rarely saw a single person. Not the Queen Mother, nor even Queen Louise, who found the feuding and intrigues at court very trying and had little sympathy for her sister-in-law. Margot did not have the same rapport with Henri's Queen as she had enjoyed with Charles's, Elisabeth of Austria, who was now back home at her father's court. Nor did many friends dare come near, in case they too might be accused of being complicit in the Princes' escape.

'It is ever thus, Lottie. When one is successful and admired in court, everyone wishes to be your friend. Adversity is solitary, while prosperity dwells in a crowd.'

Margot filled the long lonely days with reading the classics, writing letters, and applying herself to her religious devotions.

'You make me proud,' said her old governess. 'You are showing great fortitude, turning these days of persecution into an opportunity for further study.'

Margot smiled. 'I trust my love of literature and philosophy will save my sanity. Science conducts us, step by step, through the whole range of creation, until we arrive, at length, at God. Misfortune prompts us to summon our utmost strength to oppose grief and recover tranquillity.'

She was also engaged in secret correspondence with her husband. How Madame managed to spirit these letters in and out of the palace, she did not know and dare not ask, yet her loyal companion somehow achieved this seemingly impossible task without their being discovered.

Navarre wrote first, begging Margot to forget their differences, and be assured that he did wish to love her and have her as his true wife, as soon as she was able to come to him. His kind words brought tears to her eyes and, ever generous, her feelings towards him softened and Margot forgave him his indiscretions. If no one else cared for her, not the King her brother, nor even her own mother, at least she still had a husband who would welcome her back into his arms.

'Now that he is at a distance from his Circe, Madame de Sauves, perhaps he is listening to good advice. His eyes have been opened and he has discovered the plots and machinations of our enemies. Our continued disagreement can only be the ruin of us both.'

Until they could be together, he urged her to keep him informed of the state of affairs at court, and with her brother, which did generate a small doubt in her mind.

'Does he truly love me, Lottie, and want me to join him in Béarn, or am I more use to my husband as a spy here in Paris?'

Madame de Curton wisely ventured no opinion on the subject.

Margot began to sense a growing fear in her mother, and the King, that she might ultimately seek revenge for her prolonged incarceration, which caused her some amusement. In a bid to gain her much longed for freedom she prudently insisted that nothing was further from her mind.

'I would never prefer my own good to the welfare of my brothers and the State, to which I am ready to sacrifice myself. I want nothing more than peace, and would do all in my power to bring that about.'

But Margot's hatred of Henri continued unabated. Her brother claimed to have only her interests at heart, yet whenever she pleaded, with tears in her eyes, that she might join her husband in Béarn, he refused to consider it.

'You will remain a hostage until Alençon, who you so favoured, returns to court.'

Her younger brother came later in the year, accompanied by Bussy and a small army of his most notable gentlemen, and the King made a great show of receiving them with all generosity, as if he loved him dearly. Anyone watching the pair embrace would never have thought them capable of plotting against each other. But then Henri had realized the political necessity of at least a show of reconciliation.

The country was rife with rumour that the charismatic Guise was the people's choice as king, that they were turning against the Valois. This sickened and enraged him, and in a fit of pique, Henri broke with tradition and ascribed himself as leader of the Catholic League, a typically dramatic and unnecessary gesture. He went further by reminding Alençon of his duty as a Son of France who would one day wear the crown, offering him support to win a Catholic crown in the Low Countries rather than a Protestant one, for the sake of the House of Valois and of France.

Alençon instantly abandoned the Huguenots and the *Politiques*, changed sides once again, and likewise joined the League.

Margot remained under house arrest, although no longer so closely confined to her apartments. Many still turned their backs as she walked by, reluctant to acknowledge friendship with the notorious Queen of Navarre, or even speak to her. Only one old friend risked the displeasure of the King by reaffirming his support, and that was Guise.

Seeing her standing alone one morning at the back of the room during the King's *lever*, he came up behind her and gently pinched her waist. Margot let out a tiny squeal, and then, realizing who teased her, couldn't help but turn and laugh up at him.

'I've missed you,' he said, keeping his voice low and his eyes on the King.

The royal bedchamber was strewn with flower petals, the bed

gilded and decorated with cloth of silver. Henri lay back upon crimson satin pillows in his white satin *manteau-de-nuit*, richly adorned with silver spangles. The chief valet was carefully removing the mask that had been soaked in perfumed oil to protect His Majesty's face while he slept, in order to offer him a collation of sweetmeats before he rose. A second *valet-de-chambre* was standing before the fire airing a shirt worked in exquisite needlework.

'It was by your own folly that we separated.'

'But that is all in the past, and of no account,' he said dismissively, half turning away as if fascinated by the way the valet was now removing the King's embroidered night gloves and massaging his long white hands.

Margot cast a sideways glance up at him through her lashes. She remembered well the warmth of his skin, the scent of leather and sandalwood about his person. So strong, so masculine, in marked contrast to the ceremony they were now witnessing with her effeminate brother.

A shirt was being slipped over the King's head, the high collar set upright, then the doublet was pulled on, so close fitting that it took two valets to set it properly in place and fasten it. Silk stockings came next, puffed, slashed breeches, and a pair of shoes, small and dainty enough for a woman rather than a king.

'You expect me to forgive you when you treated our love so shabbily, falling at the feet of that harlot de Sauves?'

'You forgave your husband and brother, why not your lover?'

Margot sighed with exasperation. What was it about that woman? A harlot indeed, who, under the edict of the Queen Mother, had been ordered to plot and cause mischief where she could. Yet Guise was as handsome and as desirable as ever. There was something in his eyes even now, in the way his look challenged her, that she found impossible to resist. To see him about court and not be able to speak to him was painful enough; to have him press so close was robbing her of any sensible thought.

'You and I should talk,' he murmured, in that throaty tone that set her pulses racing.

'Not here. You must be mad to even attempt it in such a public place.'

The valets were decking Henri out with perfumed gloves, handkerchief, rings, chains, a mirror that hung from his girdle along with a delicate lace fan, pomander and comfit boxes. Last of all, they carefully set his Polish-style hat with its decorative plume upon the royal perfumed hair.

Guise murmured, 'We could help each other in so many ways. Should you be passing our special place this afternoon around four, I would explain further.'

Before she could catch her breath to find an answer to this, he had drifted away to speak to others; a smile here, a quiet word there. Margot remained where she was, her heart beating like a mad thing in her breast.

It was as if they had never been apart. Margot fell into his arms with only the faintest whimper of protest. She had never stopped wanting him, needing him, loving him, thinking of him every single day, and here she was at last, in his arms where she belonged.

He showered her with kisses, tracing his lips over the flutter of her translucent eyelids, pale cheeks, her rosy, eager mouth. His greed for her was such that he seemed to devour her. He couldn't get enough of her, nor she him. And to have him inside her, bringing her to those heights she could attain only with Guise, surely took her close to the realms of paradise.

Afterwards, as they lay together on the silken sheets, their hearts beating as one, they spoke quietly of their lives since last they were together. 'I have never stopped loving you, Margot,' he said, his voice a caress. 'You are a part of me, and ever will be. No matter where fate takes you, know that I am yours.'

She pressed her lips against the hard planes of his chest, a tear cooling her hot cheek. 'I have need of friends,' she murmured. 'I have need of your love, and I fear for what the future will bring. I must get away from this exalted prison, to my husband where I will at least be safe. I do not trust the King. He is more and more controlled by his squabbling *mignons*, and by his moody selfish temperament, his petty feuds and jealousies, his peevish demands and grievances.'

They understood each other perfectly. Neither had ever forgotten their hatred for Henri, from when as the Duke of Anjou he had readily listened to the malice that du Guast spilled in his ear, and destroyed the young Princess Margot's reputation by spreading vile rumour and slander against her. Nothing had changed in Henri's attitude towards his sister since that day.

'The people loathe him as much as do we,' Guise whispered, his mouth breathing the words softly against her ear. Then with a grin he added, 'They call him the King of Sodom.'

Margot widened her eyes as a mischievous smile curled her lips. 'A wicked epithet.'

'But apt.' His grin faded as he stroked her cheek. 'I too fear for your future. We could help each other, my love, so that we both get what we want: you safe in Béarn with your droll husband, and I . . .'

'Yes, what is it that you want, my lord?' she asked, trailing her fingers along his inner thigh. He smiled at her before capturing her mischievous hand with his own, saying nothing as she returned his smile, reading his thoughts only too well. 'You want the diadem.'

Guise demurred with a slight lifting of the brow. 'I want to be head of the Catholic League.'

'And that is all?' she teased.

Two heartbeats passed before he answered. 'For now. Should a time come when there is no other suitable candidate for the crown of France, I, as a Bourbon Prince, would not fail to do my duty.'

Margot smiled mockingly at him, even as she kissed his beloved mouth. 'I'm sure you would not.'

'The south belongs to your husband, to Navarre. The central provinces to Alençon, the eastern follows the House of Lorraine. But Paris bitterly resents the King's constant demands for money to pay for his excesses, and toys for his *mignons*, while the people starve. Even the bankers refuse to offer him any more credit, yet he is in dire need of funds for he is in terror that Philip II may bring his armies out of the Netherlands and invade France. He needs the strength of the League for protection, yet I am the leader they crave, not Henri Trois.'

Margot was thoughtful. 'My brother may wear the crown he so long coveted, but I wish it to feel like a crown of thorns upon his head. I would thwart his every wish, seduce both Catholic and Huguenot, and favour my younger brother in his own far-fetched ambitions, however improbable it may be for him to realize them.

The King views me as his enemy, so why should I not be so in very truth?'

Guise was grinning widely now, his eyes gleaming. 'As ever, Margot, you and I are as one.'

'I desire only to avenge the many insults Henri has inflicted upon me, and if by supporting one brother I offend and bring about the downfall of the other, so be it.'

'Then this is how we must proceed. Discord, and the threat of war, will allow the League to expand and survive, and give us the power we need.'

Margot frowned. 'We have had enough of war; it is peace we crave.'

'Think you this latest treaty will last any longer than those which came before it? While pretending to pursue peace, the King, as always, is hypocritically doing the exact opposite and preparing for war. He is setting the Huguenots against you and your brother by making Alençon turn Catholic, and by keeping you from your husband. We must make the threat of more conflict work in our favour.'

When they had done talking and scheming and planning, they made love again before going their separate ways about court, their faces blithe with innocence. But each knew that this would be only the first of many such meetings.

Margot again requested permission to go to her husband, but the King insisted he had need of her at court on State occasions whenever he wished to dazzle the opposition with her beauty and glamour. Margot knew it was not quite so simple, and when she learned that Navarre had sent an envoy to Paris to demand his Queen be allowed to come to him, she repeated her plea with some fervour.

Henri point-blank refused and dismissed the envoy with cold contempt. 'If the King of Navarre wishes to have her back, he should first become a Catholic.'

Margot put forward a stout defence. 'I did not please myself in getting married, but did so under the will and authority of King Charles, the Queen Mother, and yourself. You are against my going to him because he has again become a Huguenot.'

'What the Queen my mother and I are doing is for your own

good. I am determined to carry on the war until I exterminate this wretched religion which is of so mischievous a nature. If you, who are a Catholic, were once in their hands, you would become a hostage and they might seek revenge upon me by taking away your life. No, you shall not go amongst them.'

'He will never allow it,' she told Guise when they again met at their secret place. Margot felt on the brink of despair, finding the situation impossible. 'But I do not see how I can possibly remain at court while my brother rages war against my husband.'

'Then you must change the nature of your request,' Guise suggested, as he unhooked her corset to release her soft breasts into his hands. 'Ask to visit Sainte-Claude on a retreat, or go on a pilgrimage to Notre-Dame-de-Lorette.'

He was caressing her breasts, moving his hands down over the sweet curve of her belly, sending her mad with desire as she arched her body against his. She reached up to curl her arms about his head, but then, unable to bear any more, turned in his arms and pushed him back on to the bed. Climbing astride him wearing nothing but her silk stockings she gave herself up to pleasing her lover.

It was some time before either could speak again, but they made their plans with complete agreement.

Guise said, 'Alençon is chaffing at the restrictions imposed upon him since he foolishly returned to court. Yet with the right word, in the right ear, you could be free to help restore his lost cause in Flanders. But let the suggestion come from him. That should infuriate Henri nicely. Speak to the Queen Mother. It is essential you enlist her support.'

Margot went to see her mother and begged her to persuade the King to allow her to make a pilgrimage to take the waters at Spa.

'How can I remain at court when Henri plans to march his armies into Gascony and attack my husband? The Princess of Roche-sur-Yon is unwell and I have suffered another outbreak of erysipelas, the skin complaint which you know has always troubled me. I feel the waters would do it good, as well as keep me from causing offence to my husband by seeming to be party to my brother's plans.'

Catherine agreed this might be prudent. 'I too am concerned that the King, through the persuasion of the bishops, has resolved to break the last peace which was concluded in his name. I see already the ill effects of this hasty decision, as it has removed from the King's Council many of his ablest and best servants. I doubt you could remain at court without offending your husband, or creating jealousy and suspicion in the King's mind. I will advise Henri to give you leave to set out on this journey.'

Margot was hardly able to believe her good fortune. Their little scheme had worked exactly as they'd hoped. Henri gave his permission, probably because he'd achieved his aim of separating Alençon from the *Politiques* and Huguenots. The necessary papers for free passage were obtained, and preparations duly made.

She was to be freed from her prison at last and allowed to embark on what felt very like an adventure. Margot had always been at the beck and call of the Queen Mother, living under her domination and power, not even able to properly enjoy her marriage. Her two recent lovers, whom she'd taken in retaliation against Navarre and Guise's earlier defection, were now all but forgotten: poor La Molle gone to his death, and while Bussy was now back at court with Alençon, she had no inclination to rekindle their affair, even had she not been back with Guise.

After so many long miserable months in isolation, Margot would at last be able to conduct herself without having constantly to check her every move. She longed to join her husband in Béarn where she might at last be safe, perhaps even enjoy being Queen of her own small kingdom. In the meantime, she could at least be free and begin to live.

Yet it was in her nature to do what she could to help her younger brother, whom she loved despite his failings. And she'd never been afraid to risk dipping her fingers in the political pie.

Sadly, Alençon seemed bent on destroying his own cause before ever she got the chance to support it. Having been given command of the royal army during this, the sixth war of religion, in May he captured the Protestant stronghold of La Charité-sur-Loire. He was only prevented from doing untold slaughter by Guise's firm intervention. But Guise was not with him when the following month he sacked Issoire in the Auvergne, and had 3,000 citizens massacred. To his former Huguenot allies it seemed like a repeat of St Bartholomew's Eve and lost him all credibility.

Henri, of course, was delighted by the victory, if jealous of his brother's part in it, just as Charles IX had been of his own military glories. Nevertheless he held a magnificent ball to celebrate. Dressed like a woman, he wore a gown of gold brocade, sparkling with Polish diamonds, emeralds and pearls, his hair tinted with violet powder, easily outshining his plainer wife. It was but a mark of the dissolute style he'd adopted, paid for by the taxes wrung out of the Parisians.

And in July, when Margot set off for Flanders, the King ordered his armies to head south and make war on her husband.

Having put these matters into effect, Henri returned to his usual indolent and profligate ways, leaving his mother to deal with State affairs from her palace in the Tuileries. Catherine opened all dispatches, devised new laws, received ministers and foreign ambassadors, and paid a daily visit to the Louvre to lay documents before her son for signing. The King, meanwhile, could more likely be seen strolling about the gardens of the Louvre with a basket hung about his neck, richly lined with crimson satin, in which were curled several of his tiny dogs.

Parrots and small monkeys were also an obsession, and Henri enjoyed teaching the former to curse and use rude words, while the monkeys were trained to practise their mischief on some poor unfortunate, or to raid a lady's apartment.

Henri would often give away one of these pets to his favourites, and then buy them back for an extravagant sum. He recklessly plundered the privy purse, squandering huge sums on masques, balls and pageants. When the public treasury ran dry and the banks refused him further credit, he called upon wealthy individuals and local businesses to sponsor him in what became known as *édits bursaux*. None dared refuse as these loans were not voluntary, but compulsory.

Living at court was expensive for everyone. The King demanded high standards of dress from his courtiers, and from his *mignons*. It was a requirement that every gentleman must possess at least thirty suits, and never wear the same clothes two days running. These must be of the finest silks and satins and bright of colour.

Only old men were allowed to dress more soberly, and to wear wool. And there were strict rules of etiquette. The cloak must be placed just so over one shoulder only, and allowed to fall from the other. One sleeve of the doublet should be worn loose at the wrist, and the other tightly buttoned. When on horseback, cavaliers were expected to ride with a drawn sword in their hand, as was the fashion among the Polish magnates. Style was everything.

Henri's *mignons* favoured the tall ruff, so stiff that it crackled, a fashion which soon became the object of much satire and caricature.

One day when Henri chanced to be visiting the fair at Saint-Germain, he spotted a group of students wearing immense ruffs made out of stiff paper, clearly aping his favourites. He was hugely insulted and sentenced the young men to one week's imprisonment in the Conciergerie.

Henri loved his pretty boys, and hated to have them mocked. He felt more comfortable with them than with his Queen. Louise had suffered a miscarriage in 1576 and still longed for a child, which her husband seemed unable to give her. He claimed lovemaking exhausted him, and that he needed to rest for two days afterwards. Henri preferred taking his pleasure with his particular favourites, in ways which did not involve too much tiring emotion.

Bussy mockingly called these special elite the King's 'bed *mignons*'.

Margot's tour of Flanders was both eventful and enjoyable. She relished her new freedom, skilfully mixed business with pleasure, and made many new friends.

She travelled in a magnificent litter with glass window panes and pillars covered with ruby-red velvet embroidered with opal silk and gold, followed by a second litter for Madame de la Roche-sur-Yon, and several ladies-in-waiting. Behind them came ten maids-of-honour on horseback, her chamberlain, cooks, pages, gentlemen and household members in six coaches, an entourage fit for any queen.

She applied herself with great enthusiasm and patience to her brother's cause, sadly not helped by the atrocities carried out at Issoire. Nevertheless, she exercised her considerable charm to win over the old Flemish Noblesse, who were vehemently anti-Spanish. She sparkled and flirted, danced with boundless energy, admired the festivals and fireworks they provided, had them marvelling at her wit and oratory, and entranced them all.

In 1573 the Spanish King had adopted a less harsh policy and appointed his bastard brother, Don Juan of Austria, as Governor, in place of Alva. But despite every courtesy and the pains he took to entertain her, he remained very much on the side of his king.

Once Margot arrived at Liège she stayed for some weeks, having the waters from Spa brought to her daily, declaring that she had never felt so well in her life. In November, letters reached her from Alençon, telling her that having achieved the Peace of Bergerac, a treaty less advantageous to the Huguenots, the King now felt in a strong position to curb the ambitions of his younger brother.

Alençon also warned her that Henri had discovered she was working for him in Flanders, and was conspiring with Don Juan to thwart these efforts, had even ordered she be taken prisoner at the first opportunity.

Margot was forced to flee for her life.

It was Twelfth Night and the King was preparing for the usual feast and celebrations. The process took several hours and his favourites loved to lounge about, reading, joking, or gossiping, while he was dressed.

The *mignons* loved adornment, and, like their royal master, enjoyed dressing as women, the more extravagant the better. They curled and perfumed their hair, cut and stitched their own garments, concocted perfumes and cosmetics, sang licentious songs to the accompaniment of guitars or mandolins, and relished exchanging malicious gossip and risqué stories which would bring many a blush to the cheeks of those less amoral than themselves.

Tonight, as always, they happily advised the valets, or made comments as the King's hair was curled with hot tongues till it smoked with the heat, then dusted with violet-scented powder. One plucked his eyebrows, leaving a clearly defined arc above each elongated eye, while another prepared a paste of rose water and cypress oil to apply to his cheeks, forehead, and neck. Last of all, the chief valet knelt before the King, gently tugged on his beard to open his mouth, then after rubbing a white powder on to his gums, took some false teeth from a tiny cedar wood box and fitted each one wherever there was a space. With his beard washed with perfumed soap and water, and neatly brushed, Henri was at last ready.

But first he went along to the Queen's apartment to spend the next several hours dressing and preparing Louise's toilette with equal attention.

'Why do you bother? I shall never be beautiful,' she chided him.

'I can think of nothing that delights me more,' he said, as the plain, simple girl who was his Queen patiently submitted to being tweaked and curled into what might pass for a beauty.

The King and his *mignons* made a dramatic appearance in their most dazzling, outrageous attire, hair curled and scented, lace collars open to a low *décolleté*, as they processed from the Louvre to the Bourbon Chapel to hear Mass. Alençon, with Bussy and his entourage, arrived dressed in simple Puritan garb, followed by six pages all clothed in cloth of gold, sporting huge ruffs and plumes in the fashion of these effeminate dandies.

'It is the season,' Bussy announced in his usual insolent manner, 'when the least important are most nobly arrayed.'

Henri was furious at his impudence, and, turning to his favourites, muttered, 'It is long past time we clipped that fellow's wings.'

As tempers rose, Alençon took the precaution of dispatching his First Gentleman to meet with his sister and escort her home.

When Margot at last reached La Fère, she was relieved and delighted to be met by a party of her brother's men. She had only succeeded in returning safely to France with the help of the townspeople of Dinant, who ably assisted her in outwitting her enemies. Even during the last part of her journey, danger was still present as the Huguenots too would gladly have captured her, for they had not forgiven Alençon for changing his allegiance and taking up arms against them. Alençon himself arrived a little later, delighted to see her but complaining of the slights and insults he was once again being subjected to at court, thanks to the King's favourites and Henri's spiteful jealousy.

'They try my patience to the utmost,' he mourned.

'Let us not think of them now,' she consoled him. 'Let us relax and enjoy this time of peace.'

Brother and sister spent two happy months together, resting and discussing all she'd achieved in Flanders, and what further work still needed to be done. Margot felt no desire to return to court. She longed to continue south and join her husband in Béarn, and had every intention of doing so, but they made a stop at St Denis where, to her dismay, they were met by the King, Queen Louise, the Queen Mother, and the entire court. It was a bitter blow to her hopes.

The royal party made a great show of how delighted they were to see her again, showering her with feigned affection, devising the most sumptuous diversions, and encouraging her to tell them of her adventures.

As always Margot kept her feelings private and put on a fine show, relating how well she had been received in Flanders. As they drove onward to Paris she entertained the royal party with tales of floods, disasters and disappointments, how she narrowly escaped being captured by the Huguenots, being obliged to abandon her litter and make a perilous journey across country on horseback. She spoke of sadness when one of her ladies died, and none of them guessed how distressed she was to see them.

Later, after a welcome-home supper and celebratory ball, she begged leave of the King for her to join her husband. 'You see how well you can manage without me. Pray, allow me to go to him, as a good wife should.'

'But of course you should go to him, dear sister,' Henri agreed, much to her surprise and delight.

The Queen Mother said, 'That seems an excellent plan, daughter. I may even accompany you on the journey.'

Greatly encouraged, Margot dared make a further request. 'And if you could expedite the payment of my marriage settlement, which I have still not received, I would be most grateful, and of no further burden to you.'

'We will see that it is done,' Henri agreed.

Margot was filled with new hope and excitement, but as spring advanced and still no firm plans were made for the journey, her joy gradually faded and soured. As ever in this court of double-dealing and deceit, promises were easily made but rarely kept.

The *mignons* continued with their endless squabbles, fights and duels. They loved to swagger with great pride and bravado, thinking themselves in such high favour that even the court nobles were obliged to concede to their every whim. And they continued to spread mischief about her, claiming she was too close to her younger brother, that their relationship could not be either honest or moral.

'They are accusing me of incest now!' Margot railed to Guise.

Alençon too was continually insulted and ridiculed, his bedchamber searched on one occasion, Henri certain he was intriguing against him. To his embarrassment the King found only a letter from de Sauves tucked under his brother's pillow.

Escaping from the Louvre became of paramount importance, and once more Margot came up with a plan, this time for him to climb out of the window of her bedchamber and somehow be lowered to the moat below. She sent one of the maid's beds to be re-sprung with a new strong rope. All she had to do then was to unfasten this new rope from the bed and tie it to the old one, which would surely be long enough for the task. The escape must be made under cover of darkness, assuming Alençon could hold fast to his courage for once in his life.

Bussy was set the task of making the necessary arrangements to quickly spirit his master safely out of Paris. He would wait for him, with horses, at the monastery of Sainte-Geneviève.

The entire operation was filled with risk. Margot had already been held prisoner once in lieu of her brother, which meant that her life was as much at stake as his.

The next evening the King was fasting, so Margot and Alençon dined alone with the Queen Mother. Margot saw that her younger brother was indeed a bag of nerves, as always in tense situations. She feared he might change his mind at the last moment and not go through with the plan, as had happened before. Towards the end of the meal he rose, still jittery, and whispered in her ear that he would meet with her later in her room.

Unfortunately, this exchange was noted by several of those present and, after the Duke had left, Catherine took Margot to one side and demanded to know what he'd said to her. 'You know that I pledged my word to the King that your brother would not get away.'

Suspicion crackled between them, but Margot made no attempt to defend him. Adopting an air of perfect innocence, she calmly replied, 'Had the Prince conceived such a plan, he would certainly have confided it to me, from whom he has never concealed anything. I would answer for him with my life.'

'Consider well what you are saying, daughter. You *will* answer for it with your life.'

Dry-mouthed with fear but smiling sweetly, and with all the skill of the practised liar she had become, Margot said, 'That is just what I would wish. Goodnight, Your Majesty.'

Once in her room she quickly undressed, dismissed all her ladies save for three she could trust, and fell into bed. She was far too restless and emotionally charged to sleep, and time seemed to drag by excruciatingly slowly as she waited.

At last Alençon appeared with his valet and a friend, Simiér. With their help the rope was tied in place. The Duke went first, laughing and joking, the prospect of being free of the spiteful *mignons* overcoming his fear of falling. Simiér, quaking at the knees and pale with fright, went next, followed by the valet. It was at this moment as she looked down, that Margot thought she saw a man start to run from the moat towards the guard-room. She and her ladies at once fell into a panic.

'It must be a spy. Oh, dear God, he has been betrayed. Quick, we must dispose of the rope. Throw it on the fire in case they come to search us, then to your beds, ladies. We must pretend to be asleep.'

Margot lay on her bed, heart pounding, listening for the sound of approaching footsteps, of the clink of arms from the guards. The room beyond her bed curtains was dark save for the bright fire, the rope taking an unconscionable time to burn as it was so very thick, making her cough a little from the smoke.

Then of a sudden, a loud hammering came on the door. 'Madame, your chimney is on fire. We can see flames coming from the top of it.'

Margot and her ladies looked at each other in horror. There was nothing they could do, for the rope was still only half burned.

'One of you must go quietly to the door, apologize for having made too big a fire and explain that I am asleep and you dare not disturb me. Do not, on any account, let them in.'

The youngest, prettiest lady volunteered, and opening the door by the smallest crack, peeped out at the guards and whispered her tale of woe.

'I beg you please not to wake my mistress or she might be angry with me for making up such a big fire. We are quite safe. I'm sorry for worrying you all,' she said, tears rolling down her pale cheeks.

They took pity on her, not a little influenced by her pretty face, and agreeing to say nothing, went away. Margot and her three ladies breathed again, and, giggling a little hysterically, went back to their beds.

But their relief was short-lived.

The next morning Margot was again called to stand before the Queen Mother, recalling all the times she had suffered from intimidation and threats in the past. The King was sitting at the foot of his mother's bed, and Margot trembled at the ice-cold fury emanating from them both. Would she never be free of their malice? Henri might not fall into the mad tantrums that Charles had been prone to, yet his displeasure could still be keenly felt and exercised in more peevish, underhand ways.

Catherine was the first to speak. 'You assured me that your brother would not leave court, and pledged yourself for his stay.'

Margot began to weep, although they were very much crocodile tears on this occasion.

'He has deceived me, as he has you, Madame. He gave no indication, told me not a word of what he planned. But I am ready still to pledge my life that his departure would not prejudice the King's service.'

Henri appeared somewhat mollified by her distress, which seemed genuine. 'Do not weep, sister. Tell us where you think he might have gone?'

'I'm sure it is only to his own principality to hunt and rest awhile.'

By a miracle, they believed in her tears and her innocence, and within the hour, letters came from Alençon containing assurances of his continued loyalty, and his hopes for making yet another expedition to the Low Countries on the King's behalf, once all due preparations had been made.

Henri made a show of affording assistance to this proposed expedition, while secretly resolving to use every means in his power to frustrate and defeat it. Nothing had changed. The King remained distrustful of his brother, and fearful of offending Spain.

He need not have worried, for in July when Alençon marched into Flanders to a fanfare of trumpets, he gained only two towns and his campaign ended in miserable failure. His sister would have made a much better job of it.

It was in late summer that Margot was at last to be permitted to set out on her journey to Béarn to join her husband. Henri now considered her of no further political use at court, at least for the present, and showered her with affection and good wishes in the days before her departure, fearful of parting on bad terms which might work against him with the King of Navarre. He restored to her the lands and benefices that formed part of her dowry, and gave her money from the privy purse, to which as a Daughter of France she was rightly entitled.

'How useful our friendship could be, sister, while your brother's will lead only to your ruin.'

Margot refused to be drawn. If Henri thought she would act as spy for him, after all the ill service he had done her over the years, then he was doomed to disappointment. 'You can be sure that when I rejoin my husband, I will not in any way fail to obey *his* commands.'

Catherine was to accompany her daughter on the journey before continuing on a progress of peace in the Southern Provinces. Margot began making preparations with joy in her heart. She was to be free, at long last.

Leaving Guise was the hardest thing she had ever done. They met for one last time in their favourite place, making love with a desperate passion, and many promises of devotion.

'Why do you go? Do you not love me?' he asked, his hand-some face unusually sorrowful as they lay entwined on the black satin sheets.

Margot gently kissed his mouth, tracing the familiar feel of it beneath her own, fixing it in her memory. 'I love you more than life itself.'

He lifted the heavy curtain of her dark hair to kiss her slender neck. 'Then why leave me for some Huguenot Prince?'

'Because he is my husband, and I would be a true wife to him.'

'Ha, an impossibility! The fellow drives you to distraction with his many amours. Am I not a better man than he?' His eyes gleamed in the light from the lamp as he grinned wickedly at her. 'I am miserable when you are not at court.'

Margot gave her trilling laugh, tugged lightly at his short pointed beard and kissed him again. 'Liar! You will hardly notice I am gone. Within days you will be in de Sauves' bed.'

'Madame de Sauves is travelling with your mother in her *Escadron Volant.*'

'Is she indeed?' Margot's eyes widened, wondering how Navarre would react to seeing his erstwhile mistress again. 'I hadn't heard. Well, you will have your wife to console you instead,' she said, glancing archly at him through her lashes. It had always been an unspoken agreement between them that his wife was never mentioned, and Margot instantly regretted having done so now, even before she saw his brow pucker, darkening those mesmeric eyes of his.

She hurried on, 'But you will also have the creation and strengthening of the League to sustain you. You bring to it such power and fire, fortified by the great love that the people have for you. How could you fail to uphold the Catholic Church as you so wish to do? The people of Paris are with you. You are their champion.'

'Am I yours?' He pulled her beneath him, spreading her arms out on the pillows and capturing her hands in his, not so that he could kiss her again, but simply to look at her, as if memorizing every detail of her delectable face and body.

'You are my very parfit knight,' Margot whispered.

He laughed and sat up away from her, elbows on his knees. 'The people of Paris do love me, you speak true. Would that I had the support of the rest of the realm.'

Sensing a new tension in him she began to massage his shoulders, smoothing her soft hands over his naked back and belly.

'Why, would you oppose the King? No, do not answer that. It is a question that should never be asked, and certainly never answered.'

'I will do only what is right for God and for France,' Guise enigmatically replied, then half turned to smile at her, knowing this was no answer at all, and she smiled back, her own eyes a mirror to the passion sparkling in his.

They both knew that his power was growing, and represented as great a danger to the Queen Mother and the King as did the Protestants. Henri III was unlikely to leave an heir, nor was Alençon. Neither of her brothers were healthy, as they each suffered from the same lung complaint which had carried off her other brothers. Which left Henry of Navarre, a Huguenot, as most likely to succeed, and unless Margot fulfilled her duty he too would lack the necessary heir. After him, or if some accident should befall her husband, the next most likely candidate for the crown was Guise, a Bourbon Prince well loved by the people. All of these thoughts lay silent between them, acknowledged with nothing more than a wry smile.

He was lying beside her again, his hands caressing her trim waist, her firm breasts. She reached out a hand and stroked his cheek with the backs of her fingers, a caress which expressed all her love. How would she feel when this space in her bed was occupied by another, even if that man were her husband? Would he not seem like a stranger, an intruder?

'I must go to him, my love. I can stay no longer in this hot-house of intrigue and danger. I need to be free to live and breathe and not be constantly checking my own shadow.'

Guise captured her face between his two powerful hands. 'I too would feel happier if you were safe, my love. But not a day will go by when I will not yearn for you.'

He kissed her then, a long, gentle kiss that despite its softness was filled with passion and love. When it was done, he gazed deep into her eyes. 'Go in peace, my Queen of Hearts, and remember my promise to you. Should you ever be in need of my help, remember that I am forever yours.'

Sources

I have used many sources in the writing of this book. For readers who wish to explore the subject further I can recommend the list below as being the most useful to me. I would like to acknowledge the Project Gutenberg collection for many of the out-of-print titles.

Memoirs of Marguerite de Valois, Queen of Navarre, Written by Herself.

Henry III, King of France and Poland by Martha Walker Freer, 1888.

The Later Years of Catherine De Medici by Edith Helen Sichel, 1908.

Illustrious Dames of the Court of the Valois Kings: Marguerite, Queen of Navarre by Pierre de Bourdeille and C.A. Sainte-Beuve. Translated by Katharine Prescott Wormeley, 1912.

Queen of Hearts by Charlotte Haldane, 1968.

History of the Reign of Henry IV by Martha Walker Freer, 1860.

The Favourites of Henry of Navarre by Le Petit Homme Rouge, 1910.

The History of Protestantism by J. A. Wylie, 1878.

Nostradamus, the Man Who Saw Through Time by Lee McCann, 1941.

The French Renaissance Court by Robert J. Knecht, 2008.

Catherine de Medici by Leonie Frieda, 2003.

Renaissance Woman by Gaia Servadio, 2005.

Delightes for Ladies by Hugh Plat, 1609.